Letting Go

Go

Awakenings 1

Michele

Zurlo

Lost Goddess Publishing

This book is a work of fiction. While reference might be made to actual historical events or existing locations, the names, characters, places and incidents are either the product of the author's imagination or are used fictitiously, and any resemblance to actual persons, living or dead, business establishments, events, or locales is entirely coincidental.

Warning: This book contains sexually explicit scenes and adult language and may be considered offensive to some readers. It is not meant for underage readers.

––––––––

DISCLAIMER: Education and training are necessary in order to learn safe BDSM practices. Lost Goddess Publishing LLC is not responsible for any loss, harm, injury or death resulting from use of the information contained in any of its titles. This is a work of fiction, and license has been taken with regard to BDSM practices.

An Impulsive Proposal...

The terms of Sabrina's grandfather's will require her to be married in order to gain her inheritance. In a moment of weakness, she proposes to a handsome stranger at work. She needs someone to play a part, and she's willing to sleep with him to sweeten the deal.

A Promise of Passion...

With a failed marriage haunting him and something to prove, Jonas Spencer jumps at the chance to have sex with a beautiful, intelligent woman for a whole year. It would be fun, and he could use some fun in his life—as long as she lives by his rules. He is a Dominant, after all.

A Powerful Desire...

No man has ever satisfied Sabrina in bed, but Jonas is willing to peel away her carefully constructed façade. Layer by layer, he reveals the depths of her passion. As Sabrina falls in love with Jonas, she forces him to confront his dark secrets.

Can she help him let go of the past, or will he use it to throw away the future?

Foreword from authors Lydia Michaels and Allyson Young

With her evocative and heart-wrenching prose, Michele Zurlo is a treasure within the romance genre. Her words spin deep, sensual tales of unforgettable heroes and heroines that withstand the test of time.

The re-release of Letting Go has long been anticipated. This unforgettable story blurs the lines of traditional and erotic romance, leaving readers hungry to return to the world Zurlo has created. We're thrilled Michele has chosen to reintroduce her characters, and include never before read scenes. The account of Jonas and Sabrina remains an exciting talking point—with an edge—for erotic romance lovers. It was, after all, the catalyst that took us from fans to friends of the author herself.

The romance community has awaited the re-release of Letting Go with bated breath—and it's finally here.

A Note from Michele

Sabrina was the first character I created who wouldn't leave me alone until I wrote her story. There have been others since then, but she was the one who blazed the trail they followed. She's smart and strong, and her journey of self-discovery taught me so much about her and the emotional fortitude it takes to reach for your dreams. It took two years for me to find a publisher willing to take a chance on an unknown and untried author, and Sabrina lent me the strength to keep submitting Letting Go until I found a publisher.

Jonas was more of a mystery. I got to know him the same way she did. The original story contained no chapters from his point of view. I put those in later, on the advice of an editor who felt he needed to speak. I'm glad I did, because those chapters helped me understand the depth of pain and anguish twisting his soul. This edition had even more from him, so those of you who've claimed him as your book boyfriend can get a better look at this flawed man.

The original story was written in first person point of view, which I had to change to third person in order to get it published. I felt the story was deeper and more authentic in first person, so when I got the rights back, that was the first thing I changed. This is primarily Sabrina's story, and it's better when she tells it.

I've also expanded this edition, adding over 30K words to flesh out parts readers wanted to know more about, such as their trip abroad and the ending. I thought it was sweet to end with a proposal, but many emails from readers have let me know that they wanted more. So I expanded that scene as well. Also, at the end of the novel is bonus material, a scene from five years later in their marriage.

Over the years, Letting Go is the novel that most readers, women and men, have contacted me about. Many of the emails have discussed the highly personal, and even therapeutic, connections people make with Letting Go. There's something special about this story that really resonates with people, and so, after many years, I'm proud to bring it back to you. If you're a returning reader, I hope you love the changes I made. If you're new to Letting Go, grab a cold drink for those hot scenes and buckle up for an emotional journey.

Table of Contents

Chapter 1—Sabrina

The buzzing of the air conditioner filled the empty conference room, and a metallic noise clicked every few seconds, the soft, discordant ping like a finishing hammer on my nerves. Normally I wouldn't notice it, but today the office was deathly quiet. Being Saturday morning, the silence was unsurprising. Normally even I wouldn't be in the office, but I was hiding, and I figured this was the last place people would look for me.

Even the incessant clicking was better than the alternative. Having just lost my grandfather—the only father figure I'd known—I wanted to be alone with my grief. I wanted to simultaneously wallow and forget about it. Being at home meant endless deliveries of flowers, and being at my mother's house meant endless streams of well-wishers. It also meant dealing with her half-relatives stopping by to see if they'd inherited anything.

They hadn't. Not yet.

Grandpa had put most of his money into trusts for me, Mom, and my sister Ginny years ago. According to his will, we'd also inherited outright. Well, Mom and Ginny had, anyway.

Grandpa's will had come with stipulations attached to my inheritance. Stipulations that were cruel and unfair. Stipulations I had no hope of fulfilling. Bastard.

How was it possible to be so helplessly miffed at someone I had loved so deeply?

While I was sitting here feeling sorry for myself, in walked Jonah Something. I suck with names. In my business, that's a liability. I've developed coping mechanisms, so very few people have noticed my shortcomings. Jonah was new to the corporate world. He used to be a teacher, but he'd left the profession due to the inadequate pay. That told me he used to be an idealist, but his illusions had been shattered by reality. I didn't know him well enough to know if he was bitter or happy about it all, and I had too much going on in my life to care.

Not that it mattered. *Who the hell could I get to marry me by Wednesday?*

Have I mentioned that, in order to get my inheritance, I have to be married before I turn thirty? In other words—next Wednesday.

Jonah nodded at me, but his gaze roved down my legs, bringing my attention to the fact my skirt had ridden up, and then he sat down all the way on the other side of the room. He opened his laptop and ignored me. I understood that to mean he wanted to be left alone as much as I did, though with the emptiness of the offices, he could have gone to his desk and nobody would have bothered him. He sat facing me, though his attention was on the laptop screen, so I couldn't help but watch him. After all, I really didn't have anything pressing to do, and he was easy on the eyes.

Of course, my brain kept wandering back to the tragic unfairness of Grandpa's will. Fury burned inside me briefly, and then it turned to grief. I'd love for a chance to argue about this with him. I'd love for a chance to talk to him about anything once again. Then my brain pictured my half-aunt and half-uncles licking their lips in anticipation of gaining my inheritance when I failed to find the place where Mr. Right and Mr. Right Now intersected.

Don't get the wrong idea about me. I'm usually not so cynical, but this stunk. I knew it wasn't the end of the world. I just needed some time to wrap my head around it all.

Jonah moved, squeaking his chair in the process and distracting me from my self-pity session.

I studied Jonah. I might not have a memory for names, but I never forget a face or a conversation. I'd seen Jonah in staff meetings, but I'd never talked to him. I wasn't in the mood to talk now; looking was enough. He was about 5'10, which was a good height for a man. He had a slim, athletic build, but because he wore only suits to the office, I couldn't tell if he was muscular or just one of those people who was naturally on the lean side. He had sandy brown hair that I imagined would show golden highlights in the sun. It was cut short, but that didn't mask the beginning of corkscrew curls. I wondered whether the texture was soft or coarse. For some reason, I ached to run my fingers through them to find out.

Stop it, Sabrina. That would be sexual harassment.

I hadn't been able to get close enough to see his eye color, which was hidden behind his wire-rimmed glasses, but he did have nice lips. They were full, but not too big. I willed myself not to think about kissing him or anything like that.

Ah, willpower. Why have you abandoned me?

"Is there a reason you're staring at me?" Judging by the tone of his voice, Jonah was irritated.

"Will you marry me?" I would like to say the offer surprised me as much as it did him, but given the drift of my thoughts, it was a natural outcome. Weird and unexpected, but almost logical. Right about now, I was wishing for my better sense to make an appearance, but it seemed to be on sabbatical with my willpower.

He looked over his left shoulder, and then he turned the other way to check behind his right side. "Are you addressing me?"

"There's no one else in the room." I could have denied the whole thing and he probably would have let me get away with it, but I wasn't thinking about salvaging my pride. I really wasn't sure I was thinking at all.

"Why would I want to marry you?" His question wasn't mean. He was honestly baffled.

"Are you already married?" *Why was I digging this hole deeper?*

"No." He stopped and looked at me thoughtfully, though there was something else hidden in the depths of his eyes. Humor, maybe? "Why would you want to marry me? You don't even know my name." It was a valid question.

I liked his voice. It wasn't too deep, but it was strong and distinctly masculine. I could get used to hearing it around the house. "I do too. It's Jonah." Score one for me.

"No, it isn't."

My triumphant smile vanished.

"It's Jonas." He emphasized the *s*. "Jonas Spencer."

I sat up and smoothed my skirt down. "It's nice to meet you, Jonas Spencer. I'm—"

Of course he beat me to the punch. Who but a former teacher would know everyone's name? He even pronounced it correctly, recognizing the *szew* was closer to *chef.* "Sabrina Breszewski, Director of Client Services or something else long and boring that basically says not to mess with you. You lead the most successful team in the company, and you're unofficially in charge of several other teams.

Though you sit on the interview committee, you were not present at mine. Something about Jared Larsen sinking or swimming on his own."

I smiled again. That wasn't quite my title, but he had my duties and my attitude toward Jared nailed down. "I consult and recommend. That's all." My strength was in knowing which associates would work well with whom and on which accounts. I'd looked over his resume and rubber-stamped his application, nothing more. Most people hired to work for Jared eventually quit, so it hadn't mattered if I thought he was good or not. If he survived being on Jared's team, then he'd earned his place at Rife & Co.

He was definitely not flattered by my invitation. "I've worked here for four months, and this is the first time you've deigned to speak to me."

What grade had he taught? His tone would have hardened seniors on their knees begging for forgiveness. Not me, though. I came from tougher stock. "I didn't notice you seeking out me."

He smiled for the first time—briefly, and it was something to see. His entire face changed, brightening to reveal a truly handsome visage. I had a fleeting need to make it come back. I knew he had enjoyed my retort, but I didn't know what else to say.

He interrupted my thoughts again. "You didn't answer my question."

"Which was?"

"Why would you want to marry me?"

I sighed. "I need to get married by Wednesday in order to get an inheritance. I have to stay married for a year, and we'd need to convince people we're in love. That'll take some doing, but I'll give you half a million dollars for your time and effort."

He regarded me thoughtfully, which I found disconcerting. People weren't in the habit of openly studying me—not this intently, anyway.

He approached me slowly and in such a way that I had no doubt he owned the room. Jonas had presence, and I felt myself ceding to his authority. It was a curious development. Maybe it was the situation—I'd asked for a year of his time. Maybe it was the twelve years he'd spent as a teacher, but one thing was certain—I *liked* it. He stopped in front of me and stuck his hands in his pockets. "My apartment building caught fire last month, so I'm technically homeless right now."

I remembered hearing something about that, but I'd dismissed it as rumor when nobody took up a collection. As I studied him (he wasn't the only one who could play that game,) I realized he wouldn't have accepted the money. "I have a house," I informed him. "You can have your own room."

He looked me up and down slowly. I'm not a bad-looking woman. I'm short, but nicely put together. Long brown, gently curling hair framed my round face. My eyes were a nice deep chocolate brown, also round. I'd been told by more than one man that my lips are incredibly kissable. Jonas spread his palms in a gesture that was anything but helpless. "So this would be a platonic marriage?"

I was tired of craning my neck to look up at him, so I stood up, smoothing my skirt in the process. The added height didn't help. "You can date, have girlfriends, whatever you want. All I need you to do is to pretend you're in love with me well enough to fool my mother, my sister, and a bunch of other self-absorbed relatives, though to a lesser extent."

He must have figured that my neck was getting sore because he flopped down on the sofa and patted the seat next to him. After I sat, he continued. "I don't like to rush into things."

"Well, then I guess that's a no. I need to be married before Wednesday."

The look he gave me shut me up. Truthfully, it made me quiver a little bit too. I saw that his eyes were a vibrant shade of olive green.

"You want me to marry you this weekend so that I can pretend to be a loving husband in front of your relatives. You and I will maintain a professional relationship, and I am free to date." His summation was surprisingly non-judgmental.

It sparked the flame of hope. "And I'll pay you a half a million dollars at the end of your year of service. Since you'll be living with me, you can save your money. Maybe buy a house next year. Or, I could buy it, and you could get it in the divorce." I smiled, hoping the incentives outweighed the cost.

He scratched at the pale stubble on his chin, which I found attractive—the stubble, not the itching. "It would be nice to not live with my best friend. I mean, she's great and so is her husband and their new baby, but living there is awkward." He looked over at me with a pensive expression, and that flame flared. "I'm sorry, Sabrina. Your deal is tempting, but I can't do it."

The clatter of my hopes crashing before they were completely airborne was loud in my mind. I shrugged to cover my bewilderment. "It was a stupid proposition."

He slapped a hand on my knee, patting it a couple of times before withdrawing. I had mixed feelings about that. I mean, he didn't want to marry me, but he had no problem copping a feel? Still, he had strong hands and a firm grip. A little thrill traveled up my thigh.

"No, it's not stupid. Desperate, maybe, but not stupid."

I rolled my eyes. "Thanks." My sarcasm was unmistakable. I'd rather be called stupid than desperate.

"Don't you have a boyfriend or someone to whom you're close who might be better suited for this job?" His tone was both apologetic and concerned.

I shook my head. I burned my ex-boyfriend bridges pretty fast, yet another reason to avoid dating at work. "I guess I'll end up exactly where I've always been, minus a grandfather." I looked over at him. "Can I ask you why you said no after appearing to actually think it over? Were you amusing yourself at my expense?"

His shrug was the essence of nonchalance. "I don't want a wife I can't fuck."

My eyes grew as wide as saucers, and I blushed furiously. I honestly hadn't expected coarse language from someone who had been an English teacher.

Emboldened by my reaction, he grinned and continued. "I'm not going to lie to you, Sabrina. I do find you attractive. I've thought about laying you across that table over there and finding out what kind of underwear you have hidden under those sometimes very short skirts more than once."

He paused, the better to hear my gasp. My skirts aren't inappropriately short. They were stylish and chic.

His eyes were glued to the naked flesh above my knees. "For the record, I always hope for a lacy thong, black or peach. Black for when you're in a naughty mood, and peach for when you're feeling shy. But even if I hadn't entertained those kinds of thoughts, I would be hard pressed to marry a woman who only wanted a roommate."

First thought—he'd put more thought into my panty selection process than I ever had. I was resolutely utilitarian when it came to underclothes. I didn't even own a lacy bra.

Second thought—he was cute in a studious sort of way, and I wasn't against casual sex. It was less about the money and more about the increasingly intolerable possibility that I might murder every one of my mother's nieces and nephews who throws a superior look my way while they're living it up with Grandpa's money. The prospect took on disproportionate importance the closer it came to happening. Perhaps we could work out a deal? There had to be some way to persuade him.

"What if you meet someone you really like? Wouldn't a physical relationship between us complicate your relationship with her?"

"No."

I tilted my head, trying to figure out how to take that. "If I were to meet someone and find out he was sleeping with another woman, it would be a deal-breaker."

"I would insist on fidelity on both our parts."

I was taken aback. Okay, he did rub off on me a little. "But it's not a real marriage, Jonas. It's only for a year."

He shrugged, a casual gesture he wore well. "Still, it's a marriage. Not a 'til-death sort of thing, but a marriage nonetheless."

My eyebrows drew together. "There's no love involved either."

"No, but there should be honesty and friendship. And sex."

Sex was a mystery to me. I knew lots of people enjoyed it, and so I'd tried it with many different lovers. However, it had never worked out for me the way it did for other people. In all the years I'd been sexually active, I'd never once had an orgasm. I'd come close a few times, only to end up even more disappointed. It didn't help that most of the men I tended to date were as quick in the sack as they were in making business deals.

I studied Jonas a little longer, noting the somberness in his eyes. He was attractive, and there was something about him I really liked, but I couldn't quite put my finger on exactly what.

He was negotiating sex into the deal, and I didn't think I minded so much. After all, what was a couple of minutes once a month?

"How often are we talking about?" I asked the question as if I hadn't already talked myself into it—because I could still talk myself out of it.

He stretched out his long legs, crossing them at the ankles, but his devilish expression captured my attention. "As much as we want. I'd never kick you out of bed."

"Jonas." I strove to match the tone he'd used earlier, but I was only partially successful.

He laughed and touched my knee again. The shock of intimacy kept me from moving it out of reach. "Twice a day?"

"Once a month."

His smile was teasing. "It's not your period, Sabrina. It's wild, wet, and fun."

That description brought to mind an amusement park. Sometimes sex had amused me, but not too much and not for long. However I wasn't going to share that with him. It was my private shame. Instead I countered his offer. "Twice a month."

He laughed and moved his hand up my leg. "Twice a week. Minimum."

Slapping my hand over his wandering touch, I said, "Are you serious?"

I wasn't going to commit to something that wasn't going to happen. At this point, it wasn't even about the money. It was about wiping those greedy, smug grins off the mouths of my half-cousins, the malevolence of whom had begun to grow in my imagination in direct proportion to the absurdity of this conversation.

Casually, as if it were the most natural thing in the world, he gripped me by the shoulders. Through the thin fabric of my blouse, his fingers were warm and strong. I knew he was going to kiss me before his hands slid up and he threaded his fingers in my hair. I didn't have high expectations, and so I was pleasantly surprised. His lips were firm, not nearly as soft as they appeared, but he didn't pull me into him or otherwise touch me. The lack of a spark left me more than a little disappointed.

When he finished, he leaned back, resting one arm on the back of the couch and his other elbow on the arm of the sofa. Then he propped his chin on his hand and studied me. I had a feeling he hadn't been wowed by the kiss either. "Are you a virgin?"

Had he lost his mind? "I'm almost thirty." Then it occurred to me that I knew almost nothing about him. "How old are you?"

"Thirty-four. Answer the question."

Did he think the kiss was that lame? I'd never been accused of being a bad kisser before. "One kiss makes you think I'm a virgin? I'm a good kisser."

He shrugged again. "You're a little passive."

"It was a first kiss." It wasn't like passionate feelings had led to the kiss, and he hadn't really taken the lead either.

"So?"

This time, I grabbed him, drawing him down to my altitude. He submitted to me, letting me control the kiss. Lightly, I brushed my lips against his, gradually increasing the pressure. I licked at his lower lip before slipping inside to discover that he tasted warm and minty.

Determined to show him that I was an accomplished kisser, I threw myself into the act.

He met me halfway, toying with my tongue until either he felt he'd played with me enough or passion took over. I'm not sure what it was like for him, but passion was definitely a factor with me. Heat spread, warming my blood. My heart followed suit, its rhythmic beat thumping in my ears.

I wanted to explore this unexpected chemistry, but Jonas broke the kiss and settled back against the couch. He dragged his middle fingertip along his lower lip. "Are you opposed to role playing?"

"I'm not into Dungeons and Dragons." My breathing was just beginning to normalize, and my competitive streak faded, which meant that my shyness took over. I couldn't seem to look directly at him.

He smiled. "Neither am I, unless it involves bondage and domination. Perhaps an erotic spanking."

My eyes came close to bugging out of my head. Heat blossomed in my cheeks and spread down my neck, the tell-tale sign of a blush. The taboos to which he referred were definitely not a suitable topic for conversation, even for joking.

He chuckled again. I liked his laugh, but I didn't care to be the source of his amusement. My frustration must have shown because his tone became serious. "I meant dressing up for sex."

"Are you talking about lingerie, or a French maid's outfit?"

A rakish grin stretched the corners of his mouth, and I couldn't tell if he enjoyed my discomfort or if he liked the images in his head. "Yes."

It wasn't a clear answer, but I understood it anyway. "I've worn lingerie before, but not the other stuff. Look, I'm willing to try, but what are you going to do if I absolutely hate it?"

"Make you not hate it." His eyes, edged with topaz, held a promise that made my breath hitch.

I really didn't know where to go with this, but Jonas had figured out how to disconcert me, something that rarely happened. He sauntered across the room and grabbed his laptop before settling back next to me.

"What are you doing?"

"Booking our flight to Vegas," he said as if everything was settled. Still in shock from the most explicit discussion I'd ever had with a stranger about sex, I didn't say anything.

He found the flight, but before he booked it, he asked one last thing. "Let's recap the terms, shall we? I am to be the best, most loving

15

husband to you in front of your relatives. At least twice a week, I get to fuck you until you scream my name. The rest of the time, we're friends."

This was happening. I wasn't quite sure what I was feeling—relief, fear, disbelief, anxiety, wonder—definitely too many conflicting emotions to identify.

"Screaming isn't necessary, and I wish you wouldn't use that word." I was a huge fan of euphemisms when it came to naming sexual activities.

He moved a lock of hair that had fallen in front of my face. "Screaming is absolutely necessary, and I think I'm going to like using that word around you if you're going to blush like that."

Chapter 2—Jonas

I navigated the roads to Sabrina's house in my 10-year-old beater. It was the only possession I still had from before my ex-wife went through our savings and retirement funds. By the time she'd left me, she'd racked up considerable debt, which we split in the divorce.

I guess I did have more than just a car.

Sabrina had offered to meet me at the airport or to pick me up, but I wasn't comfortable letting her do that—or with her paying me for my services. My reasons for doing this were purely selfish. From the first time I saw her walk into a room, I'd wanted to possess her. Known for her relentless drive for perfection and her incredible creativity, she was a legend in the advertising world. I had originally applied for her team, but that query hadn't produced a thing. Instead I'd been hired to work on a team headed by someone she avoided, so I had no hope of catching her eye.

When she'd proposed, it had taken me a few minutes to realize she was serious. And then my mischievous side had kicked in, and I'd tried to see how far I could push her. She'd surprised the hell out of me with the way she'd yielded to my dominant kiss. Add that to her incredible beauty, and I would have been crazy to refuse. This was a singular opportunity—to live with a brilliant advertising mind and have sex with a gorgeous woman.

Her house was on the edge of a private subdivision, the part where the more expensive houses with larger lot sizes were located. It wasn't far from Ellen's house, maybe fifteen miles. My best friend had been allowing me to live in her basement for the past six weeks while I looked for another apartment. The arrangement couldn't last for long. As much as I loved Ellen and her husband, Ryan, they had a new baby, and I wanted to give them as much privacy as possible.

I hadn't mentioned anything about my plan to wed the lovely Sabrina tonight. I'd packed an overnight bag and told Ryan not to wait up. He'd opened his mouth to ask where I'd be, but I'd left before he could utter a syllable. Good thing Ellen hadn't been home; she wouldn't have let me leave so peacefully. As my best friend, she felt it was her duty to never keep her nose out of my business.

Parking in the driveway, I wondered if Sabrina would change her mind once she got a look at my beater, or if it would cement the choice in her head. I definitely wasn't part of her social circle, and that made me a good choice for a fake husband. I could go through the motions quite easily. I loved to role play, and so I could treat this as an extended scene.

She greeted me at the door wearing dress slacks and a shy smile. "You came." Her hair was up, coiled in a chic bun that I longed to dishevel.

Though I wasn't feeling overly confident myself, I had much experience in appearing comfortable and in control. I flashed a grin designed to put her at ease, and she visibly relaxed. "Did you think I'd change my mind?"

She shrugged and stepped back to let me inside. "Perhaps you realized how crazy this all is. I would understand if you changed your mind."

"I've done crazier things."

From the sparkle of interest in her eyes, I knew she wanted to ask, but she refrained. I admired a woman who could control herself, and I looked forward to discovering what it would take to make her lose that control.

She worried her hands. "We have a little time before we need to leave for the airport. I thought I would show you around, and you could pick out a room for yourself."

How sweet—she thought we would have separate bedrooms. That wasn't going to fly. It might take her some time to warm up to me, but I aimed to show her that sex should be a daily activity. One of the things I loved about this arrangement was the inherent honesty of it. There was no pretending—we were openly using one another. That inspired a special kind of trust, a foundation that could last the year and spark an actual friendship. I looked forward to getting to know her. If she was half as passionate as I suspected, then it wouldn't take much to get her to agree. I didn't care to sleep around, and my wife—fake or not—had a duty to see to my needs.

The house was a Victorian, painted white with violet shutters. I didn't care one way or the other for purple, and I was pleased to see that the inside had a much more contemporary look. The front door opened into the foyer, with a grand curving staircase dominating the space. An opening to the left revealed a large formal dining room, which didn't look like it was used very often. To the right was a living room that swallowed that half of the house. The large kitchen, laundry room, her office, a library, and a breakfast nook took up the rest of the space on the ground level.

The second floor had five bedrooms. Two were made up as guest bedrooms, and two more were empty. I could tell she expected me to choose one of these as mine. I would claim one—as an office. I had no plans to construct a dungeon. Though Sabrina had responded to my dominant kiss, she lived a vanilla life, and that appealed to me for several reasons. My ex-wife had used me because I was a Dom who could meet her needs. Life with Sabrina would be a strict departure from that. Sure she was using me, but she was upfront about exactly what she wanted and why. I prized honesty.

The master bedroom, like the living room below it, was massive. It had a rounded sitting area with floor-to-ceiling windows in the front. The walk-in closet in the back was almost as large as the bedroom I intended to use as an office. The master bathroom was down a short hallway, private enough so that I could come home late and shower without disturbing her.

As she gave the tour, she subconsciously held her breath. I could understand why. Her house said more about her than anything I'd learned at work. I knew she wanted me to like it. The place was damned nice—far nicer than anything I'd ever be able to afford. Sabrina came from money, and I did not. Most men might feel intimidated, but this actually made me feel better. I could sit back and enjoy this adventure because there was no chance this would get awkward. I served a utilitarian purpose for her, and she would serve one for me.

"What do you think?" She finally asked my opinion as I stood in the sitting area of her bedroom. I'd been looking out the front window, checking out the neighborhood. It was pretty private, though if we had sex right here, someone peeking out the upstairs window across the street would get one hell of a show. The idea appealed to me greatly, though I knew she'd never go for it. I thrust my hands into my pockets to keep from seeming nervous, which I was.

19

She followed her question with something different, allowing me an out if I needed one. "Which room do you want?"

Turning to look at her over my shoulder, I smiled a long, slow grin and let her in on my plans. "My dear fiancée, I'll be sleeping with you."

"But you can have your own room," she pointed out. "I don't want to encroach on your privacy."

I crossed the room and checked out her closet again. "There's plenty of room in here for my stuff, which is amazing because I think I've seen you wear at least twenty different skirts this month alone. You have the most incredibly sexy legs I've ever seen. You have no idea what I'm going to do with them."

My smile was pure triumph and jubilation, while the expression on her face bordered on pain. She had a lovely pain face. No doubt she was trying to figure out what I wanted to do with her legs. I didn't take the opportunity to enlighten her.

She came closer, her arms crossed protectively over her chest. I noted her defensive stance and stayed still. "Do you have any clothes that aren't suits?"

I grinned. She was slowly accepting that I would be a literal roommate. "Some."

She glanced around, no doubt thinking of her immaculately decorated home and picturing the charred remains of my possessions ruining the overall effect. "Do you have a lot of stuff to move in?"

I wrinkled my nose in lieu of a response and opened one of her drawers. She had a lot of underwear, but they tended toward functional instead of sexy. This wasn't surprising—I already knew she had a practical streak a mile wide.

"Are you packed yet?"

Yeah, it was an evasion. I didn't want to explain why I was almost thirty-five and had yet to accumulate many material items. I'd seen her open suitcase on the bed, so I knew she was almost finished.

She bit her lower lip and stirred my memory of the taste of her kiss. Heady. "I'm almost done. Is it time to get going?"

"We have about a half hour." I scrutinized the contents of another drawer. My nosiness didn't seem to bother her. "I saw you in a dance club a month or two ago. You were wearing this tiny denim skirt. Do you still have it?"

The scrap of fabric had barely covered her ass. My cock jerked from the image that flashed in my mind. Sabrina had a fantastic ass and sexy legs. The skirts she wore to work hinted at her assets, but that denim skirt revealed most of her secrets.

"With leggings?" She frowned, probably trying to figure out which club and the reason she hadn't noticed me. "I think I have it somewhere. Why?"

I grinned, and a blush crept up her neck as I let her picture reasons for my question. "I want you to wear it tonight."

"To our wedding?"

I'd shocked her, something I was beginning to realize wasn't all that difficult. I shook my head. "Wear something nice to the wedding. The skirt is for afterward."

She opened a lower draw on the other side of the room. Without having to dig or rummage, she extracted the exact item. Her cheeks turned scarlet as she regarded the strip of material. Wait until she saw what I actually had in mind. Her fidgety response triggered parts of me that would send her running in the other direction if I let loose. I tried to squelch it, but I wasn't entirely successful in halting the predatory stance and expression that showcased my dominant streak. Though I had no plan to indulge that side of my nature, I did have another kink I couldn't resist sharing. I'd already arranged for her to experience it.

She lowered her gaze, and her chest rose and fell rapidly. I felt my cock respond, and I didn't want to wait for our wedding night.

Chapter 3—Sabrina

On the plane, he revised our vows so they'd be accurate. "We need to always be honest with one another. That should start with our vows."

In the end, we promised to honor each other for the duration of our marriage, in sickness and in health and in all other aspects of our lives. We nixed all the love and cherish stuff, but it was honest and it did aspire to loftiness.

After we arrived, he took me to the hotel, which was above a casino. I had never been to Las Vegas before. The lights seemed garish to me, but the desert backdrop was breathtaking. We dropped our things in the room, not bothering to unpack. It was nearly eight in the evening and our return flight left at two the next afternoon.

"I can't believe I'm doing this," I said.

Jonas put his arm around me. During the three hour flight, I realized he had no reluctance about touching me. On the other hand, I was very reticent to touch him. I didn't come from a demonstrative family. I figured that would change in time, as I acclimated to his presence in my life. "This is your last opportunity to have second thoughts. Want to fuck before we do the deed? It'll relax you, perhaps soothe your nerves."

I narrowed my eyes at him. I disliked vulgar words. "I'm not sleeping with you until we're married."

"You drive a hard bargain." He grinned, not taking it personally. "Let's go."

"Wait!" I said, panicking. "We don't have rings."

He patted the pocket of his suit, which was miraculously fresh and unwrinkled after the long flight. "I brought rings. I will want them back once you divorce me."

"You'll divorce me. Will it fit?" I wasn't concerned about it being too large, only too small.

"Perfectly."

"How do you know? I haven't tried it on." I get peevish when I'm nervous. It's not my best quality, but it didn't seem to put him off.

Jonas smiled enigmatically and refused to show me. "I have an eye for these things."

We had to wait in line once we got to the chapel. Apparently, Saturday in Vegas was a big one for out-of-state marriages. Jonas kept up a steady stream of conversation. I found out that he taught for twelve years before transitioning to marketing. He hated the politics and the apathy of both the students and parents. Since the pay didn't allow him to live the kind of life he should with that amount of education, he went to college at night and during the summer, getting his masters in advertising in four years.

Everything seemed so planned in his life, even his career change. "Is this the most impulsive thing you've ever done?"

"This isn't impulsive, Sabrina. It's only for a year. I'm used to measuring my life in years." He moved a strand of my hair that had come loose from its bun, looking over my face appreciatively. "Besides, I make a habit of doing things most people would call inadvisable and I have yet to regret it."

"Such as changing careers?"

"Such as marrying an incredibly smart and attractive woman in order to live out the myriad sexual fantasies I've had about her." He held a hand up when I started to respond. "I know, I know. I can't fuck you at work; we could get caught. I can't afford to lose this job. I'm still paying off student debt."

He'd booked this flight quickly enough. "Well, you won't have to worry about those things for a year," I assured him. "I'll foot the household bills. You are responsible for your entertainment expenses and clothes. Of course we'll keep our finances separate. It'll streamline the divorce." Something else occurred to me as I went forward with this questionable action. "Did you want a prenuptial agreement?"

Instead of answering, he kissed me, slanting his lips over mine in one of the most provocative kisses I've ever experienced. It didn't scare me, but it did arouse me. A sliver of apprehension stabbed my chest. I didn't want to go to sleep disappointed tonight. I enjoyed the time I was spending with Jonas, and I didn't want that shadowed by a series of unfulfilling sexual encounters. Perhaps I should have held out for my original terms?

One thing was certain: Jonas was adept at kissing.

He grabbed a flyer from the bulletin board in the chapel and borrowed a pen from the people in line behind us. In his masculine, blocky handwriting, he wrote: *This is to certify that all of Sabrina's money, assets, possessions, and whatever else she owns before the wedding belongs to her alone. Should this marriage dissolve, I have no claim to her stuff.* He signed it, had me sign it, and then he asked the couple behind us to witness it. I wasn't sure it would hold up in a court of law, but I appreciated the gesture.

Our turn came up before I was ready, and we were married before I knew what was going on. I wasn't usually so absentminded, but this was a unique circumstance. I had only known him for twelve hours.

When he slid the rings on my finger, I gasped. Not only did they fit perfectly, but they were the most beautiful pieces of jewelry I'd ever seen. The diamond was small enough to be classy, but large enough to attract notice. Surrounded with a nest of emeralds, it reminded me of Jonas' eyes. His matching band had tiny diamond and emerald chips to show they were part of matched set.

"Where did you get these on such short notice?" And had they been purchased for someone else?

"My grandfather left them to me," he said. "They belonged to his parents."

I watched them sparkle in the Las Vegas night lights. "No wonder you want them back. I'll take good care of them." I couldn't tear my eyes away, and I wondered how his eventual real wife would feel about being Jonas' second wife to wear the rings.

"I know you will."

We went out to dinner, and I had a few drinks. By the time we got back to the hotel room, I was feeling uninhibited. I thought he would want to have sex then, but he didn't. He unzipped my suitcase and pulled out the denim skirt and a lacy camisole I hadn't seen him pack. I usually wore it under a suit jacket. Its pretty femininity was wasted because it was never seen.

"Put this on." His voice had gone a little hoarse.

My body responded to him. A fresh surge of moisture flooded between my legs. This night wasn't progressing how I'd envisioned it, and I was much more attracted to him than I thought I would be. The more time I spent with him, the more I liked him.

This wasn't an outfit I would normally wear. The skirt needed leggings, and the shirt needed something over it. Otherwise it showed too much flesh, and the straps of my bra were wider than the straps on the camisole. Taking a deep breath, I reasoned that I was dressing sexy for Jonas because we were going to consummate our marriage. If this was what he found attractive, then it was the least I could do.

I grabbed the clothes from his hands without making eye contact and headed to the powder room to change. The camisole dipped low, revealing the swell of my breasts. I was glad my bra converted to strapless. There's no way I could manage without support. I tugged at the bottom of the skirt that barely hid my mound, but it was stuck on my hips, so it didn't budge.

Giving up on modesty, I ran my fingers through my hair, brushed my teeth, and freshened my makeup.

Jonas had been doing a little freshening of his own at the vanity outside of the actual bathroom. He'd exchanged his glasses for contacts. Gone was the suit. He faced away from me and my first sight was jaw-dropping. He had changed into jeans that hugged his butt. I had wondered about his physique and this settled my question. He has the most incredible behind I had ever seen, and that was not the alcohol talking.

The rusty hued T-shirt had a logo from one of the chain stores in the mall. It clung tantalizingly to his shoulders and chest. His suits were deceiving. While he did look good in them, he looked even better in street clothes. He had an unbelievable body. The degree of his sexiness was no longer in question. I couldn't wait to show him to my sister—not that she'd properly appreciate him, but she would be happy for me.

He whistled appreciatively when he saw me. "You are even more beautiful than I imagined, and my imagination is pretty spectacular."

I stood there, uncertain how to begin. After all, I was the one who had proposed a platonic marriage. He was the one who bargained this into the deal. I liked that he saw me as sexy. I didn't want to cross the line into slutty.

He approached. I wasn't sure what he would do. The way he talked about sex didn't seem to match what I'd observed about his generally relaxed approach to life. He looked at me with those smoky green eyes as he ran his fingertips over my lips, my cheeks, my eyelids. I trembled by the time he kissed me, equal parts nerves and sexual tension.

This kiss was different from the others. It was insistent, demanding. I opened my mouth to let his tongue in, but he coaxed mine into his mouth, licking and sucking on it as if it was water and he had spent a month in the desert. I lifted my hands, running them up his chest to his shoulders, feeling his muscles ripple beneath my fingers. I was glad I seemed to affect him as much as he affected me.

He touched me as if he owned me, and I didn't flinch away from him at all. Instead, I leaned into him, pressing my breasts and hips against his firm body.

He moved his hands over my back to grasp my behind, squeezing firmly and pressing his arousal into my abdomen. I didn't let his lips away from me, but I had reversed the possessiveness of his kiss. Now I had his tongue. The harder I sucked on it, the more he made little moaning sounds in the back of his throat. I felt his hands on my thighs, sliding gently beneath my skirt, and then I felt my panties flutter around my ankles.

He stopped kissing and pushed me back, holding me at arm's length and studying me with a knowing look. I glimpsed my face in the mirror behind him. My lips were puffy, a flush stained my chest and cheeks, and my eyes held a dreamlike quality that vanished with his next words. Dropping his hand to mine, he said, "Let's go."

"Where?" I was surprised. And panty-less.

His eyes softened. "Dancing. I'd like to see you shake those hips before I shake them for you." He tugged on my hand. "I know a great club."

I knew he wanted me. I could see that he was still hard. Anyone who looked at him could see he was hard. I said the only thing that came to mind. "I don't know what kind of music you like."

"It's not about the music; it's about the company." He didn't ask about my preferences.

I crouched down to retrieve my panties, but Jonas stopped me.

"Leave them."

I raised a brow. "Jonas, I hope you don't think you get to boss me around in this marriage."

He grinned. "I know better. I've watched you for some time. You like to be in charge. I'm okay with that."

I continued crouching down, which, thanks to the micro-skirt, was a process in and of itself. It would have been nice of him to help out, but he didn't. His hands closed around my ribs and he stopped me again.

"Jonas!"

My glare seemed to arouse him even more.

His lips closed over mine again, cutting off my protest. When he finished, I was not steady on my feet. "No underwear tonight." I heard the amusement in his voice as he steadied me, and I didn't know how to respond. He smiled and closed his hands around mine. "Please?"

He had a way of asking that made it seem as if I granting his request was just a matter of time. Tentatively, I nodded. Nobody would know, and it was kind of liberating to be so naughty. Of course, with the scant coverage of this skirt, I was going to have to be extra careful about not bending too much.

He rewarded me with a smile and led me from the room.

The club was one of those ones that didn't exist in the Midwest outside of very large cities. Ginny dragged me to clubs like this when we visited New York, Los Angeles, or Paris. It wasn't exactly upscale, but nearly so. A line out front snaked around the corner. I eyed it dubiously. Clubs like this required bribery or knowing someone who could get you on the guest list. I didn't have any cash on me. "I don't think we'll get in."

Jonas must have known someone, because when he bypassed the line and gave his name to the security guard, they let us right in. I should say he gave *our* names. When he said, "Mr. and Mrs. Jonas Spencer," it took me a minute to figure out who he meant.

I hadn't changed my last name. Though Breszewski was Ginny's father's name and Spencer was far easier to pronounce, I didn't want to change it now just to change it back in a year. I suppose I could have kept it permanently, but I didn't think that was fair. After all, it was *his* name. However he couldn't have known my intentions either way because we hadn't discussed it.

The club, whose name was simply *City Club*, was dark. Music pulsated through my body, amplifying the throbbing I still felt from my almost-encounter with Jonas. I headed to the bar with the intention of getting a drink, but Jonas stopped me. "I need you sober tonight, honey. You had four glasses of wine with dinner, and you're still a little tipsy."

I frowned, but not because he'd kept track of my alcohol intake. I hadn't been counting. Was that the reason I had responded to his touch earlier? It explained a lot. Not wanting our first time together filled with drunken groping, he was killing time.

Jonas mistook my frown. He leaned in to shout over the music. "You can have as much as you want when we get back to the hotel. I won't stop you. Dance with me, Sabrina. Let's have some fun."

He threaded his fingers through mine and led me to the dance floor. The shoes he had chosen for me had very high heels that emphasized my calves. They made me stand with my hips thrust forward, which was sexy, but not an easy way to dance, especially not in that skirt. When I mentioned this to Jonas, he looked down at my feet and smiled bashfully. "Sorry. I'll make it up to you. But goddamn, you look hot."

He held me as we danced, helping me keep my balance. I think his ulterior motive was to keep me close because he never let me move more than an inch or two away from him. I was uneasy at first, but soon the crowd fell away, and all I saw was Jonas. His eyes were still a smoky green, and his lips found mine again and again as we gyrated and ground against one another.

When he'd had enough, and frankly, so had I, he leaned down. "Let's go."

Finally, we were on the same page. That was the first time I wanted a man with a desire that nearly crippled me. Completely sober, I stumbled after him as he pulled me through the crowd. It wasn't so much the heels as it was that my legs were weak with desire. Wetness dripped between my legs, smearing across my inner thighs so that I could feel the slipperiness when I walked. It was a foreign sensation, curiously erotic.

We went out through a different door. It was painted the same color black as the walls, and it was hard to find because it blended so well with the décor. I initially thought it a service entrance. Never letting go of my hand, Jonas led me through several doors and short hallways until we came to one guarded by a very large, burly man and an equally formidable woman.

Jonas handed him a plastic ID card. The woman ran it through a magnetic reader. The duo watched the display screen with expressionless faces.

The man looked us both up and down, and then he asked, "Observation only?"

Jonas smiled and shook his head.

The man nodded. He put a green band on Jonas' wrist and a red one on mine.

As I stared, wondering what they meant, the woman crooked her head at me. "Hold out your arms. No cameras, phones, or other electronic recording devices allowed."

Jonas released my hand. The man patted him down, but I didn't watch because the woman was patting me down, running her hands along my sides and underneath my breasts. I protested when she took my purse, but Jonas intervened with an assurance. "You'll get it back."

"I thought we were leaving."

That smile didn't falter once. "You'll enjoy this. I promise."

I wanted to go back to the hotel and have sex with Jonas. I didn't have much patience for whatever this was, but he wasn't exactly giving me a choice. Too focused on him earlier, I had no idea where we were, and I wasn't sure how to get back to the hotel. Still, I was curious about what could put such a satisfied grin on his face before the sex happened. I relented. "We can stay for a little while."

The big man opened the door and closed it behind us. The lock clicked with a resounding thud. We went down two flights of stairs that came out in a room that stopped me in my tracks. People in various stages of undress were draped all over, but that wasn't what made all the color drain from my face. Many of them were having sex, and all the rest were watching—openly watching. He had said we weren't there for observation only.

Offshoots from the main area created alcoves that gave the illusion of privacy. As Jonas walked me into the room, pushing me with his whole body behind mine, I saw additional places that hid more couples, or triples, or more. He must have known I was contemplating flight, because his arm snaked around my waist, and he held me tightly. His hard-on pressed into my lower back. My heart beat so hard and so fast, I thought it would break through my chest. I was as excited as I was afraid. The tableau in front of me was far outside my realm of experience and imagination.

When I spoke, my voice came out as a whisper. "Jonas, I don't want to stay here." It was a lie, but I didn't want to think about why it was a lie.

"Relax," he said, bending his head to whisper in my ear. It was as if he *knew*. "Take a minute to get used to it." I felt him smile against my neck. "Look around you, Sabrina."

I hadn't realized that my eyes were shut tight.

"Look at their faces."

I didn't open my eyes. Curiosity was the bane of my life. I wanted to open them, but admonitions from my mother popped into my head—things she would say about the kind of people who did these kinds of things, and what that meant about me if I wanted to watch them. Or if I wanted them to watch me. Taking deliberate breaths, I forced myself to relax.

His free hand came up and fondled my breasts through the fabric of my camisole. He kissed my neck, grazing it with his teeth and causing me to quiver. "I'm going to do that to you, Sabrina. I'm going to fuck you until you come with all these people here to see it."

It shouldn't have titillated me, but it did. Good God, the idea that someone might watch me come made me even wetter than I already was. I'd never guessed a place like this existed.

My eyes finally opened. To our left sat a man, his head thrown back with a dreamy expression on his face. A woman was bent over him, her mouth bouncing up and down the length of his penis while another man took her from behind. I wondered what it would be like to be in her position. Did having a man take her from behind make giving a blowjob more enjoyable?

A little farther down, another woman sat on a man's lap, riding him while he suckled her breasts. I could see various combinations of people pleasuring one another just from where we stood.

I moaned as he bit into my shoulder and pressed me against him even harder. "Do you still want to leave?"

Slowly, hesitantly, I shook my head once. Then I shook it again decisively. "I'm not very good at this." I confessed, hoping he would mistake it for anxiety and not take my words at face value. I really wasn't very good at sex, but I guess he was about to find that out for himself.

"You'll do fine," he assured me. "I'll make sure you enjoy it."

He slipped his hand under my skirt. It was short enough so that it barely moved as he parted my lips with his fingers, rubbing and pressing my slick clitoris. I couldn't breathe. Paradoxically anxious and filled with an incredible yearning, I leaned against him. One emotion fed the other, sharpening the pleasure. I whimpered.

Then I looked up and happened to meet the eyes of a woman looking at me with such undisguised fascination that I wondered what she saw. As I watched her watching me, Jonas worked his magic, slipping his finger inside me and moving it in gentle swirls. I moaned and moved against him, giving in to the fascination—the permission—in that woman's face.

"That's it, Sabrina. Let me touch you. Let me make you come." He added another finger, and I moaned, my knees weakening. The sound was small and strangled as I struggled to swallow it.

"Don't fight it." The command, murmured against the sensitive skin on my neck below my ear, made me quiver even more. "Let it out, honey. Tell me how you like it."

All around me, the sounds of sex created an erotic cacophony. Sighs, moans, demands, and climactic screams rent the air. The arm that kept me from running away now held me up as my legs liquefied. I couldn't say I was close to orgasm when he abruptly withdrew his fingers from me. It had felt good, and I moaned in protest, but he only chuckled as he turned me to face him.

I hadn't realized he had moved me from the center of the room until that moment. We were in an alcove. Not only could people in the main corridor see us, but the alcove itself was paneled with a darkened glass that I was sure hid people behind it who wanted to watch without being seen. He set me on the edge of a large, solid platform a little over three feet in height. Bent at the knees, my legs dangled down the side.

We weren't alone. The anonymous onlookers were treated to the sight of three couples in various stages of erotic play, and we were about to become the fourth. Being this close to the couples made me too shy to look at them. I concentrated on Jonas.

He wedged between my legs and kissed me hard, plunging his tongue deep into my mouth and robbing me of breath. The rough fabric of his denim-clad body rubbed against my throbbing clit and made me gasp. Heat swirled through me. I didn't know what to do with the intensity of the feeling. I'd never been this turned on in my life. I held onto him. Firmly in unexplored territory, I needed an anchor.

Drawing back, he stared deeply into my eyes. His chest moved fast, his breaths coming harder now, and his eyes were liquid gold. "Tell me what you want, Sabrina."

I licked my lips, trying to force words when my only coherent thoughts were primal needs.

He licked my ear and nibbled at my lobe, sending shivers throughout my body. His gentle whisper was husky with desire. "Tell me, honey. You're in charge here. I am your willing slave."

I didn't want him to be my slave. "I want you." My lips barely moved. He had to strain to hear me.

His eyes locked with mine, and I felt like I was the only person in the world who mattered. "How do you want me?" His hands gripped my waist, slipping beneath the soft, thin fabric of my camisole. I quivered as his warm hands explored the skin there.

My inhaled breath was sharp and tremulous. "I want you to touch me, Jonas. I want to feel you inside me."

He eased my top over my head, pausing to kiss me again when my arms were temporarily bound by the flimsy fabric. Electric heat shot through my body, and I arched closer. I never knew a kiss could ask for so much, and this was only the beginning. After some time, he released my arms.

I slipped my hands under the hem of his shirt, touching him for the first time without a barrier between us. His low moan vibrated against my mouth.

His skin was smooth and firm. Emboldened, I increased the area of my forays, pushing his shirt out of the way until he pulled it off and threw it behind me. I explored his strong shoulders and the clearly defined muscles on his chest and back. He was muscular without being bulky, inherently sexy.

He pushed the cups of my bra down, folding them beneath my breasts. Then his hot mouth was on my nipple. I arched against him, holding his head close, and wrapped him in my legs. He licked and sucked and bit me, sending jerky waves of pleasure shooting to my core. Never had a lover been so rough. My body responded feverishly to this treatment, seeking more and faster. Tension and heat coiled lower and lower. I completely forgot my audience.

His touch wandered all over my legs. Pushing me back so I lay down on the plastic-coated surface, he lifted one leg high. He bent and his mouth was on my calf, licking and nipping at skin I never knew could be an erogenous zone. Moving lower, he sucked at the back of my knee. I cried out, slamming my hands down next to me, searching for something to hold onto, but there was nothing. Reflexively, my body lifted from the table at the shock of unexpected pleasure.

I felt his lips curve in a smile. "Like that?"

"Yes," I croaked, my voice hoarse with hunger. "Very much."

He chuckled and I felt his teeth scrape the curve of my inner thigh. He caressed me with his hands, stroking higher and higher until his fingers were again inside me. Thrusting them in and out, he asked, "Is this what you want?"

It felt good, but it wasn't enough. "No," I panted. "I want you."

Withdrawing his fingers, he shook his head. "You're going to have to do better than that." He switched legs, his mouth on the back of my other knee, driving me into the air again.

I never knew that part of my body was so sensitive. I wanted him. I wanted this. I knew he felt the same way. Why was he playing hard-to-get? "What do you want me to say?"

"Tell me what you want." He barely moved his lips, leaving his words muffled against my leg.

"I want you to make love to me."

"No, you don't," he said against the skin on the side of my upraised knee. "Tell me what you really want. Tell me to fuck you."

He stopped his exploration to look in my eyes. His expression was encouraging; his eyes, unfathomable.

In the throes of equal parts desire and alarm, I lost control of my breathing. "You're going to make me say that word, aren't you?"

His eyes burned with promise. "You have no idea how much you're going to enjoy it."

My breathing came in gasps and half-sobs. I wanted him inside me. I needed him inside me. "Jonas," I begged. "Please."

"Say it, Sabrina," he urged, grazing his teeth along the back of my knee. I moaned and writhed at this torture. "Tell me what you want, and I will give it to you."

The woman to my left cried out her climax and the woman between her legs leaned back, breathing hard. The woman to my right gasped and moaned as she murmured commands to her lover, who thrust into her with excruciating slowness. I wanted what they had.

I could barely speak. "Jonas." The plea strangled me. I was afraid of asking because I didn't want to be disappointed. Not by Jonas. Not after all he made me feel. Finally, I was awake and coming alive.

His voice was silky and heavy with need. "Say the words, Sabrina. Tell me you want me to fuck you."

I wanted him more than I had ever wanted anyone in my life. He promised the same things other men promised, but he seemed capable of following through. "I need you, Jonas."

Using my shaky arms to push myself up, I unbuttoned his pants and drew down the zipper.

He didn't move.

I slid my hands into the waistband and pushed them down until they pooled at his ankles.

He still didn't move.

I touched the silky softness of his full erection, stroking him gently with my fingertips. He didn't move. He breathed harder with the effort it cost to resist me, but he didn't move.

I was desperate, an unfamiliar predicament. The reading of the will only left me depressed, not desperate. "Fuck me, Jonas." The request was quiet, and heat suffused my face. I couldn't look at him. I could barely speak.

Smiling triumphantly, he opened his hand, revealing a condom. "Put it on me."

My fingers trembled in anticipation as I unrolled it down the length of him. He pushed me back on the table and entered me slowly, savoring every inch. He stretched me by degrees, penetrating a little more with each passing second. When he was all the way in, he reversed direction, withdrawing just as slowly. At this rate, I would be insane by morning.

I itched for him to feed the heat building in my core. "Faster," I begged. "Harder."

He did as I asked, increasing the tempo and force only slightly each time I asked it. My pleasure built, and I felt the orgasm that hovered just outside my reach. I had been here before, only to be disappointed time and again.

Fear tasted bitter and metallic in my throat. I prepared myself to come close and miss, closing my eyes to hide the frustration I knew was moments away. I didn't want to ruin it for him, and so I prepared to fake an orgasm. It was what I usually did.

Jonas lifted my legs, hooking my knees over his shoulders to expose me even more, and pounded himself into me. The violent action shocked my eyes back open. He was rough, and it hurt. I was going to be sore for days, but I didn't care because with the pain came a sharp pleasure I'd never felt before. It was enough to push me closer than I had ever been, and it scared the hell out of me. I had never lost control, and I had never once been in a position to give in. Now it was a choice I had to make.

"Don't fight it," he ordered through ragged gasps. "I won't let you do this. Let go." He rammed into me harder and faster, pushing me closer despite my fears. He took over my body, making it more his than mine. I flailed, grabbing at the mat and at him. I left scratches on his arms and shoulders, but it did nothing to help me find an anchor.

I screamed as I came, the waves rolling over me, holding me down, stretching me into something I didn't recognize. I'd chased this moment my entire adult life. Tears gathered in the corners of my eyes, and I couldn't stop the tremors that rocked my body.

His orgasm followed. He pulsed and throbbed inside me with such a force that I wasn't sure the condom could contain it. I didn't worry, though. Birth control had been a staple of my diet since I was a teen.

Jonas pulled me up and held me until we were both breathing somewhat normally. He adjusted the cups of my bra to cover my breasts and slipped my camisole over my head. "You okay?"

I couldn't stop shaking. He tilted my face up to his and gently wiped the moisture from my temples, concern clouding his tawny eyes.

He searched my eyes for something. "Sabrina? I know I was rough, but you seemed to want that. Did I hurt you too much?"

I shook my head. "I'm fine. This was very different for me. Intense."

Inhaling sharply, he nodded his understanding. "But you liked it? You might want to do this again sometime?"

Nodding before I thought about it, I said, "Yes, I... I want this again." I meant the orgasm. Truthfully, the audience didn't matter to me. They had dropped away, and I didn't notice them after my attention focused on Jonas.

He held my hand as we walked back to the hotel, which was several blocks away.

We didn't talk much, even as we changed into our pajamas. Well, I changed into mine, and he stripped down to his underwear. I climbed into bed beside him. We lay in the dark, each lost in our private thoughts.

Then I broke the dark silence with a question. "How long have you been a voyeur?"

"Exhibitionist."

"Sorry?"

He chuckled, a low, tired sound. "Voyeurs like to watch. Exhibitionists like to perform, to be watched. It's a symbiotic relationship among strangers."

"Then how long have you been an exhibitionist?"

He exhaled to stall for time to calculate his years of debauchery experience. "Sixteen years."

Doing the math, I realized he had been eighteen when he began doing what we had just done. I had still been a virgin when he began fucking women in front of an audience. As I considered what his life must have been like, the slow, even breathing next to me told me he had fallen asleep.

I watched him for a little while. The curtains parted a little, letting in just enough neon light to let me see his relaxed face. I studied it and thought about what the coming year would bring.

Chapter 4—Sabrina

The next morning, I awoke refreshed, which I found incredible considering I hated sleeping on a mattress that wasn't mine. But I guessed when someone expended as much energy as we had last night, exhaustion trumped discomfort.

Jonas awakened as I contemplated climbing out of bed. He sat up and stretched, showing off his fine physique. "You can have the first shower, but I need to take a leak."

Not at the point where I felt comfortable talking about bodily functions, I merely nodded.

When he emerged a few minutes later, he slid into his jeans. "I'm going to make coffee. Do you like regular or decaf?"

"Whatever you want will be fine."

He shot me a strange look. "I'm asking what you like, Sabrina. I'm not asking you to settle for what I like."

Sliding from bed, I got to my feet slowly. "Regular. Two sugars, no cream."

"Are you still sore?"

I took stock of where I hurt. The backs of my legs were sore from being stretched when he'd thrown my knees over his shoulders. My labia was tender, but I wasn't going to mention that. "A little. Nothing a warm shower won't loosen."

Frowning, he looked me up and down. "A cool cloth will help more. I'll make you an ice pack."

"That's not necessary." Rather than argue, I went into the bathroom and showered. Afterward my legs felt fine, but my lady parts were still a little swollen. When I emerged, I found Jonas seated at the small dining table finishing off a cinnamon roll. My coffee waited next to a basket of assorted breakfast pastries. I snagged one without checking the flavor, and sipped the coffee. "Thanks for this."

"No problem." He wiped his fingers on a napkin and got up. I thought he was going to shower, but he returned in a few moments with a wet washcloth. "Take your underwear off and hold this on your pussy."

Alarmed because no man had ever pretended to have an interest in that area outside of sex—and I preferred things that way, I froze. He shook the cloth at me. Finally I swallowed. "I'm fine. Thanks anyway."

"I don't believe you. Either you do it, or I will look to make sure you're all right and then I'll do it for you." He lifted a superior brow, daring me to refuse.

Taking the cloth, I reasoned that he was just trying to be nice, to take care of me. Perhaps he felt guilty about being so rough, though I couldn't say I had any regrets. Without flashing my private parts, I removed my panties and pressed the cloth between my legs. He was right—it did feel good. "Thank you."

I sat down and finished my breakfast while he showered. Afterward he let me put my panties back on, and he asked how I wanted to spend the few hours we had before we had to be at the airport.

I didn't want to gamble, which didn't seem to surprise Jonas, so he suggested showing me some of the other tourists attractions. He opened doors, deferred to me in nearly everything, and held my hand as we walked. I was surprised he held my hand. Even though we'd shared something remarkable, we were still strangers. Hand-holding was a sign of affection. I liked him and I could tell he liked me, but I didn't see where affectionate feelings would have had the time to develop.

Still, I caught myself staring at him quite frequently. When he caught me, he would lean down and give me a light kiss.

We wandered around the town for most of the time, talking and getting to know each other. I rationalized it all by reminding myself that we would need to know personal things about each other if we were going to pull this off. I found out that he had taught high school business, technology, and writing classes, and that he had no regrets about his career change.

His parents were still living, as were his maternal grandparents, and he had two younger sisters. One was my age and the other was two years younger. I told him about my mother, who raised my sister and me alone after Ginny's father left when I was five and Ginny was two, and about Ginny and her wife, Lara.

"You're close to your sister?" he asked as we headed back to the hotel.

"She's my best friend."

"Is that who I saw you with at that dance club?"

I looked up at him, confused.

He countered my look with a devilish smile. "When you wore that skirt."

I didn't need details. Having only worn that skirt once before because Ginny had made me, I knew what he was talking about. "You were at the club that night? It's a gay bar."

"I know."

"What were you doing at a gay bar?"

He shrugged. "I was there to see a former student who had come out of the closet and needed some moral support."

Wow. Teachers were sure different now than they were when I went to school. I couldn't imagine a single one of my high school teachers at a bar with me. My disbelief was reflected in my question. "So you went to the bar with him?"

We paused on the sidewalk in front of the hotel. The street was relatively quiet. "He's twenty-five now, an adult. I ran into him about a week before that, and he invited me to his show. He was the drummer in the band that played."

It hadn't been a memorable band. I shrugged and shook my head to let him know I had no recollection.

"Anyway, I saw you there, dancing, and I ended up watching you instead." He opened the door to their hotel for me. "I watched your sister a little too. She looks a lot like you, only not as gorgeous."

I ignored his compliment, not liking that it came at Ginny's expense. "Why didn't you talk to me?"

He smiled shyly. "I was afraid of you."

My jaw dropped. After last night, I found that very hard to believe.

"No, really—I was. I had been at Rife and Company for about six weeks. I'd seen you around, listened to you speak at staff meetings, but you didn't notice me at all. I didn't take it personally; you don't seem to notice anyone unless you need them for something. Anyway, you have quite the reputation for not being tolerant when it comes to small talk. People warned me to stay out of your way." As he explained his reasoning, he guided me into the hotel and to the bank of elevators in the lobby.

I frowned. I hadn't been aware of my grim reputation. "People at work don't like me?"

He pushed the button for the elevator. "I didn't say that. You're known for being driven, focused on work. You expect the best from everybody around you and you don't accept excuses for less than spectacular work. I wasn't sure I was up to your standards. I was waiting for my spectacular marketing genius to catch your attention."

The elevator chimed, and we got in with too many other people. I waited until we exited on our floor before continuing. "So you avoided me. Why did you talk to me yesterday?"

He put the card in the slot to open the door. "I thought you would ignore me, but when you kept staring, I couldn't concentrate. I have a presentation due tomorrow, which is why I'll be working my ass off tonight while you're sleeping." He pushed the door open. "At any rate, talking to you worked out fine. Unexpected, but nothing I regret. I had a nice time this weekend, Sabrina. Thank you."

I lingered in the doorway. "For what?"

"For everything." Reaching behind me to close the door, he trapped me between it and his body, claiming me with his lips. It only lasted a minute, but fire raced through me. The way he caged me with his arms excited me instead of making me feel trapped. It was a new sensation, one I liked. But then he released me abruptly and didn't attempt it again.

Later, on the plane, I asked him about the club to which he had taken me. He had given his name at the door, and he knew exactly what was behind door number three.

He smiled enigmatically. "There are clubs like that all over the world. Any time you want to take a road trip, just say the word."

I flushed red and turned to look out the window, letting the subject drop. It was too much, too soon.

That evening, I helped him move his things from his friend's house. Ryan, who still taught at the high school Jonas had left, loaned his truck. His wife, Ellen, was at work, and so he was alone with their four-month-old son, Jake, and couldn't help. It didn't matter. We had all of Jonas' things to my house in one load. The fire must have been bad.

"Did you have renters' insurance?"

He grinned ironically. "For the first time in four years, I let it lapse. How's that for fate?"

I put away his clothes in my closet—our closet—while he got to work on his presentation. Later in the week, I would make one of the extra bedrooms over into an office for him. He didn't have a desk, but I had an extra one in the basement. In the meantime, I made dinner, which he didn't properly appreciate.

"It came from the freezer. You didn't make it; you heated it up."

Throwing back my shoulders and drawing myself up to my full height, I said, "If you expect better fare, then you'll have to do the cooking." That should have taken some of the wind from his sails.

It didn't. He laughed at me, but I didn't mind so much. I was growing used to it, and I liked his laugh. "As long as you do the dishes."

I liked to clean. In fact, I preferred it to cooking, which was why I didn't often cook. Maybe we were a perfect match after all. By the time he finished his presentation, it was nearly eleven. His supervisor was a jerk by the name of Jared Larsen who didn't do a good job of checking over the presentations made by the people on his team before presenting them to the client. I had been assigned to that team when I had first started at Rife & Co, so I knew what Jonas was up against.

"Would you like me to look it over?"

"No." No laugh this time. He rubbed a hand over his tired eyes.

"Why not?"

"It's unfair to have the big boss check over my work."

It was my turn to laugh. "I'm not technically Jared's boss. We have equal standing."

"Yet you do the hiring, and you often assign accounts or determine who gets to compete for the accounts. You have more power than Larsen, and you have a better title. He's just a team leader."

Though I did have a better title, I shook my head. "I may have more of a say, but I don't have carte blanche. Jared's input is considered, as is that of every team leader. And I don't make the final decision on anything. That comes from above me."

He studied my face as he thought. "It's like being a department head. You're expected to do additional things, but you can be undermined or ignored at any time."

"Exactly." I smiled encouragingly. "Look, if you have a connection, Jonas, use it. Nobody else who has my ear would hesitate to use it."

He hovered nervously over me as I clicked through his slides. I figured he was anxious about the kind of feedback I might give.

"Give me some space," I said, shooing him away. "Go brush your teeth or get into your pajamas."

"I know my work isn't up to your standards." He eyed me nervously before leaving the room.

I tweaked a few things without his permission. They were beginner's mistakes, things Jared should catch if he was thorough about his job. By the time Jonas returned, I had feedback for him. "It's good. I changed a few things that are common errors. Your slides should only have a few words on them—the essence of your idea. The rest should be verbal, and you have all the details written out in the proposal."

Jonas only stared at me with that same thoughtful, appraising expression he had used when he considered my proposal of marriage. It was disconcerting because I couldn't fathom what he might be thinking.

Finally, I snapped. "What?"

He settled next to me at the dining room table and leaned forward, searching my eyes. "I don't want people to doubt my work. I don't want people to even think to themselves that any success I have is because I'm married to an executive. You've already proven yourself. You started where I am now and earned your position."

"I had some good mentors."

"You worked on Larsen's team," he countered. "I know he didn't help you out."

"He certainly didn't, but other people did. Don't be afraid to use your resources."

He scowled. "I don't see you as a resource."

"You should. It's a perk of being married to me." I closed his laptop and shifted to face him. "Look, I have no intention of hovering over you or getting involved in your career. But there is no reason you can't ask me my opinion or to check over something. I have more experience in these matters, and I'm willing to help however I can."

He stood, his green eyes clouded with doubt. "Well, if you ever want to know how to split your infinitives with dynamite results, you can ask me."

I had no idea what that meant, and I didn't ask. Some things were better left to the imagination.

We drove to work together. I let him drive my car because I had a better parking spot and because I could work while he navigated the roads for twenty-five minutes. Plus his car wasn't very reliable. We didn't talk about how things might change at work. He wished me a productive day, I wished him luck on his presentation, and we parted ways.

I didn't realize until I was going through my messages with my assistant that I didn't know where in the building he worked. I knew it was on my floor, but that was all. I made a mental note to wander by Jared's hideout around lunch time, but I never got a chance to get over there. Missing a week for my grandfather's funeral had put me behind on too many things. I probably should have been working Saturday morning instead of lounging around and propositioning strangers.

I was still working when Minnie, my assistant, buzzed. "Mr. Spencer is here to see you. He doesn't have an appointment." She sounded annoyed. It was unusual for someone in an entry level position to see someone in my position without an invitation.

"It's okay. Send him in." I smoothed my hair back and made sure nothing was out of place. Jonas came in. "Sorry about that. She doesn't know who you are."

He sat across from me and took off his glasses. "You're keeping it a secret?"

I frowned. "No, I just haven't had a chance to say anything. It's been a hectic day, and I don't make a habit of revealing personal information at work."

The look he gave me was one of profound disbelief. "You opened up to me pretty quickly."

My mind went to a different place than what he meant, and I blushed. "A fluke."

I didn't realize until I said it that I meant two things. First, confiding in someone at work had been a fluke. Second, I was sure the single night of amazing sex had been a fluke. I threw down my pen, stretched, and gave him my full attention. "What brings you to these parts?"

He smiled. "The dinner bell."

I blinked at him. "The what?"

"It's nearly six. Time to go home. Your secretary is one of the only people out there." The corner of his mouth twitched in amusement.

I looked at the clock on my computer. The last time I had looked up, it had been near three. I still had so much to do. If Jonas hadn't insisted I leave, I would have stayed until after dark. I rang Minnie and told her to go home.

Jonas waited patiently while I gathered the things I wanted to take with me. He surveyed the pile of papers dubiously. "You think you're going to get any of that done?"

I sighed, resigned. "Some of it I have to get done."

We didn't make it home until after eight. Jonas insisted on stopping off to eat. "I saw the inside of your refrigerator, Sabrina," he said as he pulled into a sit-down restaurant. "You seriously lack food in your house."

"I'm not home much."

"At least it explains all the frozen lasagna."

I shot him a dirty look, but all he did was grin at me. He was easy to be with. I liked that he didn't take me too seriously, especially given his revelation about how intimidating people found me. I relaxed and enjoyed both dinner and my companion.

The phone was ringing when we got home. Jonas looked at me and then answered it when I showed no sign of doing it myself. As I headed up the stairs to change out of my work clothes, I heard him talking. I didn't know who would be calling my house that he would have anything to say to, and I knew Ellen and Ryan didn't have my number because Jonas didn't even have it.

I turned around when he came into the bedroom. "We should probably give each other our phone numbers." I would have said more, but he handed me the phone.

"Your sister and your mother are in the driveway wondering if they can come in to see you." He disappeared into the closet as he said it, no doubt to change out of his suit.

I was tempted to swear, but I didn't. I held the phone to my ear. Ginny was on the other end. "Yes, you can come in."

"Are you sure?" I heard the laughter in her voice. "It looks like you're entertaining someone special."

"I'm not entertaining anyone right now, except you."

"Honey, I'm in the driveway. He answered the phone. I saw him through the living room window. And when I drove by yesterday, I saw a strange car in the driveway. I assume it was his car. Anyway, we can come back later if you want."

"He lives here," I said. "If you come back later, he'll still be here." I hung up the phone and abandoned my plan to change into comfy pajamas. Ginny and Mom were at the door by the time I unlocked it.

Ginny and I looked remarkably alike. For as long as I could remember, random people have assumed we were twins. Except where I let my hair grow until it spilled halfway down my back, she cut hers in a short style that made her resemble a pixie. Fortunately we both take after our mother. At fifty-eight, she was still every bit as beautiful as she had been when I was a little girl. When the three of us went out together, she was often mistaken for our older sister.

Ginny threw her arms around me. "You look really, really good considering everything that's happened."

Mom joined the hug.

I was trying unsuccessfully to disentangle myself when suddenly Ginny and Mom let go. They stared, mouths agape, toward the bottom of the curving staircase where Jonas stood. Then Ginny noticed the boxes still stacked on the hardwood floor in the foyer. We had not yet unpacked all of his things. "You weren't lying, were you?"

I motioned Jonas closer. He smiled and draped his arm around my shoulder. I reached up to hold his hand. So much depended on this moment. I did want them to like Jonas. "Jonas, this is my mother, Melinda, and my sister, Ginny. And this is my husband, Jonas." It was the first time I had ever used the word husband in describing him, and yet, the word rolled naturally from my tongue.

Jonas extended a hand to my mother first. "It's very nice to meet you, Melinda. I hope you don't mind if I call you Melinda? Sabrina has told me so much about you."

Mom reluctantly shook his hand. Manners dictated her behavior. She harbored a skeptical, cynical soul, which I had inherited. "Husband? Sabrina, tell me you didn't do something stupid."

I looked at Jonas. He smiled reassuringly. He'd go along with whatever story I concocted. "I think it's working out good so far." I smiled back at him. "What do you think?"

"I would say it's working out *well*." Without much effort, he kept his face open and friendly. He turned his charm on my mother. "Ideally we would have waited and invited our families to the wedding, but Sabrina was in a hurry, so we went to Vegas on Saturday."

Tonight, Mom was in particularly high dudgeon. She hated surprises, even the good kind, not that she considered this a positive development. "Is that where you've been all weekend?" Mom's nose wrinkled in disgust.

A headache began to form at the base of my skull. "We got back yesterday and moved some of his stuff in. We haven't had a chance to unpack it yet." I hated feeling like I had to explain the boxes in my foyer, yet I did it anyway.

Jonas turned up the charm, and I appreciated his attempt to divert attention from me. "Ginny, Melinda, would you both like to sit? Can I get you something to drink? I think I saw some Scotch in the freezer."

Mom wasn't buying it, and not just the fact that I would store Scotch in the freezer. I liked it cold, but she would consider that a poor way to treat alcohol. I could tell by the way she narrowed her eyes at him that she had already decided against liking Jonas. She crossed her arms. "Nothing for me."

Ginny had a different reaction. She was amused. "I'll take some water. Really we can't stay long. I have to be at work early tomorrow. Drew and I are getting ready for a competition." Ginny co-owned a successful pastry shop and catering company in Royal Oak called *Sensual Secrets,* and the competition would be televised on the Food Channel. It wasn't her first, but she always practiced for them as if it were. I was surprised to see her out this late at all. She had most likely tagged along because I hadn't returned calls all weekend, and she knew I wasn't in a place where I could handle our mother alone.

Jonas didn't seem to take my mom's reception personally. If it was possible, his smile widened before he went into the kitchen to get drinks. It had been a long weekend and a busy day. Maybe he was glad they weren't going to stay late because he wanted to go to sleep. I sure did.

Ginny and I followed my mother into the living room. It might have been my house, but she had a way of taking over. Mom settled on an antique chair I recently had reupholstered, her spine ramrod straight and her hands folded neatly in her lap. "Sabrina, did you think about this carefully before you married someone you obviously don't know?"

I thought Jonas and I got along pretty well. However, something happened to my synapses around my mother. I loved her dearly, but no one has ever had the ability to turn me into an incompetent child faster. "I didn't think it was obvious, because I do know him."

"He's cute," Ginny whispered. "Where did you find him?"

"At work," I said in a normal voice. Mom wasn't bothering to whisper. I don't know why Ginny felt she should do so. Jonas had left the room so we could talk about him. "Jonas came to work at Rife and Company about four months ago."

I could have made up some lie about how we'd flirted for months and how we'd been out several times, and so he'd seemed like a natural choice. Jonas would have backed me up, but I hated to lie, especially since I was so bad at lying to my mother, and so I said told Ginny about him seeing me when she had dragged me out to the bar with her and Lara. It wasn't a lie, but it was misdirection.

Ginny's eyes sparkled triumphantly. "I told you that was a great skirt. You never listen to me."

Jonas returned in time to hear her comment. "It is a great skirt. She wears it well. Then again, she wears them all well." He handed Ginny a glass of water, and he put a shorter glass in my hand. He had sized up my mom correctly and brought me alcohol. "Thanks."

"You married some guy because he likes the way you look in a skirt? I gave you credit for more brains than that." Mom managed to sound outraged and bitter.

Jonas settled on the couch between me and the arm of the sofa. He rested one arm behind me, but I was sitting on the edge of the cushion, so he wasn't touching me. However his nearness had a curiously calming influence.

"No, Mom. I didn't know about the skirt until later. I married him because he agreed." I took a sip of expensive Scotch, a gift from an appreciative client. Cold fire. It went down smoothly.

Much like me, Mom wore a blouse and a skirt. Her legs were neatly crossed at the ankle. So were mine. I uncrossed them.

She turned her venom on Jonas. "Do you know why she asked you to marry her? Didn't it surprise you that someone you barely knew proposed marriage?"

"Certainly," he admitted. "I wasn't sure she was talking to me at first. I didn't agree until we negotiated terms."

"Terms? You do realize that according to the terms of my father's will, her inheritance cannot be split due to divorce? You won't get a penny from her." Mom folded her hands in her lap. She had just played her trump card.

Jonas was singularly unexcitable. I was impressed with his calm. I wanted to pick her up and throw her out. I entertained fantasies, but I would never have the courage to stand up to her. "She didn't say that, but I figured. I turned her down when she offered me money, and I signed a contract saying all of her stuff is hers."

Ginny's eyebrows rose at his confession. I knew she was impressed by him as well. I twisted to face him, my knees brushing against his thigh. "That's not why you turned me down."

His eyes softened, and he moved a lock of my hair, tucking it behind my shoulder. It hadn't been in my face. I think he just wanted to touch me, but he knew I wouldn't be comfortable with it in front of my mother. "There's only one reason I accepted." His grin grew smug. "Maybe two."

"And what was that?" Mom wasn't going to be happy until he admitted it had been the money I'd offered. I didn't know if that was still part of our bargain, but I had every intention of honoring it.

Jonas leaned forward and met my mother's hard glare. "Why, Melinda, for the oldest reason there is. She agreed to have lots of sex with me. When a beautiful, strong, vibrant woman offers unlimited sex for a year, only a fool would refuse."

My face and neck burned pink. I closed my eyes and studied the floor, letting my hair fall forward to curtain my face and hide my blush. Thinking back to our conversation in the conference room, sex had been his primary concern. Mom nearly had a stroke when he said it. I gulped my drink, and Jonas took the empty glass.

"You want some more?"

I didn't want more Scotch, and I didn't want him to continue provoking my mother. We needed her on our side, or all of this would be for nothing.

Ginny watched this all with amused fascination. She sat in one of my wingback chairs, her head lolling against the back and her denim-clad legs crossed at the knee, which annoyed Mom to no end. Her question was, like her, blunt. "Besides the occasional roll in the sheets, what do you get out of this?"

I should have known when he turned his attention directly to me that I wasn't going to like his response. He began slowly, thinking as he went along. "Well, my apartment burned down, so I have a roof over my head. And..." He leaned closer to me, speaking in a low voice, but loud enough so that everyone heard. The color of his eyes had shifted to smoky green. They mesmerized me. "Maybe we should try it in a bed next time?"

If my face wasn't on fire before, it was now. I needed more Scotch. Before I could choke on his words, he kissed me—right there in front of my mother, who never so much as allowed that sex might happen in a marriage. To this day, Ginny and I were convinced we were born via Immaculate Conception.

Mom shot to her feet. "I don't believe I approve of you. Sabrina, I think you have made a mistake in marrying this man. I hope for your sake that you have the sense to rectify your lapse in judgment before it is too late."

I knew she meant children. Her big regret in life was having children and then failing in her marriages. I had no doubt that if Ginny and I had not been born, she would have blithely gone through life as if she had never been married. When I was younger, I used to think that she should have remarried, and that a good man would have made her happy, but I knew that wasn't true. Nothing and nobody could make my mother happy. The best for which anyone could hope would be a little less bitter.

Jonas stood when my mother did. "Melinda, you know and I know that you made up your mind to dislike me the moment Sabrina introduced me. I understand why, and I don't blame you at all. If some stranger married my daughter in order to help her get an inheritance, I would be wary of him as well."

He had Mom's attention. Twin spots of anger stained each cheek. She did not like being called on her prejudgments, even when they were obvious. "How dare you!"

But he wasn't finished. I honestly didn't think someone so quiet and seemingly reserved would go up against my mother, his penchant for exhibitionism notwithstanding. I fell for him a little that night.

His face remained neutral, a mask. "Under the circumstances, I don't expect you to like me after one meeting. However I am your son-in-law, and that isn't going to change. I think the least you could do is give me a chance."

Ginny met my eyes and mouthed *wow*. It had taken her nearly seven years to get Mom to the point where she was civilized to Lara, whose only crime had been to fall in love with my sister. Mom didn't care about gender; she hated every person either of us ever dated, even Stephen. She was the only one who hadn't been upset when I'd ended that relationship.

Mom didn't respond, but Jonas had more to say. He turned to Ginny. "Sabrina's birthday is Wednesday. She told me how horribly your cousins have treated her. I'd like to invite them over for a small celebration. Can you take care of the invitations? I'll do all the rest."

"I don't want a party." My stomach muscles tightened, threatening to return dinner. I loathed the idea of a birthday party.

"You only turn thirty once," Ginny said. "I wanted to throw you a surprise party, but I canceled it when all this happened." She turned her thousand-kilowatt grin on Jonas. "I'd be happy to handle the invites and the cake. What's your cell number so we can plan this without Sabrina around? She can be such a wet blanket."

I didn't have a good feeling about this. Ginny had inherited a love for all of the social things in life, while I'd inherited a driving need to do well in school and succeed in my career. Whenever Ginny got an idea in her head, it grew and grew. By Wednesday, I had no doubt it would either be a formal dinner party or something with a beer keg and a musical act. Jonas and I would need to have a little chat before this got out of hand.

Ginny and Jonas talked about general plans for the party, ignoring my attempts to cancel it before they could spread the word. Mom studied them both carefully, sizing Jonas up differently than she had before. She had decided to postpone judgment.

On the way out, she hugged me and said, "Maybe you didn't completely mess up your life after all. We'll see. And don't worry about Ginny. I'll keep her under control." She bade Jonas a good evening, and they left.

He closed the door behind them and locked it for the night before leading me up the stairs, all of my intentions to do work forgotten. "That wasn't so bad, was it? I see why you're so close to Ginny. She's great. And your mom... Well, I see now why you are the way you are."

We had just reached the door to the bedroom when he said that, slowing his pace so that I could enter the room first. I stopped, blocking his path. "What is that supposed to mean?"

He smiled maddeningly before picking me up and moving me out of his way. He went into the dressing area and began untying his tie. "You didn't ask me how the presentation went."

"It went fine." I followed him without thinking. "Joy was impressed. I heard her congratulating Jared on it." I stopped suddenly. Jared would have presented the material without giving credit to Jonas or anyone else on his team. It was part of the reason people left his team as soon as they had a choice. "Oh. This was your first presentation, wasn't it?"

He hung his tie on a wooden spinning rack I had left empty because I had no idea what it was for. I had a jewelry chest for necklaces, and my stockings were in a drawer. "No, it wasn't. But it was better than the others, thanks to your input."

I waved away the compliment. "I didn't make any significant changes, Jonas. You do good work."

He unbuttoned his shirt. He had a magnificent, strong chest hidden under those suits. Patches of light, gently curling hair began at his navel and thickened as it traveled downward. The rest of him was recently tanned from the sun. I caught a glimpse of his tan line when he dropped his pants. There was so much I had been too preoccupied to notice.

"How does he get away with it?"

I tore my eyes away from his body as he finished undressing. "I'd like to say he doesn't, but he does. He's Joy's nephew. At least they don't advance him, but he doesn't seem to care."

Before I made a fool of myself, I went into the powder room to remove my makeup, closing the door for privacy. I didn't want to start something I knew wouldn't end satisfactorily for me, and I didn't want to take the chance it wouldn't be fulfilling for him. Though men were different, weren't they? Things like duration and quality didn't matter so much.

When I climbed into bed, he was already there, absorbed in a paperback novel, and the cream-colored sheet was pulled to his waist. He was shirtless, but that didn't surprise me. I had turned off the air conditioning. It wasn't warm for a June night, but it was too warm for a lot of clothing. Out of curiosity, I checked the cover of his novel. It was a popular mystery. He tossed it on the nightstand and turned out the light. I wondered if he was wearing anything under the sheet.

Thoughts of work and of my personal life whirled through my head. I waited for them to settle down so I could sleep, but one thing kept nagging at me. "Jonas?"

"Hmmm?" He was half asleep.

"I really don't want you to make a big deal out of this."

"Out of what?" he mumbled.

"Out of my birthday. I don't care for parties."

He didn't reply. I thought he was asleep until he pulled me to him and kissed me, cradling my face in his hands before he let them roam my body. I wore a thin cotton nightgown, and though he didn't move it out of the way, his hands burned through. I touched his bare chest, giving myself permission to touch him the way he touched me, and I kissed him back. When I let my hands roam over his hips, I found out he was wearing boxer shorts. I don't know if he knew I was holding back. I couldn't help but hold back. Things were different now. There was no audience, no urgency.

Finally he ended the kiss and his exploration of my body, falling asleep with his arm still draped across my midsection. For some reason, I left it there.

He half listened to my plea for not having a party. I felt a phone call was sufficient for informing my cousins about my current marital situation, preferably one delivered by the lawyer, but Jonas felt they needed to have their noses rubbed in it. He probably thought they should have their behinds smacked with a rolled-up newspaper as well.

When I arrived home on Wednesday, he and Ginny had arranged for a buffet-style dinner spread. Ginny brought an intricately decorated cake that had a combined birthday/wedding theme. It was way too much food for the nine of us. My three cousins and their parents all made it to the party. They probably thought we were trying to build a bridge because they were going to be wealthy.

Ginny accosted me with a big hug and smacked a kiss on my cheek. I smelled Scotch on her breath already. Mom must have been in rare form. I wasn't looking forward to seeing her, and I felt guilty about it.

"The cake looks wonderful, Gin." I recognized Drew's handiwork in the white chocolate bride and groom figures situated on the second tier, and Ginny's in the piping and pulled sugar flowers. Separately, they were amazing artists. As a team, they were unstoppable. "You guys are going to win that contest for sure."

"At least you and Lara have confidence in us," she said with a shrug. "But then again, you sort of have to." She liked to pretend it didn't matter to her, but I knew it did. Winning competitions like this not only brought them more business, which they didn't actually need, but also international acclaim, which they both craved. Drew was in negotiations to showcase the catering side of the business with a syndicated cooking show.

Ginny had been with Drew longer than she had been with Lara, having buddied up with Drew in middle school. They'd gone to pastry school together, but Drew had transferred to culinary school after a while. Ginny and Lara had met when Lara's mother hired the pastry school to cater her fiftieth birthday bash. It was love at first sight. Only later did Ginny find out Lara didn't have a sweet tooth. Being with a pastry chef, it was a waste, but at least Ginny knew Lara wasn't with her for the sweetness of her confections.

"Shut up," I said playfully. "You'll do fine."

The doorbell rang, and we both looked toward the foyer, then to one another. Ginny squared her shoulders and squeezed my hand.

"It's only one night," she said, letting out a long breath. "With a stranger here, they should be on their best behavior."

"We can hope," I said. I didn't have much hope, but I wanted to. Jonas had gone out of his way to make sure everything was perfect for tonight. He hadn't let me do a thing, shooing me from the kitchen last night while he prepared most of the meal.

I pasted a welcoming smile on my face and opened the door. There stood my mother's half brother and half sister with the three children they had between them. All five of them had arrived together, forgoing the bringing of spouses or other family members. I took that to indicate they didn't mean to stay very long.

Jonas joined me as I greeted the guests. I introduced Aunt Ingrid and Uncle Randolph first, then my cousins: Timmy, Tommy, and Regina.

I motioned to Jonas. "This is my husband, Jonas Spencer." Just as he had that fateful day, I emphasized the *S* sound to separate his names. Still dressed in his suit and tie, minus only his jacket, he had a very distinguished air about him.

Jaws opened in shock and outrage. I could hear them thinking about how close they'd come to a windfall, and then their looks turned speculative. They searched Jonas for flaws, but he didn't have any. He smiled graciously and shook hands.

I happened to catch my mother's eye as I turned. She had been in the kitchen with Jonas, but I hadn't made it back there to see her yet. The expression of smug satisfaction on her face did my heart some good. I didn't extrapolate that to mean she was warming up to Jonas, only that she loved witnessing the moment I brought down her estranged relatives' arrogance one notch.

If Jonas was shocked by the ages of my cousins, he managed to keep it under wrap. Having been so busy the last couple of days, I neglected to mention that my grandfather had been forty-two when he married my grandmother. It had been his first wedding, but her second. Ingrid and Randolph had both been in their early twenties when Grandma remarried. Grandma had been a widow, but since her kids were older and didn't live with them, Grandpa had never developed a close relationship with either of them.

The average age of my cousins was north of fifty, and my mother's siblings were firmly entrenched in their seventies. I wasn't close to any of them, and neither was she. The only time Grandpa had seen them after Grandma passed away was when they wanted money.

Jonas hid his surprise well, graciously greeting each person by name. Timmy and Tommy weren't twins, but they may have well as been. Less than a year apart in age, they were difficult to distinguish. Both short, rotund, and bald, they were even more difficult to tell apart now than when they were younger. It didn't help that they still dressed the same. Tommy's face was slightly more round, but that was the only significant difference.

Regina had fared better. Where Aunt Ingrid overindulged her boys from the beginning, Uncle Randolph was a much stricter parent. Regina reaped the benefits from personal discipline, but she was rather rigid in demeanor, and she had been raised to look upon my mother, two years her elder, with a disdain that carried over to Ginny and me.

"Dinner is served," Lara said, appearing from the kitchen and saving us from the awkward moment. Like Ginny, she dressed casually for the occasion, in jeans and a flower print T-shirt with the name of Ginny's bakery emblazoned on the back. I think they did this to get on my mother's nerves. She hated the sexual connotation behind *Sensual Secrets'* name.

Dinner conversation was strained. Jonas did a wonderful job keeping up a steady stream of topics. Lara complimented him on the dinner, which was homemade lasagna. "Did you make the sauce as well?"

"Yes. It's a Spencer family recipe. I'd tell you what's in it, but then I'd have to kill you. Then Ginny would kill me, and my parents would come after her. When all is said and done, the carnage wouldn't be unlike that at the end of *MacBeth*. It's better for everyone if I don't say too much."

Lara and Ginny shared a mercy laugh with him.

Aunt Ingrid said, "Well, that's wonderful. She's gone and married the hired help. He is not *our* kind. Dress it up all you want, dear, but trash is still trash."

Inhaling sharply, I trembled with buried anger. I struggled to contain it. Nothing good ever came of a display of temper around these people. Gradually, the fury subsided to annoyance, and then it receded to numbness. I felt as if I was made of ice and nothing could crack me. It was both comforting and disturbing.

Mom came to the rescue. "That kind of statement is not only untrue, but extremely rude."

Regina came to her aunt's defense. "Melinda, everybody employs a cook and a housekeeper. It's all right to cook recreationally, but not like this. We have people to do these things. I told you no good would come letting Sabrina pursue a sales job."

Though it was more of a swipe at Ginny than at me, the fact that she put down my talented sister made me hate Regina even more.

At work, when someone crossed a boundary or challenged me, I had no problem calling them out or putting them in their place. I couldn't seem to do it in my own home. My insides turned to ice, and my tongue was paralyzed. A thousand thoughts zoomed through my brain, but I couldn't utter a word. I stared at the remnants of sauce on my plate and wished this evening was over.

"I cook," Ginny returned frostily. "And when you can cook as well as this, it's a sign of affection and generosity to prepare a loved one's favorite meal."

Jonas had no way of knowing this was my favorite meal. I thought he'd made it because he wanted to show me how much better it was when it didn't come premade and frozen. Either way, it was a nice gesture. The entire evening was a nice gesture on both Jonas' and Ginny's parts. That brought no comfort.

"Not to mention that it's extremely ill-mannered to be so judgmental," Jonas added dryly. "Especially with someone you've known a total of twenty minutes."

He shot a concerned glance at me. I caught it from the corner of my eye, but I couldn't move. His hand crept over to take mine under the table. I stared down at it, unable to acknowledge his kindness or accept his reassurance. I wanted them to all leave, and I knew Jonas wasn't going to make them go. I had to do it.

Suddenly, I glanced up, catching everyone in a sweeping look, my cold smile frozen on my lips. "Well, now that dinner is finished, you'd best be getting on your way. Ginny will cut you a piece of cake to take home."

I stood, pushing back my chair, and began to clear the table. Jonas helped me. I snatched plates from Uncle Randolph and Regina that were only half-eaten. Timmy and Tommy gulped down their remaining bites before I made it around the table to them. Aunt Ingrid, despite her remarks about the dinner, slurped it down like a greedy pig at the trough.

Ginny, knowing I had reached the end of my endurance, retreated to the kitchen with Lara to prepare pieces of cake for everyone to take home. Mom handled the pleasantries until the five of them disappeared into their respective cars.

After closing the door behind them, I eyed the stairs. A long bath sounded good right now. I could light candles and use my scented oils. I could play soft jazz until I dozed in the cooling water.

"I know you're tired, honey," Mom said sympathetically. She took my hand and led me into the living room. "We have a few gifts, and then we'll leave you alone."

I didn't want gifts. I hated the obligation that went with forced gift-giving. Birthdays and Christmas were the two worst times of the year. I was forced to purchase gifts for people, and they were forced to do the same for me. When all was said and done, it was a wash. I had things I didn't want, and so did they.

I lowered myself to the edge of the sofa and softened my smile because it was expected of me. Ginny, Lara, and Jonas gathered around to watch as Mom put a slender box into my hands.

Carefully, I untied the ribbon. The plain, black box had no logo to mark it as a necklace or a watch or a pair of gloves. It was June. I hoped it wasn't a pair of gloves. Similarly, my mother and I had completely different tastes in jewelry, and I didn't wear a watch.

Slipping off the cover revealed folded papers—a legal document. Mom had signed the affidavit attesting to the fact that Jonas and I were in love. I had the twelve million dollars as long as we stuck it out for a year.

Stunned, I looked up at her. "But why?"

She smiled at me sadly. "Maybe I'm hoping. Either way, you deserve it, Sabrina. Dad had good intentions—he wanted to see you settled and happy—but it was a stupid provision."

Ginny hugged me and threw a larger box on my lap. "That's a little something for the both of you. It's a combination wedding and birthday present."

From the self-satisfied smirk on her face, I knew I was in trouble. Ginny knew I hated gift-giving. Long ago, she stopped buying things she thought I *would* like and started buying things she thought I *should* like.

Just to annoy her, I opened the wrapping paper at the seams, ripping nothing in the slow, painful process. "Bitch," she said good-naturedly. "Wait 'til you see what's inside."

It was filled with assorted colors and styles of silk, thigh-high stockings, matching garter belts, thong underwear, and bras. I raised a questioning brow at Jonas.

He shrugged. "That's all her. I can't say I have a problem with her taste, though."

Later, when everyone had gone, Jonas apologized for not giving me a gift. "I haven't had a chance to get to the store."

I was in the midst of shedding my work clothes. Presently, I wore only a skirt and bra. He leaned against the frame of the closet door, watching me. I liked the appreciative gleam in his eyes, and so I didn't protest the invasion of privacy. I tried to smile, but I wasn't sure how successful I was. "You've already given me the only thing I wanted."

He most likely thought I was referring to the fact he married me, but I meant the orgasm, and I had no intention of clarifying anything.

The smoke in his eyes should have made me wet with remembered passion and the promise of more to come, but it failed to move me. Still numb from the encounter with my relatives, I turned away from him to unzip my skirt. Still, he had done so much for me. When I felt his arms come around me from behind, I let my head fall back against his shoulder.

He kissed my neck and worked his way across my shoulders. His large, warm hands cupped my breasts. When I turned to face him, I tilted my face to meet his kiss, and I tackled the rest of the buttons on his shirt. We made our way to the bed, slowly undressing one another to explore and caress more skin. Though he didn't arouse me, I didn't mind his touch. It comforted me to be held and to hold him in return. Slowly, I began to unthaw.

After a while, when his green eyes turned tawny with his arousal, I ripped open a condom. He moaned when I touched him to put it on, and he kissed me as he entered me. When he was completely in, he stopped, looking down at me uncertainly. I was barely wet. I didn't know how he knew that through the lubricated condom, but he did.

"Don't stop," I said as I ran my fingertips down his chest and thrust my hips against him, wanting to get this part over with as quickly as possible. If he asked, I would blame hormones. I'm not sure if it would have counted as a lie, and I was glad when he didn't question me.

He thrust into me. I matched his rhythm as the heat built inside. I clung to him as his pace approached frenzy, and he whispered my name. I imagined it was an exclamation of passion, not the plea I so clearly heard. I did my best to fake pleasure, but I didn't overdo it. He knew he wasn't driving me insane as he had before. Eventually he came and collapsed next to me.

After a few minutes, I rose to complete my evening toilette. When I rejoined him, Jonas was laying on his side of the bed. I arranged the covers over us and turned off the light. Jonas lay next to me. I thought he was sleeping until he pulled me close and spooned me from behind.

"You didn't have an orgasm," he said, his voice muffled by my hair.

I really didn't want to discuss my sexual shortcomings with him. "But you did," I said. "That's all that matters."

He was quiet after that. Too quiet.

Chapter 5—Sabrina

We settled into the routine of the terribly busy. Jonas worked a second job tending bar at Ellen's club. Though I would have happily given him the extra money he seemed to need, I didn't feel it was my place to interfere with the life he had before he met me. Besides, I knew he wouldn't take money from me.

I woke Saturday morning to an empty bed. This surprised me because Jonas hadn't come home until after midnight. I lay staring at his vacant pillow, marveling at how much my life had changed—again—in one short week. Last weekend, I woke thinking I really should get to the office to begin to wade through the mountain of paperwork awaiting me. I had wanted something to take my mind away from the slap in the face that passed for my grandfather's will.

It wasn't that he left me out completely. From the day I was born, he'd paid into a trust for me. Mom and Ginny each had one as well. Twelve million was a symbolic inheritance. To me, that will might as well have meant that reading to him when his eyesight went and holding his hand through the pain and feeling as if part of me was dying right along with him didn't mean much because I lacked a life partner. I didn't want a life partner, not then and not now. Jonas wasn't bad company, but I would have rather been given a choice. Under different circumstances, who knows what would have happened?

When I was at work, nothing was different. Nobody knew I was married. Jonas hadn't said a word to anyone, either. We carpooled most days, separating and meeting at the elevator before and after work. Except for that first day, he hadn't appeared at my office again. Now he texted me if I wasn't at the elevators when he was ready to go, and I did the same with him.

I didn't know why neither of us said anything to anyone. Perhaps we wanted to avoid questions. He'd said he didn't want people to think the quality of his work was a reflection of me instead of him. Maybe he was ashamed of me.

Even the staff meeting was the same. He came in with his team, sat in the back, listened politely, asked relevant questions, and left when the meeting was over.

At home, some things were different and others were the same. The nights he was home, he cooked dinner, finished any work he brought home, and socialized with me. The nights he worked, he left right after dinner, and I didn't see him until the next morning when he magically appeared in my bed. I wondered how long it would be before he realized that it would be easier for him to stay in the city for dinner on the nights he had to work. Would he want me to dine with him, or would he send me home? In only a weeks' time, we hadn't settled into a firm routine, so it was hard to say.

This was our first weekend home together. I convinced myself to get out of bed and go for a swim. My pool was twenty-five meters, the standard competition length, and three lanes wide. Today promised to be sticky and warm. I turned on the air conditioning before heading out.

Jonas was nowhere to be found. I found no used dishes in the kitchen. It was as if he'd vanished. I grabbed a towel from the laundry room and headed outside. It was only nine in the morning, and the temperature was already in the nineties.

"Sleeping Beauty awakens."

I looked over to find the voice, shielding my eyes from the sun. I found him in the garage. Since it was an older home, the garage was a backyard feature instead of attached. I only minded in the dead of winter when the wind chill was far too cold. "What time did you get up?"

"Six." He walked toward me, dressed in cutoff shorts and an old T-shirt with a Woodhaven High School logo across the front. His glasses were missing, but from the way he looked up at me standing on the deck in my one-piece, I knew he could see me clearly. He stopped and rested an arm on the deck railing. His hair glinted with blond highlights in the bright sun, and his gaze wandered down the length of my body. "Is there a reason you pay someone to cut your lawn?"

It was an odd question. Unless he was talking about my bikini waxing habits, the answer was obvious. "Because if they cut my lawn, I don't have to."

"You don't have a lawn mower."

"The service has their own. They also deal with the weeds and fertilizer and all the stuff I want nothing to do with." I didn't like activities involving dirt or other places where bodies decomposed.

Jonas nodded once, the look on his face that of someone who should've known better than to ask. "So it's an exercise in futility to continue to look for gardening items?"

I shot him a sympathetic look. "I'm afraid so. I might have a little shovel somewhere, but that might be for snow."

He sighed, looking over my head, then back to me. "You hire out your snow removal, too?"

I descended the three steps to the flagstone path that split into two directions, one leading toward the garage, the other leading to the pool. It was probably not a good time to tell him I was seriously considering hiring that company to replace the path with pavement. "It's the same service."

He pulled me closer, resting his hands on my hips. "Going for a swim?"

"Obviously."

"You could be sunbathing," he said. "You do have a nice tan. And given your lack of interest in the outdoors, it wouldn't be much of a stretch to think you wouldn't want to get that suit wet." He tore his eyes from my chest and lifted my braid with one hand. "Or chlorine in your hair."

"Maybe you need to go back to sleep," I suggested. "You're condescending and cranky."

Abruptly, he let go. "I got up early so I could plant your birthday present, but I've spent the last three hours digging through the mass of junk in your shed and searching every inch of your ironically clean garage."

Hoping to soothe his mood, I took his hand lightly in mine. "You didn't have to get me a present, Jonas. You've done enough."

"I like to garden," he said. "I find it relaxing to plant something, nurture it, and watch it bloom into something beautiful. I wanted to give you something beautiful."

Words failed me. He filled my silence with a kiss. It was the first time he'd touched me since my birthday. I didn't realize until then that

I missed having physical contact with him. The kiss was soft and undemanding.

"You found nothing in the shed?" It was all I could think to say. The shed seemed like a logical place to find gardening equipment.

He shook his head. "A ton of old junk, magazines, trash, broken hoses, and cracked pots."

I made some kind of thoughtful sound.

"You have no idea what's out there, do you?"

I bristled at the laughter behind his words. "I don't think I've ever been in the shed."

"Then you won't be upset by the fact that I threw out most of it?"

The shed was toward the rear of my property. It was so far from the house that I never thought about it. It could have fallen down, and I wouldn't have noticed until my groundskeepers brought it to my attention. "You can do whatever you want with the shed and the stuff in it. Do you want me to have the guys finish cleaning it out on Thursday?"

"The guys?" He lifted an amused brow, something that didn't look right on him.

I was beginning to feel defensive. Who was he to judge the way I lived my life? I didn't hire out a lot of tasks, but there were some I simply didn't have the time or inclination to take on. "The guys who do the lawn. I sometimes hire them to do extra things. They do a good job."

This time he laughed. "Do you happen to know their names?"

"Yes, I know their names. There are only three of them. If you stop being mean to me, maybe I'll introduce you." I jerked my hand away and flounced down the path to the pool. If I had used their names, how the hell would he have known who I was talking about? He didn't know them.

I swam for a good two hours. It was one activity where I could lose myself, and given the way Jonas made my temper flare, it was a good way to work out my aggressions.

The midday sun blazed overhead, setting the pavement on fire, and I had forgotten to wear sandals. I hopped across the pavement around the pool to the grass and padded back to the house, avoiding the flagstone path. Maybe pavement wasn't a good idea.

Jonas was just returning to the house when I mounted the cooler wooden steps to the deck. Completely ignoring me, he opened his trunk and unloaded a shovel, gardening tools, and bags of dirt. I couldn't imagine why he needed bags of dirt. Under the grass, the entire yard was filled with dirt.

I went inside and ate lunch. After a shower, I called Ginny to wish her luck on her competition. Though it was on Monday, she was leaving tonight so she wouldn't feel rushed once she got to Atlanta. I wished I could take the day off work, but I was still so behind from my grandfather's funeral, and we had a large presentation due Tuesday. Mom would return with a camera full of pictures.

When Jonas came in later, he was sweaty and dirty. He stood in front of me, hands on his hips, and waited for me to finish talking to Ginny. It was amazing how quickly someone waiting in impatient silence could end a conversation.

"Did you want something?" I was still mad at him for treating me like I was less of a person because I hired out my lawn care and snow removal.

Wordlessly he grabbed my hand and dragged me out the back door, across the deck, and down the steps. Releasing me with an apparent carelessness, he gestured in front of us.

It was hard to miss, which was why I was even more discomfited when I realized what he had done. A trellis, stained to match the deck, sprouted from the freshly turned ground. In front of it was a rose bush in full bloom. The flowers were breathtaking, tangerine toward the bottom with a burst of pink at the tips. Jonas had threaded the thorny branches through the rungs of the trellis so they climbed up. In a few years, it would be covered with blooms. It touched me so much more than twelve million dollars.

When he'd said he wanted to give me something beautiful, I'd thought he wanted to cut the lawn and trim the bushes. After all, he did ask for the lawn mower. Now I understood why he got up so early. It was much cooler at six in the morning than it was in the afternoon, especially for this kind of work.

I stuttered trying to form words to thank him, to express how lovely it was—not only the flowers, but the gesture. Every time I returned to the house from a swim from now until the day I died, I would think of this moment. I choked on emotion.

Jonas had been watching the play of expressions cross my face. He took my hand in his sweaty one. I hung on tightly.

"I'm glad you like it," he said.

Finally, I found words. "It's beautiful."

He kissed me again, crushing my body to him. I was shocked by his hunger, and a little afraid. When he released me, I took a step back to steady myself. He bent to gather the last of his equipment.

"Jonas?"

He paused to look up at me, his eyes green in the bright light.

"Thank you."

He stood. "I'm sorry I was such a dick earlier," he said, leaning down to plant another kiss on me. "I don't suppose you're up to going to the lake tomorrow and meeting my family?"

Understanding dawned. I hadn't met his parents or his two sisters. He was nervous about introducing me, that's why he was behaving so oddly. My earlier fear came back to haunt me. Was he embarrassed about having me for a wife?

The idea followed me for the rest of the day and kept me up half the night. Jonas left after dinner to go to work. I was still awake when he returned at two, though I pretended to be asleep. He crept in quietly and disappeared in the bathroom. In minutes, I heard the shower. By the time he joined me in bed, I was asleep for real.

The next morning, we arrived at the lake before his parents to find that his sister, Amanda, and her husband, Richard, had already claimed a spot under a stand of trees. They had spread blankets on the grassy ground next to the picnic table and were busy unpacking a cooler. Amanda greatly resembled Jonas. She had the same curly light brown hair that shone with blonde highlights, only hers fell past her shoulders, and the same changeable green eyes. But where he was frequently introspective and quiet, she was outgoing and vivacious.

Amanda saw us approach as we topped the crest of the low hill between the beach and the parking area. She ran toward us and scooped me up in a heartfelt hug before we had been introduced. Luckily Jonas had insisted on carrying our cooler. All I had was the bag with our towels and a change of clothing.

"I'm so happy to finally meet you," she gushed. "Jonas has been talking about you for months and months. It's about time he brought you around to meet us."

She was still hugging me as she said this, lifting me slightly off the ground. At five foot seven, she was the short one in the family. I quirked my brows at Jonas, questioning her greeting. He shrugged in response.

"That's interesting," I said. "We've only known each other for a week."

That threw her for a loop. She let go, holding me at arm's length to study me. When she did that, she looked so much like Jonas that I was surprised she didn't follow it up with a kiss. Then she frowned and looked at him. "Joan?"

"Don't call me that," he said, ignoring the question completely.

"Hey!" Another voice called from behind us. "I thought that was you."

I turned to find a leggy, blonde-haired, blue-eyed beauty bearing down on us. She had a bag slung over one tan, athletic shoulder. She approached without varying her pace. She seemed like the kind of woman who never hurried anywhere because she knew that nothing truly began until she arrived. Despite that, I liked her immediately.

"Sam," Jonas said, handing his cooler to Richard and throwing an arm around her. She was nearly his height. "This is Sabrina. Sabrina, this is my baby sister, Sam."

"It's very nice to meet you." I expanded my gesture to include Amanda. "Both of you."

Jonas had prepared me for his family by disclosing general information like names and ages. The three siblings and Richard quickly fell into the kind of conversation people who've known each other for a very long time have. I found out Richard and Amanda had been dating since the eighth grade. She was my age and had been married for ten years. They had two kids, four and two, who had stayed the night with their grandparents, and so they would show up whenever the elder Spencers arrived. That might have been my life if I had accepted Stephen's proposal.

Sam was a couple years younger than me. She was currently flying solo. She threw all the bags at Jonas and Richard, then dragged Amanda and me to the blanket, insisting she wanted to get to know me better.

It didn't take long to decide I liked his sisters. They had a million questions about our impulsive wedding. I wasn't sure what Jonas had told them, and I didn't want to reveal anything he wanted to keep hidden, so I tried to turn the conversation around.

"What did Jonas tell you?"

"Are you pregnant?" Sam asked, leveling a serious look at me.

My eyebrows shot skyward. "We've only known each other for a week."

Amanda tilted her head and leaned back. "You have to admit this is weird. I mean, he's been talking about how much he wanted to ask you out for months, and now here you are—married. How did it happen?"

I answered honestly. "I don't know. He was there, and I asked him to marry me. There was no forethought or planning of any kind involved. It was literally the first thing I said to him."

Sam's blue eyes sparkled. "That's so romantic."

Amanda rolled her green ones. "That's so unlike Jonas. He just agreed to it? He didn't ask for time to think it over?"

"He thought it over," I said. "He asked questions, negotiated terms, and then he agreed."

Amanda snorted. "That's more like him. He's terribly analytical."

"Annoyingly so. What were the terms?" Sam asked.

I refused to tell them the terms, but I think they guessed something from the blush I couldn't stop. A shadow fell over us.

"Are you guys being mean to my woman?" Jonas frowned with mock severity.

"No. Go away," Sam said, waving her hand to shoo at him.

He crouched down in front of me. "Sabrina?"

I still had to look up at him. Luckily, the sun was off to the side somewhere. "They want to know why I married you."

"And you said?"

I didn't fight my impish impulse or a smile. "You were the hottest guy in the room."

"Ha, ha," he said without a trace of amusement.

"He must have been the only guy in the room," Sam said. She turned to Jonas. "So what would you have done if she had ignored you?"

"Ignored me?" he asked as if it were the most outrageous idea in the world. "She couldn't keep her eyes off me. She just sat there in that short skirt, showing off her legs and staring at me. I couldn't ignore an invitation like that."

"The skirt was knee length," I said.

He laughed. "If your knee was in the middle of your incredibly sexy thigh, then it was knee length."

I would have responded, but Amanda beat me to it. "Okay, you two, we get it. We're just glad Jonas is finally with someone. He hasn't had a girlfriend in more than five years."

I looked from Amanda to Jonas and back again. "I don't believe that."

He pulled me to my feet. "She didn't say I didn't date, Sabrina, only that I didn't have anyone steady."

"Then it's a good thing you met me," I joked.

His response was to study me silently. "Come on," he said softly after what seemed like forever. "Let's swim."

It was amazing how something so quietly stated could be so disquieting. I followed him to the water, pensive until he scooped me up and dived beneath a wave. Then all bets were off. I squirmed out of his hold and swam off, daring him to chase after me. We had fun.

His parents didn't arrive until after lunch. They had called to let Amanda and Richard know that their children were not easy to motivate in the morning. Richard had laughed, an infectious sound, saying they got it from their mother. Amanda shot him a look, but it was more playful than indignant.

Brandon and Alyssa Spencer were both tall and good-looking. Jonas and Amanda resembled their father, while Sam seemed to favor Alyssa's classic beauty.

Alyssa Spencer was the opposite of my mother in every way. Like Amanda, she was instantly friendly, welcoming me with a genuine hug. When she smiled, she meant it, and when she asked me about myself, it was because she wanted to know more about me. I didn't get the sense that she judged me. I was a little less sure of myself around Brandon. I had been close to my grandfather, but I always seemed to be ill at ease around other people's fathers.

Perhaps it was because I saw so much of Jonas in Brandon that his constantly friendly overtures won me over before the day ended. Brandon was a very handsome man. I found myself wondering how Jonas would age, but I shook away the thought. He was mine only for a year.

"I know it's only been a week," Alyssa said as she unloaded the lunch items from the cooler we had just packed away, "but how do you like being married to a former teacher?"

I shrugged. "I didn't know Jonas when he was a teacher. He's a little bossy, but he's nothing compared to me."

Jonas had just finished racing Ricky, Amanda's five-year-old, back from the shore. Ricky won, but Jonas made a good show of it. He overheard my remark.

"I'm not bossy," he said. "You're just not used to having another person in your house."

While that was true, it wasn't enough to cloud my judgment. "Picky, then," I amended. "Particular."

Alyssa laughed. "That's my son. You can add stubborn, bull-headed…"

"Those are synonyms, Mom," Jonas said, popping the lid of an energy drink and taking a long pull.

"Whiny and irritable, especially when he doesn't get enough sleep," Sam added.

"Enough," Jonas said. "Sabrina has plenty of time to experience all of my faults on her own."

"Yes," I agreed. "I met irritable yesterday."

"You're supposed to be on my side," Jonas added with a pointed look at me. "You know, being married to me and all."

I refrained from pointing out that he was back to being bossy. Smiling in remembrance, I said, "I've also met kind, generous, and thoughtful. He planted a rose bush for my birthday."

Jonas paused in the midst of finishing his drink to return my smile.

"That's my son," Brandon said, throwing an arm around Jonas' shoulders and clapping him on the back. "I'll take credit for that."

I felt dishonest and hypocritical as the day wore on. His family welcomed me like I was a real daughter-in-law. At least my family knew this was a temporary arrangement. I didn't have to pretend so much around them. I didn't mean I pretended to like them or Jonas; I wholeheartedly liked every one of his relatives. But I did have to watch what I said. I knew we didn't have a future, and that made it difficult to participate in talk about the future. Perhaps we would continue to be friends afterward, but that was doubtful. Whatever the outcome, we would remain friendly. After all, we were colleagues.

I must have been frowning into the distance as I sat on a blanket and looked out over the lake, because Jonas joined me before too long.

"You okay?" He had just come from swimming and droplets of water fell on me, cooling my skin where the sun had warmed it.

"Fine. Why?"

"You have a brooding look about you. Serious thoughts?"

I saw that his eyes were the prettiest shade of green in the brightness of the sun. I smiled a quick, reassuring smile. "The pessimist in me is wondering why your family is being so nice."

"They must like you," he said, laying down next to me and closing his eyes against the bright sun. "Don't be so hard on yourself. Lots of people like you."

"You said people at work are afraid of me," I reminded him.

"Afraid of disappointing you," he corrected. "That's an important distinction." He reached up, grabbed my ponytail, and pulled me down to him. It was an awkward position to hold, and I fell onto his chest. He laughed as he kissed me. "Nobody wants to disappoint you."

I closed my eyes. I knew he was referring to the other night. He had kissed me a couple of times since then, but he hadn't tried to go any further. I wasn't sure if it was because he was adhering to the agreement and he wanted to space out the twice weekly promise of sex, or if he thought he had been inadequate in bed.

"You don't disappoint me."

A frown wrinkled between his brows. "I shouldn't have pushed you. I knew you were stressed out by the dinner and everything. I thought I could help you relax."

Nothing would have helped me relax. Even the prospect of the bath I'd imagined to soothe myself was iffy. I shook my head. "It's me, not you. I probably should have told you sooner, but I didn't think it would bother you so much."

"You've had this problem before?"

I rolled to lay next to him. Most men would have been happy that I put out. Most men wouldn't have noticed I wasn't overly enthusiastic. Most men wouldn't bring up the topic or want to discuss it.

Jonas wasn't most men.

"I really don't want to talk about this."

"We'll get to it sooner or later," he said, reaching over to turn my face to him. "Wouldn't you rather sooner?"

"No," I said. "I'd rather not at all." His silence was deafening, so I added a plea. "Look, I'm having a nice time here with your family. Let's not ruin it, okay?"

He propped himself up on one elbow to kiss me slowly and deeply. "Okay, Sabrina, but I'm not going to let it go. We will resolve this before the day is over."

I hoped that meant he would leave it alone until we got home. Whatever the case, he didn't bring it up for the rest of the day.

We all left together, packing up everything in a whirlwind of activity. I helped Amanda carry her tired children to her car. Richard had already been loaded up like a pack mule. Faith snuggled into my shoulder. She was an energetic two-year-old, and she had taken an instant liking to me.

"Are you gonna come to my house?" she asked sleepily. "You can sit in the back with me."

"Sorry, honey," I said gently. "Not today. I have to go home with Uncle Jonas. We came together."

"So he doesn't have to drive alone?"

"Right." I settled her into her seat and secured the complicated belt over her. Turning to Amanda, I said, "You might want to check to make sure I did this right."

She laughed, but she followed my suggestion. As I looked on to see whether or not I made an error, I caught sight of Jonas talking to two very young, bikini-clad women. He was laughing at something one of them said. The girl leaned in closer. It was obvious they knew each other.

Amanda, who had been talking to me, backed out of the car. She might have asked me something, but I had ceased listening. Perhaps I had no right to the possessiveness and jealousy I felt, but there was no denying I was in their grip.

Following my line of vision, Amanda grabbed my arm. "Students."

"What?"

She squeezed my arm tighter, demanding my attention. "They're students."

"What does that mean?" I was truly lost.

Sympathy emanated from her eyes. "Until January, Jonas taught high school. We can't go anywhere without him bumping into a student or one of their parents. Those are probably high school students."

"They're not wearing enough to be high school students," I said. And they were awfully close to him. I'd never stood that close to a teacher.

She laughed at me, the same way Jonas did when he found me amusing. "We're at the beach. It's summer. Don't tell me you wore a muumuu to the beach when you were sixteen."

"I didn't talk to my teachers in public, even if I liked them," I said. "I pretended I didn't see them, and they cooperated fully."

Amanda laughed again. "He was well-liked by his students and respected by his colleagues and the parents of his students. They were sorry to see him go."

"I thought Jonas left teaching because he didn't like it anymore."

"Who told you that?" She closed Faith's door and opened her own. "Jonas loved teaching, and he was very good at it."

I wondered why he told me he left because he was tired of it. I hadn't been aware he'd left in the middle of the school year. As I approached my car, I could see that his smile was genuine. Everything about his body language conveyed a liking for the company, the conversation, or both.

"Mr. Kubina said you might come back next year." The slim blonde sounded hopeful as she sucked on the end of a stand of hair.

"No," he said. "I won't be coming back."

"But why? You're such a good teacher." This was from the other blonde.

Jonas hadn't seen me coming. I didn't want to interrupt, so I reached into his pocket for the car key. If our car was anything like Amanda's, it would be baking hot on the inside. I intended to get the air conditioning going.

Without missing a beat, he snagged my wrist and pulled me closer, throwing an arm around my waist. "Sabrina, this is Rebecca and this is Brooke, both former students of mine. Girls, this is my wife, Sabrina."

"You really did get married?" the one I thought was Brooke exclaimed. "Mr. Spencer, you swore you'd never get married! You said they'd have to drag your rotting corpse to the church and hope hell froze over!"

Both girls gaped at me as if I were an exhibit in an oddities museum that suddenly sprang to life, proving for once and all that I wasn't wax. Suddenly the one who was probably Rebecca remembered her manners. "It's nice to meet you, Mrs. Spencer."

We exchanged basic pleasantries for about thirty seconds before the girls beat a retreat. As they walked away, I overheard one of them say, "Well, she's hot, that's why he married her."

"They've got you pegged," I said.

He kissed me and opened the passenger door for me. "I'm not complicated."

As we drove home, I couldn't help but wonder at his claim. He didn't seem complicated, but the more I got to know him, the more complicated he became. If what Amanda had said was true, why had he given up teaching? The students obviously liked him, and he seemed to have a good relationship with them. Starting pay at Rife and

Company wasn't very much, so that couldn't have been a lure, and our benefits weren't all that great.

It wasn't really my business, but I couldn't help my curiosity.

Chapter 6—Sabrina

When we got home, I went upstairs to shower. I shampooed my hair, washing out the sand and the smell of lake. Letting the water beat its rhythm into my face, I tried to relax. The day had been nice. I hadn't been kidding when I told him I liked his family. They were the kind I always wished I had.

It wasn't that I didn't love my mother and Ginny, because I did love them very much. The Spencers knew how to have fun, how to enjoy being together. I liked his sisters, and I knew Ginny would as well. I had an adorable niece and a cute little nephew who were openly affectionate with their new aunt even though I was essentially a stranger.

Ginny had given Jonas the benefit of the doubt, but she still doubted him. Mom hadn't been more than polite to Jonas, which was how she would treat anyone she didn't like. I was the same way. If I liked someone, I was a little more relaxed around them, but not much. I often wondered if people could tell the difference. They weren't supposed to be able to discern anything. Manners had always been of foremost importance in my upbringing. Ginny had escaped those strictures. I think weekends with her father helped. It would explain the difference between us.

I wondered if my mother's marriage would have lasted longer if she'd ever been playful and affectionate with Ginny's father, as Jonas' parents were with one another. I wondered if she'd felt affection for him at all, or resentment because Grandpa had essentially forced her to marry, or was she just cold like me? I didn't want to be cold and unfeeling, I just didn't feel anything very deeply.

I tried to feel pride in my accomplishments, but I did not. I wanted to feel something for Jonas. I liked him. He was attractive and intelligent and fun. I wanted to look at him and feel desire, but I didn't anymore. Only that first night had been magic. It was as if I had been allotted one good night of sex. I knew I'd used it well, but I resented not being able to have more. I wanted to feel an orgasm again.

The door to the bathroom opened and closed. A cool breeze brushed against me as Jonas opened the curtain to the shower. It wasn't unusual for him to poke his head into the bathroom to talk to me or ask something, but he didn't usually open the curtain. I did the math and prepared myself to meet his sexual demands.

He put his arms around me from behind, pressing his naked body to mine. "You okay?"

Warm water sluiced over us. When I'd had the bathroom remodeled last year, I'd put in a shower easily large enough to accommodate two. I liked open spaces. "Yeah," I said, laying my head back against his shoulder and forcing my body to relax.

He dropped a kiss on my temple. "Dinner will be ready in about fifteen minutes. It's warming in the oven." With that, he patted my hip dismissively and reached for the soap.

I was relieved. Failure wasn't something I enjoyed. I wondered if he'd be okay with a blowjob instead, but I didn't ask. I was sure he hadn't given up on me yet. This stubborn man would take time to convince, and I didn't look forward to the process.

After dinner, he suggested a movie. We agreed on something, and as I set it up, he turned off most of the lights, leaving only the one in the upstairs hall lit. The gentle, soft light spilled into the living room, relieving the darkness enough so that we could see each other. I sat at one end of the sofa. Jonas stretched out, rested his head on my leg, and fell asleep.

The movie was one I liked, so I kept watching, letting him sleep undisturbed on my lap. I did remove his glasses, but otherwise I left him alone. He had worked last night after getting up so early to plant my rosebush. He hadn't been scheduled, but Ellen had called, desperate because someone else had canceled.

"I've worked at Elle's club since I was in college," he had said. "It pays well, and it's work I enjoy, so I never quit."

"You don't owe me an explanation," I had assured him. "I don't want you to change your life for me."

When the movie was nearly finished, I became aware that he was awake and watching me. I concentrated on the finale, trying to ignore him, but he was too distracting. I moved my hand, which had been resting on his shoulder, to cover his penetrating stare.

He chuckled, and I felt the low rumble on my leg. "Do I make you nervous?"

"You're distracting me."

"You didn't mind being watched last week." His voice was low and husky with remembered desire.

My skin burned. My face heated, and I lied. "I didn't pay attention to any of that."

"You did when we first got there."

"Jonas," I protested.

"Is it safe to say being watched wasn't what turned you on?"

I was thankful he hadn't moved my hand from his eyes. My pink cheeks weren't going away anytime soon if he wanted to pursue this line of conversation. "You liked it. It didn't affect me one way or another."

That wasn't entirely true. While they didn't distract me, something about the fact that everyone was enjoying themselves made it seem like it was okay for me to do so. I didn't think anyone there would judge me. This brought up an exasperating paradox. There was no one here to judge me either, so why couldn't I have an orgasm? I wanted to have one. Jonas wanted me to have one. Besides my inability to perform, there didn't seem to be a real conflict.

He didn't respond except to pick my hand up. He stared at me as he put my finger in his mouth, suckling and nipping at it. I know he meant it to be erotic, but the only thought running through my head was a thankfulness that I'd already seen the end of the movie. I closed my eyes and tried to enjoy what he was doing to me.

Lifting and turning, he pulled me under him, and his lips found mine. I kissed him back. His kisses always affected me. I gave myself permission to touch him, to run my hands over his chest, shoulders, back, and neck. He felt good. He was soft and hard in all the right places.

When he lifted again to let me remove his shirt, I saw the raw desire written in his eyes. It gave me pause. How could he want me so much when I knew I'd disappointed him last time, and he had to know this time would be no different?

He slid my lightweight sweats down my legs, stroking his hands over flesh I desperately wished was more sensitive to his touch. It was pleasant, but that was all.

My bare legs were next to feel the gift of his kisses, and all the places that made me wet when he had touched me at that club failed to react in the privacy of my own home. Ever so lightly, he grazed his teeth along the back of my knee. The last time he'd done that, my body had shot into the air at the electric pleasure. Now—nothing. He dropped my leg and wedged himself between me and the back of the sofa, popping himself up on one hand.

"What's wrong?"

I did my best to look innocent and puzzled. "Nothing." I didn't push my luck by asking why he'd stopped. I knew the reason all too well. If he asked to see other people, I wouldn't protest, though part of me wanted to. I'd accepted his terms and promised to abide by them, and I took my promises to heart.

He gave me that look. It was deeply penetrating. I felt naked, as if he could see my soul, which wasn't something I was sure I'd even seen. I lifted my hand to my heart, covering the place where it seemed likely a soul would reside.

Guessing he was giving up for the night, I tried to sit up, but he rolled on top of me, pinning me to the sofa with his hands and his tawny eyes. Instantly I was wet. What was wrong with me? If he got angry, would that fuel my desire? The thought brought no comfort, especially when I questioned whether I was desperate enough to try to push him.

"Do you want to have sex or don't you?" The harsh tone was a cover for the embarrassment I felt over being aroused by something he clearly hadn't meant as a sexual move.

He studied me a moment longer. "I think the question isn't whether *I* want to have sex, Sabrina. I think the question is whether *you* want to have sex."

I shrugged. "I wasn't stopping you."

He growled. "Are you attracted to me at all?"

The question took me by surprise, and his growl sent pleasant shivers down my inner thighs. "Of course I find you attractive."

He shook his head. "That's not what I asked."

"Then I don't know what you're asking." Frustrated, I pushed against him, but he didn't budge. I pushed harder, still with no result. Curiously, my heart sped up, shooting excitement to my core. It only excited me more to know my attempt to free myself was futile. I had no power over the situation right now.

"I'm asking if you feel attraction for me. That would be the physical response—desire. I know I can turn you on, but I have no idea how I accomplished it before. If it wasn't the audience, and it wasn't the way I touched you, Sabrina, what was it?"

His voice was soft; his eyes, patient. He actually wanted to know. Unfortunately I had no idea what to tell him. I squirmed, pushing with all the strength I had and refusing to meet his gaze. I wasn't strong enough to move him, and so I closed my eyes against the tide of desire sweeping through me. He was getting the response he wanted, only this wasn't how he wanted it. It couldn't be. I was more messed up than I'd ever guessed.

Finally growing impatient, he captured my hands and pressed them to the sofa. Heat spiraled to my pussy, and all he'd done was try to talk to me. I felt my control slipping, and it scared the hell out of me.

"Sabrina, I only want to make you feel good." He issued the assurance somewhere between a growl and a plea. "But you have to tell me what you like. You have to tell me how you like to be touched. When I say I'll do anything you want, I mean it. There are no boundaries I won't cross to make you come."

My breathing was ragged with effort. It could have been the desire, but I didn't want to admit to it. "Let go of me."

Instantly I was free. I fled the room. Like a coward, I wanted to hide in my room, close the door, and have a good cry. I made it as far as the foyer before he caught me.

He pressed me to the wall, caging me with his arms, but otherwise not touching me. I closed my eyes against the suddenly insistent throbbing between my legs. What was *wrong* with me? A man is tender and gentle with me, and my body fails to respond. He pins me in place to demand answers, and all I can picture is him lifting me and fucking me against the wall. I trembled at the thought.

"I'm not going to hurt you," he said, trying to soothe me with his tone and his words. "I just want to know how to make you come. It's something we'll both enjoy. I promise, Sabrina. That's all I want."

I refused to look at him, keeping my gaze downcast. "I don't have answers for you. Why can't you just have sex with me and not worry about anything else? I'm willing to let you have my body, Jonas. Don't overthink this."

He smiled sadly. "I'm not that kind of lover. The more you enjoy it, the more I enjoy it. I want you to lose control in my arms, Sabrina. I want to feel you come on me until I can't hold back anymore."

I hazarded a brief look in his eyes. He was sincere, but I had nothing to give him. "You didn't seem to have a problem last time."

"Ejaculating isn't the same as coming. It feels good, but it isn't enough. Was it enough for you?" He traced his thumb lightly along the edge of my lower lip. He wanted to kiss me, but he wasn't going to do it until he was sure I wanted it. Perhaps he wanted me to beg? He'd liked it a lot when I'd begged in the club.

My cheeks flamed. "I didn't hate it, Jonas. It was pleasant."

He exhaled his frustration. "The smell of roses is pleasant. Sex should be orgasmic, which is a far cry from pleasant."

Closing my eyes and turning my face away again, I said, "It isn't you. It's me. You're doing everything right."

"Obviously not."

I didn't know how to respond. So many reasons winged their way through my thoughts, most of them true, but none of them things I wanted to say out loud. I could fake it better for him, couldn't I? I'd faked it plenty of times with Stephen and various other men over the years. Jonas wanted more of a show, and I could do that. It was only for a year.

"Tell me about a time you've had an orgasm, Sabrina. What happened? Where were you? How and where did he touch you? What did he say to you?"

My jaw dropped, and I stared at him in amazement. Never had one of my lovers asked me to tell them about my experiences with other men.

He knew he'd shocked me. His mouth curved with amusement. "I'm not jealous or naïve. I know you've had other lovers. So have I. I'm willing to tell you anything you want to know. I like a lot of different things, but mostly I like when my lover gets off. Nothing compares to the feel of woman coming around my cock." Leaning closer, he spoke near my ear. He brushed back my hair, his fingers gently caressing, and his warm breath fanned my neck. "I like it when you squeeze me with your cunt. The feel of you pulsing around me is unparalleled. I want you to come on my fingers and in my mouth. I want to know how to touch you to make you do that, Sabrina. Tell me. Let me give that to you."

I choked back a sob. I wanted that too. My desperate confession was filled with years of repressed longing. "I don't know."

He stepped back, no longer caging me, and studied me with that look. "You mean to tell me that the only orgasm you've ever had was last week?" He didn't bother to temper his incredulity.

Mortified I nodded once, my gaze firmly on the cherry flooring I'd installed before last winter. The dim light from the upstairs hall reflected from it unevenly. He was quiet for so long, I had to say something. "I told you it was me, not you."

He wrapped his arms around me in a comforting hug. I didn't want his pity, and so I tried to squirm away. He didn't let go, and I gave up trying to escape.

"What about when you masturbate? Do you prefer your fingers, or do you use a vibrator? A clitoral simulator? Do you prefer to be stimulated from the outside or the inside?" He spoke the words into my hair, murmuring them in a tone meant to comfort me.

Masturbation was a joke. I'd tried it several times over the years, but nothing happened. I'd tried fantasizing, but to no avail. I shook my head against his chest.

He was quiet for a long time, no doubt hunting his mind for an answer. I gave him credit for perseverance. "Okay, something turned you on last week. Let's take this apart." He let me go and stepped back to study me. "We made out at the hotel. Did that turn you on?"

I shrugged, blushing furiously. I wished more than anything for him to let this go. Why couldn't he just take what was offered and not question it?

"Sabrina, now is not the time to be shy."

"I don't think you understand that this isn't something that's supposed to be talked about." I snapped at him, the words leaving my mouth without consulting my brain.

His lips parted and his eyes widened. I'd managed to shock him. "Why not? Just because you were raised by a sexually repressed, uptight woman doesn't mean you have to be one too."

I saw red. He was right, of course. I didn't want to be that woman, but I didn't want to talk about it either. "I'm finished with this conversation, Jonas. I'm going to bed."

He caught me again, caging me against the wall. Not trusting me to refrain from ducking under his arm and running for the stairs, he held me in place with the press of his body. I closed my eyes as my panties became soaked with juices.

"I'm not going to let you have your way in this. You're stuck with me for a year. I was very open about the fact that I like sex. Active sex, where we both enjoy each other's bodies to the fullest, not crappy, passive sex. I'm perfectly capable of masturbating by myself. Of course, you're always welcome to watch. You know how I like an audience."

He kept his voice low, meaning it to be erotic. It was, but it didn't affect me nearly as much as the fact that he was holding me in place. I looked up at him and saw his tawny eyes light as he recognized the desire in mine.

"What am I doing that's turning you on?" He didn't move a muscle.

For the life of me, I didn't want to tell him. It was too humiliating. I was an intelligent, capable, successful woman. Why did a man holding me immobile make my legs weak? I closed my eyes and turned my face away.

He didn't move for the longest time, and then I felt his strong hands encircling my wrists. He forced them above my head and pinned them to the wall. I couldn't stop the whimper that escaped or the tear that labeled my shame. I fought him, but he only tightened his grip. My limbs weakened with desire. I stopped struggling.

"Look at me." He issued the command in a tone that left no doubt who was in charge.

Reluctantly I did as he said, letting him see my misery. "This isn't right."

He searched my face, wonder and hope lighting his features. "There's nothing wrong with this, Sabrina. Don't judge what turns you on, and don't try to rationalize it. Desire isn't a rational thing. Have you ever been held down? Tied up?"

I shook my head. None of my lovers had been the kind of men who would think of anything outside of the realm of what was considered normal.

"I didn't hold you down last week." He frowned.

"You did." My volume approached a whisper. "When we danced, you held me close. You didn't let me get more than a few inches from you."

"You were wearing high heels after having a little too much wine. I was helping you balance. That wasn't aggressive or possessive. Well, maybe a little bit possessive. Do you like knowing you belong to me?"

I ignored his question, dismissing the absurdity. "When you first took me into that room, I wanted to leave, but you wouldn't let me." He had wrapped his arms around me and held me immobile. I was wet then, and I was wet now.

"I wouldn't have held you there if I thought you really wanted to leave. Was I wrong?" The frown hadn't left his face.

"At first. But no, I wanted to stay. I knew you would have left if I asked."

He lowered his head slowly, brushing his lips against mine. Electricity raced through me, and a fire ignited. I nearly sobbed with relief. In holding me down, he set me free. I didn't understand it, and I didn't want to.

I opened to him, deepening the kiss. I tried to move my arms, to embrace him, but he didn't let me move. I moaned, a small sound, but it got his attention. He broke the kiss and, breathing hard, grinned at me. I wanted his lips back. I tried for them, but he evaded my attempt.

"Onion."

Onions had not been on the menu at dinner, so I had no idea what he was talking about. He laughed at my puzzled expression and kissed me, hard and brief.

Regarding me with complete sobriety, he said, "If we're going to do this right, we need a safeword. If I do something to you that you don't like, you want me to stop, or if I hurt you, say onion and I'll stop immediately. If you protest or say no, I will ignore it."

"Why would you hurt me?"

He shrugged. "You're a sexual mystery, but I like mysteries. If I'm going to push your boundaries, it stands to reason I may go too far. I already know you like it rough, and I can be very rough, perhaps more so than you can take. A safeword will stop the action, temporarily or permanently."

The idea of something like this wasn't new to me, but I'd always dismissed it as deviant and absurd. Now it opened the door to something denied me for so long. I opened my mouth and closed it, and then I tried again. "How do I know if it's temporary or permanent?"

"We decide that during the time out. Now, if you understand the rules, I'd really like to fuck you." He was hard against me. Too preoccupied with my own budding desire, I hadn't noticed that this turned him on just as much as it aroused me.

My blushes were becoming a permanent thing around him. Would I ever grow used to hearing that word? Probably not. I nodded, giving my consent to begin. He dropped his hands from my wrists, which I found disappointing. He used his body to hold me in place as he explored and left behind trails of quivering flesh.

He stroked me over my panties. Chuckling at how wet they were, he pushed them down my hips until they pooled at my ankles. I kicked them aside, and he slipped his hand between my legs, parting me and stroking until I panted and held onto him for balance.

When he slid one arm around me and lifted, I really thought he meant to lower his pants with his free hand, but he surprised me by thrusting several fingers all the way inside. I exhaled a gasp at the sudden and violent intrusion.

Pausing, he locked eyes with me, waiting for me to say the word to tell him he'd gone too far. I stared silently, waiting for him to continue. He separated his fingers and slowly slid them down until they were almost out. The sensation was incredible. I let my head fall back against the foyer wall and dug my fingers into his shoulders. He had become my anchor.

By the time he thrust upward, the tension inside had coiled so tightly I had to concentrate on not panicking. He repeated his movements, drawing sighs and moans from places I hadn't known existed. My hips moved, thrusting against him to the rhythm he established. It pushed me so close, but it wasn't enough.

"Jonas?" I struggled to utter the single word, not because I was speechless with desire, but because I was about to ask him to share something, and I didn't know how he felt about it. Okay, maybe it was a little bit of both.

Without missing a beat or pausing in his actions, he pressed his temple to mine. "Yes?"

"You said that you fantasized about me." Was it wrong to bring that up now?

He smiled, his breaths coming soft against my cheek. "Frequently."

"Will you..." I licked my lower lip nervously. "Will you tell me about it? Or is that too personal?"

He stilled his fingers inside me. He withdrew, and I whimpered in protest before I thought about what I was doing. The kiss was slow and deep, but not unexpected. I didn't anticipate him letting me slide to the floor.

"You're allowed to get personal," he said at last.

He roamed my thighs, trailing his fingertips across my hips to caress my waist and stomach. He sealed his forehead to mine and kept his eyes on my body. "The first time I saw you, you were standing in the hall behind your office talking to Jared."

The lightness of his touch and the fact that I knew he wasn't going to let me go anywhere combined in a curiously erotic fashion. He knew it. I don't know how, but he did, and he fanned the flames inside me higher.

"Your skirt was cream-colored. It had about an inch of lace at the hem that ended just above your knee. You were wearing matching stockings. Thigh-highs, the kind you hold up with a garter belt."

I loosened the tie on his sweats and watched them slither to the floor. I knew he had shifted from reality to his fantasy. The skirt was real, but thigh-highs were a recent thing. I had yet to wear Ginny's gifts.

"You saw me coming and got rid of him. It was just the two of us. You asked me into your office to reach something." He said the last two words slowly, as if they were an inside joke.

I gave his underwear the same treatment he'd given mine. He looked very sexy in boxer briefs, but I wanted to touch him. Taking him in my hands, I caressed the extra soft skin of his erection lightly. "What did I want you to help me reach?"

His wolfish grin gave away the answer. "Orgasm, honey. You closed the door, and I knew you only wanted me for my body. The way you looked at me brought me to my knees."

He lifted me, impaling me quickly and forcefully. I cried out, ignoring the coolness of the wall along my back as he trapped me and slowly thrust in and out. How had I looked at him? I wanted him to continue, but I didn't have enough control of the fire running rampant in my veins to form words. My eyelids were heavy, and I knew I wouldn't be able to deny him what he wanted.

"You licked your lips, but it was a wasted gesture. I was already hard from just that one look, Sabrina—the one you have now that says, *Jonas, I'm hot and ready for you. I want you to fuck me until I can't remember my name.*"

He thrust harder and faster. The heat spiraled until even my fingertips trembled. If he hadn't been holding me up, I would have turned to a pool of liquid jelly on the floor. The feeling both scared and titillated me. He increased his tempo again, and I came on him, crying out my climax right there in the foyer.

"Yes, that's it, honey. Let it come to you. Don't fight it."

He slowed his thrusts. I thought he might climax too, but he didn't come, and he didn't stop. I looked at him questioningly. Surely he knew I had an orgasm?

His lips covered mine—seeking, demanding, taking more and more. The pulsing inside me grew, lengthening, and I knew he'd only just begun. "Say it, honey. Tell me to fuck you until you can't remember your name."

I wasn't sure I wanted that. I liked what he had done for me so far, but I was terrified of the place he was pushing me. Reaching deep inside, I convinced myself to trust him, just this once. I opened my eyes and stared into his liquid gold ones. The light was dim and his face was shadowed, but I knew the color of his desire.

"Fuck me until I can't remember my name or yours." The words were breathy and labored, but they drove him higher. I reveled in my power. The thought that he really did want me, that he really did fantasize about me, was a powerful aphrodisiac. I wanted to feel him come inside me more than I wanted to come again.

I wanted to urge him faster, but I knew he wouldn't listen to me. We were caught between his fantasy and the feel of him fucking me for real.

"I am on my knees in front of you, Sabrina. I lift your skirt out of the way, tracing patterns on your bare inner thighs. I part the lips of your pussy with my fingers and you tremble in anticipation. You want my mouth on your pussy as much as I want to know the smoky, musky flavor of you coating my tongue and filling my senses."

His eyes never left mine. I didn't need to tell him I'd never come with a man's tongue stimulating me. And now, he was making me come at the idea of his tongue circling my tender, throbbing nub and plunging deep inside me to take me over the edge.

Though I never once broke his gaze and the power he had over me, I pictured his fantasy vividly, and I wanted it too. I wanted to call him out of the hallway and into my office, where he would lick me until my legs were weak and I had to lean against my desk for support.

The throbbing of the first orgasm was a starting point as he thrust into me, forcing me to another precipice. Words became impossible, and he stopped talking, but the movie he had begun in my head refused to stop playing. I pictured him kneeling before me with a dozen expressions on his face, anything from cocky and confident to shy and pleading.

Sounds penetrated the haze of my pleasure—sobs, cries, demands—and I realized it was me. I wanted him to go faster, to fuck me harder, but he wouldn't, even when I used crude language. He kept his pace slow and steady, driving me up the sheer face of the cliff on his terms.

Suddenly his pace grew frenzied. I hooked my legs around him and hung on for dear life. My vision went black, and the scream that escaped came from deep inside. His cry joined mine, and I felt the jetting of his orgasm. His body jerked, spasming in time to the pulsing of my pussy.

He was right. Last time hadn't been anything like this for him. He sank to the floor, taking me with him. We were quiet, unable to speak or move for the longest time. My body cooled before I regained control of my muscles.

"Damn it, woman. You are far hotter than you know." He said the words into my neck.

I wasn't sure I heard him correctly. "Is that a good thing or a bad thing?"

He breathed the laugh of a man who knew he was lost but hadn't accepted it. "I'm not sure."

Later, when the house was closed up for the night and we lay in bed, I gathered enough courage to ask Jonas the question that had begun burning in me since he'd narrated his fantasy.

"Jonas?" I whispered his name in case he was already asleep. It would be a valid coward's escape.

He wasn't quite out yet. "Hmmm?"

"Would you really do that? If I asked you into my office and locked the door, would you really do *that?*" I bit my lip, hoping he'd let me get away with alluding to his fantasy. He was quiet for so long, I'd begun to think I imagined his acknowledgement.

When I'd given up, he spoke, his voice muffled by a face half turned into his pillow. "Hell, yes. You wouldn't even have to lock the door. If you recall, I said nothing about you locking the main door to your office. Anyone could have come in and watched."

I blushed in the safety of the darkness, but somehow, I knew he was aware of my pinkened complexion.

Chapter 7—Jonas

In my time, I'd encountered many people who had a kinky side. The difference with Sabrina lay in her complete ignorance of her submissiveness. Watching her with her mother and sister, I witnessed a woman who doubted her self-worth because she didn't understand why she acquiesced. As an outsider, I recognized their dominant personalities, and I felt bad for Sabrina. If she could embrace that side of herself, then she could find the strength to stand up to her mother and sister.

Or she'd have someone to take care of her and help her find the words and courage to take a stand. I may have overstepped my bounds when I'd met her family, but she hadn't seemed to mind. When I'd held back at her birthday dinner, she'd retreated into a turtle shell made of ice.

I liked bondage. I liked it a lot, but she wasn't ready for it. She was barely ready to accept domination, openly challenging me when I stepped over her invisible, unstated lines. Part of me looked forward to the challenge of getting her to realize what she needed to be happy and fulfilled. And part of me wanted to pack my bags and leave. Awakening a submissive was a dangerous endeavor. What if she became too attached? What if she mistook the pleasure of submission for love? I didn't want to break her heart, and at the same time, I didn't want to fall into the same trap with her that I'd escaped with my ex-wife.

Except that Sabrina didn't possess an inherent ruthlessness. Even at work, she had a reputation for fairness and level-headedness. I could work with that. No way would I talk to her about it, though. In my world, the rules dictated that I needed to be open and honest. In the sanctity of my home, I knew that abiding by those guidelines would send her running. Besides, I didn't want to put labels on the things I was going to do to her. If she wanted to be dominated and perhaps bound, then that's all we would do. These were bedroom games, nothing more.

Monday I let her rest. I'd left her in a vulnerable place, and I wanted her to feel emotionally safe before I pushed her again. We had dinner together, and then she helped me set up a home office. For a little thing, she was surprisingly strong. We carried an old desk up two flights of stairs, and she didn't need a break. I made her take one anyway. No sense in allowing her to injure herself.

On Tuesday, I couldn't hold out any longer. It wasn't an ideal time to strike. I had to leave after dinner to work at Ellen's club. The prospect of spending all night imagining her gorgeous curves in front of me drove me to seek satisfaction before I left. It didn't guarantee I wouldn't think of her, but it did increase the chance I would be able to keep my mind on my job.

We'd just come home from work. I liked driving with her, though grabbing a quick dinner in the city and heading straight to my second job would streamline my daily travels. Spending that time with her allowed me to ask questions and get her perspective without seeming too obvious. We both liked having philosophical discussions about myriad topics, many of which had direct bearing on the projects I was working on. She stimulated my brain and got my creative juices flowing.

Opening the back door, I let her enter the house first. Not only was it good manners, but it allowed a prime view of her backside. She had a great ass. I cupped one cheek, giving it a squeeze. She shot a frown over her shoulder. After work, she liked to decompress by changing into something less formal and having a glass of wine. If she was stressed, she'd go for a swim first. She swam a lot.

Not at all recalcitrant, I smirked.

She bit her lower lip, a subconscious response to a promise I hadn't verbalized. I let her put her phone and purse on the kitchen counter before I struck again. The kitchen had a large island in the middle with seating at the other end. Last night as I made dinner, I realized the cold, hard granite surface would provide a good shock to her system. Twice she'd orgasmed for me against hard surfaces. It was likely they compounded how imprisoned she felt.

Moving in close, I herded her against the counter. She gripped the edge. "I was going to swim."

I closed my hands around her upper arms and pressed my chest to her back. "I won't stop you." Grazing my teeth along her nape, I held her still.

A shiver moved down her spine. "It feels like you're stopping me."

"Delaying." I pulled a pin from her hair and unraveled a long, silky coil. I liked the way her hair looked when she wore it down, something she rarely did. "You can say no."

She froze. "But that won't stop you."

Reaching around, I gripped her breast and squeezed through the layers of clothing hiding her from me. "No, it won't stop me."

She swallowed, and I couldn't tell whether from fear or desire. Or both. I had time to discover all her secrets. "What if I scream?"

"You'll scream." Tugging at her waist, I lifted her shirt so I could get beneath it. I slipped my hand into her bra and kneaded. She inhaled a ragged breath, and I knew I had her. Pinching her nipple sharply, I proved my point when she yelped. "Not quite as loud as I know you can get, but it's a good start."

"That hurt."

I pinched again, this time holding it. "Breathe through the pain."

She trembled and pushed against me, seeking relief I wouldn't allow. At last she relaxed, accepting what I chose to give. "Please," she whimpered.

Releasing slowly, I gave a temporary respite. "More?" She nodded. I didn't make her vocalize the request or beg. She wasn't there yet. I wasn't sure she could even look at me and ask for more. I pinched her other nipple, and this time, she didn't struggle. "That's it, honey."

I removed her blouse and bra, baring her to give me unfettered access. Though she didn't cooperate, she didn't fight either. Gripping a handful of hair, I tipped her head back and kissed her thoroughly. She kissed me back, her fingers scratching against the back of my neck because that's all she could reach. My chest heaved before hers did, probably due to all that swimming, and I released her abruptly. She responded with a desperate mew, and so I licked the column of her throat.

My cock had been hard from the moment she'd bitten her lip. I wanted her more than just twice a week, and I resolved to stop holding back. If she wanted to protest, she could, but unless she safeworded, I would take what I wanted. I ground my hips against her ass, giving her a taste of what she was going to get.

Lifting the hem of her skirt, I slipped my hand along her stockings. I eased them over her hips slowly, stretching the moment to toy with her. She held her breath at first, but when I took so long, her breath came in short pants, and then when I came into contact with her skin, her breathing hitched. I could do this all day—a different kind of breath play.

Gooseflesh traveled up her arms, and she shivered violently. Giving in to an urge, I bit her shoulder. She jerked and moaned, reaching up reflexively to push my head away. I grabbed her wrist, twisted her arm behind her back, and bent her over the counter. She was short, and my action lifted her off her feet. Screeching a protest, she flailed her legs. I stepped on the crotch of her stockings, which I'd lowered to just below her knees, to trap her limbs. Her shoes, sexy tangerine heels that had strategically placed straps, kept her nylons from slipping off.

Seeing her in this vulnerable state, wearing only a skirt and heels, turned my dick into a rock. I threw my tie over my shoulder, opened my pants, and pushed into her weeping pussy. It amazed me how well she responded to bondage and dominance. She had been made for this.

Her vaginal walls quivered around me, signaling the start of an orgasm. I fucked her, taking my pleasure as she shouted. Partially coherent words echoed from the granite, and I recognized some of the sounds of my name. And then she swore. "J—Jo—Fuck—Oh!" I'd made her forget the manners and maddening propriety that had been relentlessly pounded into her. Hearing that vulgar word from her sweet mouth sent me over the edge. I surged forward, burying myself deeply and taking her with me.

Afterward, I helped her take off her shoes and stockings. She put her shirt back on but not her bra. I looked her up and down, admiring the sex blush staining her chest and the brightness of her eyes. "Going for a swim?"

She ran her tongue along her upper lip. "Yes. I—Yes. Thank you." With that, she took her shoes, stockings, and bra, and she disappeared up the stairs.

That night at work, Ellen accosted me under the guise of delivering my mail. She came to my work station between clients and handed over the stack. Wearing stiletto boots that came to the middle of her thigh put her at the same height as me. It wasn't her height that made her an imposing figure; it was her larger-than-life personality, which I both loved and hated. She looked me square in the eye, and I realized this wouldn't be a short visit.

"When you asked for Saturday night off, I had no idea it was so you could get married."

It was bad form to get married and not tell my best friend, not that I'd ever admit it aloud. "I brought her by when I came for my stuff, but you were out."

"No, you jackass. It was the end of the month. I was locked in a tiny room with Sophia while she tortured me with accounting crap. You knew I wouldn't be home. You should have called me before you tied the knot with someone you just met."

I'd known she wouldn't be home. All things considered, I didn't want to expose Sabrina to Ellen until Sabrina had a chance to know me better. "It was an all-of-a-sudden thing. I wasn't sure she would go through with it. Besides, it's only for a year."

Ellen came closer. The music wasn't too loud, and nothing could drown out her scowl. "Marriage is serious, Jonas."

I didn't need a reminder. "No shit."

"I don't want to see you get hurt again."

I rolled my eyes. "Elle, it's fine. She needed someone to play husband for a year so she could get some inheritance, and I'm sick of people trying to set me up on blind dates."

Ellen's dark brown eyes looked black. She studied me, assessing what I'd said and what I left unsaid. "You're getting something out of this."

Yeah, I was. "I took her to City Club in Vegas, the exhibitionist section."

Well used to my brand of kink, she pressed her lips together and exhaled. "This is the hot chick from Rife you're always talking about?"

Sabrina might not have noticed me very much before she'd asked me to marry her, but she'd caught my eye the first time I saw her. Over the past few months, she'd become my fall-back, my reason for not taking an interest in whomever my friends or family wanted me to meet. Ellen and Ryan had teased me more than once by calling her my fake girlfriend. Now she was my fake wife. "At first I didn't think she'd stay, but once she got used to it, she was amazing. She focused completely on me, trusting me to take care of her."

A dominant's role was to protect his submissive. Perhaps those labels didn't quite apply to this situation, but I couldn't deny being affected by how much she trusted me.

"Ryan said she looks just like Helene."

The little spitfire sharing my bed had nothing in common with that icy bitch who passed for human. "She does not. I have a type. I like short women with long, dark hair. She fits the mold. Other than that, she has nothing in common with Major Bitch." As I sorted through the stack, I exhaled hard at the amount of bright red ink on the envelopes. It was going to take me at least another three to five years to pay off these debts. Living with Sabrina helped a lot. If I were a better man, I'd insist on splitting the household bills. At least I'd refused the money she'd offered.

"Are you calling my husband a liar?" She arched an eyebrow. Ryan and I had met Ellen our freshmen year of college after we'd been put on academic probation for partying too hard. She'd whipped our asses into shape, helping me discover my dominant side and showing Ryan that he was meant to be her submissive. I was one hell of a service top, and I owed my skills to her. The friendship we'd forged was solid and strong. Ellen might give me hell, but there's no one I trusted more to have my back.

I growled a warning. "She's nothing like Helene."

"Then why haven't we met her? You've been married for a little over a week. Are you afraid to let me see for myself?"

My fear came from a different place. I didn't want her to know about this part of my life. While Ryan would keep the conversation vanilla, Ellen would take every opportunity to insert probing and leading questions. Sabrina didn't stand a chance. "You can meet her, but don't mention Helene or anything about working here."

Ellen twisted her lips in a frown. "Where does she think you are?"

"Here. Tending bar." I laid out a heavy flogger and a crop on my table. My next client, a woman who went by the pseudonym "Cherry," was scheduled to begin in a few minutes. Sometimes she came alone, and sometimes she brought her current boyfriend. Depending on the proclivities of the man, he either watched or ended up bound with her while I topped them both. I didn't mind an audience, but I refused to share top duties with anyone.

With a laugh, Ellen ran her fingertip along the flap of the crop. "Hell of a way to pour a drink."

That night, as a parade of submissives and bottoms came through my station, I couldn't keep from imagining Sabrina in their places. What would she look like bound to a spanking bench? Tied to a cross?

Would she trust me as much when real bondage was involved? I didn't know.

When I arrived home, she was asleep. I showered and crawled into bed. Needing her closer, I put my arm around her and scooted her to me. It didn't take long to realize she was naked. I smiled into the darkness, but I was too damned tired to wake her up, so I fell asleep with a silly grin on my face.

Over the course of the next couple weeks, I surprised Sabrina daily with demands for sex. I experimented with catching her in the midst of an activity and between them, hoping to figure out when she was more receptive. Though she protested and sometimes fought back, she never once refused. It seemed my beautiful fake wife was ready to submit any time I wanted.

One weekend morning after working late, I woke the feel of Sabrina's fingertips tracing down my chest. I cracked an eye to see what she was about. The hungry expression on her face was a pleasant surprise. This was the first time she'd initiated sex. The knowledge that I'd created this sexually self-confident woman made me proud. It was a heady experience, for both of us, I was sure. She sat up, exposing her breasts. If I lifted my head, I could have her nipple in my mouth in a second, but I wanted to see what she had planned.

She pushed the sheet down, feathering her light touch as she went. Taking my cock in hand, her eyes widened when I hardened instantly. She looked up to find me watching her. "I want you to fuck me. Hard and fast. No foreplay."

Before she could change her mind, I pinned her to the bed, entering her as hard and fast as she'd asked. She wasn't very dry, and she was sopping wet before my second violent thrust.

She struggled against me, and I understood this was a test. She trusted me not to let her win the physical battle. If I let her win, she wouldn't have an orgasm. She needed me to force her to it, and I had no problem fulfilling that role.

The sounds she made came faster and harder, ripped from her with each thrust. In the morning, my stamina wasn't as good as it was in the afternoon. Suddenly, I let go of her. I reached down, lifted her legs, and hooked her knees over my shoulders. This new position let me into her far deeper than before. She thrashed and fought, but I had her pinned, and she wasn't going to get away. She arched and shouted, coming almost immediately. Her pussy convulsed around me, and I surrendered to her sweetness. I cried out as I climaxed, but I made sure to fall next to her instead of on top. The sky outside was barely light. I closed my eyes and fell back to sleep.

Chapter 8--Sabrina

I'd always wanted to sleep naked, but I lacked courage in light of the number of admonitions running through my head. What if the house caught fire? What if there was some emergency, and I had to leap from bed to attend to it? What if someone came to the door? In all likelihood, I would grab a robe first anyway. I liked the way the soft silk of the sheet caressed my breasts, my stomach, and my backside. It made me feel sexy and alive. And Jonas seemed to like it as well. There was less in the way when he wanted to hold me down in the morning and have his way with me.

While he slept, I took a shower, stroking the tender, abused flesh between my legs. He'd been too tired to show much restraint, and I found I liked it lot. Making him lose control gave me power and a satisfaction I hadn't known I craved. My pussy was sore to the touch, but the pain brought pleasure and excitement I didn't expect. Giving in to the urge, I closed my eyes and continued stroking my clitoris. Heat coiled in my loins, and my breaths came faster.

Bracing one hand against the wall, I ventured lower, where I was more swollen and raw. The pain was worse there, but I fought against my inclination to stop. The pressure inside me increased until it released suddenly, my body stiffening as I climaxed on my own for the first time in my life. I rested my head against my arm on the tiled shower wall, weeping with the relief of so many kinds of release.

My success gave me courage in other respects. Jonas had an amazing imagination. I loved the fantasies he liked to tell me about when he had me pressed to a wall, trapped in his arms. Where I once thought he was ignoring me or politely listening at staff meetings, I now knew he was picturing me naked, beckoning to him across the room, begging him to pleasure me in front of the entire staff. There was no way in hell that would ever happen, but some of his other fantasies were more plausible, especially the first one he'd narrated.

We'd been sleeping together for nearly a month, and he hadn't once tried to act out that particular fantasy, either at work or anywhere else. Stephen had gone down on me several times, and neither of us had enjoyed it. I knew Jonas would be different. Everything with him was. I wanted to know what it would be like to have his face between my legs.

The first obstacle was the layout of our offices. Because he was stationed on the opposite end of the floor, he was rarely found in the area around my office. Nobody knew we were married, and now I wondered if enticing him to me would fuel rumors of a relationship between us. He would probably like that, but I wouldn't.

Not wanting to send anything untoward on the company's email, I texted him with a simple message: *I have no appointments between two and three.*

His reply came quickly: *Do you need help reaching something?*

I replied with a smiley face. Of course, as luck would have it, my schedule changed unexpectedly. A meeting that was supposed to end well before two did not. When I finally opened my back door, fifteen minutes had elapsed. I found Jonas in the hall, leaning casually against the opposite wall, conversing with Randall, a member of my team.

Randall had been with me the longest. He wasn't my first acquisition, but he was my best. Like me, he had come to Rife fresh from college, accepting an internship to get his foot in the door. He was short enough to look me directly in the eye when he spoke, and he was as square as a brick house. His looks and his tenacity reminded me of a bulldog.

They both looked over as soon as my door opened. One of the perks of being the boss was that I didn't have to explain my actions. I cocked one brow at Randall, which implied a question I had no interest in asking.

"I'm working." He held up his hands in mock defense.

I mimicked his gesture. "I didn't say a word."

"You don't have to." He flashed a smile and turned to catch Jonas' eye. "Catch you later, man."

Jonas nodded. "Let me know how it goes." He watched Randall walk away, and then he turned the same look on me that I'd just given to Randall. "Need help with anything?"

I smiled. "Now that you mention it."

Leaving the sentence dangling, I gestured into my office. He sauntered in, and I closed the door behind us, locking it. I'd already secured the main door. He eyed it with a cocky grin.

"Chicken."

"We'll call it job security. Now I think we've wasted enough time on pleasantries. How about we get to work?" I was able to get the entire statement out without giggling. The laughter that threatened was of both the amused and the nervous varieties. Amusement didn't lead to orgasm with me. I needed him to take charge and set the tone. He was good at it.

But this time, he just looked at me with an expectant expression on his face and his hands in his pockets. He had dressed in a suit that morning, but sometime during the day, he'd lost the jacket. The white, pinstriped shirt and the emerald tie brought out the green in eyes hidden behind his wire-rimmed frames.

I realized the tables had been turned. I was supposed to be in charge. I had no idea how to give him a look that would say I wanted him on his knees in front of me. I only knew how to want it.

At a complete loss, I fumbled for how to proceed. Finally I thought about how, when he set me free at home, I always felt like I was someone else. Taking a breath, I became someone else. Office slut seemed to be the appropriate label for what I wanted.

Cocking my head, I turned on my flirtiest smile. "You're relatively new here, aren't you?"

"I've been here six months, Ms. Breszewski." He caught on quickly.

"I've heard good things about you. Can I call you Jonas?" I didn't wait for a response. Approaching him, I fingered his tie, letting the smooth fabric caress my skin. Inches separated us. "Jonas, I'd like to see what you're made of."

A knowing light came into his eyes. He grasped my hips and pressed them to his pelvis, lifting me in the process. I had to grab his arms to keep from losing my balance. "I'll bet you would."

I imagined him throwing me on the black leather sofa in the corner of my office and holding my hands hostage as he groped under my skirt. It worked. When I looked up at him, I had the right look in on my face, the one that begged him in the way he liked. Slowly, deliberately, he sank to his knees.

He caressed me over my stockings, starting at the knee and gradually disappearing under my skirt. I hadn't worn the cream one with the lace hem. This one was black. It flared under my hips, making me seem curvier than I was. I always thought it made me look a little plump, but Jonas had merely stared at me with disbelief this morning when I'd responded that way to his suggestion I wear it.

He stopped, his hands stuttering when they reached bare flesh. I wore a pair of thigh-highs, and I knew without looking that his cock was swelling. He glanced up, burning me with his tawny eyes.

He retreated, but only for a moment. This time, when he ran his hands up my legs, he raised my skirt as well. I watched his face as he discovered I wore no panties—only a garter to hold up the stockings. He stared at the V of curls pointing to his destination, mesmerized.

I was becoming heady with power. "Lick me," I commanded.

"Spread your legs." His voice came out strangled, his breathing uneven.

I thought he would want me to lie on the couch or at least lean against my desk, but we were in the middle of the room, and nothing was nearby. With a move that was much more decisive and confident than I felt, I widened my stance.

He rotated my hips forward, spreading me wider with the movement and parting me with his thumbs. Without hesitating, he opened his mouth. I watched, loving the view of his sun-kissed head nestled against my deep brown curls.

The first sensation was heat, pure molten lava. I inhaled sharply. Strong and talented, his tongue caressed me as erotically as he promised. My legs trembled, and I swayed. He broke off sharply, catching me before I fell, and guided me back several steps to lean against the front of my desk.

He returned to his exploits, and I gripped my desk, luxuriating in the tiny pain the edge caused as it dug into the palms of my hands. I needed more. I loved when he handled me roughly. Several times he'd left bruises, and I couldn't find a way to regret them. Now he was gentle, almost reverent. It wasn't enough. I needed more if I was going to come. Letting the desk dig into my hands went a small way toward that end.

The pressure between my legs changed. His mouth opened more, biting my clitoris sharply. I yelped at the unexpectedness of the pain, and wetness flooded me. I felt self-conscious at the thought of my juices pouring into his mouth, but he moaned into my flesh, sucking harder and harder.

Capturing my swollen and throbbing nub between his teeth, he drew it into his mouth, stretching it. Cold fire raced through me, passion mixed with a titillating sharpness. I moaned and leaned back, not to escape him, but because my knees would no longer support my weight.

Without seeming to move, he thrust a finger inside and pinched me with the thumb that remained on the outside. The tension in my abdomen coiled tighter. I was so close.

Two more fingers joined the first, stretching me from the inside as his strong lips kept my clit elongated. I came on him, just like he wanted, my juices soaking his fingers and filling his mouth. My cries were louder than intended, and there was a better than even chance that someone standing near one of my doors would hear, but I didn't care.

He stood, kissing me as hard as he'd sucked me a moment ago. The musky taste of me lingered on his lips and tongue. I knew he wanted me to know my own flavor, to revel in my essential femaleness, and I did.

Reaching between us, I loosed his belt and opened his pants. He was inside me before I could to fully move his boxer briefs out of the way, riding the waves of my waning orgasm. He pushed my knees up so that my feet rested on the edge of the desk, and he held them there with his shoulders as he leaned over me.

I couldn't hang on to him in this position. I was forced to balance by resting my weight on my hands behind me. I let my head fall back and concentrated on the growing tension, forgetting everything except Jonas and the way he made me feel.

The first distraction was momentary. He pulled the pins out of my hair, freeing long strands to cascade down my back. I pushed it out of my mind, knowing he wanted to leave a tangible mark, a *Jonas was here* sign. He knew I wouldn't have time to put it back up before my next meeting.

The second distraction nearly undid me. The phone rang, my direct line. The only people who used that number were my myriad bosses. It was most likely Joy, Vice-President of Marketing and my immediate supervisor. I liked Joy; she was largely responsible for promoting me as far as I had come this fast. Her only downfall was the fact that she was Jared's aunt, and she definitely watched out for him, making sure he looked good no matter what. I often took flack for his mistakes, which pissed me off.

I turned toward the sound.

"Don't," he said, his lips lingering near mine, ready to capture them. "You're almost there."

"It's Joy," I said, the face of the cliff already receding into unreachable territory. "I have to take it."

He imprisoned my hands behind me, forcing me to use my stomach muscles to balance. Immediately the tension increased. I moaned out loud, a long, low sound that was far too loud to not be heard outside my four walls.

Jonas chuckled and closed his mouth over mine, swallowing my sounds and demanding my soul. I know it sounds dramatic, but that's exactly what he did, and it was the first time he did it. I fought him—not the fact that he was holding me so that I couldn't move even to meet his thrusts, but the fact that I didn't want to share such an intimate part of myself.

"Give it to me," he murmured, losing himself in me. His tawny eyes took on a dreamlike quality. He was lost in the fantasy. "Give it all to me."

The phone stopped ringing and I gave him most of what he wanted. I drew the line at my soul. He had no right to it.

I whimpered, trying to control the volume of my orgasm.

He thrust harder, knowing it would push me higher. "Let it go, Sabrina. Let me have it."

I bit him. Hard. I wasn't aware of what I had done until it was too late. With my teeth firmly entrenched in his shoulder muffling the sounds of my orgasm and his face buried in my neck for the same reason, we came together. It was the first time this happened. I was used to him following me, sometimes a great deal of time later. It was an amazing feeling.

I think he got a little bit of my soul in that moment. He definitely gave me a piece of his. Either way, it terrified me. It terrified me long after we fixed our clothing and parted ways, a pink stain of lipstick on his shirt where I bit him.

Joy breezed into my office moments after Jonas slipped out the back door. At sixty-three, she was a powerhouse of energy and drive. Tall, with a willowy figure and a chronic smoker's cough, she was my opposite in so many ways.

She was loud, forceful, and unreserved. She had a presence that demanded immediate attention. I envied her many things, but being related to Jared Larsen was not one of them. If my weakness was that I was too reserved and too controlling, then hers was that she fawned over her dead sister's overgrown child. Otherwise she was a talented ad woman.

"Where have you been?" she demanded. "I called, but you didn't answer."

I shrugged away the question. "What did you need?"

"I have someone for your team," she said. "I want her to start immediately."

I bristled at this. My team was hand-chosen, by me, and they were easily the best group of people in the company. Their skills complemented one another, making the sum of us much greater than what we brought to the table individually. Adding a new member would tinker with that chemistry. As talented as I knew Jonas to be, I never considered adding him to my team because I didn't know how he would change the group's dynamic. I might have been the unknown quantity in that equation, but if I wasn't sure it would work out well, I generally didn't give someone a chance.

"Joy," I protested. "There is an interview process."

She pushed aside my concern. "Veronica will be a great addition to your team. There will be some problems as you adjust, naturally, but I expect you'll straighten them out in no time."

I stole Jonas' penetrating stare, turning it on Joy until she grew uncomfortable.

"Sabrina, she's very talented. Just sometimes she lets her mouth get away from her."

Great. I needed someone with a talent for alienating others, as if I didn't already have enough to worry about. Usually I was the one who made clients wary. My shy, reserved nature often came across as aloof and cold. Many people didn't realize that a person could be both confident and shy, or that a shy person could hide behind a façade of confidence. My posture and body language exuded the conviction that I was in charge. My icy demeanor often hid an underlying fear that people wouldn't like me.

That was one of the reasons Ty and I worked so well together. When I first met Ty four years ago, he had me smiling immediately. Tall to my short, he was also a mesmerizing shade of dark chocolate, and he was handsome, but that wasn't why I liked him. Something about him put me at ease, and then he used his incredible sense of humor to keep me there. He was golden with clients. I used his charm and presence extensively in presentations. He balanced my introverted nature perfectly.

Then I had Clare. Clare had worked for several advertising firms before I lured her away three years ago with the promise of equal treatment and respect for her ideas. She was incredibly creative, and she brought the perspective of a working mother with teenaged and college-aged children.

Though they were both level-headed and talented, Clare was a counterweight to Randall. He was in his late thirties with two young children. Clare balanced Randall's inherent unattractiveness with her smooth, motherly charm.

The rotating member of my team was my intern. Right now, I had Ophelia. It wasn't a paid position, and I wanted her to have the full experience, so I rotated her around the team as an assistant. At twenty-one, she was still optimistic and full of the possibilities in life. I had been too. That was about the time Stephen had asked me to marry him, forcing me to take stock of the deficiencies in our otherwise perfect relationship. I still regretted breaking his heart—and mine too. Ophelia often made me wonder what had become Stephen. I heard about him occasionally because our parents moved in the same circles, but I didn't truly know how he was.

"Joy," I cajoled. "I have all I can handle right now."

"Why? Did you suddenly get a personal life?"

She meant it as a joke, but it stung nonetheless. It had been a while since I had a date, and she knew Jared had a thing for me. She'd looked the other way when I was on his team, ignoring it because Jared had still been married. Now she thought we'd make the perfect couple, and I had no idea why.

Jared was a large man. He often bragged about playing the position of outside linebacker in college. Now in his early forties, I don't think he had hit the gym since graduation. His waistline seemed to have increased in direct proportion to his recollection of his feats on the field. He kept his sparse hair shaved close to his head and he never wore a jacket over his shirt and the single red tie he seemed to own. I didn't have a problem with large people, but he was a jerk. Qualities like that were hard to overlook.

"Yes," I answered Joy without changing my expression. "I have acquired a personal life."

The dismissive way she looked at me said she didn't believe me. "Well, too bad. I have Veronica here with me." She flung open my door and motioned Veronica inside.

I recognized her. In her mid-forties, Veronica Russell was a familiar figure in the advertising community. She was talented. She had a strong personality. And she had a knack for not filtering anything she said.

"You're smaller than I remembered," she said, shaking my hand. "We met last year when you stole that automotive parts account from under me."

I threw a look at Joy. She owed me, big time. Screwing on a smile, I withdrew my hand from Veronica's iron grip. "What brings you to Rife and Company?"

She jabbed a thumb in Joy's direction. "She said I would be a perfect addition to this team, but I don't know."

"You have doubts?" I raised a polite brow. Was there a way out of this?

"You have a reputation for being a bitch." She tossed her bright red, frizzy hair over her shoulder. "I like that in a woman, but men find it off-putting. It seems you and I have the same problem in this field."

Except I had manners. I refrained from amending her statement. It brought to mind what Jonas said about people being afraid of disappointing me. Was he putting a good face on the way people viewed me because he'd married me and wanted to keep the peace?

The polite expression frozen on my face was all the encouragement she needed to continue.

"Except for the fact that you're pretty. Men will overlook many flaws if they come with a pretty face. That must be how you've gotten this far this fast. In me, they only see the flaws."

"Well, then," I began, "you'll just have to keep your mouth closed when we're with a client. Let everyone else do the talking."

Unlike Jared, I required my team to be part of the presentation. Nobody failed to receive credit or accolades for their work. Jared liked to complain that I micromanaged my team, but we were, by far, the company's most productive team. Only since the addition of Jonas had Jared's team even begun to approach the average in productivity.

I had never been so happy to see five o'clock. Jonas and I continued to carpool, as it was working out well for us both. We were quiet on the drive home. I didn't know the drift of his thoughts, but mine were in turmoil over the things Veronica had said. Was my reputation really so bad? I knew I could come off as cold, but I worked hard to mitigate that perception.

Successful women in this business still had the problem of being perceived as a bitch or slut. I wasn't sure which was worse, but so far I guess I had traveled the bitch route. I had certainly proved myself a slut this afternoon, and though nobody had said anything, I knew they had to have heard. My stomach roiled with regret. How did Jonas really see me? Perhaps it was unfair to cast him in the same pool as the rest of men, but he had mentioned, albeit diplomatically, that my coworkers considered me unapproachable. It was a euphemism for the word Veronica used.

Out of nowhere, Jonas interrupted the self-deprecating flow of my thoughts. "I can't believe you're not wearing underwear."

I stiffened, stung by the judgment inherent in his words. I guess I'd moved from "bitch" to "slut" in his estimation. Either way, it stung. I was quiet for the rest of the ride, pushing my hurt into a ball of anger that I could stow safely away. It would come in handy the next time he demanded a piece of my soul.

When we got home, I headed straight for my underwear drawer. This had been a grave mistake. I wasn't the woman I'd been pretending to be, and I hated admitting this had all been a sham.

He followed me, but I didn't think anything of it. He was in the habit of changing into jeans to make dinner. Sometimes he wandered outside to do yard work or walk the property. Other days, he went to work right after dinner.

I opened a drawer. Before I could reach inside, he slammed it shut and leaned his weight against the facing. He didn't cage me with his arms or try to intimidate me with his presence as he did when he approached me for sex, so I knew he wasn't trying to turn me on.

"What are you doing?" His voice came at me from just above my right ear.

Still angry and stiff, I kept my back straight and my shoulders square. "What does it look like I'm doing?" My inner ice queen was in charge. Life was safer that way.

"Don't answer a question with a question."

I whirled on him. "Don't ask stupid questions."

The muscle in his jaw flexed, and his eyes glittered with green anger. Slowly, the look turned cold, matching my frostiness. "It won't help, you know. It's far too late."

No matter how much I wanted to, I refused to break the glare between us by looking down in shame. "Leave me alone."

He dropped his arm, making sure I knew my escape path wasn't blocked from either direction. "You can't undo what you did today." His tone was deceptively soft.

Anger made me shake. I struggled to control it, to turn it inward. "How dare you?"

"How dare I what?" he sneered. "How dare I take advantage of what's offered? You, of all people, should know a woman without panties is demanding to be fucked."

My face flamed scarlet with anger, so the embarrassment was camouflaged.

"You'll never make a good whore if you don't realize that right now," he continued.

I curled my hands into fists, digging my nails into my palm to prevent the tears that pricked my eyes from falling. He wasn't saying anything I hadn't already thought, berating myself all the way home for the way I'd acted today. What the hell had I been thinking?

"You... You... You..." I stammered, unable to think of something to call him that would sting him the way he hurt me.

"Bastard? Son of a bitch? Asshole?" He supplied those suggestions and more, never taking his eyes from mine.

None of those words were ones I particularly liked. I abandoned the name-calling route. No epithet I could throw at him would do anything more than amuse him. "You didn't seem to mind this afternoon."

I wanted to close my eyes and shrink into nothing the moment I said it. Breaking down, I looked away, turning my head to sever his hold over me.

"My God, you suck at this," he said. "Come on, Sabrina. I've seen you take on Jared with no problem, yet you can't think of a single comeback now?"

My eyes widened with shock. Slowly, I looked up at him. I had no idea what he was talking about.

"How are we ever going to have a good fight if you refuse to shout at me? I gave you every opportunity to call me names, but you didn't. Then I thought you would take the high road and rip me a new one using polysyllabic words. You headed for it, but you stalled before you made any progress." He perched his hands on his hips, again mocking me with fake displeasure.

"What are you talking about?" My anger hadn't vanished, but bafflement temporarily won out.

"What are *you* talking about?" he returned. "I thought we were having our first fight. For the record, this doesn't count. I thought I had you when you clenched your fists. You were ripe to take a swing at me, or at least call me something nasty, but you didn't." He looked me up and down. "I gave you every opening, Sabrina. I even tried to help you out with things to call me. Why didn't you?"

My eyes were still wide with shock. "What good does name-calling or violence do? You're stronger than me and you know worse things to say."

He laughed, a real, deep-down belly laugh. He fell against the row of drawers behind me. I turned to leave, but he caught me and wrapped me in his arms. "You are a rare woman."

I didn't like the game he was playing. I didn't understand the rules, but I knew when I was out of my depth. I pushed against his arms, trying to dislodge them. "Let go of me."

"First tell me why you're mad at me."

I thought it was obvious. "You won't let go of me."

He ignored me. "I told you I couldn't believe you weren't wearing panties. You gave me the silent treatment the rest of the way home and marched up here to cover yourself. Why?"

I stiffened anew, not that I had been relaxed before. He wanted to know, so I went for it. "You judged me. How could you do that?"

"I did nothing of the kind," he said. "Who put it into your head that a woman who goes commando is asking for it?"

As wonderful as things had been between us, he had to know I was still innately uncomfortable discussing personal issues. Hoping he would give up, let me go, and drop the subject, I didn't answer.

"Stupid question. Of course it was your mother."

Pride reared its head. "Leave my mother out of this. She's a good person."

"I know she is," he said. "But she's passed some pretty uptight notions to you."

He let me go so abruptly I had to reach for the chest of drawers to steady myself. I looked up, my eyes shooting unasked questions I wasn't sure I wanted answered.

"For the record, I did not pass judgment on you. I thought what you did today was incredibly hot. I know how much courage it took for you to break through your antiquated barriers to proposition me in the first place. The more I know you, the more I'm amazed you agreed to marry me after you heard my terms."

He walked around me, intending to exit the closet. I didn't watch him go, but I felt him pause.

"Not wearing underwear, sleeping naked... Those things don't make you a slut any more than wearing underwear or sleeping in a high-necked flannel nightgown makes you virtuous. If you like it, Sabrina, there is no reason in the world you shouldn't do it. It's also perfectly okay to enjoy having sex with me and to be the one to initiate it. There is a lot of passion in you. Don't fear it."

He spoke softly, using a tone that washed through my senses and affected me in a way I didn't understand. He would have stayed with me if I'd asked, but he knew I needed space. He left, and I didn't move for the longest time, thinking about what he'd said. I had been unaware of exactly how many hang-ups I had until I met Jonas.

In the short time I'd known him, he had done so much for me. I was grateful, though it only illuminated how much more work needed to be done. It was a painful thought and a painful prospect. I had no desire to face my demons. I wouldn't have faked my way through therapy when I was a teenager if I did.

He didn't bring up the subject again that evening, turning the topic of dinner conversation to our families. He had invited his parents and my mother to dine with us the following evening.

"Do you think your mother will bring up your grandfather's will at all?"

I shrugged. "She might."

"Can you ask her not to?"

Something in the tenor of his question gave me pause. "Why don't you want your family to know about any of that? It's more believable than love at first sight. As affectionate as you were to me at the beach, I don't think they bought it."

"We all have our own crosses to bear," he said. "I didn't marry you for altruistic reasons, Sabrina. I could give a damn about your inheritance."

"Yes, I know," I said, the tell-tale blush creeping up my neck. I hated that damn thing. "You married me for the sex. Little did you know it was going to be so much work."

He laughed. "I don't mind the work. You could say I get off on it. But seriously, I bought myself a year of peace, probably more. Now they can't nag me to settle down with someone and get married. I've already done it."

I couldn't imagine his parents or his sisters nagging him to get married. Then I remembered Sam and Amanda talking about how he hadn't had a serious relationship in years. He must have had his heart broken pretty badly. This marriage was just as much a refuge for him as it was for me. I reached over and squeezed his hand sympathetically.

He looked at me in surprise. "It amazes me how perceptive you can be with other people when you're so blind to things that directly affect you."

"Yes," I agreed. "I don't know how you put up with me. You're such a saint." I was proud of myself for the note of sarcasm that crept into my voice. It usually took me years to warm up to someone enough to banter with them.

"A fallen saint," he said, rising to clear the dishes. "I can't have you putting me up on a pedestal."

Later that night, as we lay in the dark, I wrestled with my demons. "Jonas?" I whispered. I don't know why I whispered. He always seemed to hear me, even when I thought he was sleeping.

"Mmmm?"

"Did you... Was today at work... I mean, did you mind?" I bit my lip to keep from fumbling further.

"No," he said, turning his face out of his pillow so I could understand him. "Text me anytime. I should warn you I have a meeting tomorrow afternoon, so I won't be free. I can spare you a half hour at lunch, though."

"You didn't have to hold me down." It wasn't an accusation, but he took it as one.

"I wasn't about to let you answer the phone. There's no way you would have had that orgasm if you had."

"I know. I meant that it wasn't what did it for me."

I felt more than heard his head rise from his pillow. "Really?"

I didn't know how to explain it, but I tried anyway. "It's like I wasn't me. I was someone else, and so were you."

"You were playing a role?"

It sounded so awful. "I... Yes. I was. Does that upset you?"

A short burst of laughter preceded his response. "No. I'm all for role playing. We can do more if you want. Much, much more."

The idea did appeal to me, but I chewed my lip, uncertain. When would his patience with me end? "I wouldn't know how."

"You did a fine job today. Did you give yourself a different name?"

Frowning, I said, "Why would I do that?"

"To complete the illusion. Role playing is all about fantasy. You made one of my fantasies come true today. I meant to thank you. You can't know what it meant to me." He moved closer, his lips only a breath from mine. "I've always wanted to kneel before the great Sabrina Breszewski."

"Who was pretending to be the office slut." I laughed, but it was of the self-deprecating variety.

He winced in the faint light from the full moon seeping in the curtains we'd left open. "Maybe you should choose a persona that doesn't make you feel dirty afterward."

My smile was painfully thin. "That's probably a good idea."

He kissed me. It was full of tenderness, and it scared the hell out of me. Desire, I could handle. I didn't want affection or the complications it would arouse. I was relieved when he draped an arm across me and fell asleep. I don't think I could have responded to him if he'd tried to make love to me.

Chapter 9—Sabrina

The next couple of weeks passed quickly. I didn't see him much at work. Our paths had never crossed before and fate didn't conspire to change anything. We were both far too busy to meet more than a couple of times each week.

Since I was raised with a social conscience, I invited his family over regularly. Sam was in Toronto with her boyfriend, but Amanda and Richard brought the kids over whenever I invited them, as did Ryan and Ellen.

Ellen was different. While Ryan seemed at ease around me, Ellen seemed to always be studying me. Sometimes she got the same quietly thoughtful look Jonas used that disconcerted me. It was no less effective coming from her.

I was hopping out of the pool after having spent a good portion of my afternoon turning into a prune so that Faith and Ricky could cavort in the water, when Ryan's shadow fell over me.

He was every bit as tall as Jonas, only he was thinner and his skin was covered with freckles that matched his shock of strawberry hair. In one arm, he cradled his son, Jake. In the other, he had a towel, which he held out to me.

"Thanks," I said, wrapping it around my waist. Ricky and Faith disappeared into the distance, each with one hand threaded through Amanda's.

"I'd like to say you're welcome, but I came down here with an ulterior motive. I have a favor to ask." He grimaced apologetically.

I waited for him to continue, hoping he didn't want me to take Jake into the pool. The infant was not housebroken.

"Can you loan Ellen a swimsuit? She didn't bring one because she hasn't lost all of her weight from the baby, and she still feels self-conscious about her appearance, though I have no idea why. I keep telling her she's every bit as attractive as the day we met."

Mentally, I searched my closet. Ellen was easily five inches taller than me and, as Ryan pointed out, she was curvier. Having decided on a diplomatic answer, I opened my mouth, but Ellen interrupted. As I was facing Ryan, I hadn't seen her approach.

"Ryan Kubina, your ass is mine."

He looked over my head and smiled. "There was never a question about that, Elle."

Dark, shoulder-length hair jumped out of the way as she tossed her head, reminding me of a moody horse. Her glare could have melted ice cubes in winter. She turned the blast of hellfire on me, toning it down a tiny bit. "You. Come with me."

Without waiting for my response, she linked her arm through mine and dragged me off, not stopping until we were upstairs in my bedroom. She locked the door behind us. "Those bastards have a bet going."

I lifted a brow as someone knocked on the door.

"Ellen? Sabrina? It's Amanda. Open up."

Skirting Ellen, who quite frankly scared me, I unlocked the door to admit Amanda. She breezed in, and Ellen whipped the door closed again, making sure it was locked.

"What did they do this time?" Amanda asked.

"They bet I couldn't fit into one of Sabrina's swimsuits." Her deep brown eyes narrowed with displeasure.

If I were Ryan, I'd never upset her out of mortal fear.

"You can't," Amanda calmly pointed out. "She's short and petite."

"Thanks," Ellen retorted dryly. "That wasn't what pissed me off. Ryan bet he could get Sabrina to drag me up here to try one on. Jonas didn't think she'd do it."

Amanda's mouth rounded as if to say *Oh, that explains everything*, but no sound came out.

I watched from the sidelines, dripping chlorinated water onto my carpet. Then I disappeared into the bathroom to rinse and change. Closing the door behind me was a wasted effort. It burst open before I was able to step into the shower. A blush stained, I was sure, the majority of my body.

Ellen waved my embarrassment away. "Oh, don't worry. I've seen it all before."

"Did you need to use the powder room?" I asked, my manners kicking in automatically. "I can change elsewhere."

"You see," she continued, "you're so formal and well-mannered. You were going to offer me a suit, weren't you?"

"I don't think I have anything that will fit you," I apologized. "But you're welcome to look." I resolved to purchase suits in a variety of sizes for guest use.

Her mouth twitched. "Get dressed," she commanded as she closed the door.

I felt as if I were the subject of a joke and I didn't know the punch line, only that people were laughing at me. I emerged a few minutes later, a towel around my shoulders to catch the drips from my damp ponytail. Ellen and Amanda lounged on the window seats.

Ellen didn't look too upset anymore.

"Are you still angry with Ryan and Jonas?"

"No," she said, turning to lay on her stomach. "But this does give us some quiet time. No kids, no husbands. Just the girls. We should do a girls' night out next weekend."

"You can invite your sister," Amanda added. "And Lara. They were so nice when we met them last week. They seem like fun."

They could bet the planet I would bring Ginny and Lara with me. Then I would understand at least two people.

"Okay," Ellen said, pinning me with a knowing look. "Let's hear it."

Uncertain as to what she meant, I said, "Next weekend sounds okay. Jonas is working Friday, so that's probably a better night. I think Ginny is free, but I'll have to call."

"No, silly," Ellen said. "I mean, tell us how you snagged Jonas. He swore he'd never get married."

I thought about the scar he had over his broken heart and the fact that he'd asked me to not tell his family anything about the real reasons we married. "I guess I caught him on a good day."

"What Ellen is so tactlessly trying to ask," Amanda interjected, "is if you know about Helene."

I'd never heard the name before. Wordlessly, I shook my head.

"Bastard," Ellen said.

"Quite the asshole," Amanda agreed. She sat up to face me, patting the cushion next to her. "Come sit, Sabrina."

"You know," Ellen said, shifting to sit up, her legs crossed in front of her, "when I first met you, I thought you would be just like her. You look that much alike."

Amanda cocked her head to one side. "Not that much alike."

"Same coloring, same build." Ellen shook her head. "Ryan and I were shocked that Jonas would suddenly get married, but when we saw you, we understood."

"And you were so stiff when we first met," Amanda said apologetically. "You barely returned my hug at all."

Both women stared at me, as if their observations should mean something significant. I addressed Amanda first. "I had no idea who you were. And I've never been one of those people who hugs strangers. Your family is very different from mine. We aren't demonstrative."

"The point is," Ellen said, "we thought you were just like her until we got to know you a little better."

"Well, I didn't," Amanda said. "Not with the way Faith clung to you. Not once during that whole day did you lose your patience with her."

"She's a sweet girl," I said quietly.

Ellen waved in my direction. "And you didn't get upset when Jake spit up on you."

"Babies spit up. It comes with the territory." If their intent was to let me know I looked like Helene, but didn't act like her, mission accomplished. Except for the fact I had no idea who they were talking about, everything was fine.

"Sit," Amanda ordered, again patting the cushion next to her.

Sitting as ordered, I put up a hand. "Wait. Are you talking about the woman who broke his heart?"

"He *did* tell you," Ellen said, pressing her hand to her chest in relief. "Thank goodness. I thought he was just going to use you and throw you away."

She made him sound heartless. The man I knew was anything but. "I guessed. Anything he hasn't told me is none of my business."

"Don't be so quick to dismiss this," Amanda warned. "I love my brother, but he can be the biggest jerk where women are concerned."

I eyed her warily. "He's been nothing but kind to me."

Ellen frowned at this. "Kind? That doesn't sound like Jonas. He's a lot of things. Kind isn't one of them."

"I don't like the direction of this conversation." I folded my hands on my lap, ready to defend Jonas and our life together. "I think your intentions are good, but you know nothing about my relationship with Jonas."

"Are you in love with him?" Amanda's eyes filled with sympathy.

I answered her honestly. "I like him. We're friends."

"With benefits," Ellen added with a suggestive laugh.

"There is that," I confirmed. Turning to Amanda, I tried to allay her fears. "He isn't in love with me either."

"I know," she said softly, apologetically. "That's what concerns us. We didn't know if you could see it or not."

I stood. "Neither one of us went into this with illusions about the other. While I certainly don't know everything about Jonas—nor does he know much about me—it doesn't change anything. We may not have discussed previous relationships, but that doesn't mean I'm ignorant of the baggage he carries. Perhaps he agreed to marry me because he's tired of defending his decisions to you. I don't know, but I'm certainly not going to make him answer to me."

I would have said more, but a knock at the door interrupted. Ellen flew past me to answer it.

"You rang?" She opened it a crack, placing her foot behind it to bar him from entering.

Good luck keeping him out of this bedroom. Jonas shoved the door open. Ellen yelped and hopped out of the way.

"That trick works better if you're wearing shoes." He strode across the room and stopped at my side.

Without a word, he bent me backward and kissed me. It was an odd kiss to begin with. His lips were icy cold, and so was the tongue he teased past my lips. Then something else followed. I realized it was the last of the Italian ice he had just eaten.

He set me back on my feet with a grin. "How was that?"

Swallowing the lemon-flavored ice, I smiled back. "The ice was good, but the kiss needs a little work."

"You walked right into that one," Ellen said as she plopped back on the window seat. "Why are you interrupting our girl time? By the way, you can tell Ryan he lost the bet. Sabrina hasn't tried to talk me into wearing any of her suits."

Ignoring the last part of her statement, Jonas looked down, taking in his shorts and T-shirt. "Can't you see the shining armor? I've come to rescue my lady fair from the clutches of my evil sister and the Wicked Witch of the West."

Amanda kicked his shin. I moved out of the way. My family may not be physical with one another, but his family didn't share those values. He kicked her back, missing because she rolled to dodge his retaliatory strike. He went after her again, but I pulled on his arm, distracting him.

"Why do I need a shiny knight?"

He took my hand and fell to one knee, dramatically pressing the backs of my fingers to his lips before he spoke. "Because I'm sure these two are filling your head with nonsense. They'll cloak it cleverly, but it's nonsense no matter how they style it. Pay no attention to the women behind the glass. Beware of dog. It all applies to Ellen and Amanda, especially when they have you under their control."

"I'm not under anyone's control," I countered.

Jonas rose to his feet. "Oh yeah? Then what were they telling you?"

"We were making plans for next weekend," Ellen answered in a voice I didn't dare interrupt. "A girls' night out. No kids, no husbands. Just five hot women and a pulsating dance floor."

He looked from Ellen to me. I wasn't about to lie to Jonas. "Apparently I resemble your ex-girlfriend upon first sight. Further examination vindicates me."

I had never seen Jonas angry before. Annoyed, frustrated, focused—but never truly angry. His eyes darkened to olive green and the cords in his neck stood out. And he shouted.

"You had no right." Amazingly, he projected his anger toward both women, neither of whom seemed impressed by his display.

Ellen sprang to her feet. She stood inches from him and planted one hand firmly on her hip, while the other jabbed at his chest. Her volume matched his. "You can't treat her this way, Jonas. It isn't fair."

"You don't know what you're talking about," he said through his teeth. "I haven't done anything."

Seriously alarmed, I put a hand on each combatant's arm. "There's no need to get upset," I said without raising my voice. In addition to years of reminders to never yell, I simply didn't have the voice for it. My volume was pitiful, and my tone was not only high-pitched, my voice cracked when I became distressed. Jonas and Ellen fighting distressed me.

They went on as if they hadn't heard me. There was a good chance neither one had.

Ellen narrowed her eyes. "You haven't?"

"No," he said in the quietest venom-filled voice I've ever heard. "I haven't."

114

Ellen studied him, critically assessing him for something I had no clue about. At last, she was satisfied. "I misjudged the situation. I apologize."

She stepped back and looked at me. "You must think I'm completely loony. I'm sorry. I just didn't want you to get hurt."

That comment did nothing to quell Jonas' anger.

"I'm an adult," I assured her. "I can take care of myself." Looking from Amanda to Ellen, I added, "Maybe it's best if you give us a moment alone."

Contrite and a little embarrassed, both women exited the room. I closed the door behind them, and then I returned to Jonas. He hadn't moved, and the furious expression on his face was unaltered. His mind seemed miles away.

"Care to talk about it?" I ventured.

"No," he said with no less venom than he'd used with Ellen.

Stung, I stepped back. "Are you angry with me?"

"No," he said. Finally, he moved. His eyes pinned me with their intensity. "But I am interested in knowing what they said to you."

I shook my head slowly, careful not to break his gaze. "Nothing more than what I already told you. Why does it upset you so much?"

Desperation and pain edged the anger that was beginning to recede. "You're nothing like her."

"I didn't think I was." Even though I had broken Stephen's heart, I had done it honestly and as gently as I could. No description of or reference to Helene had been at all flattering.

He crushed me in his arms, kissing me savagely. It didn't scare me like he had when his kiss was tender and understanding. Instinctively I knew he sought those things from me. Unfortunately I responded to his brutality, forgetting myself for long moments.

When I did force myself away from passion, I softened my body to his, and he responded in kind, gentling his kiss. He let me go and ran a hand through his damp curls, breathing raggedly. When he finally looked at me, regret and sadness crept across his features. He ran a thumb over my swollen lips. "I was too rough."

"It's all right," I assured him. "I know the safeword."

The tension broke as we both laughed.

Later that day, as we lounged on the patio after eating far too much barbeque, Amanda asked what I planned to pack for Kentucky.

"It can get really cold at night," she warned, tying back her long curls in an attempt to make Faith stop pulling at them.

I stared at her blankly. Often Jonas and his family fell into the kind of talk that excluded me. I didn't mind, as they usually stopped long enough to fill me in on the backstory if I didn't figure it out for myself. I felt as if I had tuned out during the backstory, and now I was failing the pop quiz.

"We're not going," Jonas said from the other end of the patio. The steady scrape of metal on metal worked its way over to me as he cleaned the grill, something I had never done before. "I haven't been at work long enough to be eligible for vacation time."

"What?" Richard exclaimed. He was a normally quiet person, but in a comfortable way. I greatly hoped to pick up on his style. I was quiet as well, but my silence usually made people dislike me or assume I disliked them.

"You have to go," Ricky said. "Uncle Jonas, we always go."

Amanda, seeing my usual confusion, filled me in. For as long as she could remember, their parents rented a huge log cabin in Kentucky near two sizable lakes. They spent the last two weeks of the summer there, including Labor Day weekend. This would be the first year Jonas missed.

I turned to Jonas. "You could probably get the time, but you wouldn't get paid."

He waved my words away. "Don't worry about it."

"It won't be the same," Amanda said, cajolingly. "Sabrina, you have to make him change his mind."

"You would think, Amanda, that you've put Sabrina on the spot enough today." Jonas's acid tone matched the look he threw at Amanda. "Leave her alone."

Chapter 10—Sabrina

As it turned out, any discussion of me accompanying the Spencer family to Kentucky was pointless. Jared chose that time to take his vacation, and Joy informed me that I was covering for him. I sat in her upscale office, so much larger than mine, and fumed at the breathtaking view of the city. I had no windows at all. One day, this office would be mine. I would earn it, and it would take time, but it would still be mine.

"He has a major presentation next week." It was a whiny protest, but I had my own presentations to mastermind. Jared had timed his vacation just right. All of the groundwork should have been done already. This time now should have been for practicing and refining the pitch. Jonas had said nothing about the project, so I had the sinking feeling he knew nothing about it, which meant Jared was sitting on it. A tension headache started in the back of my head.

Joy sat back in her chair and adjusted her lapel. "It's two weeks, Sabrina, and he always covers for you."

I refrained from telling her that when I prepared to leave for vacation, I made sure my team knew everything that needed to be done, and I trusted them to do it. Whoever covered for me didn't have anything to do.

I didn't know Timothy, Jonas' partner, or the intern for the team, but I knew Jared. This meant a lot of work for me. I grimaced and caved, lacking grace completely. "Fine, but you owe me."

Joy leaned forward. She had every intention of reminding me how she advocated for me to be put in charge of a team. It was her way of telling me that I owed my success and my position to her. It was at times like these that I seriously considered starting my own firm. Or taking over this one. I could afford to buy the stock.

117

I held up my hand to stall her. "You just dumped Veronica on me and you know as well as I do that Jared is going to leave a mess to straighten out. I'll be calling in my favor soon." Rising to leave, I threw a last glance at her. "Next time, it's someone else's turn."

Taking my frustration out on the elevator buttons didn't alleviate any of my tension. Perversely, I headed toward Jared's office when I reached my floor. Realistically I did need to meet with him so that he could bring me up to speed on his projects and his schedule. I would instruct Minnie to meet with Jared's assistant to coordinate those meetings with the ones I already had scheduled.

The growing list of tasks in my head was rudely interrupted by the fact that Jared's office was empty. As he shared his assistant with another team leader, I couldn't find him either. I stared at his open door through narrowed eyes, trying to decide whether or not it would be ethical to go in and start poking through his things.

That was the moment I heard a familiar laugh. The answering laugh was familiar, too, but not in a good way. It was a feminine laugh, young and flirty. It answered Jonas' laugh. On a whim, or driven by an inexplicable surge of jealousy, I traversed the short corridor to the open area where Jared's team shared space with another small team.

Leaning back in his chair, Jonas watched as the pretty, buxom blonde intern bent over something on his desk, ostensibly for a closer look. I couldn't see his expression, but I did know that he had a clear view of her ass and her long, shapely legs. He had expressed enough appreciation for mine to make it clear he was a leg man.

I reined in my jealousy when I rounded his desk and saw his slightly bored expression.

He clicked his pen impatiently. "Tina, I need to finish this."

"It's really, really good," she cooed. Then she looked up at me, straightening suddenly. "Ms. Breszewski, I'm sorry. I didn't see you standing there."

Jonas smiled, something slow and admiring. "What brings you to this part of town?"

"I'm firing your boss and taking over his accounts and his team." I delivered it deadpan. The intern bought it.

"Oh, no! You already have an intern. What happens to me?" Her big blue eyes grew two sizes, and her mouth shaped to match.

Jonas rolled his eyes. "Don't tease like that, Sabrina. It's cruel on so many levels."

118

"Breszewski!" Jared's booming voice called my name. He was twenty feet away, but he used enough volume to cover a much larger distance. "What the hell are you doing? I heard rumors you were trying to steal my people, but this is ridiculous."

I ignored his insinuation. No doubt Jonas had been seen outside my office on several occasions, and those toadying for better favor with Joy via Jared probably ran to him to report. "I've come for your files. I don't suppose you're ready to debrief?"

"I'm not leaving until tomorrow."

Glaring at him dubiously, I said, "You have nothing prepared at all, do you?"

With a curt jerk of his head he asked me into his office. I knew he was going to get rude, and I was glad he wasn't going to do it in front of Jonas. I could hold my own against him, but I didn't think Jonas would put up with it very well. Brandon Spencer passed to his son some very specific ideas about women and respect. The door behind me slammed shut. Jared's office was in a nicer location than mine. He had a bank of windows, but the room was much smaller. I frequently worked with my whole team inside my office. Six people would never comfortably fit inside Jared's tiny space.

Jared's area was more centrally located, whereas mine was off the beaten path. Anyone near my office was lost or meant to be there. It had its advantages in the lack of interruption, but I found myself often left out of the loop on office affairs not directly related to business. While I had only found out about his vacation today, it probably wasn't news to anyone else.

He threw a folded newspaper on his desk. It was open to a half-finished crossword puzzle. "I don't need your attitude, Breszewski."

"Jared, if I'm going to manage your accounts for two weeks, I need lead time. I need to look them over while you're still here so that I can access you when I have questions." This was old, worn ground.

He gestured to a chair across from his desk, but I didn't take it. I'd long ago learned when to remain standing to move things along. I waved away the invitation. "How many accounts do you have?" Last year, there had been four. Three of those had been badly neglected.

"Five. We're pitching a cat food project." Without sitting, he rounded his desk to put something official between us to indicate we were in his territory. I wondered if he had peed on the thing as well. He tossed the file across his desk.

I opened it. Everything was as I thought. "Your pitch is next Wednesday and you haven't even given this to Jonas and Tim."

He shrugged. "It's cat food. I let Tina take a crack at it."

"Tina?" I desperately hoped he hadn't let a potentially large account like this, or even a small one, rest in the hands on an untried intern.

"My intern. You saw her out there." Something in the way he said it made me think Tina was more willing to give Jared what he wanted than I had been when I was stuck with him. I discounted the implication on the basis that Jared was a misogynist bastard.

My sigh had him scrambling.

"She's coming along nicely. I gave her to the teacher. He's good with the whole mentor thing." He rearranged some papers on his desk. I thought one looked like an off track betting receipt. My grandfather had taken me to the races several times, but we'd gone to larger places than the Hazel Park Racetrack.

I closed my eyes against the pain that wrapped around my head and squeezed. "You handed her over to someone who has been in the advertising business for less than a year?"

Resentment colored Jared's neck red. He didn't care for my judgment. "He's good at it."

I knew he was good at it. I frequently looked over his work. After the first time, he had hesitantly begun coming to me with questions. I knew he hated relying on me the way he did. He wanted a clear delineation between work and home, but Jared was no good to him. If Jared's accounts were in good shape, I had no doubt it was due to Jonas' diligence and not Jared's sudden leadership abilities. Tapping the file in my hand impatiently, I jettisoned the topic. "What else do you have going on?"

He dug into his file cabinet and tossed the remaining dossiers to me. "These two are dormant and these two have something coming up, but not for another month or so."

I couldn't believe he still had a job. I took the files and left without thanking him for his time or insight. I headed back to my office, which was in the opposite direction of Jonas' desk.

He waited for me in the hall that linked the two halves of our floor together. It skirted the large main conference room where we had first met. Without a word, he pushed me into a supply closet and leaned against the door to keep anyone from entering. It was dim and cooler in here. My oncoming migraine appreciated the low light.

Before I could tell him this was not the time for a quickie, he said, "You look stressed."

Bitter was a better descriptor. It was nice of him to not use it. "It seems Jared is planning to go on vacation."

"I know," he grinned. "I'm looking forward to it."

"I'll be covering for him."

His grin grew. "Now I'm really looking forward to it."

"Were you aware that you have a major presentation next Wednesday?"

The grin dropped from his face. My headache throbbed. He struggled to keep his voice from becoming a growl. "If you tell me it has anything to do with cat food, I'm going to kill him."

It was my turn to grin. "Then I guess I won't tell you it has anything to do with cat food. If they arrest you for murder, who will I get to take your place?" I meant to tease him, and he took it that way, but the words crashed into me with startling clarity. After Jonas was finished with me, what would I become? Where would I find a man who understood what I needed like he did? For this reason and because of my headache, my grin wasn't successful.

"You can't replace me," he said, taking the files I held too tightly. He shoved them on a shelf full of toilet paper rolls and turned me around. "That bastard has had Tina working on this. I thought he made it up so she could practice developing a campaign. Here I was thinking he was doing something right for a change."

"He was looking for cheap labor," I said. "He used to do things like that to me when I was his intern. Luckily I made some choices that turned out to be fortuitous for me and for the company." I shouldn't have been surprised that his habits hadn't changed. He hadn't had an intern in years. I wondered who let him have one. It wasn't Joy's responsibility to place interns.

Jonas dug his thumbs into the middle of my back, finding knots of tension I hadn't known were there. I yelped.

"Breathe into it," he said, pressing harder.

The pain grew worse before it lessened and disappeared. He moved his thumbs up, chasing the knots away. By the time he finished with the back of my head, I leaned against him. He wrapped his arms around me and dropped kisses onto my neck.

"I've ruined your hair," he said, pulling the pins from it and stowing them in his pocket. His fingers played across my lips. "Let me finish relaxing you."

121

I opened my mouth to capture the tip of his middle finger. Turning to face him, I said, "I think you need it more than me."

Before he could correct my English, I pulled his face down and kissed him. My other hand wandered down to loosen his belt and open his pants. I slipped my hand inside to find him already hard. I smiled in the middle of the kiss, pleased with the effect I had on him.

Heady with power, I sank to my knees and licked the length of him. He smelled of my scented soap and fresh laundry mixed with something musky and masculine.

He quivered. "Sabrina, you don't have to—"

Whatever he wanted to say was forgotten. I took him inside my mouth, sucking gently, exploring his slanted, soft head with my tongue. I let him set the pace to some extent. He rested one hand on the back of my head, encouraging me and letting me know I was in command.

I reveled in the taste of him and in the sounds he made—sounds I ripped from him. The change in pressure of his hand on my head and the crescendo of moans he issued let me know he was about to come. I gripped his ass hard, sealing him to me, and he came.

Instantly he hauled me to my feet and kissed me, his tongue dueling with mine for possession of the semen I had yet to swallow. Unlike him, I wasn't in a generous mood. I felt unaccountably possessive, and I didn't want to share. I fought and won.

The tempestuous kiss ended, and he held me close, resting his chin on the top of my head. "You didn't have to do that."

"I wanted to."

His embrace tightened. He ran his fingers through my hair in long strokes. He liked when I wore it down, which I didn't often do.

Before he could get maudlin, I added, "Plus, I'm good at it. I wanted to show you I was good at something."

"Don't underestimate yourself," he said into my hair. "You're good at a lot of things, and you're much more passionate than you seem to think."

After informing my team of the impending, albeit temporary, changes, I spent the rest of the day in my office poring over Jared's files. Some were in better shape than I thought they'd be, mostly due to Jonas. The cat food account was going to be the majority of the problem. One of my team members would need to help.

I didn't know Veronica that well, so I couldn't move her. Ty was the logical choice. He was smart and worked well with others. The more I considered it, the more I could see him meshing with Jonas. The two of them would feed ideas to each other and come up with something wonderful. The only unknown in this scenario was Tim.

I would need to pump Jonas for information about his partner. The fact he rarely mentioned Tim didn't surprise me. Our conversations at home largely excluded work.

My cell phone rang as I finished informing Ty of his temporary reassignment and the rest of the team that they'd have to pick up the slack related to Ty's absence. I listened to the customary grumbling, most of which was directed toward Jared, with grace and silent aplomb.

The number on my caller ID was unfamiliar. "Hello?"

"Sabrina? This is Alyssa Spencer. I'm so sorry to bother you at work, but I didn't want to chance Jonas overhearing. Is this a bad time?" She sounded truly apologetic, and I had the sense that she would sound that way no matter where she called me. She didn't yet know me well enough to feel comfortable contacting me for no reason.

"No, this is fine," I assured her. "Can you hold for a minute?"

Without waiting for her reply, I muted the call and handed the cat food file to Ty. "Look this over. I'll send you to meet with Jonas and Tim tomorrow."

As I walked away, I resumed the conversation. "Thanks for waiting, Alyssa. What's wrong?"

"Nothing is wrong, dear. Amanda told me about what happened yesterday at your house. She's really sorry for putting you on the spot."

I frowned. Amanda had already apologized, though it was Jonas she had upset, not me. "Jonas was the one who was annoyed. I wasn't mad at her."

She made a motherly sound of concern. "Brandon and I are extremely sorry you can't make it to Kentucky this year. We were so looking forward to having a chance to get to know you better."

Jonas hadn't consulted me about it one way or another. "I'm sorry," I said. "One of my colleagues is on vacation that week, and we can't both be gone at the same time." I refrained from mentioning Jonas' looming presentation that would win or lose the account. "I could pull a few strings, though, and get Jonas down there after next Wednesday."

Alyssa sighed on the other end. I felt bad. If I had known about this even a week earlier, I could have arranged for us both to go.

"What about his birthday?"

This one, I fumbled. "His birthday?"

"He didn't tell you." It was a statement. Alyssa knew her son.

This time, *I* sighed. "He probably didn't think it was important."

She laughed sympathetically. "I'll have to keep you in the loop, Sabrina. Wednesday is Jonas' birthday. We usually wait and celebrate it in Kentucky. We do Sam's at the same time. Her birthday is the second week in September."

"Wednesday as in 'the day after tomorrow,' or next week?" I ground my teeth. Why hadn't he mentioned it?

"The day after tomorrow. I can't believe he didn't tell you."

I could. "I'll have to retaliate appropriately. Let's surprise him. Nobody mention anything."

"I usually call him in the morning," she said. "Just to wish him a good day."

I smiled wickedly. "Do that, but don't ask him out to dinner or anything. If he asks, you have plans. You meant to keep up the tradition of celebrating his birthday in Kentucky, so you didn't keep your schedule clear."

A plan formed in my head. I sucked at lying, but he hadn't told me anything about this, so I wouldn't be forced to pretend to have forgotten. Alyssa and I mapped out a plan for a surprise party. I enlisted Ginny's help, and not only for her cake skills. She had an extra key to my house and knew the alarm code.

Then there was the bonus that Drew Snow, her business partner of four years and close friend, was one of the country's top chefs. He'd recently clinched a deal to film six episodes of a cooking show for the Food Channel. I wanted him to cater. Alyssa would handle the decorations and help Drew and Ginny with the food preparations.

My job would be to get him home on time.

Wednesday began like any other day. Alyssa called while we were in the car driving to work. Jonas had worked the evening before and was dozing as I drove. He let it go to voice mail. Sneaky devil probably didn't want me to hear his end of the conversation. It annoyed me that he wouldn't tell me about his birthday. After all, I'd told him about mine.

I moved Tim and Jonas to the smaller conference room near my office so I wouldn't have to travel to the other side of the floor to see them. Tina came with them. I asked Ophelia to change places with her for the duration, knowing she was the more competent intern. It wasn't her fault, or Tina's; I had simply trained Ophelia better than Jared had trained Tina. If she kept her eyes open, she would learn a lot in the two weeks she would be with me.

Ty moved into the conference room. I was pleased to see him take a leadership role. It didn't take me long to figure out that Tim was a follower. He did whatever he was told, and he did it to the specifications given. I didn't see him ever progressing to a better position.

I didn't realize how much Jonas was bristling under the changes until he snapped at me. He and Ty had brainstormed a variety of approaches. They were hunched over a spread of sketched ideas when I came by to check on them. I commented on several that I liked and pointed out the major problems with the rest of them.

"Are you going to be looking over my shoulder for the whole two weeks?" He forced the question through gritted teeth, his green eyes shooting daggers at me.

I struggled to react as his superior and not his wife, but I couldn't stop my eyes from widening in surprise. At least my voice was strong and even when I answered. "Yes."

He threw down his pencil and rested both hands on the table between us. "I can't work like this. Stay out of my way. If I need something from you, I'll ask."

My mouth tightened and my eyes narrowed.

Ty put a hand on Jonas' shoulder, but he addressed me. "Sabrina, Jonas didn't mean it the way it sounded. We're working under a deadline, as you know, and it's stressful."

Jonas' eyes hadn't left mine and his expression hadn't changed. "No, that's not the problem. I'm used to deadlines and stress. I don't appreciate having someone constantly micromanaging my work."

I wasn't about to let this go further. "My office. Now." I turned and left without looking back to make sure he followed. If he hesitated, I'm sure Ty would remind him that I wasn't known for my patience with insubordination and that I was well within my rights to fire him.

I opened the door and it slammed behind me. I whirled, intending to let him have it, but he opened fire first.

"You didn't even let us have a chance to discuss any of the ideas. Brainstorming and discussion are the most important part of the creative process. We could have combined ideas, or altered others to come up with something we really liked, but you can't let that happen, can you? You may give your team credit for their ideas, but you make sure your hand is in every single piece, don't you? I prefer to have my work stolen than to have it hijacked!"

I saw red. If he wanted to push me over the edge, he'd found the right buttons. "I don't have time to massage your ego, Jonas. I not only have Jared's five accounts to maintain, including this pitch project which wasn't even started until I told you about it Monday, I have the eight my team normally handles. If you can't handle the way I do things, then maybe you need to go back to teaching."

Though he stood less than two feet away, I shouted at him every bit as vehemently as he had shouted at me. He was right—yelling did relieve stress. I had more ammunition in store. I was also working with four new people, and I didn't know their skill sets. I might know what Jonas was capable of in the bedroom, but I didn't have a clear picture of what he was like at work.

"Wow," he said. "I wondered if you had claws, kitten."

It was a low blow. "Asshole." I whispered in anger, not pain. I would have called him something worse, like "bastard," or "son of a bitch," or "motherfucker," but I liked his mother, and so I saw no reason to cast a shadow on her character.

"Finally, you see the real me." His eyes glittered hard. He closed the distance between us with half a step. Grabbing my wrists, he pinned them behind me and kissed me solidly.

I fought him, struggling against the direction he was trying to take my passion. For someone who was so against bringing work home, he didn't have a problem bringing home to work. It probably wasn't very nice, but I couldn't remember ever being so angry and out of control. I bit his lip.

Without releasing me, he pulled back and looked at me, his eyes tawny with arousal and the ghost of a smile curving his mouth. "Are you opting to not use the safeword?"

I stifled the urge to kick his shin. My heels featured pointed toes. I could do some real damage. "We're at work, Jonas. This is neither the time nor the place."

"I'm pissed at you, Sabrina. The way I see it, we could continue yelling, probably both say things we'll regret, or we could use this passion for something more fun."

He was still angry. I could see it in the firmness of his mouth and feel it in the stiffness of his body against mine. I was just as angry. While I couldn't deny his kiss and his rough treatment aroused me, I wasn't going to let him use sex to control me.

He kissed me again, softer, letting passion supersede anger. I drew my foot back to kick him, but the door opened. I was glad for the interruption because I didn't want to kick him, but I was mortified to be caught in this situation.

"Sabrina?" It was Ty. "Is everything okay?"

Jonas let go and stepped back. I smoothed the hem of my shirt, taking in Ty's flexing fist and the way he watched Jonas through narrowed eyes.

"Yes, Ty. Can you give us a minute?"

He stared at Jonas a long time, a clear warning in his eyes. Reluctantly, he nodded. "I'll be right outside." He kept his gaze on Jonas as he backed out the door.

I turned on Jonas as soon as the catch clicked. "Don't you ever do that again. I am your boss for the next two weeks. I expect you to treat me with dignity and respect. You can't kiss me just because you're unhappy about the way I do things."

He wandered over to my sofa and sat down. "I kissed you because you look so damn hot when you get mad that I couldn't resist. For the record, that was the first time I've ever seen you lose your temper. You should do it more often. I bet you'd scare the hell out of your mother."

I was dangerously close to losing it again, and his nonchalant attitude wasn't helping. I stalked over to stand in front of him. "You may not like the way I do things, but we don't have time to ease into this. If we snag this account, Jared gets all the credit. However if we lose this account, I'll get all the blame. Check your ego at the door, or it will get bruised."

"It's already bruised," he mumbled. Looking up at me, he continued in a clear voice. "It amazes me that you engender such loyalty and devotion when you obviously don't trust anyone but yourself."

I huffed out a breath. "That's not true. I trust my team implicitly. You're forgetting that you are not a member of my team."

"Veronica—"

I cut him off. "Has been with me less than a week. She's also enduring trial by fire. The sooner you realize the way I treat you has nothing to do with you, we'll get along better."

He scooted forward to perch on the edge of the sofa, all business. "Therein lies the problem. Sabrina, you *do* know me, and I know you. Pretending otherwise will only create problems that neither of us wants. I need you to trust me to come to you when I have a problem and let me work through this on my own. Ty and I are making progress. We should have a proposal by Friday if you leave us alone."

Letting my breath loose in a long, thoughtful exhale, I settled onto the couch next to Jonas. He was asking for a lot. He wasn't far from the mark when he accused me of micromanaging. The only difference was my team knew how to deal with me. Ty suffered in silence. Randall ignored me. Clare tolerated me. Veronica had shot me more than a few dirty looks, and I was sure her tongue had holes in it from the number of times she'd bitten it. I could tell she was going to be a challenge.

"Fine, but if you fail, I will kill you." I used the appropriate gravity when I said this. "And believe me when I say that no one will find the body."

"That lacked your characteristic grace." His hand closed over mine. "Thank you. I know it's hard for you to give what I'm asking."

I looked at his hand, appreciating the long, strong fingers and the way they felt on me. "Yes, well, it'll be easier than explaining to Ty what you were doing to me."

His thumb traced circles on my wrist where my pulse beat. "I think it was obvious what we were doing."

"It looked like you were attacking me, which you were, and I was trying to break free, which I was. He doesn't know anything about my personal life, and you don't seem comfortable with anyone knowing about us." I shot him a pointed look as I said the last part.

"If you explain the marriage, you're going to have to explain the divorce."

"People don't ask about divorce, and people don't make a habit of asking me personal questions." I was completely sincere, and he burst out laughing. Exasperating man. "I don't see what's funny about any of this."

Raising my hand to his lips, he pried open my fingers to kiss the palm. "You're priceless. Never change, Sabrina. I like you just the way you are."

He left, and I stared after him, unable to fathom what in the world he found amusing. Ty came in, and I motioned him over. "What did you need?"

He gave me a pained look. "Sabrina, did he try to assault you?"

My eyes widened. I knew what he had seen, but when he put it in legal terms, it sounded so ominous and wrong. "No, Ty. No. Jonas would never do something like that."

Those chocolate eyes that usually smiled with inner joy were serious. Even at our most important presentations, I'd never seen him so worried. "You've known him for a day. You don't know what he will or won't do."

"I've known him for longer than a day." I hoped the look that went with my statement was meaningful and uninvited further questions. "I'd really appreciate it if you kept this to yourself. We don't really want this getting out."

He stroked his smooth chin, his elbows resting on his knees. "How long has 'this' been going on?"

In the three years I'd worked with Ty, this was our first personal conversation. I'd been surprised when he'd come to my grandfather's funeral, now here we were, discussing my love life. "Two months. I never expected to work with him. It seems the different dynamic isn't an easy change for either of us."

"Okay, there's not a delicate way to say this," he said, leaning toward me and taking my hand in his. I was unused to being touched like this, and now it had happened twice in one day. "When a man holds a woman the way he was holding you—"

I cut him off. "Then he really knows how to please that woman." I hadn't thought about how that would sound before I said it, and now my trademark blush made its appearance.

"Sabrina," he began in protest.

"Ty, trust me when I say you really don't want to know the details of my sex life. Jonas is a gentleman. He's kind and thoughtful and generous. You weren't meant to see what you saw. Nobody was." I bit my lip to keep from saying more.

It seemed now that I had acknowledged there was something between us, the floodgates opened. Before, I hadn't felt the need to confide anything about my relationship with Jonas to anyone. Now I couldn't seem to stop. It was time I phoned Ginny for a heart-to-heart. She was good at this kind of thing.

The look Ty gave me was doubtful at best. "I'll be watching him, Sabrina. He has a way to go before he wins my vote. What I saw today doesn't earn him any points."

I flopped back onto the sofa and put my legs on the coffee table, crossing them at the ankle. It was the least composed I had ever been in front of an employee, but I wasn't feeling overly composed.

"Ty? Can I ask you a question, and you give me an honest answer?" I didn't look at him. I didn't want to pressure him either way.

"As long as you promise not to hold it against me."

I looked up. The humor was back in his eyes, but I wasn't fooled. I knew he would be watching Jonas and me closely. "I promise."

He leaned back beside me and rested his legs next to mine. They extended much farther onto the table. "Then go for it."

"Am I too involved with your work?"

"You're going to let his crack about micromanaging get under your skin?"

"Ty," I pleaded. Jonas wasn't frequently wrong. "Jonas asked me to step back and let you guys do this without my feedback until you have a proposal."

"That's gotta hurt," he teased.

"So it's true." I sighed. "It is hard for me to give up control. I don't want to get in the way of the work you guys do, but I don't want to step back and have it all blow up in my face."

"There is a happy medium," Ty said. "But you're going to have to find it through trial and error."

I scrubbed a hand down my face, careful to not smear my makeup. "I like how you told me I was a bitch without ever saying the word. That's some talent you have for diplomacy."

He laughed. "Did you honestly just crack a joke?" He whipped out his cell phone. "Let me record this."

He punched some buttons, but I took it away and set it by his feet. "I won't say that twice in a row."

"Just to be clear," he said, "I would never call you a bitch. You're smart, talented, and beautiful, inside and out. You have a wicked business sense, and you pursue your goal with a startling single-mindedness. If you cross the line from time to time, nobody who's ever worked with you for any length of time is going to second-guess you. You've pissed me off more than once, but I trust your judgment, so I swallow my pride and move on. I know in the long run, I'm going to learn so much from you that I'll come out ahead in the end."

I squeezed his hand, which hadn't left mine. "When I die, I want you to speak at my funeral."

He lifted a thick brow at me. "Two jokes. He really rattled you, didn't he?"

"He always rattles me," I said. "That's one of the things I like about him. He's observant and smart, and he's not afraid to argue with me."

"Is that an invitation to argue with you?" he asked. "Because I have no problem arguing with anybody."

I pushed away all mirth to regard him with complete sincerity. "If you think your idea is better than mine, or if you want to question something I say, I think you should do it." If nothing else, it would improve my team's morale and confidence. At best, I would see an overall improvement in our bottom line. "Nicely," I added. "Be gentle with me, Ty. I'm fragile."

He laughed uncomfortably, and I knew he was thinking of the rough way Jonas had been holding me when he'd walked in on us earlier.

Chapter 11—Sabrina

I put Veronica with Tim and refrained from checking on anyone until it was nearly time to call it a day. I was pleasantly surprised to find nothing amiss, and I was able to accomplish many other things I would normally end up taking home to finish. Perhaps Jonas had a point.

When I made it to the conference room where he and Ty were working, he looked up at me, an unspoken warning in his eyes. I ignored it. "Let me see what you guys have so far," I directed.

Ty waved me over to show me the storyboard he had nearly completed. Jonas came over to tape the last three sketches in place. I studied them carefully, impressed with the idea and the sketches, but I said nothing. I looked up at them both. "It's five o'clock. Time to call it a day." I turned to leave the room, when Ty's voice stopped me.

"A happy medium, Sabrina." His pointed look was less sharp because of the amusement in his eyes.

"It looks good." Ignoring Jonas, I winked at Ty and left the room. Within five minutes, Jonas was in my office.

"Are you ready to go home?" he asked tightly. "I thought waiting by the elevator would be a little stupid given the fact I'm working so close to your office."

I grabbed my purse and smiled at him. "Let's go."

He was quiet and aloof for most of the ride home. I was fiddling with the radio when he finally broke his silence.

"You didn't say anything about the presentation so far," he said accusingly.

"You asked me not to say anything until Friday," I reminded him.

"I didn't mean... Christ. You're pouting about this, aren't you?"

There was an edge to him, an anger I didn't understand. "No, but you are."

He turned the radio off in the middle of a song I liked. "You winked at him."

Frowning, I asked, "I winked at who?"

"At whom. 'Who' is a subject. 'Whom' is an object." He didn't take his eyes from the road. His response seemed automatic, but I knew it was a defense. That didn't make it less aggravating.

"Don't correct my grammar, Jonas. It's annoying. Answer the damn question."

A muscle in his lower jaw twitched. "Ty. You were in your office with him for quite a while, and I know you didn't tell him we were married."

"You didn't want me to," I reminded him. "You're the one who's embarrassed to be married to me, not the other way around."

"I'm not embarrassed to be married to you," he snapped. "And I don't think it's right for you to flirt like that right in front of me."

I narrowed my eyes. That wasn't flirting. I could flirt with the best of them, or the worst, depending on the point of view. I just didn't do it often. "You sound jealous."

"He's younger and better looking, and he'll probably get a promotion long before I do. For Christ's sake, I'm five years older than you."

Stifling a grin, I said, "Four years. I just turned thirty."

"I'm thirty-five," he said. "Today is my birthday."

I let a moment pass before I made a knowing sound. "So this is why you've been so cranky all day. Why didn't you tell me it was your birthday? Do you know how inconsiderate this is? I didn't have a chance to make reservations or buy something sexy to wear. I had my eye on this black lacy thong I thought you'd like, but I haven't had the nerve to purchase it. This would have been the perfect motivation."

Folding my arms over my chest, I pouted for a few moments. When we pulled into the garage, I turned to him. "I don't even know what to get for you."

Flouncing out of the car, I made it to the garage door before he caught me. "Let me make it up to you." The vinegar was gone, and Jonas was contrite—or, as contrite as he got.

From his tone, I knew what he had in mind, but I still asked. "How?"

"Buy the thong. Wear it tonight and let me tie you up."

I was wet from the way his voice turned husky when he breathed the request against the sensitive skin at my nape. "Why would you want to tie me up?"

He ran a light caress up and down my arms. "When I hold you down, it inhibits my movements as well as yours. This way, I could hold you down and still have my hands free. I promise you'll like it."

I already liked it, and he hadn't done anything. "Let's go inside. I need to get my other purse, and you need to get dinner started."

We went in the back way, through the laundry room, but I had already warned Ginny and Alyssa of the path we usually took to enter the house. During the time I pretended to pout, I had been unable to detect anyone's car nearby. Either they had changed their minds, or they'd hidden their vehicles well.

As soon as we stepped into the kitchen, I turned to watch Jonas. Though I was sure the rich, mouthwatering smells of Drew's cooking tipped him off the moment he'd walked into the house, the candid surprise in his eyes as everyone yelled to him made me smile.

Family and friends thronged around him. I scooted away to greet Ginny and my mother, and to thank Drew for throwing dinner together for twenty people on short notice. At 5'10, with spiky blond hair and startling blue eyes, Drew's show was sure to be a success with anyone who enjoyed a pretty face and a dynamic personality. Once they tried his recipes, they'd be hooked.

Jonas tore himself away from everybody and wrapped his body around mine, laying a long, slow, open-mouthed kiss on me that was pornographic in its heat and intensity.

"You made me feel guilty," he accused.

"Serves you right," I said. "This wasn't easy to throw together in two days."

"Does this mean I don't get my gift?" His hands were strong on my waist, and his warmth penetrated the fabric.

"It means you have to wait until tomorrow," I laughed. "Come, and meet Drew. You'll never come across a better chef."

Jonas wasn't offended, especially after he tasted Drew's smothered chicken and Ginny's signature Wicked Berry Tart.

Later, after everyone had eaten too much, finished all the wine, and left, Jonas tried to thank me for the party as we cleared away the remnants of the mess.

"It was the best present anyone's ever given me," he said.

I waved away the compliment. "Your mother and Ginny did most of the work. I only wrote the checks." Heading to the dining room, where I had a hutch that hid more than it revealed, I riffled through a drawer of junk to find his gifts. "I did get you something."

He sat down at the dining room table and opened the envelope. The first piece of paper was a notice that his student loans were paid in full. The second was a round-trip ticket to Lexington, Kentucky.

"I could only get you next Thursday and Friday off," I explained, "but I figured it was better than missing your family vacation for the first time in thirty-three years. A rental car is waiting for you in Lexington. You can drive the rest of the way."

He looked at me, a flurry of emotions mixing across his features. "You paid off my student loans?"

He hadn't owed much, only about ten thousand. I nodded.

He shook his head. "I'll pay you back."

"It's a gift."

"I can't accept this," he argued. "It's far too expensive. You don't have your inheritance yet, and even if you did, I wouldn't accept this from you."

I hadn't anticipated this reaction. It stung. "Why can't you?"

Lightly, he caressed my cheek. "I don't want your money."

Frustrated, I tried to point out rational reasons for him to accept the gift and move on. "This way, you won't have to work a second job. You're so tired on the days after you work, Jonas. Now you'll have more time to do the things you want to do."

He stared at me, a strange emotion glittering from his green eyes. "I like working at Ellen's club."

"I know," I said, amending my logic. I'd stumbled into a sore spot. "But you can cut back your hours."

He stood, taking me in his arms. "If you want me to work less, honey, all you needed to do was ask."

"I didn't do this to interfere with your life. I don't want you to change things for me. I did this to give you more options."

"You keep spending large amounts of money on me," he said testily.

I drew back. "I do not. This is the first time I've spent over a thousand."

He raised a brow. "I have several pairs of three-hundred dollar jeans that say differently."

"Did anyone ever tell you it's rude to fish in the trash for price tags?" I didn't see his point about the jeans. "You had one pair of jeans when you moved in here. You may have saved your suits from that fire, but you let your casual clothes burn."

"My suits cost about three hundred each, Sabrina. I saved them because they were the most expensive things I owned. Now I have designer jeans, countless designer shirts, and silk ties—and that just to begin with. You need to stop or you'll have spent your inheritance before you get it." Firm lines settled in around his mouth. If he didn't watch it, he would have a disapproving scowl set into his face permanently.

I waved away his concern. "The twelve million is nothing to me. I have plenty of money, and I get to spend it however I choose. If you don't like the clothes I buy you, all you need to do is say something." My pique was evident. I didn't add that I felt compelled to shop when he was gone at work. He frequently returned home to find something new I thought would look good on him. It always did.

I didn't draw the line at clothes, either. He was constantly absorbed in some kind of thriller or mystery novel. His favorite authors were easy to identify. I picked up new releases for him, as well as tools and electronic items. His new laptop was in the mail. I hadn't meant it as a birthday gift. I had been shopping online when I'd noticed how beat-up his looked.

He pressed his lips together, ready to keep taking me to task, but I wasn't having any of it. I flounced away and went upstairs. It had been a long, long day and I didn't feel like fighting with him—again. I hadn't walked away from our first tiff unscathed.

I stood at the vanity and pulled the pins from my hair, tossing them carelessly on the marble surface. I had paid his student loans before I knew his birthday was coming. The real gift was time in Kentucky with his family. I had thrown the statement closing the loan into the envelope at the last minute. Somewhere in the back of my mind, I knew he wouldn't be pleased by that gift, and I didn't want him to think I was being manipulative.

Jonas appeared behind me in the mirror, his expression heavy with meaning. He pushed my hands away and finished freeing my hair. When he was done, he pulled me back against him and massaged my scalp.

"I'm sorry," he said quietly into my hair. "I didn't mean to hurt your feelings."

136

I didn't reply. I didn't know what to say. His hands moved to my neck and shoulders, kneading the knots I carried there. "I don't want you to think you have to buy me things to keep me with you." His lips grazed my throat as his hands worked their magic on my arms.

I stiffened at the insinuation. "I know you won't leave before the year is over."

"Relax, honey. I wasn't talking about sex, either. I don't want you to think I married you for your money. You have to know it doesn't matter to me." His voice caught a little. He had meant to keep from me how important this was to him.

I turned in his arms. "I never thought it mattered to you. You need to stop worrying about it, Jonas. I give more to charity each year than I've spent on you."

He looked at me oddly, his hands never stopping as he smoothed the stress from my lower back. "You can't possibly make that much money."

Shrugging, I said, "The money I make at Rife is inconsequential. My grandfather set me up with a very large trust fund on the day I was born."

His hands stopped. "That's some kind of favoritism."

"No," I said. "Grandpa took care of Ginny and Mom as well. Even his step-children have trust funds, though they're smaller than ours. The twelve million he gave Ginny outright came with strings when it came to me. That's why Ginny and Mom thought it was so unfair. But mostly, the way he did this was to make my cousins think there was nothing left so we wouldn't get caught in a costly legal battle."

Thoughts raced through his head, reflecting on his face. "If you're so damn wealthy, then why did you only give me one ticket to Kentucky?"

"What do you mean?"

"I mean, you can obviously afford to take time away from work. Why aren't you coming with me?"

I bit my lip, knowing that however I answered, it was going to come out wrong. "You didn't invite me."

"Amanda invited you. My mother invited you. I thought it was a given that you were expected to be there too."

I tried to pull away, but he didn't let me. "You didn't tell me about the trip for a reason."

"So you assume it was because I don't want you there?"

"You don't." I said it with certainty. He had a serious problem leaving me alone with his family members. He'd stayed by my side the entire evening, tensing whenever I slipped away and he saw me in conversation with one of his relatives. He didn't have a problem with me speaking to Ginny, my mother, Lara, or Drew, who had stayed for the party.

After much thought, he spoke, forcing the words out painfully. "I haven't told you about Helene. I don't want you to hear about her from them."

Empathy surged through me. I wanted to take away his anguish. It may have been years old, but the pain was still fresh. "Maybe you should tell me."

He let go and tugged at his tie.

I pushed his hands away to loosen it for him. "You don't have to if you don't want to, Jonas. I haven't exactly told you anything about me, either."

"Aren't we a dysfunctional pair?" The ghostly smile on his lips didn't reach his eyes. "She isn't my ex-girlfriend. She's my ex-wife."

I felt an insane urge to strangle him with the now-loosened tie in my hands. It was none of my business, and I hated the surge of jealousy I felt. He'd married her because he'd loved her. Somehow, it made it worse to know they'd been married, that they'd planned to spend the rest of their lives together. He'd never once referred to me as his wife. I wasn't the first to wear his grandmother's wedding rings. It wouldn't be his second wife wearing them after me; it would be his third. I wasn't special to him in any way.

I watched the maroon silk slither through my fingers and pool on the floor. I might have said something like, "Oh," or it might have remained inside my head. I rubbed at my eyes, and then I stared at the black smudges on my hands. Abruptly, I turned and went into the bathroom to wash the makeup from my face.

I looked like her.

It didn't matter what he said. His sisters, his friends, even his parents saw the resemblance when they looked at me. It explained the hesitance that lasted a second every time they saw me again. I thought it was due to the fact that maybe I wasn't his usual type, but now I knew I was thoroughly his type. It was unsettling and hard to process.

He followed me. His reflection in the mirror eyed me regretfully. "I meant to tell you, but as time passed, it didn't seem relevant. Then I didn't want you to know. It was selfish of me, and I can't explain why I didn't want you to know."

My patience for games vanished. "You don't want me to know because I look like her. That's why I caught your eye in the first place, isn't it?" I rinsed my face, the icy water a punishment for having been so gullible.

He snatched my towel and dried my face. "You don't look like her. You look nothing like her." His hand trembled, and his denial had been too vehement.

I took the towel from him and finished with my face and hands. "Don't lie to me. You're the one who insisted honesty be part of this thing between us." I disappeared into the closet to change my clothes.

The things he insisted on made so much more sense now. He wanted a monogamous relationship. He'd wanted to sleep with me from the beginning—and it had nothing to do with me. Most likely, he closed his eyes and pretended I was her. That stung more than anything. I didn't expect him to feel anything tender for me, but I'd believed him when he said we were friends, and that he desired me.

Jonas gripped my shoulders, forcing me to look at his face. "I am being honest, Sabrina. Maybe at first, I wanted you to replace her. But you haven't. You can't, and I don't want you to. I didn't know you then, but I know you now."

Abruptly he released me, his shoulders slumped in defeat. "She left me almost five years ago. We were married for eighteen months."

"But you dated for a long time," I guessed. "Three years? Four?"

"Five."

Five. I'd spent more than five years with Stephen. It was a significant chunk of time, not something easily dismissed. I hadn't even seen Stephen in eight years, and the memory of him haunted me, full of regret and a sense of failure.

"Why did she leave?" It was an unfair question. If anyone asked Stephen why I had dumped him, he wouldn't be able to do more than guess.

He drew a hand through his hair and took a ragged breath. "Because she said she couldn't survive on a teacher's salary. I didn't make enough to buy her the expensive things she wanted. We weren't poor, but I couldn't make enough to satisfy her desire for material items."

That gave me pause. It explained his reluctance to accept expensive gifts from me. "You left teaching so you could shower your next wife with expensive things?"

He nodded, a short burst of movement from an otherwise frozen man.

I pulled on my nightgown and went to him, resting my hands on his chest. "Jonas, accepting gifts from me doesn't make you materialistic. Besides, you've given me something worth more than anything I could spend on you."

He looked down at me, searching my eyes. "What's that?"

"I thought there was something really wrong with me until I met you. You opened an entire world to me, one I thought I'd never know. For the first time in my life, I feel truly alive, and it's all because of you."

Shaking his head, he said, "Anyone could—"

I cut him off. "No, Jonas. I've had far more lovers than you can possibly guess. Nobody has. That's my point. You didn't pretend to love me, and you didn't judge me. You don't question what I want, what I need. You give it to me without reservation. Maybe this is something that's always come easy to you, and you can't appreciate what you've given me, but don't brush it aside or belittle it."

I trembled, thinking about how empty, how inadequate, how dead inside I'd felt for so long. Even now, I wasn't fully ready to face my feelings, or the fact that I had any. He pushed me to anger, to jealousy, and to pain—all in one day. They weren't comfortable emotions. I couldn't control them, and that terrified me.

But it also freed me. When I didn't know anger, I couldn't know joy. Without jealousy, I didn't recognize that the security I always thought I felt was a sham. Without pain, I felt no pleasure. I wasn't done. I wasn't at a place where I felt whole or fully alive, but I was on my way, and it was due to him.

He held me, kissing me tenderly as he led me to bed. If he made love to me, I ignored it, pushing it away because I couldn't accept that from him. When he held my hands immobile above my head and whispered in my ear, urging me higher, I came, crying out my orgasm as I arched beneath him.

Afterward I lay in his arms with my head resting on his shoulder, and I passively explored his chest. He captured my hand and brought it to his lips.

"Come to Kentucky with me." His mouth curved into a large smile beneath my fingertips. "There's a club in Lexington I think you'd love."

Chapter 12—Sabrina

The next day went smoother than the previous one. I practiced stepping back with everyone, not just Jonas and Ty. Randall and Clare shot me strange looks, but they didn't comment. Veronica began to smile at me instead of scowl.

Overall I found nothing was lost from the experience. Work progressed. I offered my opinion when I couldn't hold my tongue and found it better received. Perhaps Jonas was onto something with this. After all, he had undeniable leadership experience. I pondered the difference between being bossy and being the boss.

Toward the end of the day, I heard raised voices coming from the conference room where Jonas and Ty were working. The sound triggered alarm bells in my head. I didn't need a shrink to tell me that one of the reasons I kept such tight control over my team was to prevent arguments like this.

I entered the room and closed the door behind me. Ophelia sat at one end of the table, watching the disagreement. She twisted a strand of her long, frosted hair around her finger. I stopped next to her. "What are they fighting about?"

She looked up, startled, and sat up straight. She was easily six inches taller than me, and the sight of me made her tremble. I wasn't sure I liked that. "Oh, they can't decide which concept they want to use for the commercial. Jonas thinks Ty's idea isn't versatile enough and Ty thinks Jonas' idea is too versatile."

Without waiting for an invitation, I rounded the long table and lifted sketches, coolly assessing each with an eye toward the client profile. Jonas automatically stepped back to let me access the ones in front of him, never missing a beat in his passionate debate with Ty.

"Look at the data. Gay people are more likely than straight people to spend the money to purchase expensive food for their pets," Jonas said. "It's insane to ignore the sales potential in this area."

"The client didn't name the LGBT subgroup as a direct marketing target," Ty argued. "Don't compromise the integrity of the campaign just to put a commercial or two in liberal-leaning shows."

In studying the sketches, I saw their point of contention. Jonas wanted to run a spot where the players were interchangeable. A heterosexual couple could become a gay or lesbian couple with only the change of actor or actress. Ty wanted something with a single actor and a cat. It didn't exclude the LGBT target group, but it didn't include them, either.

"Ty is right, Jonas. The client didn't specify this audience." I turned to look at him, to face the fury I knew I would find. "They're just starting up. They don't have the budget for something like this. Although simple to accomplish, it would cost more money to shoot, and it might be the difference between us landing this account and another firm who can bring it in for less."

He regarded me dispassionately, and I was relieved. At least he wasn't taking any of this personally. I recognized the brilliance of his plan. If only the cat food company had a little more to spend, this would explode them into a lucrative niche market.

Pleased with his reaction, I continued. "However, I think you should keep this idea as an addendum. We can add it as a modifier to the original proposal. You'll need to research the added sales potential in order to really sell this."

Without a word, Jonas handed me a short stack of papers. He'd already done the necessary research. I had no idea when he might have fit it into his packed schedule, but it was thorough.

"We'd need a name if you want to go the LGBT route," Ty said. "The anonymous commercials don't pack as much of a punch, especially when you use women."

"Yes," Jonas agreed drily. "People tend to overlook generic grown women who live together. We could use Ginny in the mock-up."

That caught my attention. "Ginny?"

"Ginny." He uncrossed his arms and spread his palms wide. "She's all fired up because Drew is getting his own show. She said he's too much of a prima donna already. If she turns it down, we threaten to ask Drew. He seemed open to it when we discussed it last night."

Immediately I held up a finger and pointed out the flaws. "Drew isn't gay, and he's using sex to sell his show. Coming out of a closet he may not even be in wouldn't help his ratings."

Jonas lifted his brows in doubt. "He hit on me."

He propositioned me often enough as well, but I knew better. Squelching my urge to laugh, I reoriented his perception of the conversation. "If you reexamine the conversation you two had, you will no doubt realize he hit on us."

"Us?"

Ignoring his question, I ticked off my next point on another finger. "Second, did you tell Ginny you were planning to out her to the entire world? She may seem like a free spirit, but she values her privacy. She's not truly jealous of Drew's impending success. After all, he's not doing it as a pastry chef." Ginny wanted her success to be based on the quality of her goods, not her sex life. "And she's on board as a producer anyway."

He nodded. "Good point. We can use you. I'll bet very few people would know the difference."

I stared at him with uncharacteristic stoicism. I wondered if he would be surprised to know I'd explored that avenue already. It would most likely turn him on, and he'd want me to repeat it for his benefit. Then there was the fact that Ginny needed to give permission for her name or her likeness to be used, whether or not I was the temporary stand-in. And, mostly, there was the lack of budget to consider. No matter how we phrased this part of the proposal, it wasn't in the budget.

Ty watched us in silence, sizing up our relationship through our interaction. Finally he broke in. "This is taking shape awfully fast for something that's supposed to be a theoretical add-on. If you'll kindly tell us which direction to take, we'll work on finishing this proposal tonight for your personal edification."

Trading my creative shoes for my pragmatic ones, I pronounced judgment. "Go with Ty's idea." I handed the papers to Jonas. "Add this in with a separate cost analysis, and don't attach anyone's name to it. Use a stock photo."

I flashed a quick smile at Ty. "You're doing a great job."

His smug smile let me know that he approved of my new management style.

"I'm leaving in a half hour," I murmured to Jonas as I brushed past him.

"Yes, ma'am," he said.

Before I left, I caught sight of Ophelia. I had completely forgotten she was there. My lapse in discretion was uncharacteristic and unforgivable. I'd relaxed my guard because not only did Ty put me at ease, but he knew my secret. I didn't care to keep it a secret, but it was important to Jonas. Maybe he didn't want people to look at him and see two failed marriages. Maybe he would pretend this one never happened.

Whatever the case, I owed him my loyalty. Ophelia would keep her mouth shut.

Once we were safely ensconced in the car, an apology was my first order of business. He smirked a little bit, but I caught the short gesture.

"What is so amusing?"

"People have seen me entering your office from the back door, and they've seen us duck into several different rooms. The whole office thinks we're having an affair."

I glared at him, seething inside. "You're fine with people thinking we're having an illicit affair, but you don't want them to know we're married?"

"It isn't illicit."

White-hot anger surged through me. "I don't find this amusing. I could lose my job for this, Jonas."

"You don't need to work," he reasoned. "Besides, we're married. It's not technically an affair."

My fingers flexed, and I pictured punching him in the arm so vividly my fist hurt. "That isn't the point. I have a reputation at this company and in this business, a reputation I've worked hard to build. The last thing I need is for it to be destroyed with charges of sexual harassment."

That hit home. He was quiet for several miles as he considered it from my point of view. I was in management and it appeared that I was having an affair with a subordinate. By definition, it was sexual harassment even if it was consensual.

"I'll have those rumors quashed in a week," he said.

"Just in time for us both to take off early so we can catch a flight together." My sarcasm was not lost on him.

He turned into the driveway, stopping the car outside of the garage. He put his arm on the back of my seat and looked deeply into my eyes. "Does this mean you won't let me tie you up tonight?"

I slammed the car door and was in the house before he could cut the engine. Fuming, I realized I was more than a little anxious about what he proposed to do to me that evening. The realization did nothing to calm me down. Neither did the fact that Jonas didn't follow me inside. I looked out the front window to see my car disappear from the driveway.

My spirits were in a freefall. He hadn't told me he was working tonight. Besides, I reasoned, he didn't have a change of clothes in my car. The suit would stand out at a bar, particularly on a bartender.

I changed my clothes and went for a swim. I don't know how long I was there, but a shadow looming over the shallow end caught my attention. Poking my head up, I saw Jonas crouched down, waiting for me.

He had changed into jeans, a pair I'd bought him, and a T-shirt. He looked too good. I regretted buying the jeans, especially knowing he primarily wore them to the bar where I wouldn't see him in them.

"Are you going to come in for dinner? I made your favorite."

"My favorite?" I wasn't in the mood for frozen lasagna.

He shrugged. "It's something new, destined to become a classic."

I rolled my eyes. "You heated up Drew's leftovers."

"You betcha. Come on, Sabrina. After dinner, I'll show you the present I bought for you. It's something every woman should have, but you don't."

I chalked the self-satisfied grin on his face to his anticipation of Drew's cooking, but I shouldn't have.

As we ate, Jonas tried to apologize. "I didn't realize the harm, Sabrina. At least give me a chance to fix this before you expend all this energy being mad at me, okay?"

"What if you can't fix it?" I pushed my plate away before I burst.

"I can fix it," he said confidently. "Why don't you head upstairs? I've laid out an outfit on the bed for you."

"What if I don't want to wear it?" I knew I was being a pain, but the trepidation that had disappeared as I swam was back in full force.

"It's a role. You have to dress for the role." He rose and carried our plates to the sink. We had developed a habit of eating in the kitchen, ignoring both the breakfast nook and the dining room unless we had company.

"What is the role?" I hid my excitement. The whole concept of playing a role made me heady with some kind of floating feeling. I

146

liked leaving Sabrina Breszewski, and all that she represented, in the dust.

"Your husband has been out of town. You've taken the opportunity to entertain strange men in your bedroom. Tonight's lover knows you'll never truly be his, and so he's hell-bent on making sure you can think of nothing but him—no matter who you're with."

He gave me the scenario in the same tone as an afterthought, but I wasn't fooled. I wondered how he would play the role of the husband who caught me with one of my lovers. The idea of a spanking made me squirm with unexpected desire.

"What's my name?"

He closed the dishwasher. "You don't share that information with your lovers. You don't know his name, and he doesn't know yours."

I was wearing a towel over my damp swimsuit, but the way he stared at me made me feel like it was all transparent. I liked this fantasy. After hurrying up the stairs, I scooped up the clothes he had left on the bed and jumped in the shower. I wanted to look perfect for my anonymous lover who burned for me and only me.

The white lacy bra and matching thong were easy to put on, but I had no idea what he wanted me to do with the black leather cuffs. They were thick and strong, and not sexy. The clasps were metal buckles. I assumed they went on my wrists, but it would take two hands to secure them.

I found Jonas waiting for me on the bed, absorbed in one of his thriller novels. "You're late," he said without looking up. He was already in character.

I arched a brow and scoffed. He was my lover, here at my behest. "I wasn't sure when you would arrive, and I wasn't going to wait around."

Wordlessly, he held out his hand. I handed over the cuffs, which he tossed carelessly onto the bed next to his novel. Standing, he checked me over as if I were a piece of prime rib or real estate. I passed inspection, but just barely. "You'll do."

"I'll do?" My tone betrayed outrage. "Who do you think you are? You are here for my pleasure."

His emotionless eyes met my haughty ones. A thrill ran through me at the hardness there. He lifted a hand to caress my cheek. I batted it away.

"I don't think I like you," I said, sizing him up the same way he had appraised me.

He wound his hand in the hair at the base of my neck and forced me to my knees. That was the moment I realized we were playing a domination game, and he was the much more experienced party. It was a battle of wills, and I was determined to win. Or lose—whatever felt better.

"You don't have to like me," he said. "But make no mistake: You are here for my pleasure." With his free hand, he traced the outline of my lips, which parted slightly because I was already panting in anticipation.

"Unzip my pants."

He had my head pulled back to look up at his face. He released me the tiniest bit so I could see what I was doing. My hands were clumsy as I fumbled with his snap and zipper. I expected him to be hard, to spring out at me as he had done so often, but he wasn't the least bit aroused.

I glanced up at him in surprise.

"You're going to have to do better than that," he said. "Touch my cock. Take it in your mouth."

I thought back to his surprise in the supply closet when I first did this to him only four days ago. The power I had over him lent me strength now. The fear and trepidation he temporarily engendered in me vanished, and my look turned sultry.

Deftly, I pushed down his pants and boxers to claim my prize. I touched him with expert hands, caressing the sensitive skin of his sac with a light touch. I was the queen of hand jobs. I had given more than my fair share in lieu of actual sex. By the time I added my lips to the mix, his eyes had turned tawny. He struggled to keep from murmuring my name. I knew nothing would make him stop me now, and I hadn't begun to use my tongue.

He came moments after I took him in my mouth, surging so deeply that I had to swallow to keep from gagging. Hauling me to my feet, he kissed me furiously. I knew he had planned to hold out for far longer. I smiled a great Cheshire smile and resisted telling him that he was at my mercy.

My grin must have incensed him further. Before I knew it, I sailed through the air, weightless for a moment before I hit the bed, bouncing twice before the momentum played out. He joined me, lifting me to snatch his novel, which he tossed to the floor, and straddling my stomach so I couldn't move.

I closed my eyes against the tug of desire that negated the sense of power quickly vanishing from my veins. He captured one wrist, securing the cuff to it. There wasn't much I could do to distract him. He had fastened his pants before joining me on the bed. The other cuff encircled my wrist tightly before I knew he had changed hands. He had definitely done this before.

Flipping around, he slapped cuffs onto my ankles before hopping to the floor. He held a hand out to me. "Come on."

"Where?"

He scowled, grabbed me, and tossed me over his shoulder. "When I tell you to do something, you do it without question. You've earned a punishment."

His tone, his promise, and his arrogance combined in a way that left me drenched. I'd been with arrogant men before, but they didn't promise nearly what Jonas delivered. The domineering way he handled me helped also. I half-wished he would gag and spank me, but I checked that thought at the door. Even though he cautioned me that I should never be ashamed of what turned me on, he would think I was too kinky if I voiced that naughty desire. Hell, I thought it was iniquitous, and it was my thought.

He whistled as he carried me down the long hall to the room we'd converted into his office. It was the same tune I often heard him whistling when he worked in the yard. I had no idea what it was, but it spent enough time stuck in my head for me to recognize it anywhere.

I wasn't sure why he needed a home office. Strangely reticent to bring work home, he almost never used it. For that matter, my own office downstairs had been grossly neglected since Jonas became part of my life.

Jonas had a narrow, drop-leaf table in his office. It was scratched and warped, and it had sustained smoke damage in the fire. I had offered to have it refinished, but he'd refused. Four handles were bolted to the top, one in each corner of the main surface. Four more could be found if the leaves were unfolded. They resembled the kind I'd seen on boats, and now I saw a new use for them. Not only could they hold a rope and a sailor's knot nicely, the eye in the middle was the perfect place to secure the kind of hook often found at the end of a dog's leash.

With a swift click, two short hooks were fastened to the cuffs on my wrists. I stood at one end of the table, where he set me, and looked up at him. I schooled my expression to be cool and impertinent. His chest brushed against mine lightly, and my nipples responded instantly, hardening to ripe peaks.

The hands on my waist traveled upward possessively. This lover might not have had me before, but he knew my body and he wanted me to know he owned it. I shivered in anticipation as he cupped my breasts through the delicate lace, his thumbs grazing the hard pebbles at the tips. As if he were caught in my thrall, his head dipped, and I felt the heat of his mouth close over each nipple, dampening the fabric and spilling fire in my core. He pushed me backward, arching my body over the table. I tried to lift myself onto the table, but he stopped me with a slight pressure at my waist.

His hands retraced their path, extending the foray until my arms were raised above my head. Deftly, he moved around the table, securing my wrists to the hooks. Satisfied, he stepped back to survey his work. My toes were on the ground, my butt was against the edge of the table, and my back arched over the top. The entire arrangement was held in place by my wrists. I could neither twist nor lift myself into a comfortable posture.

I protested the awkward position, but he only smiled absently and left the room. This time, he was gone much longer. Minutes passed like hours. The muscles in my shoulders screamed for release, and I had no idea what this had to do with sex. Yes, pain turned me on, but not this kind. Besides, he was unaware I liked when he got too rough, when his fingers bit into my shoulders, arms, or wrists as he held me down, or when he left me tender and bruised, the only time I could successfully masturbate. He always apologized anxiously for losing control, while I assured him I was fine. Then he would avoid me for days, giving me time to heal. The one time I'd tried to seduce him while I was still sore, he'd stopped when tears came to my eyes, even though I had begged him to continue.

This was annoying, undignified, and not at all sensual. What did he hope to accomplish by leaving me like this? Then I remembered. Power. Domination.

Just when my thighs and calves began to ache, he strode into the room. The rectangular box in his hand was tied with a single red ribbon.

He leaned his elbows on the table next to me and held up the box for me to see.

Ignoring his offering, I spoke without thinking. "If you think leaving me like this will make me at all contrite, you are sorely mistaken."

Pride leapt into his green eyes, only to disappear into the hardness. "You haven't begun to learn contrition, my dear."

He placed the box carefully on the table and straightened to his full height. His hands traced along my muscles, igniting me everywhere he touched. I knew when he came to my crotch that my subterfuge was over. The thin strap of the thong was drenched, useless, not that it ever had a purpose.

He fingered my wetness, pinching, pressing, and pulling at my clitoris until I moaned and whimpered. I was not going to beg. Not yet.

His exploration continued down my legs to the bottom of my feet. My toes were sore from holding me, and I was sure I had a crease across my ass from where I rested my weight to give my toes some relief. I congratulated myself on my dedication to swimming. My muscles were strong, and I had punished them far worse than this.

Then he was next to me again, holding the box. "Inside this box is the next item I will use to torture you. Call me when you're ready." Then he was gone.

I don't know how long I held out. I thought about what might be in the box, but my imagination was too limited. I was already tied down, so it wouldn't be rope. Handcuffs were too wide. In the end, curiosity got the better of me. Then it was only a matter of figuring out what to call my mystery man whose name I didn't know.

Finally, I decided on a simple statement. "I'm ready."

He took his own sweet time in coming. I couldn't see the door, so he might have been there all along and I wouldn't have known. At any rate, he looked far too relaxed. That was the worst part of the wait, knowing he'd heard me, and I had to wait until he decided it pleased him to give me his attention.

Placing one hand under my back and another under my rear, he lifted me onto the table. The muscles in my shoulders and lower back screamed in protest as they unbent and my weight was redistributed along the length of the table. A moan escaped.

He clicked his tongue at me and rearranged my tresses to suit him. "If you weren't so stubborn, you wouldn't be so sore. Never question me again."

Lifting my legs by the ankles, he secured them to the hooks at that end of the table. Now I was bound at each wrist and each ankle.

My knees were bent and in the air. I let them fall together, but he wrenched them apart, pushing them until I was completely open to him. It was an inelegant position, and I didn't like feeling so vulnerable.

Holding the box aloft again, he urged me. "Open it."

I stared at him. My arms were bound to the table. "How?"

"Use that luscious mouth of yours," he suggested.

Lifting my head, I took the end of the ribbon between my teeth and pulled. He enjoyed my discomfort and all the reasons for it. "Now what?"

"Now you ask for help," he said, resting his chin on one palm. "I like to hear women like you beg."

I viewed him through narrowed eyes. *Women like me.* Bored housewives or well-mannered, successful wives? I struggled to remind myself it was a role. We were both playing roles, and he had obviously done this many times before. Okay, I needed to stop thinking about that too.

"Would you be so good as to open the box?" I went for haughty with that statement and succeeded.

He shot back with a perfect mockery of me. "Would you be so good as to beg?"

A beat passed. "Please."

Amused, he said, "That's not begging."

I licked my lips nervously, my eyes flickering from his to the box and back again. I wasn't sure I wanted to know what was in the plain white box. Screwing in my courage, I tried again. "Please?"

He smiled and lifted the lid. "Was that so hard?"

Reaching inside, he withdrew a flesh-colored, phallic-shaped item that was slightly longer and thicker than any penis I'd ever encountered. I had my suspicions about what it was and what he intended to do with it, but I said nothing as I threw him a questioning look. I was careful to not actually question him. Frowning at the item, I gave a tentative response. "Thank you?"

"Is your husband really so neglectful? Should I have more sympathy for you? Do you honestly not know what this is?" Jonas wasn't surprised, but his character openly mocked me.

"I assume you're going to fuck me with it."

His mouth twisted sourly. "Such language from such beauty. You really should refrain from speaking that way. It ruins your attempt to appear better than me."

Twisting a dial near the base produced a humming sound. He set it on my stomach so I could feel the vibrations. He twisted the dial again and the rate of vibration increased. My insides clenched and a fresh wave of moisture gathered between my spread legs. It was hard and plastic against my skin, and I wanted to know what it felt like inside me.

He watched me, gauging my reaction. I knew he wouldn't move until I asked. Begged. My breathing came harder and my eyelids wouldn't open beyond halfway. "Please," I panted. "Put it inside me. Make me come."

"I will grant part of your wish, my dear."

I felt the hard tip nudging my vaginal lips farther apart. It moved, the vibrations stimulating me outside, finding my clitoris and the sensitive flesh leading from there to my opening. My hips lifted from the table and the word spilled out. "Please."

It slid inside, needing no extra lubrication. I thrust against it, wanting the vibrations deeper. He moved it slowly, maddeningly negating my attempts to draw it deeper, faster. Tension coiled in every muscle of my body. I trembled with need and strained against my bonds.

Ignoring the riot he fueled, he continued thrusting the damn thing into me with excruciating lassitude. When he took me hard and fast, the orgasm came the same way. Now he urged me up the side of that mountain in a way that didn't assure me I'd make it. I hated the uncertainty. I hated the lack of control. I hated that I had surrendered to his domination so quickly. I vowed to hold out much longer next time. I knew there would be a next time, that there would be many next times. There had to be.

I sobbed. I begged. Mindlessly, I pleaded and fought my bonds. Patiently, he ignored me. Or maybe I did affect him. I was too wrapped up in my own internal struggle to process anything other than the sensations that had taken control from me.

Finally he turned the dial, making the vibrations come faster as he rotated it inside me. I lifted from the table, the climax stretching longer and more intensely than anything I'd ever experienced. Before I could come down, my feet were free.

I don't recall when he switched the way he'd secured my wrists. They had exchanged places. I was once again on my feet, bound only by my wrists. This time I was bent over with my breasts pressing into the table. He lifted my hips and entered me from behind, thrusting, riding the waves of my climax with me.

"Harder," I gasped. "Please."

He didn't thrust harder or faster, but he did reach around me, and I felt his fingers on my clitoris, pressing and rotating the way I liked.

The only sounds were our mingled moans and the wet slap of his hips against my ass. I was damp everywhere with the effort, and so was he. Even the bottoms of my feet were slick against the cherry flooring.

I rested my head on the table, relaxed my arms, and let him take me where he wanted. Sensing I had given over to him completely, he varied his rhythm, using me for his own pleasure. I came again and again, each more intense than the last. I lost track of how many times he made me scream my climax against the surprisingly smooth grain of the table.

I was liquid, malleable and molten. No place inside me escaped the inferno. For the first time in my life, even for the first time with Jonas, I held back nothing. Everything exploded in white, and that was the last thing I remembered.

When I awoke, I was lying on the black sofa in his office, wrapped in his naked body. I was too weak to move or speak or let the slight chill in the few places he didn't touch bother me. I reveled in the safety of his arms, listening to his even breathing until I couldn't keep my eyes open anymore.

The next time I woke, the grandfather clock in my foyer was chiming five. The thin light of dawn streamed in the windows, competing with the lights we'd left on in the hall and in his office where we lay in exhausted slumber.

Turning my head slightly, I studied his face relaxed in sleep. It was something I hadn't done since our first night together. He was truly a beautiful man. I didn't know how he ever escaped my notice before that fateful morning in June. I regretted it, not only because it was time I'd lost with him, but because I knew my grandfather would have liked Jonas. They were from vastly different worlds, but they were both good men.

"Serious thoughts?" His voice was hoarse with sleep and probably from all the screaming he'd been doing the night before.

Not wanting to share the drift of my thoughts with him, I smiled. "I was thinking this thong isn't nearly as comfortable the next morning when it's damp and stiff."

154

Chuckling, he planted a kiss on my forehead and tightened his embrace. "You have far more stamina than I gave you credit for."

"I don't know why," I teased. "I've put up with you for two months now. My fortitude is astounding."

"So are your blowjobs. I thought Monday was a fluke, but I see that you do have some unexpected hidden talents."

I peered at him through narrowed eyes. "I'm not sure that's a compliment."

"Oh, it is," he assured me. "The highest kind." Caressing my hip, he added, "Come shower with me. We haven't had sex in there yet."

We were late to work.

I tried to work in the car on the way there, as I frequently did, but he confiscated my phone, severing my lifeline.

"Hey," I protested. "I need that."

"You want it," he corrected. "We need to talk about last night."

It might be a stereotype, but I thought this was an odd statement coming from a man. "Seriously? We both had a good time. What is there to talk about?"

He wasn't fooled by my attempt to brush him off. He reached over the console and threaded his fingers through mine. It had been a long time since he'd held my hand just to hold it. "It amazes me that you're still so shy about sex."

"It's not shyness," I argued. "I just don't see what there is to discuss."

"I need to know what worked for you and what didn't."

I bristled. "It was fine. But you should know that. This wasn't your first time using that table of yours. I always wondered about the hooks."

"I'm an old hand at bondage," he agreed. "So trust me when I say I need to know what you liked and what you didn't."

I thought about what we had done in detail. Out loud. I knew if I was quiet for too long, he'd probably pull the car over and we'd be even later to work. "I like when you get that look in your eyes, the one that says, 'I'm in charge.' It makes me know that when I challenge you, you won't let me have my way. Even though I know that when I give in, the sex will be incredible, I just can't. I've never been able to just give

155

in, but you already know that. I like that you can make me let go and enjoy what you're doing to me. I didn't know you could actually pass out from climaxing."

A self-satisfied smile settled on his lips and lit his light green eyes. "I did wonder what your threshold was. You nearly bested me."

"Really?" This caught my interest. I wondered if I could wear him out as he had me. Then I recalled where we'd slept. He hadn't removed my wrist cuffs or taken me to bed. He must have been exhausted as well. "Was it the blowjob?"

Pink stained his cheeks. It was the first time I'd seen him blush. "It was extremely difficult to maintain my role afterward. I wanted so badly to make you feel the way you made me feel. Where did you learn to do that?"

My lips twisted wryly. "You'd be amazed at what a woman will do to avoid sex with a man she likes when she knows it will be disappointing."

He glanced over at me, and then he changed the direction of the conversation. "What about the role playing?"

"I like it," I said. "I like that I can be anyone I want with you. I expect the bored housewife will need to take other lovers. I was thinking that she might like to try the gardener next." The sight of his shirtless form working in the warm August sun never failed to arouse me. So far, I had left him alone when he was playing in the dirt.

"The gardener?"

"Yes," I said, caught up in the possibilities. "Then someone else's bored husband in the changing room of the department store. An eager college student, maybe an intern looking to sleep his way into the company. Oh, and the tech support guy. She wouldn't know how to address issues that arise with her computer. And a lumberjack. I should get you a flannel shirt. The pool boy is always a hottie."

His laughter cut my musings short. "And I was worried you wouldn't like role playing."

"No." I shook my head. "I need the role playing. I need to not be myself."

"Threesomes?" he ventured.

"Absolutely not." My answer came with conviction. I knew I wouldn't be able to let myself go with anyone but Jonas. No matter what persona he assumed, it was essentially Jonas who gave me permission to be free.

"Good," he said, relieved. "I don't think I could handle sharing you."

The quiet way he spoke the words made me look over and study him. Something permanent in the way he stated his possession of me was as comforting as it was terrifying. "It's only a year, you know." My words were equally quiet.

"No, it's not," he said, never taking his eyes from the road. "It's a fever, something that burns from the inside. Do you honestly think either of us can walk away before it has run its course?"

I had no response to his passionate sentiment.

Chapter 13—Jonas

I was agitated when I met Ellen for lunch at a café around the corner from the Rife and Company offices, and I didn't like thinking about the reasons why.

"I'm glad you came to your senses." She shoved the lettuce back into her BLT and took a huge bite.

We tried to meet at least once a week. This would be one of our last meetings alone. When the school year started up again after Labor Day and Ryan went back to school, Jake would join us. I liked kids. I liked them a lot. The dream of having a couple of my own had died years before, having walked out the door with Helene.

It wasn't that I thought Sabrina would be against having kids, just that she wouldn't want to have kids with me. Our relationship, as she had reminded me that morning, was temporary, and I had ten months left on my contract. Then what? I harbored no illusion that I would be able to find someone like her again. The thought was both soothing and horrifying. Falling for Sabrina was not an option, for so many reasons.

"Sabrina's loaded." I made the statement casually. Ellen was the only person to whom I would dare say something like that. Too many people would take it as a statement only a gold-digger would make. "Apparently we can afford the time and the travel."

Ellen thought about that for a minute, mostly because she wanted to finish chewing before she spoke. "I get the sense you're not talking about that huge inheritance she has coming her way next summer. Oh, that reminds me..." Voice trailing off, Ellen plopped her purse on her lap and dug through it.

I refrained from commenting on the size of her bag. Most of the stuff through which she sifted was baby-related. A drop of jealousy

158

squeezed through my defensive denial. The image of Sabrina in a similar position flickered for a moment, and then it was gone. Shaking my head to clear away the cobwebs, I reflected on the need for sleep. There was no way Sabrina would ever be caught looking as unorganized as Ellen did at that moment.

Ellen hit pay dirt. Extracting a pile of unopened envelopes, she handed them across the table. "I don't see why you can't change your address from mine to yours on these."

Taking the stack of what I knew were bills, I muttered an insincere thanks. "For starters, Sabrina saw my student loan statement lying around and paid it off for my birthday. She claims ten thousand isn't much money."

The shadow of confusion crossed Ellen's face, gone almost before I could really register it. "Maybe she wants you to stay home more? You do work a lot, and she seems to actually like you."

Anyone else would have earned a cold glare. "I have bills to pay. Besides, I've already cut back on my hours at the club."

Ellen snorted. "You still work there three and four nights a week."

"And make more than I do in advertising," I reminded her. "Working for you is paying off the majority of my debt. With Sabrina covering my living expenses, I'll have this paid off in about two years."

Stuffing another bite into her mouth, Ellen refrained from saying what we were both thinking. That debt was Helene's. The fact I was paying it down instead of declaring bankruptcy said much about my character, but it definitely exacted a toll.

She changed the subject. "So, are you taking her to that club in Lexington? I can call down there and get your name on the list."

Thinking about last night, I smiled, but then that unsettled feeling returned.

"What?" Ellen dug into me the same way she attacked her salad. Normally she ate fries, but for some reason she was on a diet. I didn't understand some things about women, and that was one of them. I watched her fork stab lettuce, and I imagined her coming after me with a sharp point. "What's bothering you?"

Not wanting to put it into words, I shrugged.

"You either do or don't want to take her to the club."

"I do, but I don't. It's a fetish club. What if she gets ideas?"

Ellen stared. "Living with you, she's bound to get ideas. I don't understand why you're introducing her to the lifestyle without introducing her to the lifestyle."

I scowled. "I'm not introducing her to the lifestyle. She just has a difficult time achieving orgasm if she's not restrained."

"Physically or mentally?" With that barbed can of worms, Ellen finished off her sandwich. "She's submissive, Jonas. When I give her my Domme look, she even submits to me."

Waving away her observation—mostly because she was right—I scowled harder. "I know she's submissive, but she has no interest in exploring that side of her personality."

"So you've discussed this with her? Does she know you're a Dom?"

Sabrina was blissfully ignorant about kink and BDSM, and I aimed to keep her that way. Perhaps after the fire that burned between us petered out, I would introduce her to someone who could initiate her into the wonders of submission. Still, Ellen had made an interesting point. I wondered if Sabrina would respond as well to mental domination. Could I drive her to orgasm—without restraints—simply by ordering her there?

Ellen correctly interpreted my silence. "Jonas, you're playing with fire, and you're both going to get burned. Have an open and honest discussion with her. I think she'll surprise you."

"And then what?" I scoffed. "Submissives are work. They have expectations and make demands."

She stared at me in disbelief. "You're working now. She currently has expectations, and she makes demands—demands you're more than willing to meet."

I shook my head. "Her demands aren't unreasonable. She just wants to climax." Thinking over our scene from the night before, I convinced myself that's all she'd wanted. "I tied her to my table last night."

Exhaling hard through her nose, Ellen communicated displeasure. "So you used bondage and domination to make her submit. How did it go?"

"We were role-playing, so it's not the same thing. She liked it. We had a nice time."

"Let me guess—she was the woman who needed a lover who would take over and make her his alone. Did you need a shrink to point this one out to you, or is reality smacking you in the face yet?" She snagged one of my fries and dragged it through my pool of ketchup.

"You have it all wrong." Wheels in my head spun. "She's at a point where she's learning about herself, about what she wants and what makes her tick. I'm helping her explore her sexuality and learn how to own it."

"The altruistic mentor." Ellen piped in from sarcasm-land.

I ignored her tone. "Not altruistic, but definitely a mentor. I don't want to be her Dominant. I don't want that kind of relationship with her. I like her. We have fun together. I'm going to help her as much as I can. And when the year is up and we go our separate ways, I hope she meets someone who can take her to the next level."

Thinking about this morning in the shower, I hadn't demanded her submission, and she hadn't wanted me to be very dominant. We'd washed one another, and then I'd lifted her up and fucked her against the wet marble shower wall. She'd wrapped her arms and legs around me out of trust, not submission.

"So you're going to stick to role playing scenarios that involve domination and submission, but you're not going to actually have a conversation, use the correct terms, and get this all out in the open." Ellen sighed into her salad, probably at her wit's end with both it and me. "Don't you want to see her kneel at your feet? Address you by title? Don't you think she'll find peace in knowing that what she wants—how she thinks and feels—is normal? You say you want an honest relationship, but Jonas, what you're doing isn't honest."

I didn't see things her way. I was being as honest with Sabrina as I could be, and she was reaping the benefits. I would continue to push her, to help her explore her wants and needs, but within limits. "It's only for a year. Besides, I can't see Sabrina embracing a D/s relationship that way. She's not ready for something like that. Maybe a few years down the road, she'll want it, but by then I'll be long gone."

"Stubborn jackass," she muttered. "Are you going to take her to the club or are you too afraid she's going to get ideas that you won't be comfortable with?"

"You're wrong about her," I said. "You don't know her like I do, Elle. I'm in a position to judge what she wants and needs, not you. She wants a little bondage and light domination games—nothing more."

"So you're taking her to the club?" Casually, she took two more fries.

"Yes. I'm taking her to the club. Are you going to make the arrangements?"

Ellen grinned. "What are you going to do if she asks for a spanking?"

I snorted. "She might like rough sex, but she wouldn't go for a spanking. She'd find it humiliating, and she's not into that."

She snagged another fry. "What if she wants to be flogged?"

This conversation was getting out of hand. I smacked her hand as she reached for my plate again. "Stop stealing my fries. Order your own."

"Stop avoiding the questions." Ellen inhaled sharply. "You've already done it."

This conversation had nowhere good to go. I wiped my hands on my napkin and got up. "Thanks for lunch."

Chapter 14—Sabrina

The day flew. I had forgotten that Amanda and Ellen wanted to have a girls' night out. Ellen called to remind me around noon, and I spent the next several hours exchanging texts to arrange things with Ginny and Amanda.

Jonas would take the car home so he could change and go to work. I would stay in the city and have dinner with the girls. We planned to go clubbing that evening and shopping the next morning. Amanda bowed out of the shopping since they were leaving for Kentucky bright and early. She was thrilled to find out that Jonas and I would be joining them for the holiday weekend.

Ty, Ophelia, and Jonas presented to me in the early afternoon. I liked the majority of their proposal. After some tweaks—under which Jonas bristled—I sent them off to finish the project. Without some serious help, they would fail to meet their deadline. I pulled Randall, Clare, and Veronica from our projects, which were in much better shape, and put them with the cat food account. I couldn't find Timothy anywhere.

I also reassigned the ditzy intern whose name I couldn't remember. She glued herself to Jonas as soon as she entered the conference room. No doubt she thought the nasty look with which I nailed her had to do with restrictions on inter-office dating and not the cold strands of jealousy stabbing through me.

At five o'clock, Jonas came into my office. Minnie didn't stop him. She was exceptionally good at her job. When my predecessor had moved on, he'd left Minnie in limbo. Snatching her up was one of the best decisions I'd ever made. She had obviously figured out that Jonas was welcome in my office, and she had begun treating him rather warmly.

"I put Tina to work with Clare," he said. "Clare seems to have more patience with her than anyone else."

I had been in the middle of sorting an enormous amount of paperwork. It littered my desk in piles. Peering up at him with my brows drawn in confusion, I asked, "Who?"

"Tina. Blonde hair, long legs. The attractive intern on my team you seem to like glaring at."

I narrowed my eyes at his description. I might have nice legs, but I was nowhere near tall.

"Sheathe your claws, kitten. She doesn't hold a candle to you." He came around my desk and took the papers from my hands to throw in my chair. I stepped into his arms, missing him already.

"When will Ginny be here?" His voice was muffled because his face was buried in my neck.

"Ellen's picking me up."

He stiffened. "Promise me you won't take everything Ellen says too seriously, okay? She can be overly intense."

"What are you so worried about? You already told me about Helene." Placing my hands on either side of his face, I maneuvered him in position for a kiss. "Do you really have so many dark secrets?"

"A few."

I wanted to ask about them and assure him I wouldn't pry, but the conflicting urges never had a chance to fight it out. He kissed me like a lover, giving me more than I ever thought I deserved. His lips massaged mine, and his tongue teased sighs and moans from me. It wasn't a passionate kiss. It wasn't meant to start anything we didn't have the time to finish, but it left me weak. My heart pounded with the same sense of comfort and fear I had earlier when he'd told me I was a fever inside him.

Ellen texted from the street outside moments after Jonas left. I climbed into the passenger seat of her green minivan to find the inside transformed. Gone were the car seat and the baby paraphernalia. It was as if the odor of diaper wipes and Cheerios never existed, which I found oddly deflating.

Ellen grinned at me. "Ryan detailed the van. I love it when he gets a bug up his butt."

"What brought it on?"

"The promise of mind-blowing sex. He likes it when I tie him up and punish him. We haven't been adventurous lately." She related this as if she were telling me what color she had selected for her living room walls. Either she was pleased with the new color or she was just happy to look at something different.

The memory brought a fond blush to her cheeks. She glanced over at me, but I had already successfully hidden my shock. "I'm not scandalizing you, am I?" Laughter hid behind her question.

"No," I said. "I am familiar with the concept of bondage."

"So, where are we going for dinner?" she asked, abruptly changing the subject.

She reminded me of that girl in high school who convinced the entire senior class to donate an impossibly large stone bench with some pithy saying on it one day and convinced the mascot to wear something shocking to the state finals the next day. She was glib and adept at controlling the conversation. Subtleties and pleasantries were lost on her. I wasn't sure if I liked her or not, but I would make the effort for Jonas.

"Riverside."

The name of the upscale and exclusive bistro silenced her for all of five seconds. "Well, it's a good thing I listened to you and wore my little black dress. I almost didn't. I can't seem to lose this last little bit in front."

"Yes, well, that'll teach you to get pregnant," I said dryly.

She burst in a tide of laughter. "I didn't think you had it in you. You're so painfully polite all the time."

"I barely know you," I argued.

"You know me better than you think," she said. "I'm Jonas' best friend. We're a lot alike."

I looked over at her in surprise. "I thought Ryan was his best friend."

She flashed me a knowing smile. "Second best. Jonas and I formed a bond in college that can never be broken. Plus, he introduced me to Ryan. They both failed the same American Lit class."

I didn't know if I was more surprised that Ellen was his best friend or that he had failed a literature class and still ended up with a degree in English. Ellen noted my surprise and chattered away. By the time we met Amanda, Ginny, and Lara at the restaurant, I found out more about Jonas than I had ever thought to ask.

Uncovering a knack for finding every party on campus, he had blown off his first semester of college, landing himself on academic probation. Ellen had been part of a student organization that mentored struggling freshmen. Jonas had been a handful from the beginning, thinking he was the authority on everything.

One day, Ellen had enough of his attitude. She had taken him down with a move that pinched a nerve in his upper arm and informed him that she would hurt him very badly if he didn't straighten up and fly right. Then she'd put him to work at her club. At the time, it had belonged to her parents, who had since passed the business to Ellen. The discipline he learned there carried over into his academic life. His grades straightened out, and he discovered his love of teaching.

"It was the saddest day of his life when he quit teaching," Ellen said. "I'll never understand why he went through with it."

I had listened to her entire story without interrupting, a courtesy I knew she would never return. Curiously, I didn't mind. Now I had something to add. I could defend his decision to change his career. "He's very good at advertising. He has good ideas, and people like him. It would take a miracle for anyone to land that cat food account next Wednesday. He knows this, and he won't give it anything but his best effort. If we do land the account, it will be largely due to him."

"I have no doubt," she said. "It's just... He was such a good teacher."

I had never heard Jonas express anything approaching regret for leaving teaching, so I let the subject drop. I directed Ellen to valet park. Shedding the suit jacket I wore to the office, I revealed a black dress of my own.

Ellen lifted a dark brow when she joined me on the sidewalk. "You look hot in pretty much anything, don't you?"

"It's the Breszewski curse," Ginny said, coming up suddenly behind us. She enveloped me in a tight hug, and then she held me at arm's length to study my dress.

"I came from work," I said, knowing her objection before she said a word. The hem of the skirt came down to my knees and the short-sleeved dress was very plain. Her dress was scarlet and silver, the pattern and cut perfect for a hot August night on the town.

"You can't wear clothes with personality to work?"

"Not really." I turned her attention to Ellen so I could introduce them.

Ellen looked from Ginny to me. Except for the fact that Ginny was a little taller than me, her face was slightly rounder, and her hair fell only to her ears, we looked very much alike. "I'd like a piece of that curse."

166

Ginny linked her arm through Ellen's and dragged her to the door. "If you share yours. I'd give almost anything for curves like yours."

"Is Lara inside?" I asked before Ginny could say more. She had a knack for hitting on women and not even realizing it. More than once, she'd found herself surprised by a bouquet of roses or some other romantic gift. Lara took it in stride. I didn't know where she found the patience.

Amanda was waiting in the lobby with Lara. Both tall, athletic blondes, they made a striking pair. Men waiting with their wives turned their heads to look at them more than they should have. Ginny abandoned Ellen immediately, gluing herself to Lara's side.

We were seated quickly. Ginny was well-known in culinary circles. I was frequently able to get reservations at exclusive restaurants on the strength of our last name alone. The chef himself came out to greet us and tell us what we would order for dinner.

After we ate, Amanda excused herself. She had to make sure Richard packed everything correctly and also get her beauty rest. Richard liked to leave at the crack of dawn. I made a mental note to buy her a portable movie player for the kids and an herbal eye mask for the drive home.

As we waited for the valet to bring the cars, Ginny suggested some of her favorite dance clubs, listing the attributes and drawbacks of each one.

Lara raised a brow and said, "I thought Ellen owned a club?"

"I don't think you want to go there," Ellen said, looking at me.

I hadn't been to the club at all. Shrugging, I said, "I can't see why Jonas would mind. He's working. It's not like he'll even know we're there."

Maybe I'd flirt with a handsome bartender while my husband was working late, and we'd end up sneaking off to a secluded corner or an abandoned break room for a quick hook-up.

The club was housed in the lower floors of a high-rise, five-star hotel and day spa. I hadn't realized how posh it was, and I knew that was the snob in me. Though she lived in a very large home not far from me, I discounted the classiness of her club based on her brash personality and the lack of creativity in its name. The club in Vegas has also been called City Club. They simply added the location to the title to differentiate.

The club's entrance was down the street from the hotel's main doors, clearly marking them as separate entities. A line of hopeful patrons waited in a cordoned line outside. Ellen handed her keys to the valet. We waited for Ginny and Lara to do the same. At her signal, the security guard moved the thick red rope to admit us.

The inside mirrored the stylish exclusivity of the area. The furniture was new, glistening, and modern. The inside was arranged in several distinctive sections, each playing a different type of music. Though it was open, the acoustics remained where they were meant to be.

Ellen waded through the crowd of dancers, leading us up several short flights of stairs to a restricted lounge. A line of security kept the general public outside. They parted as soon as they saw Ellen approach. Ellen indicated which table she wanted, and then a girl took our drink order and left us alone.

"Wow," Ginny said. "This is better than the red carpet treatment I get at Riverside."

Ellen shrugged. "They know who signs their paychecks."

Ginny and Lara enjoyed the VIP treatment for all of five minutes before they drifted off to the dance floor, lost in each other. I watched them wistfully. Other than our first night together, Jonas hadn't taken me dancing. He hadn't taken me anywhere. He hadn't even intended to take me to Kentucky. I frowned.

Ellen leaned closer to speak to me, her words in opposition to the elegant jazz that rocked the room. "Jonas works too much."

"I know," I said. "I told him there was no reason for him to keep working, but he said he likes his job."

She downed her second shot of tequila. "That's no reason to neglect his wife."

I could tell she was about to mount a soapbox campaign as to the things he did wrong in our marriage. Ellen was nothing if not opinionated. Desperately I searched for a way to change the direction of the conversation. "He doesn't neglect me."

She laughed. "He spends a lot of time avoiding you because he's afraid he might fall for you. I tried cutting his hours more, but, well, he's in demand."

Alarm bells sounded, and they weren't from the dance floor. "Ellen, I don't think—"

She cut me off. "He's not here to interrupt me, so I'm going to take this opportunity to put my nose where you both seem to think it doesn't belong."

I tried again. "Ellen—" How much could I tell her without revealing things he didn't want his friends and family to know? Her heart seemed in the right place.

"I've never seen him so happy," she said. "It scares the hell out of him. Helene did a number on that boy."

"He told me," I said, trying to placate her. "She didn't want to be married to a teacher."

"And what do you think about that?" she asked with uncharacteristic detachment.

"I think she couldn't have loved him if she couldn't accept him as he was."

She sat back, a satisfied smile on her face. "I knew I liked you."

I sipped my fruity drink and watched Lara gaze adoringly at Ginny. "I think you're getting ahead of yourself. I told you our marriage was an arrangement. We're not in love with each other."

"Call it what you want," she said. "I've seen you together. You were just as unhappy before you met him."

"No, I wasn't," I argued. She hadn't known me before I'd married Jonas. I hadn't been happy or sad. I had focused on a goal—furthering my career—and pursued it relentlessly, disregarding inconsequential things like emotions.

She relaxed, watching me use my drink as a shield from this conversation. Why couldn't she talk about normal things like fashion, hot movie stars, or politics? I had a definite opinion about the Hemsworth brothers, and I was prepared to share it. Something she said replayed in my head. Jonas wasn't here to interrupt her. Of course, she meant Jonas wasn't in the immediate vicinity.

Didn't she?

I excused myself to wander the floors. He had to be at one of the bars scattered throughout the different levels of the club. I just wanted a peek. However I was doomed to disappointment. I seemed to miss him at every station.

When I returned to Ellen a good twenty minutes later, I found her deep in conversation with a sultry brunette in an extremely short leather skirt and cotton tank top. Leather bands encircled her wrists. They looked remarkably like the ones Jonas had used on me.

Ellen smiled as I took an empty chair next to her. "Sabrina, this is Sophia, one of my best."

I greeted Sophia with a polite smile and a handshake. She wasn't a bartender. Ellen's bartenders were dressed in uniform. Every single one of them wore a black lawn shirt with the club's name emblazoned on the front. There were various styles, but they were easy to spot. Jonas didn't own a shirt with the club's name on it. I felt slightly nauseous. Why would he lie to me?

Clearing my throat, I concentrated on the conversation. "One of Ellen's best what?"

Sophia's lush lips curved in a pouty smile. "Dominatrixes, of course."

My face froze. My body turned to stone. "Of course," I managed to choke out.

Her dark brows drew together in a confused frown. She looked even lovelier when she frowned. "Ellen tells me you're Jonas' wife. It's very nice to meet you. That naughty boy didn't tell me he got married. I didn't even know he was seeing anyone."

I couldn't respond. It should have been easy. I turned to Ellen, who regarded me with wary concern. "Ellen, why did you say Jonas wasn't here? Isn't he working tonight?"

"Of course he is!" Sophia laughed. "I just left him a little bit ago. He had two lined up and one in the stocks. He won't be finished for quite a while."

I stared at Sophia, who apparently spoke a version of English I didn't know. The music and the crowd became nothing more than background noise. I couldn't take my eyes from the cuffs on her wrists.

"Sabrina?"

Ellen's voice called to me, but my mind had stalled. Images flashed before me: The remote look in his olive green eyes when he gripped me by the back of my head and forced me to my knees. The surety of his voice when he promised I would like my punishment. He'd bought me a vibrator. They were little things, but they added up.

How would he know about that club in Las Vegas? It was so similar to the setup here—an upscale dance club with a room for exhibitionists and voyeurs in back. I didn't remember seeing anyone dressed as Sophia was, but Jonas wore jeans to work, so what the hell did I know? Was he doing those things here, with other women? Why would he insist on monogamy when I had been willing to let him live his life unaltered?

Ellen gripped my shoulders hard. I concentrated on the pain and focused on her concerned brown eyes. "Sabrina, you said you knew."

"He doesn't tend bar for you, does he?" I whispered the words and she had to strain, but she heard them.

"He told you he was still a bartender?" She pressed her lips together. Though her frown was stern, she didn't seem at all surprised.

I shook my head. "He didn't tell me anything. He just said he worked for you."

"But you said you were familiar with bondage and domination."

Feeling began to flow back into my limbs as the shock receded. There had to be a simple explanation. "The concepts, yes."

"Oh my God," she gasped. "He was telling the truth."

"Was he?" Right now, the idea of Jonas telling the truth was foreign to me.

"He's never flogged you, has he?"

I glanced at Sophia, the Dominatrix. "Is that what you do? You flog people for money?"

Her worried and concerned face mirrored Ellen's. "Sometimes I tie them up, tell them they're naughty, and let them sit a while. It depends on the client."

"Do you have sex with them?" It was a crude question, but I had to know. I had to know if my husband had sex with strangers for money. Somehow I couldn't reconcile the idea of Jonas doing something like that with the man who caged me against a wall and made me believe I could have an orgasm.

Sophia's delicate nose wrinkled in disdain. It was one of the nastiest looks anyone had ever given me, and it lifted a huge weight from my shoulders.

"Is that what you thought?" Ellen asked. "Jonas would never cheat on you."

I pierced her with an intense look. Confusion, anger, and helplessness competed for dominance. Anger won. "I wouldn't know. It appears I don't know him at all."

Sophia squirmed uncomfortably.

Ellen patted her hand sympathetically. "Sophia, why don't you leave us alone for a while? And do me a favor? Don't mention any of this to Jonas."

"Any of what?" she asked with a plastic smile. "It was nice to not have met you, Sabrina."

"Wait," I called before she turned away. "I'm sorry for offending you. I didn't know."

"Don't worry about it," she said, flashing me a genuinely friendly smile. "I'm sure things will go much smoother when we meet for real."

"Come on," Ellen said. "I want to show you something."

I followed her through the club, numbness and apprehension taking turns mixing the remnants of dinner in my stomach. She led me through a door that gave me a sense of déjà vu. It looked like a service entrance with security guards. I braced myself for the worst.

The first room was a nicely appointed waiting room. Men and women perused magazines, browsed the internet, and watched television as they waited. Some of them were dressed up and some of them barely wore anything. Ellen ignored everyone and continued past the receptionist, through a locked door that read her handprint.

She led me down a long hallway and up a set of stairs. I really didn't want to see people having sex, not with Ellen. I walked behind her on the catwalk, watching her crane her neck over the side as she searched for something. I kept my eyes firmly on the back of her head.

She stopped suddenly and pointed. "There."

I looked only at her. "Ellen, I don't want to see—"

Her eyes turned hard. "It was wrong of him to keep this from you. It's one thing if you two go for straight vanilla sex with a few sprinkles on top. It's another to hide your true self from your life partner."

"It's only a year, and we're both entitled to our secrets." The image of Jonas in my office earlier this evening replayed before my eyes. He had secrets. Ellen knew them. He wasn't ready for me to know them.

"Are you sure he's never flogged you? I saw the way you looked at Sophia's wrist cuffs. She likes the way they look, but she also uses them to restrain clients." The harshness of her voice matched her eyes. I couldn't believe this was the same woman who blew raspberries on her infant son's round belly.

"I think I would remember that," I said. "He did tie me up once."

"And you didn't like it?" she ventured.

I answered candidly. "I loved it." I also knew he was experienced. This explained why he was so damn good at it.

"Lots of people like it, Sabrina. Jonas is a service top. The bottom directs the fantasy by requesting a scenario and specific actions they want taken, like punishment, bondage, flogging, or humiliation. Within limits, of course. This is a private club, and I do have strict standards for what kind of play is allowed. Edge play is limited with regard to blood and bodily fluids. I have experts in wax, needle, or knife play available, but I have strict rules and protocols in place. And there are other boundaries—none of my service tops are allowed to have sex with clients, and Jonas doesn't want to. He never has. And I've never seen him look at a client the way he looks at you." She took my hand in hers. "Look over the railing."

She'd dropped a lot of information on me. I was going to Google "service top" and a few other terms as soon as I got home. Mostly I was happy that sex wasn't part of the equation. "Can he see me?"

"Only if he looks up, which he won't." She could tell I was about to argue with that thin assurance. "He is one of the best, Sabrina. His ability to concentrate on the client is amazing."

I believed it. Hesitantly, I peered over the railing, gripping it tightly. I wasn't afraid of heights or of falling. I was afraid of seeing Jonas do something with someone else he should only do with me.

The sight that greeted me stopped time. He was shirtless, wearing only the jeans I'd bought him. Sweat glistened from his torso, reflecting in the dim light that suffused the entire area. He wielded a whip, swinging it back and forth with a practiced precision against the fleshy backside of a person whose face I couldn't see. The body appeared to belong to a male.

As I watched, he switched hands with a flawlessness that left me no doubt that the man he punished was unaware of any change. If the man cried out, I couldn't hear it over the pulsing of the bass-heavy music.

I wasn't sure how long I watched, but the man was eventually taken away by others clad in leather bondage gear. His back and butt, which I could see when he turned, was a mass of welts, but the skin was unbroken.

Alone for the time being, Jonas rolled his shoulders, stretching muscles that had to be exhausted. He cleaned and coiled his whip, and then he hung his head for a moment, looking utterly lost and lonely. My heart went out to him.

A couple, barely dressed, entered his arena, and the vulnerable man disappeared. He chatted with the man while the woman waited silently. Suddenly he grabbed her by the hair, forcing her to her knees. I held my breath, my entire body tense as I battled insane jealousy. I knew what it felt like when he did that to me, and I didn't want to share that part of our relationship with anybody.

He buckled wrists cuffs on her—different than the ones he used with me—and secured her to a chain bolted from the ceiling above where Ellen and I stood. In a swift series of movements, he grabbed the man, subdued him, and secured him to a chain next to the woman. The man struggled and shouted. His voice carried to me, but not his words. They didn't matter anyway.

"Do they use a safeword?"

"Onion."

My head snapped up and my eyes met Ellen's. Of course he would use the same one. He was trained to use it. A giggle bubbled from me, coming louder and more forcefully the more I thought about it. *This* was where he came to exorcise his demons. No wonder he didn't want to quit. I didn't know if he was over Helene, but I did know he was still reeling from what she'd done to him. If he needed this, I wasn't going to take it from him.

My giggle grew louder. Ellen clapped her hand over my mouth to stifle the sound. She dragged me from the edge of the railing, where I collapsed on the floor, forcing her to follow me down if she was going to keep me quiet.

She hugged me, thinking I was becoming hysterical. Tears bubbled from my eyes. I couldn't remember the last time I'd laughed so hard. "Oh, Ellen," I said when the compulsion to laugh had passed. "Jonas tied me up two nights ago. He put those cuffs on me and threw me over his shoulder. He was taking me to his office where he has this table, which I'm sure you've seen. I remember thinking how nice it would be if he would spank me too."

Her brows rose, encouraging me to continue. "Did he?"

I smiled wanly. "No. He was very gentle."

"If you want him to," she grinned, "all you have to do is ask."

Again I shook my head. "No. He hasn't shared this part of himself with me for a reason. Whatever it is, I'm going to respect his privacy. He'll either tell me in his own time, or he won't tell me at all." It made me sad to ponder the possibility that he'd never tell me, that he would never trust me enough to show me this side of him.

She helped me to my feet. "Does that mean you don't want him to know I told you about any of this?"

"I would appreciate it," I said. He was so worried about me finding out. Why? Did he think I wouldn't understand? That I would disapprove? Make him stop? How little he knew me, and how little I knew him.

Ellen put a gentle hand on my shoulder. "How about a drink?"

"A very strong drink," I agreed. It wasn't every day I found out that people paid my husband to beat them. I downed two shots of tequila in a row, and then I sat back, waiting for it to hit me.

"Do you have questions?" Ellen removed the umbrella and sipped a mango drink.

I had a shitload of questions for Jonas, but I couldn't ask them. Chewing at my lip, I stared into the empty shot glass. "Do they climax?"

Ellen eyed me with a practiced calm. "Sometimes. A service top doesn't provide those kinds of services directly, not here, but if someone can orgasm from having their ass flogged, there's a pretty good chance they'll get there."

I didn't like the idea that he was dispensing orgasms to other women. I'd seen men there as well. Did their orgasms bother me? Yes. No. Man or woman, their climaxes meant nothing to Jonas. I frowned. "Does Jonas get off on it?" Ellen opened her mouth to answer, but I cut her off before anything came out. "No, don't answer that. It's better if I don't know."

"Sabrina, you really should discuss this with Jonas. Not everybody can handle their Dom servicing others."

He wasn't really mine, so I didn't feel I had a say either way. I shook my head, rejecting the idea outright.

Ellen exhaled a long stream through her mouth. "Christ. You're just as stubborn as he is. Then at least ask me. I'll be honest with you."

I wasn't sure I could handle her brand of brutal honesty. I stuck with a few safe questions. "What does he get out of it?"

"He's well-known, a Master in the field. When he consents to do a workshop, which is rare, people come from all over to see him. If he'd travel, I could loan him out all over the country, but he doesn't want this for a career." She sighed. "Before he met you, he did it primarily for money."

My eyes widened as I thought of his ex-wife. She was responsible for at least one demon riding his back. I wished he would believe that his income didn't matter to me.

Ellen frowned. "After he met you... I think he uses it as a pressure valve release so that he goes easier on you. You're not in the lifestyle, and he won't force it on you."

Though the alcohol had taken effect and I was starting to float, I understood that I would have to make the first move. I didn't know how that could happen considering I wasn't even supposed to know about this part of his life. What a complicated mess my marriage was turning out to be. I downed another shot. "He didn't have a problem making me have sex in public."

With a snort and a blast of laughter, Ellen's face transformed to something stunningly beautiful. "Well, that's one kink he can't indulge in here. Did you mind so terribly much?"

Scorching heat traveled up my neck. I blamed the alcohol. "No." I leaned closer to confide something very personal. "There's a club in Louisville he wants to take me to. I'm kind of looking forward to it."

Ellen flashed a smile that rivaled the Mona Lisa's.

I had to switch her to another topic. "Do you and Ryan... *You know?*"

"Are we in the lifestyle? Yes. I'm his Domme, and he's my sub."

My eyes widened again. I hadn't considered their dynamic would be like that, but it did explain why Jonas was closer to Ellen than Ryan. "Does he mind that you work here?"

"He's okay if I have to fill in, but I need to let him know first. We've negotiated hard limits, lines I can't cross when I'm working as a service top." She went on to explain some other things. I tried to make a mental list of words to look up, but most of them floated out of my head, propelled by fumes of alcohol.

Many drinks later, we went home with Ginny and Lara, leaving the freshly detailed minivan in the city overnight.

Chapter 15—Jonas

When my shift ended, I waited around for Sophia. Though the parking garage was just behind the club, the workers made a point to walk out in pairs or more. Sophia had been attacked in the parking lot a few years earlier, before she'd become a Dominatrix. Though she never said anything, I knew she was wary of being alone out there. I always made it a point to look out for her.

I was bone-tired, but reluctant to go home. For the first time since I'd met Sabrina, my bed would be empty. The idea of not having her warm little body next to me was oddly depressing.

Just now, Sophia was too quiet. While she was never the most talkative person in the room, when it was just the two of us, she usually opened up. "What's wrong?"

She shrugged. "Just tired. I work both jobs on Fridays." Fully aware that I also did double-duty on Friday, she wasn't complaining.

I slung my arm around her shoulders and squeezed. She flinched a little at the unexpected gesture. I didn't take it personally because I knew that Sophia didn't care to be touched. "And yet, my crystal ball tells me that's not what's wrong."

She smiled up at me, her deep brown tresses pulling from under my arm as she turned her head. "I didn't know you were into the occult."

"I deal in magic and illusion, Sophie DiMarco. So do you. That's why we get along so well. We're both equally fucked-up, and we both hide it quite well." We came to a stop at the door to her car. "Spill."

She reached for my hand. When I tried to close my fingers over hers in a supportive gesture, she raised my hand between us and pointed to the simply adorned platinum band on my fourth finger. "You got married and didn't tell me."

Sophia was one of the only people I had let into my life after Helene left. She was aware of my baggage, but she'd missed the worst of it. I smiled apologetically. "Sorry. It happened kinda suddenly."

"So sudden you wouldn't even invite me to your wedding?"

My expression morphed from contrite to concerned. I hadn't meant to hurt her feelings. I hadn't meant to hurt anyone's feelings. My parents had been more baffled than hurt. "We eloped, Sophia. Nobody was invited."

That mollified her a little. "I didn't even know you were dating anyone seriously."

I hung my head, not so much in shame, but in thought. I had bonded with Sophia over our mutual desire to never become seriously involved with another person again. For different reasons, we'd taken vows of casual sex and no strings. I had definitely broken that promise. "We didn't date," I said. "I went to work one morning, this beautiful woman asked me to marry her, and I took a chance."

Sophia's brows rose. "Because she was hot?"

I shook my head. "Because I wanted her."

I wanted to find her, drag her home, and turn her ass pink, not stopping until she admitted that she belonged to me.

An hour later, as I showered away evidence of exertion, I thought about Sabrina. She was a strong submissive, the kind of woman who turned me on and made me want to run in the opposite direction.

Helene had been strong as well. Both women knew what they wanted and went after it. Only Sabrina cared about people too much to trample over them. She was a safer bet, but only because she didn't understand the submissive part of her nature. If she did, I had no doubt she'd turn on me too. She'd use me for the pleasure I could give her, and when I was no longer of use, she would cast me aside. Helene had fallen for my gift with a flogger, not for me. Given the fact that Sabrina liked rough sex, she would be easily seduced by the flogger as well. I would cease to be a person and become an extension of that instrument or a similar implement.

I couldn't let that happen, but I could fantasize about it. I let the warm spray pulse over my skin as I took my cock in hand. Closing my eyes, I pictured Sabrina naked. Her wrists were bound to a hook hanging overhead. She stood on her toes to relieve the pressure in her shoulders, but she couldn't rise up as far as she wanted because her ankles were bound to a spreader bar. I would kiss her breathless, and then I'd force a ball gag between her lips to stifle her cries.

First I'd use the deerskin to warm her up, get the blood flowing. I'd concentrate on her thighs and ass. Then I'd move on to something with more bite. Between floggers, I'd spank her with my bare hand. It had been years since I'd done something that intimate. At the club, I had to use paddles, which suited me just fine. Helene had loved being spanked, and that fact soured the idea for me.

I'd break out other toys—a bamboo cane or a tawse to make stunning marks on her beautiful skin. Maybe I'd juxtapose that with light sensation play—a feather, ticklers, perhaps even a pinwheel. Through the gag, she'd make the most glorious noises. I'd revel in her screams and cries, and then I'd remove the gag to hear her beg for more. Only when she reached the breaking point would I take her down, carry her to the bed, and use her for my pleasure.

I came hard, but opening my eyes left me feeling empty and alone. I couldn't want those things with Sabrina. She was the perfect woman, and I would only ruin her if I turned her on to all my kinks. I finished showering and went to bed without thinking about why it was okay to indulge in exhibitionism and light bondage, but not anything else.

Chapter 16—Sabrina

Ginny had to work in the afternoon, so we got up early, medicated our hangovers and went shopping. Ellen came with us. Our adventure seemed to have bonded us, creating a new understanding. Suddenly the little things that had annoyed me about her disappeared, magnifying her generous heart and blithe spirit.

I remembered to pick up a movie player and herbal sleep mask for Amanda. Perhaps I overdid it, but I also bought Jonas some summer clothes and a set of luggage. I could only recall him in one pair of swim trunks and two different pairs of shorts. He seemed to have a plethora of t-shirts from mall chain stores. I bought him a few more.

We parted ways in the City Club parking garage, and Ellen drove me home. It was a wonder we made it in one piece, given the fact that we kept giggling over things that weren't funny in retrospect. She helped me carry my bags into the house. The two of us were a cacophony of dropping bags and uproarious laughter. We ended up in a heap on the floor of the foyer.

I looked up to find Jonas peering down at us, hands in pockets and a perplexed expression on his face. He was wearing contacts today, and I had no trouble seeing his eyes were a brilliant light green. I stopped laughing

"You have the sexiest eyes I've ever seen," I said softly. I probably had a dreamy look in my eyes. I certainly felt maudlin enough.

He reached down and plucked me from the floor to set me on my feet. Leaning in, he sniffed me. For a woman expecting a kiss, it was a definite disappointment.

"What are you doing?"

"Sobriety check. Would you mind standing with your arms out to the side and seeing if you can touch your nose with your index finger while counting backward from one hundred in increments of seven?"

Ellen grabbed my hand, and I helped her up. She shot him a look of disdain that bounced right off. "Somebody didn't get his beauty rest last night. What's wrong? Are you exhausted from a long night of tending bar?"

I stiffened at her jab. "Ellen," I warned.

Jonas cut her off for reasons all his own. "Ryan called here three times today looking for you. Don't you have a baby or something like that to take care of?"

She wrinkled her nose at him. "You definitely didn't get enough sleep. Does Sabrina know what a prick you are when you don't get your eight hours? And why the hell is Ryan calling you? I told him I was going shopping with Sabrina, Ginny, and Lara."

"He didn't want to bother you, but he wondered if Sabrina had given me an ETA." He pointed a look at me. "She didn't."

Ellen rolled her eyes dramatically, gave me a hug, and left.

I faced Jonas, aware he wasn't pleased with me. I chalked it up to his anxiety about not knowing what Ellen might have told me.

"It looks like you two bonded." I eyed me warily.

"Don't worry," I said. "She's still your best friend."

His face darkened—outlook ominous.

I stepped over several bags, stopping inches from him. Dropping my head back so I could see him, I rested my hands against his chest. "If we get in a fight right now, can we have make-up sex right after?"

The corners of his mouth turned up and his arms encircled me. "If I had time. My boss gave me an impossible amount of work to do in a very short time."

"Surely you can make some time for a roll in the sheets?" I asked. "She can't be that heartless."

His mouth closed over mine, and he kissed me, a starving man given a feast. I kissed him back, seeking to soothe his fears and tap into the passion simmering just below the surface. I was successful.

One hand threaded through the hair at the back of my head, cradling me. The other hand gripped half of my rear end and lifted me against him. I cupped the sides of his face in my hands and gave in to the demands of the kiss.

"Jonas? Whoops. I so gotta start knocking."

The sound of Ty's voice brought our activities to a screeching halt. Jonas put me down, and I stepped back, tripping over the mountain of shopping bags on the floor. He caught me before I crash landed in an awkward position.

"Hello, Ty," I said. "What brings you over on such a fine summer day?"

"Cat food," he said without cracking a smile. He was dressed casually in light blue cargo shorts and a white T-shirt extolling the virtues of Aruba. It was the first time I'd seen him in something other than a suit. "You didn't, by any chance, come over to help, did you?"

I shot Jonas a look clearly indicating he was dead. Now I was a guest in my own home. "I can help. Just give me a little time to stow this stuff and grab some lunch."

"You didn't eat?" Jonas asked. "It's nearly four o'clock!"

It did explain why Ellen and I were so slap-happy. I shrugged. "Okay, how about dinner? What are you making?"

"I was going to order pizza," he said, leaning down to help gather up the bags. "If that's okay with you. I'm working tonight."

I'd forgotten. Ty disappeared into the kitchen, and Jonas helped carry my purchases to our bedroom. Or was it *his* bedroom now?

"Look, Sabrina, I didn't know when you'd be home."

I waved away his explanation. "Just let me know when I get to move back in." I pushed aside the hurt I felt and disappeared into the bathroom to splash cold water on my face.

He followed me, leaning against the door jamb. "Are you mad that I have Ty over to work on this? It needs to get done."

"You can have anyone you want over," I said into a towel. "It's your house. Normally, I would say, 'It's your house too,' only that doesn't seem to apply in this case."

"Sabrina," he began.

"Don't," I countered. "Anything you might say is only going to exacerbate the situation. Let's go downstairs and work on the presentation and eat pizza. Then Ty will leave, and you'll go to work, and I'll get to know my new vibrator."

The evening progressed as I had anticipated, but I wasn't able to get anywhere with the vibrator. In direct opposition to the actual clients I had seen, visions of Jonas flogging faceless sexy women ruined my concentration. The more I thought about it, the more I wanted it to be me. I didn't want to end up with welts, like that man. I knew there was something lighter, something that wouldn't leave that kind of mark but that I would find incredibly erotic.

My fantasies were woefully inadequate. I wondered if Ellen would let me go back and watch on Tuesday when he worked again.

In the meantime, I swam until I was tired enough to sleep, and then I hugged Jonas' lonely pillow to my naked body and drifted off.

I woke to the feeling of something slipping beyond my reach. Opening my eyes, I found Jonas' lanky silhouette leaning over me. He slid a hand between my knees to lift the one on top, which would free his pillow if I wasn't also holding it tightly.

"Want something?" I asked sleepily.

He froze, then chuckled, low and quiet. "What are you offering?"

I released his pillow, pushing it toward him. In the dark, his groping hand met mine. I turned over and pretended to fall back asleep. In reality, I was fuming. I hated lying to people, especially people like Ty, who I needed to trust me. And who might one day be my friend.

He lifted the sheet and slid underneath, scooting across the bed until his body spooned mine. "Ryan stopped by the club."

An image of the lanky redhead hanging from one of those hooks, dancing under the sting of a whip, filled the dark space when I closed my eyes. I opened them to banish the picture. Either way, I was acutely aware that Jonas was naked, and that I missed the feel of his skin against mine.

"He let me know what a jerk I was to you this afternoon."

I thought I had been pretty clear about that, but I said nothing.

He smoothed my hair away from my face and shoulder. "Apparently, it is acceptable to miss the hell out of one's wife when she's gone for a whole night. It is not acceptable to treat her like shit when she returns."

When the hell did he get a wife? My anger at his denial of our relationship receded as I realized he was admitting to missing me. Emotions didn't scare him the way they scared me. According to Ellen, the only thing he feared was falling for me. Falling for him frightened me just as much. As a tremor of panic ran through me, I realized it was too late for me.

"He wasn't upset about the way you talked to Ellen?"

His arm tightened around me and his fingers splayed across my stomach. "Ellen gives as good as she gets. You should have heard some of the things she screamed at me when I lived with them."

"If you were half as nasty as you were this afternoon, I don't blame her."

He sighed. "Sabrina, I don't want to fight with you. I'm trying to apologize."

The mushy feelings fueled my panic, which made me extra snarky. "Is that what this is? I thought it sounded a lot like you were trying to justify your behavior this afternoon."

Leaning up on one elbow, he rolled me onto my back, cupped my cheek and brushed his lips against mine in a gentle kiss. His body was one long line of tension, and I knew what it cost him to hold back.

"I'm sorry," he said, rising back up to hover above me, a shadow in the darkness.

He might have wanted to say more, but I pulled him back down and let loose my frustrated passion. I was rough with him, digging my fingers into his lean, corded muscles and raking my nails down his back. He responded in kind, brutalizing me with his lips and nipping at the sensitive skin along my neck and shoulders. Pushing me onto my stomach, he shoved a pillow beneath my breasts and entered me from behind.

He held his weight away from me. "Close your legs."

We'd never done this before. I was worried that he couldn't be rough with me like I wanted, and I would be disappointed yet again tonight.

He started slow, feeling his way around in this new position. It didn't take long to realize he didn't have to hold me down. Except to lift my hips the slightest bit, I couldn't move. Immediately, heat coiled inside. I gripped the pillow he positioned under me as the fire grew. A cry escaped.

"Faster," I breathed.

"No," he said, his hot breath fanning my neck. "Stop fighting it. Stop fighting me."

The urgency pressed inside, begging for release. I couldn't let it go. Every cell in my body, from the soles of my feet to the hair follicles on my scalp, demanded release. Tears pressed against my closed eyelids and a sob escaped.

I pressed my palms to the mattress, pushing against him, wiggling and fighting us both. He gripped my hips, immobilizing them so he could resume his rhythm.

"I can't," I said desperately. "I can't."

"Yes, you can. Tell me what you need." His honeyed voice sent shivers down my spine where they mingled with the trembling in the rest of my body.

Tears spilled, wetting the sheet next to my face. "I don't know."

He let go of my hip on one side to thread his fingers through mine. Squeezing my hand reassuringly, he said, "You do know. You always know. Trust yourself, honey. You're so close."

Gently, so he wouldn't think I was rejecting him, I disentangled my hand from his and slid it downward. He lifted me slightly so I could fit it between my body and the sheet. With one finger, I parted my vaginal lips and found my slick and swollen clitoris. I pressed and rotated, rubbing it hard, punishing it until I crested. It throbbed beneath my fingertip as I screamed my release and Jonas came, pulsing inside me, jerking against my hard contractions.

He held me afterward, stroking his hands over my cooling body and letting me trace patterns over his smooth chest.

"You did that on purpose," I said. I didn't have to explain that I referred to the fact he made me take control—he made me masturbate while he fucked me.

He kissed the top of my head. "I did."

I luxuriated in the soapy and lightly musky smell of him. "Why?"

"The vibrator didn't work for you, did it?"

He had such an innocuous way of asking something I found threatening. I stiffened anyway, but his knowing hands soothed me.

"How did you know?"

"It'll take practice," he said. "Don't be discouraged."

I could tell he was tired. Given his job and the hours he had kept this week, I didn't know how he was still awake. "Most men would feel replaced if their lover masturbated without them."

"I'm not most men," he murmured. "I want to watch."

No, I thought as he surrendered to sleep, he wasn't most men.

The next morning, I woke to an empty bed. Since it was Sunday, it didn't alarm me. Jonas was in the habit of gardening on Sunday mornings. He had let his disapproval of the lawn service go, since he found he really didn't have time to tend to it himself, but he refused to let anyone touch the three flower beds he had put in.

My roses flourished and the yard looked nice, so I didn't comment and I didn't worry about what would happen to them when he was no longer around. If I did, I would have to think about what would happen to me when he was no longer around.

He worked on the cat food account the rest of the day. I helped him and found myself developing a new admiration for his talent and skill, not only as an ad man, but as a teacher. I approached him as an assistant, not his boss, and he treated me the way I thought he might treat any of this students. He had the authoritative air of a natural leader and an honest appreciation for anything I had to add.

Maybe this was why Tina liked working with him. Maybe this was why those girls at the lake had looked so disappointed. I'd chalked it up to the fact that he was handsome and built. Maybe they weren't as shallow as I'd originally thought.

"Are you happy in advertising?" I asked him suddenly.

I knew he heard me, but he took his time answering. When he did, it was without looking at me. "Happy enough."

"Do you miss teaching?" I pressed.

Now he looked at me with wary green eyes. "Ellen got to you, didn't she?"

I didn't bother to deny it.

"Let it go," he said. "What's done is done."

"You could teach college," I suggested. "If you didn't want to deal with high school politics anymore." I didn't add that he was going to deal with those kinds of politics anywhere he went.

Even now, I knew the cat food proposal wouldn't net us the account because the team hadn't been given enough time to prepare. I knew Joy would have my head on a platter as soon as word came through that they were going with a different company. Jared would completely escape blame because Joy was his aunt. She may have helped my career along, but that didn't mean anything when it came to her nephew. *That* was office politics.

"College politics are the same. Let it go."

Reluctantly, I did.

Jonas, Ophelia, and Ty worked their asses off to get the presentation ready by Wednesday afternoon. Randall, Veronica, Clare, and Tina pitched in to take it to the point where we wouldn't be laughed out of town. Filming and artwork took some serious time if it was done right. It was a serious proposal, but I knew any firm that had used the entire month to prepare would be in a better position.

I packed our suitcases Tuesday night. I had every intention of whisking Jonas away to the airport as soon as the presentation was over.

After the tepid reception of our proposal, I thanked the cat food people for their time and gave my team the rest of the day off. Jonas and I made our three-forty flight out of Metro, and by seven-thirty, I'd introduced him to the luxury hotel lifestyle.

He lay, stretched across the incredibly soft, king-sized bed and said, "I think I could grow to like having a wealthy wife. How about we continue to vacation together after the divorce?"

"Jonas," I laughed as I hung up the outfit I wanted to wear to dinner. "I have a healthy trust fund. We can vacation anywhere you want, and we don't have to wait until next summer."

He twisted around to watch me undress, the light in his tawny eyes jumping the distance between us. "These clubs are found in major cities all over the world."

"Give me a list," I said as I shook out a black lace bra. It was transparent in all the places the lace didn't cover. I hadn't shown him this purchase yet. "It'll be the perfect Christmas present."

From the expression on his face, I wasn't sure he heard anything I said. With the grace and eroticism of a classically-trained enticement artist, I donned a matching thong and unrolled thigh-high stockings to cover my legs. I remembered what he said about what he'd hoped was under my skirt when I asked him to marry me.

"My God," he said. "You expect me to wait until after dinner?"

I gave him the most seductive, sultry smile I could muster and slid into the little black dress Ginny bought for me after she'd spent Friday evening disapproving of my outfit.

"I love it when Ginny takes you shopping." The huskiness in his voice cancelled out his implication that I would never pick this out for myself. I resisted the urge to take credit for the lingerie.

"Are you going to get dressed?" I gestured to my garment bag. "I packed something nice for you to wear." Shooting him a pointed look, I disappeared into the bathroom to fix my face and hair. Just because I liked it when he pulled out the pins to free long strands of hair, I arranged it in a classic upsweep.

When I emerged, Jonas was wrestling with his cuff links. I helped him, and then I retied his bow tie and smoothed the lines of his jacket. Ginny wasn't the only one with a good eye.

"I feel like a kept man," he said.

I smiled up at him. Nothing was going to ruin tonight. He didn't realize it yet, but this was our first date. "If I feel like a kept woman, does it make us even?"

A skirmish flashed through his eyes, and I recognized some of his dark secrets. Lifting a hand to my cheek, he said, "No man could ever keep you."

Oh, yes he could. I kissed his fingertips and held his gaze. "Maybe something precious shouldn't be treated as a possession."

"Where are you taking me for dinner?" he asked, changing the subject without taking his hand from me.

I refrained from calling him a coward. Amazingly I'd spent years running from something like what I had with Jonas, and here I was, trying to figure out how to convince him that running wasn't the best course of action.

I grabbed my handbag and led him to the elevators. Ginny had arranged for us to dine at a restaurant owned by a friend of hers. They were normally booked months in advance, but they could always make room for the sister of a friend and respected pastry chef.

We dined slowly, savoring the food and the company. I couldn't remember ever having a nicer time on a date. I couldn't remember ever being on a date where my date wasn't aware it was one. There were so many things we left unsaid.

Afterward, he took me to the Lexington City Club. Like the club in Vegas and Ellen's club in Southfield, a line snaked around the corner. We skipped it, heading right to the front. Jonas smiled and gave our names. The well-muscled man in black checked his list and opened the barrier for us to pass.

We didn't waste time dancing. Both of us had waited too long for this. I found the hidden door before he did. One thing was certain: I would never look at a service entrance the same way again.

Jonas greeted the twin guards with a stoic face. He looked from one to the other, and then he handed over a blank card with a magnetic strip. The guard nearest me waved the card over a scanner, handed it back, and opened the door.

Ellen's secret club opened to a waiting area. This one did not. We were searched and pointed to a unisex locker room where we stowed the majority of our clothes. I kept my underclothes, though I lost the thigh-highs. Jonas watched wistfully as I shoved them into our locker, but he didn't comment.

He stripped down to the black silk boxers I couldn't resist getting for him. He looked every bit as delicious as I thought he would. "It's a nicer place," he said. "But the people are friendlier." He added the last part as a warning.

I thought it was an odd warning. What was wrong with friendly people?

Jonas held my hand as we entered the main room. He was right; it was a nicer place. The dim lighting obscured people's faces, but it was larger, cleaner, and more colorful. I tugged on his arm. "I want to watch for a while."

"Whatever you want, honey. Tonight is all about what you want."

We walked around, Jonas following wherever my interest led. I was looking for that spark, that permission, the eroticism I found at the Vegas club. I saw a variety of sexual positions, some of which I filed away for when Jonas trusted me more. I watched him as well, looking for signs he found something particularly hot, but every time I looked at him, I found him studying me.

A pretty woman approached us, or rather, me. I didn't see her coming until it was too late to avoid her. She was about five-nine with short auburn hair and a dusting of freckles over her pert nose. The smile on her face reminded me of a fan at the point in the game when it became clear nothing could defeat her team. Without warning, she grasped the sides of my face and kissed me full on the mouth.

It wasn't the first time I'd kissed a girl, so that wasn't a shock. It really wasn't different from kissing a man until you got to the breasts. She ended the kiss and moved to Jonas. I'd never seen him kiss another woman, and I decided right then that I never wanted to see it again. He had the sense to gently disengage her before I got violent. She flashed that winsome smile at each of us and disappeared into the crowd.

Jonas looked at me, shrugged and said, "I told you they were friendly." Before I could respond, he pointed to a couple on the far side of the room. "I want you to do that to me."

I craned my neck, but I couldn't see anything. It was one drawback to being short. He led me closer. The crowd parted to reveal a man lying on his back while a woman undulated on top of him. Nowhere was she being restrained. She was in complete control of the situation. The sinking of my heart was painfully palpable.

I studied them for several minutes before I turned to Jonas with regret etched in my face. "I can't. I wish I could, but I can't."

"You can do anything you set your mind to."

"Jonas, I can't even masturbate successfully."

He grinned down at me, his eyes already liquid gold. "Yes, you can, and you did." He gestured to the woman. "Look at her."

189

"I see her," I snapped. The fun was quickly disappearing.

"No," he said. "*Look* at her. She isn't half of what you are, Sabrina. She isn't beautiful. She isn't powerful. When you walk into a room, people take notice. I want you to own me like you own a room."

I looked at her, but I thought about what he said. The parts about beauty and power didn't impress me. He wanted me to own him. He wanted to look up at me and know I controlled his destiny. He was asking me to give him what he regularly, and without reservation, gave to me.

I thought about the first time he fucked me in my office, and I remembered the dizzying rush of power I felt when I saw his head between my legs. I didn't think I would climax then, either.

Taking a tremendous leap of faith, I indicated an empty platform near the couple he wanted to emulate. He sat down and helped me climb up to straddle him. The table was surprisingly soft, a plastic-coated foam mattress instead of a hard surface.

"Relax," he said, pulling a pin from my hair. "We can take our time."

Focusing on the desire written across his face, I let him slowly remove the pins and hand them to one of the spectators that had gathered around us. When he finished, he ran his fingers through my long tresses, scattering them around us in a halo. He played with my hair until I couldn't stand it anymore. I gripped his face and kissed him. Passion exploded between us, fueled by my trepidation and the ecstasy he derived from our admiring audience. His hands were everywhere, teasing, touching, and stoking the flames higher, yet his lips never left mine.

Wrapped in the things he made me feel, I forgot the audience. I explored him, touching him everywhere I wanted and luxuriating in the deceptive softness that surrounded his iron muscles.

Tucking the cup of my demi-bra under my breasts, he lifted me and captured one sensitive peak in his mouth. Tendrils of heat raced to my core. I dripped for him. The moan that escaped wasn't merely a reaction to my arousal, it was proof that I was right to trust him. He certainly knew how to choose a moment to push me to become more.

Wiggling urgently, I made him lower me back to the table. I drove him insane with my tongue around his ear before I whispered my request. He was already hard against me.

"I want you to make me come with your mouth first." I kissed him before he could reply, giving him time to think. Barely breaking the rhythm of the kiss and of our bodies rocking together, I added to my request. "Lie down, Jonas. I want to be on top."

The world moved as he lifted me again, this time to move us back, and he did as I asked. I worked my way up his body with my mouth. When I moved to straddle his face, his hands came up to hold my hips in position. He looked up at me, patiently proud.

Reaching down, I parted my lips and traced figure-eights through my wetness. My hips rocked over him until he groaned, and I stuck my finger in his mouth, letting him have a sample of what was to come. Doing this didn't make me feel heady with power because I wasn't in control—Jonas was the one in control. I did these things because he wanted me to, and his will became mine. *That* gave me the heady feeling.

With his elbows, he widened my knees to force me lower. I gasped when his tongue began its forays. He began gently, but quickly turned rough, sucking and biting me until I shouted my release.

Panting with the exertion, I slid down his sweat-slickened body and helped him out of his boxers. Kneeling above him, I touched him, drawing my fingertips lightly over his erection and spreading the moisture at the tip around the slanted head. He thrust against me, moaning.

"Honey, you're killing me."

I smiled. He knew crude language wasn't going to get him anywhere with me on top. I positioned my opening over his penis and began masturbating with it. Ever so slowly, I slipped the tip inside and teased him until he was completely surrounded. His hips rose and his fingers dug into my hips as he tried to establish a rhythm.

The power-mad princess inside me thwarted his efforts. I smirked to remind him that I was still calling the shots. "You haven't begun to die." This was the monster he'd created and now he would have to deal with it. I looked forward to seeing how he would tame me, but instead he cheered me on and encouraged me to explore this side of my sexuality.

I lifted myself and slammed down onto him, again and again, until tears wet the corners of my eyes. The nearly-gone orgasm was reborn. The start of another orgasm began pulsing, but I didn't falter. I wanted more. I wanted him to beg, to plead, to scream my name.

Changing the rhythm, I rotated my hips, grinding into him. I snapped them back and forth as another climax stole my rhythm. Riding the waves of this smaller orgasm, I leaned forward, swinging my

Setting out, he helped arrange my clothes back into place. "I can

legs back to bring them together on top of him. Except that I was
facing him, it wasn't very different from the position he'd introduce to
me the weekend before.

Using my arms, which were thankfully strong from my relentless
swimming, I moved up and down. The position intensified the
sensations, ripping incoherent sounds from us both. He writhed and
arched beneath me, his hands clutching at me. In that moment, I knew
he was mine. His demons were at temporary rest, and he was
completely mine.

The headiness of the power rush fueled my climax, sending me
higher than I'd ever been. He cried out, his body lifting fully from the
table, taking me with him. I collapsed against his chest, thankful I was
too small to crush him. When I opened my eyes, I noticed the crowd
around us had mostly dispersed. My hairpins were in a neat pile next to
Jonas' head.

He stroked a lazy path down my back. "How are you doing,
honey?"

I grinned against his chest. "I came three times, but I'm not
making the mistake of thinking I was in control. You may have let me
be on top, and you made it seem like I was taking the lead, but you
had it all along."

"How do you figure?" His caress never stuttered.

"Because, Jonas, you're always in control. Everything I did, I did
because you wanted it."

"You wanted it too." He hugged me to him.

"Yes, but you wanted the voyeurs to see me in a certain role, and
they did. I wouldn't have done any of this if you hadn't wanted it."

He didn't argue the point. Cupping my face, he kissed me softly.
"You don't need an audience to take control or to assume this role."

I giggled. "I can see you tying my wrists together if I overstep my
authority."

Sitting up, he helped arrange my clothes back into place. "I can
see that happening too." A brief frown flashed across his face, but I
couldn't tell if it was directed at his boxers or at my acknowledgment
that he'd still been in control. "Sabrina, you were in control tonight.
You chose the pace. You determined what and how you wanted it, and
you made it happen."

"Because you're strong enough to prop me up emotionally."

He shook his head. "I encouraged you, but I didn't prop you up.
You don't need props, honey."

192

I thought about that as we drove back to the hotel. Yes, he had been there to guide me. He'd given me the tools for success and stood back to watch as I owned them. He'd freed me, but not by handing over the keys. He'd shown me how to use the ones I had all along. Later, as we lay in bed at the hotel, I let my hands roam his body, arousing him until at last I climbed on top and rode him hard. I was liberated.

He never once gloated about being right. He gave everything to me without strings attached. Maybe that's why I finally admitted I was in love with him.

Chapter 17—Sabrina

The short vacation flew. Jonas led Ricky and Faith against me in a pillow fight the first night. I retaliated by introducing them to water balloons. Sam, Amanda, and Richard joined my side. Six against one might not have been fair, but I think it only evened the odds. It didn't help that Ricky and Faith's loyalties were up for grabs, or that a water balloon hurled by a young child didn't often burst, which had the net result of supplying live ammunition for Jonas.

We all ended up in the lake.

I impressed them with my boating expertise when the engine on the rented pontoon quit in the middle of the vast lake, and I learned to bait my own hook. The night before we left, Alyssa presented me with a wedding-ring quilt she had made for me. She clarified that it was for me. If she had been given any kind of warning—here she threw a reproving glare at Jonas—she would have given it to me as a wedding present.

I was so touched by the gesture and the beauty of the quilt, I couldn't prevent tears from welling in my eyes. I could definitely see where Jonas inherited his talent for gift-giving. It was rare, and I wished I had it.

Amanda was pleased with the movie player and the sleeping mask, but those weren't gifts from the heart. They were easily obtained at any store. As I still didn't know Samantha that well, Jonas had chosen her gift. He'd bought her a nice set of paintbrushes, and I'd thrown in a gift card to an art supply store near her apartment.

On the way home, I called my mother from the airport. She was also in an airport, but hers was in Milan. She had always loved traveling. Ever since Ginny and I had moved out, she'd resumed her

194

passion. It was not unusual for her to be away more than she was home.

I shared Alyssa's thoughtfulness with her, and we chatted about other things. The waiting area was crowded with holiday travelers returning home, and the rows of chairs were full. Next to me, Jonas battled to keep his eyes open. I didn't have much sympathy. He and Richard had spent most of the night on the dock with Brandon finishing all the alcohol in the cabin. From the periphery of my vision, I noticed a woman stop in front of Jonas. His slouched posture suddenly straightened, and he became amazingly alert.

She was a few years older than me, pretty, and dressed to kill in a slinky red number and spiked heels. The most striking thing about her was how much she looked like me. Though I was wearing jeans and a nice top, people would think we were related if we stood near one another.

Sure, there were basic differences in our faces, but we answered to the same physical description. I was sure she was 5'2 and a little over a hundred pounds. Her caramel brown hair floated halfway down her back, and she peered at him with large brown eyes. It looked like we even had the same bra size.

"Hey, stranger," she said, tilting her head in the way women do when they know they're beautiful. Still, there was something icy about her. My heart stopped. There was something icy about me. *That was Helene.*

I glanced at Jonas. He was pale beneath his tan. "Hi," he said uncertainly.

Her smile became more predatory. "What brings you to these parts?" She answered her own question without giving him a chance to respond. "Ahhh, the annual Spencer family vacation. I'm still a Spencer, you know. You could invite me."

My mother chattered on the other end of the phone, describing how Milan had changed since the last time she'd visited. She was heading to Edinburgh next, and she planned to be home in late September. She'd love to take Ginny and me out to dinner when she returned.

"How have you been?" Color was returning to his cheeks. I'd never seen him not in control of a situation, and it disturbed me to see how much she threw him off balance.

"Just fabulous," she beamed. "It's not like you to fly down. I thought you liked the road trip aspect of the whole thing so you could have spontaneous sex stops." She looked around, sweeping the room with her eyes. "Who are you here with?"

"No one," he said.

I started at that. I was *No One*. That said so much about the state of our relationship. I was in love with a man who had either discounted my presence or forgotten my existence.

They spoke for a few more minutes, but all I noticed was that she worked her way closer to him, and how he reacted like he was the high school nerd and the prom queen had suddenly taken an interest. I turned away because I didn't want to see more, yet I didn't turn far enough so that I couldn't see her in my peripheral vision. And though I tried to focus on my mom, I was too distracted to pay complete attention.

I hung up from my conversation with Mom when they called our flight to board. It was a quiet flight because I was hurt and fuming. He picked up on the fact I had overheard his entire exchange with Helene, and he left me alone. Things exploded at home as I unpacked our clothes by dumping them on the laundry room floor the moment we walked in.

"Come on, Sabrina," he cajoled. "How long are you going to act like this?"

I looked left and right. It was a large airy room that had originally been a mud room. It had a door at one end that led to a covered walkway to the garage, and the other end led to the hall behind the kitchen. I leaned toward him conspiratorially. "You know, they put people away for talking to *no one*."

He winced. "Look, I'm sorry about that, but—"

"But *nothing*." I glared at him through narrowed eyes and stalked upstairs to unpack the rest of our things, which were mixed together in the luggage.

He followed me after a little while. I hoped he started the washing machine. It was the only way his clothes were going to get washed because there was *no one* else to do it. He found me in the closet, trying to toss the suitcase onto a high shelf. Without a word, he took it from me and easily stowed it. I turned to leave, but he stopped me with the iron grip of his hand on my arm.

"Sabrina, you can't not talk to me."

I whirled on him, breaking his grip in a way that ensured I would have the bruises to show for it. "You don't want to hear what I have to say."

His olive green eyes glittered with hardness and danger. "Try me."

"Fine," I gritted out. "You referred to me as *no one*."

"She was asking if my parents or sisters were around."

"*Don't* interrupt me," I shouted. "It doesn't matter who you thought she meant; you were with me, *your wife*, whether you want to admit it or not."

He stepped closer, but I was savvy to his tricks. He thought he could use his proximity to distract me from my anger. I took a step toward the door and continued.

"Did you think that denying I existed would make me not notice that you married a replica of your first wife? Ellen and Amanda told me I looked like her, but I stupidly believed you when you said I didn't." I raked a hand through my hair, tugging viciously at the long strands that were so like Helene's. "Oh sure, there are basic differences. My face is more oval, her eyes are a little smaller." Her nose was stubby as well, but it would have been petty to point that out. "But we're easily the same height. We have the same build, hair, coloring." I scrubbed a hand over my eyes. "I bet we even have the same bra size."

"Hers are fake," he supplied.

The look I gave him shut him up. I did not need to be reminded he'd seen her naked and probably done many of the same things with her that he did with me. "You won't tell your family our marriage is an arrangement. They treat me as if I belong. You don't, but they do." I swallowed the pain unsuccessfully. "Yet you don't want anyone at work to know about us. I don't understand you at all."

He stood with his arms crossed as I fell silent. "Are you finished?"

Technically, I had to stay with him until next June, but I wished to God I was finished with him. I gave an icy nod.

"If I had introduced you as my wife, you would be here accusing me of using you to throw it in her face. She would have laughed and said something inherently cruel to you. I wasn't about to let her do that."

My blood pressure shot skyward. I didn't think it could get worse, but it did. "Friend, lover, wife, boss. You had more to choose from than just one thing. I thought that no matter what else was between us, at least we were friends. Isn't that what you said when we began this? That at the very least we should be *friends*?"

My body shook uncontrollably. He reached out for me, but checked his response, knowing I would probably punch him if he touched me. The gravity of my hurt finally got through to him.

"Sabrina, I never meant—"

"I don't care what you *meant,* Jonas. I only care about what you *did.*" I hugged my arms across my torso, knowing it was a defensive gesture but not caring. I needed some kind of protection against him. He held more cards than he knew.

"I saw the way you reacted to her. You're still in love. I get that." I focused on a knot in the face plate of a drawer, swallowed my tears, and drew on all my strength to keep my voice steady. "What I don't like is knowing that I'm her replacement. I don't like knowing that when you look at me, you see her. When you're with me, you're pretending it's her. I don't like being *no one.*"

I exited the room, and he didn't follow. It was a wise move on his part. There was nothing he could say to negate the hurt I felt. Any denial would sound false, even if it were true. Empty platitudes would only hurt more.

I spent Monday at Ginny's. She had a few people over for Labor Day and didn't press when I explained away Jonas' absence with a vague, "He's busy."

Jared returned from his vacation on Tuesday, so Timothy, Jonas, and Tina returned to their own side of the floor. Tina visited me at lunch and crushed me in a hug.

"I learned more from you in a week than I've learned from Mr. Larsen in two months. Thank you." She gave me a dozen mini-carnations before she left.

Jonas worked Tuesday night as he usually did.

I stayed home, restlessly wandering the empty house and wondering if he pictured Helene's face on his clients. Did he punish her with every swish of his flogger? Did he punish himself for losing her? I couldn't stop torturing myself. In a moment of desperation, I called Ellen and told her everything. She knocked on my door before I finished pouring out my heart, her cell phone pressed to her ear and her face twisted in sympathy.

The moment I saw her, I realized my mistake. She was *his* best friend. My face flamed. I tossed my cell phone on the hall table and buried my face in my hands. "I'm sorry. I shouldn't have called you. I shouldn't have put you in this position."

198

"I won't breathe a word to Jonas." She steered me into the living room and settled me on the sofa. "If it's any consolation, he already told me everything."

"Everything?" I found that hard to believe. If I'd acted like an ass, I wouldn't voluntarily disclose my dickishness to anybody.

"Yes," she said. "I know why you asked him to marry you. I know about your arrangement, though he will refuse to take the half million you seem to think you're going to pay him."

I tested the waters. "How long have you known?"

"Since the beginning." She waved away my concern. "Jonas usually tells me everything, Sabrina. I know he isn't exactly forthcoming with you, but believe me—I've been working on that with him."

"You've known from the beginning that I was only a temporary event in Jonas's life? Why would you bother to be friends with me?"

She spoke with characteristic surety. "Because you care about him, and he cares about you. I haven't seen him this happy in a long time. I like you, and I think you're good for him."

My face folded into one of those frowns my mother was forever telling me would leave permanent lines one day. "Still, it's only for a year."

Ellen shook her head. "You're in love with him. You may not know it yet, but you are. I had to know what kind of a person you are—if you have what it takes to make this work out. I wasn't going to do anything to push him toward you if you didn't. But you do." Then she flashed me a brilliant smile. It was one of those smiles that transformed a face from ordinary to beautiful. I could see why Ryan spent so much time trying to amuse her.

I gaped at her, but not because of the smile. "He's still in love with Helene."

"No," she said, her smile fading like a shaft of sunlight on an overcast day. "He isn't. But he is still damaged by what she did to him. Gun shy. You have a lot of scar tissue to penetrate, but you have Ryan and me to help. Then there's the fact that his parents and his sisters think you're the miracle for which they've been hoping. They never liked Helene."

Lying to them weighed heavily on me. I liked them too. "Alyssa made me a quilt." I wondered if she'd made one for Helene as well, but I didn't ask. "They don't know about our arrangement. He won't tell them."

Ellen took my hands in hers. "He knows he'll never hear the end of it, especially not now that they know you. Jonas isn't stupid, Sabrina. He knows they won't care that this was supposed to be a business deal. Anyone can see it's not."

I disengaged my hands from hers. I hadn't realized I was so transparent. For someone who'd spent my entire life being branded cold and distant because I was shy, I'd apparently met my match with his friends and family.

"He isn't in love with me. I'm not stupid, either. I know what a man in love looks like and how he behaves. I'm not even sure he likes me." I might have said he probably liked me in the bedroom, but I still wasn't sure he was with *me* when he was with me.

"No, he isn't," she agreed. "He's singularly resistant to anything that might leave him a shattered, shell of a man. Again. You're going to have to find the secret entrance and winnow your way into his heart."

I knew what she was dancing around. I sighed. "I won't play manipulative games with him. That's not how I want him." Sure, I could stop taking birth control. With the way we went at it, I could be pregnant inside of a month. Jonas was a good man. He would do the right thing and stick it out for the sake of the kid. But then I would always know he was here for the child and not for me. It wasn't fair to the theoretical child, to me, or to him.

"Well then it's going to take a little longer, but I have faith that you'll succeed."

I exhaled a laugh. At least someone had faith in fairy tale endings. I didn't know what to say, but I did remember my manners. "Want something to drink?"

"How about some tea? I'm hungry too." She stayed with me until we were both rubbing our eyes and yawning, talking about anything but Jonas. I felt better when she left. Most of my anger was gone, but not all of it, and my doubts lingered.

The Thursday morning staff meeting was going to be an ordeal. There was no way around it. Joy called me to her office beforehand, and I braced myself to take the heat for the lost cat food account. Her assistant showed me inside, and Joy waved me to the seat opposite her desk. The assistant, whose name I could never recall, hovered nearby. That was never a good sign.

Joy pressed her thin lips together, covering her nicotine-stained teeth. The tense evenings at home this week had worn my nerves, and I didn't have the patience to bear her unfair disapproval.

"Sabrina, I took a chance with you." She steepled her hands in front of her face. "I plucked you from the talent pool and put you in charge of an entire team. You manage a good number of accounts, and you generally keep the clients happy. I thought you could handle putting the finishing touches on one little cat food account, but I was mistaken."

First, it wasn't really a little account. It was a gateway account. The cat food company was the sister holding of a very large, very well-funded dog food company. The dog food was also another gateway. If they liked what we did with the cat food, they would throw more accounts our way. An entire division would be needed to service them.

I choked on my tongue, so I stopped biting it. "Finishing touches? What the hell are you talking about? Nothing had been done on the account at all. I had to pull my entire team from their work to even come up with the presentation they saw. I had a week!"

"That's not what Jared told me." The hard expression in her eyes dared me to challenge her. Before Jonas, I might have backed down. She was my boss, and she had been my mentor.

I confronted her coolly, indignation quelling any fear or trepidation. "Jared lied. He gave the work to his intern who had been there all of a month. Neither Timothy nor Jonas had any idea about the account until I told them."

"I refuse to believe that," she said. "His work has been spectacular, especially in the last six months."

"That's Jonas' work," I said. "Jared, as he always does, is taking credit for his team's work. He's logged more time on the golf course than in the office this summer."

She sneered at me. She actually *sneered* at me. "I've heard the rumors about you and this Jonas. The office is ripe with news of the two of you sneaking into closets and meeting clandestinely."

I stood slowly, parking my hands on my hips. "It must not be very sneaky or clandestine if there are rumors about it. I can't believe you would sink to the level of throwing rumors at me instead of addressing the real issue, which is that Jared dropped the ball on this one, not me."

She stood, and we glared across the desk at each other. Then she spoke, and her words were slow and measured. "I'll give you this one piece of warning, Sabrina. Having an affair with a subordinate, even if he isn't directly under you, is grounds for dismissal."

"I am not," I said through clenched teeth, "having an affair with *anyone*." And if she asked Jonas, he could tell her he was having an affair with *no one*.

The staff meeting immediately followed. Everyone was assembled by the time I breezed in, late. Joy wasn't there, but that wasn't a shocker. She rarely attended these meetings. Jared was missing as well, so I began the meeting. I didn't have the most seniority, but people paid attention when I spoke, so I dove into the agenda.

I went through the items on the agenda rapidly, not bothering to hide the fact that I was seething. I felt Jonas' gaze boring into me from across the room. He never looked at me in a staff meeting, opting instead to stare at the notebook he always brought. He always appeared to be taking copious notes, but I was certain he was probably doodling.

Then I declared the last three items stupid (they were) and dismissed everyone. It was the shortest meeting in Rife and Company history. If I took into account the fact we started fifteen minutes late, then it was a four-minute meeting. Jared chose that moment to show up.

He lumbered through the door, more red-faced than usual, scattering would-be executives in his wake. "Breszewski!" he bellowed.

Everyone who hadn't run from the room the moment I blew the whistle suddenly slowed in their movements. Haste was easily forgotten when one could witness what promised to be a juicy altercation.

I stood, squared my shoulders and glared across the room at him. A few months ago, I would have tried to placate him until I could get him behind a closed door. Now I didn't care if we had an audience. My change in attitude threw him off his game for a second.

"You goddamn bitch! What the hell do you think you're doing? You're not going to win this." The veins in his neck stood out, making him look like some obscene scientific experiment gone awry.

Jonas stood. Jared might not have recognized the icy calm in those green eyes, but I did. He put a hand on Jared's arm. "Back up and try again." He said it quietly, but there was no mistaking his authority.

"Stay out of this, Spencer," Jared growled, shaking off Jonas' hand. He rounded the table, stopping inches from my face, forcing me to tilt my head back to look up at him. He was in my personal space, but I wasn't going to give him the satisfaction of taking a step backward.

"I'm finished cleaning up after you," I said venomously. "You're going to take the heat for this one, not me."

Jared's volume didn't decrease with his proximity to me. "YOU lost the account, Breszewski. This one is all on you. I handed you a perfectly good pitch, and you dropped the ball."

I wiped spittle from my forehead and shouted back. "Don't be an ass. You handed me nothing but an empty file, two men, and an intern who didn't know the difference between copy and film. It was because of *me* that we avoided looking completely incompetent, which is an image that would damage the reputation of this firm."

"Your incompetence lost the account," he bellowed.

I lowered my volume in direct proportion to the amount he raised his. "Oh, shut up. You don't have a leg to stand on."

"You goddamn frigid, icy bitch." He clenched his fists, probably meaning to intimidate me, but it didn't work. I wasn't afraid of him.

A deceptively calm voice interrupted. "You have exactly five seconds to move away from my wife."

I hadn't seen Jonas follow Jared, but he was standing right next to me. Jared's eyes rose, meeting Jonas' and finding nothing but green ice. Even I was chilled. The room, which had quieted to witness the exchange, became tomblike.

Sneering in a perfect replica of Joy, Jared didn't budge. Five seconds passed—exactly five seconds—and Jonas' arm shot out. He gripped Jared's wrist, twisting his arm and taking him down in one swift motion. Jared was on his knees before the sixth second finished.

"When you speak to my wife, you will refrain from using obscene language, and when you argue with my wife, you will remain at least three feet away. If you even think about hitting her, I will make your life miserable."

Immobilized by Jonas' hold on a nerve running along the underside of his arm, Jared just stared, unable to alter the incredulous expression on his face. If Jonas was under the delusion I would be impressed with his chivalry or his sudden acknowledgment of our relationship, my look of wrath mixed with disgust set him straight. I didn't need him to fight my battles.

He released Jared, but he didn't help him to his feet. The two clashed silently with their eyes in what might have been a moment of truth for one of them if I had cared to let it continue. Snapping my fingers between their faces, I refocused their attention on me. "This ends now, Jared. I'm through covering for you. The next time you're in over your head, don't expect me to lift a finger to bail you out."

"I'll have your job, Breszewski," he threatened before turning his venom on Jonas. "Don't expect to get anywhere in this firm, Spencer. You've messed with the wrong man."

I let the threat against me go, but the threat against Jonas concerned me. I might be angry with him, but I wasn't vindictive. "Stow it, Larson. Everyone knows your winning streak the last six months is directly due to Jonas."

Jared turned and left. I watched him go, noting that his shirt wasn't tucked in the back and that his pants didn't fit right. The room emptied pretty quickly. My team lingered the longest, each person except Ty throwing me wounded looks. Ty just looked confused.

When we were alone, I faced Jonas, turning the full force of my anger on him. "Never do anything like that again."

His brows shot into his hairline. "He was going to hit you."

"He was thinking about hitting me," I clarified. "He wouldn't have done it with a room full of witnesses, but that is beside the point. You had no right to undermine me like that." I jabbed a finger toward him to punctuate my point.

"Undermine you? What the hell are you talking about? Did you expect me to just sit there and let him talk to you like that?" His fists clenched and released. He was more frustrated than angry. He raised a hand to touch my arm. It hovered indecisively in the air before dropping back down.

I understood why he felt the need to come to my aid. It was more than the fact that Jared was threatening me—he was trying to make up for what happened at the airport. He was trying to show me that he wasn't embarrassed to be married to me. Claiming me in front of the entire office took our relationship public in a way that also quelled the gossip. If I wasn't so completely irate, it might have mattered.

I kept my voice low and even. "I am good at my job. I have spent years cultivating the respect and admiration of my peers and coworkers. In one minute, you undid years of hard work. Do you honestly think anyone is going to take me seriously anymore? Do you honestly think that every person in this firm isn't going to laugh at me behind my back every time they see me?"

I could hear the snickers now. *Don't piss off Sabrina, her husband will come after you.* Every time I asked for a favor or ran a meeting or threw out an idea, a thought akin to that flitter through the head of every person in the room.

I plopped heavily onto the chair I had so recently vacated and put my head in my hands, grateful that the conference room was wood paneled and not enclosed in glass.

"Sabrina," he said, putting a hand on my shoulder.

I shook him off. "Just go away, Jonas. Every time we have a conversation, things only get worse."

He hesitated, his hand hovering inches from me before it dropped, and he left.

I was alone for all of two seconds before my team filed in. Minnie sat next to me and patted my shoulder in a display of motherly concern. She was well past sixty and I would miss the hell out of her when she retired next year.

Randall sat on the other side. Clare, Veronica, and Ophelia sat across from me. Ty locked the door and joined us.

"You've had one extraordinary day," Minnie said. "You stood up to Joy White and Jared Larsen." At my questioning look, she explained, "Oh, secretaries miss nothing. Joy's secretary is a real gossip. But not me. I discovered months ago that you were married. All your paperwork goes through me."

"Plus there's all that chemistry between you," Ophelia added. "A blind person couldn't miss it."

"I must be blind," Randall muttered.

"I wish I was," Ty said. "How come you didn't tell me? You let me think you were having an affair, and all the time, you were married."

"I can't believe you didn't tell us," Clare said quietly. "How long ago did this happen?"

"June," I sighed. "Right after my grandfather's funeral."

They demanded the story, and I gave them the abridged version, leaving out any mention of wills or money. "It was a whim. He didn't want anyone to know."

"He was ashamed of you?" Randall exclaimed. His neck, which was never significant to begin with, disappeared in his outrage. His loyalty gave me a warm, fuzzy feeling, which was a nice change. "What's wrong with him?"

I found myself defending a decision I didn't completely understand. "He didn't want people to think I was doing his work. He wants credit for his own ideas, especially at this point in his career, and he deserves it."

Veronica tapped her fingernail on the desk pointedly. "At least we won't have to defend you anymore to everyone who thinks it's okay to deride you for having an affair with the hot new guy."

I found it ironic that Veronica would refer to Jonas as new when she'd been with me for less than a month. My smile was tight. "There is that."

The ride home was silent and tense. I headed right for the pool, hoping some serious laps could put things in perspective.

"Dinner will be ready in one hour." Jonas called after me as I cruised through the kitchen on my way out the back door.

Knowing he wouldn't indulge me in missing a meal, I made sure to be on time for dinner. I wouldn't put it past him to drag me from the pool and carry me back to the house in order to eat. We dined in the breakfast nook, which overlooked the back patio. Having skipped lunch, I was famished. I had no trouble ignoring him for the duration of the meal, at least until he spoke.

"I'm sorry, Sabrina. I didn't think. I just reacted."

I raised my head for the first time since dinner began, and I watched him struggle for the right words. He played with his fork, pushing remnants of food around his plate.

"I've never once referred to you as my wife. Maybe I didn't want to put you into that category because I have such a dim view of wives. Maybe I was afraid that if I said it, it would be true. I was completely serious when I swore to never marry again. I honestly don't know."

He looked up to find me watching him.

"I only know that when I said the words, I realized for the first time that I actually married you. This whole summer has been a kind of dream for me. It has an unreal quality to it. Maybe because this is temporary, because we've put a time limit on it, maybe my mind has had trouble processing it all."

He threw his fork on his plate and leaned back in his chair. "You've never been married, Sabrina. You don't know what a failure of those

206

proportions is like. And we're in uncharted territory. I'm not sure how to define our relationship. When you threw out to me the other night that you thought we were friends, it really brought it home for the first time. Are we friends? I wonder how we could possibly be friends, and then I wonder how it's possible that we couldn't be."

I bit my lip. His last sentiment was a bit vague, but I knew exactly what he meant. We talked about so many things—politics, ideals, what to have for dinner. But we never talked about ourselves. Nobody knew me like Jonas knew me. He had given me so much, but in many ways we were strangers. I set my napkin on my plate. "I may not have been married, but I know what it's like to fail at a long-term relationship."

"How long?" The question wasn't a judgment, though it easily could have been.

"Six years."

He rose and collected our plates. "What was his name?"

"Stephen."

I followed him into the kitchen and helped tidy the mess. He was a clean cook, so it didn't take long. He grabbed two beers from the refrigerator and directed me to the patio. "How about you tell me all about Stephen?"

Though I would have preferred wine, I accepted the beer. "Only if you tell me about Helene."

He went first. It was only fair. We watched the sky streak purple as the sun set, and I learned all about Helene. He had met her when he was doing his student teaching and was instantly blown away by the fact that she'd noticed him at all. She was a couple of years older and that held an exotic charm—he'd never dated an older woman before. She was a regular at Ellen's bar, and they'd flirted for several weeks before he'd asked her out.

I was certain that if she was a regular at Ellen's and Jonas encountered her, then she probably had been a client. The thought disturbed me because I'd entertained such fantasies myself, and I didn't like the similarities.

They'd dated for several years. Helene was glamorous. (I took that to mean high-maintenance.) Jonas worked five nights a week for Ellen, longer shifts than he worked now. (He'd cut back his hours when he'd married me. I hadn't known.) He made more money working for Ellen than he did teaching in those early years. Helene worked as a receptionist at a dentist office. Together they made enough to buy a modest house in a nice neighborhood.

After they married, he quit working for Ellen. He'd made it clear he wanted a family, but Helene did an about-face after the wedding. She wanted to wait. Then she didn't want to spoil her figure. Finally she didn't want to deal with kids. Not now, not ever. It was a crushing blow to Jonas, but he'd loved her, so he adjusted.

Helene liked material things. She shopped incessantly, burning through everything he'd made working for Ellen. The credit card debt became unmanageable. Then he found out she'd been having affairs, and that was the final nail in the marital coffin.

When they divorced, everything had to be sold to pay creditors. They split the rest of the debt, but she'd defaulted on her portion, and they came after him. He'd been paying down her debt for five years, and he was almost done. The heavy confession lingered in the air. "So," I began, trying to alleviate the tension, "I take it you're not still in love with her?"

His laugh was tinged with bitterness. "No. I'm not still in love with her. I haven't been for a long, long time. Even now, when I think about it, I was going through the motions, not wanting to admit failure. I think I knew before the wedding that I didn't love her. She was beautiful, a geek's dream. Not real."

I frowned, thinking of Stephen and thankful I hadn't tried to make it work when I knew it wouldn't be fair to him or to me. Jonas mistook my frown. He reached across the table and squeezed my hand.

"The first time I saw you, it was from the back. You were at the other end of a corridor, and I couldn't see all of you. With your hair down and given your general shape and size, I did a double take, thinking she had somehow followed me to Rife and Company." He shook his head at the ridiculousness of it all.

"Then you turned around, and I saw that you were very different from her. Classy in an authentic way. You had something she could only hope to have, some quality I still can't name." His gaze roamed my face as if the word might be written there. "Maybe it has to do with your grace and poise, or the way you really listen to whomever is speaking to you. It was daunting. I remember thinking that perhaps it was good that I hadn't been placed on your team. I'd be constantly doubting myself and clamoring for your approval."

I laughed at him. I couldn't help it. For the two weeks he'd worked under me, he hadn't doubted himself once, and he hadn't clamored for anyone's approval. Having been intensely serious, he pressed his lips together and frowned with severe disapproval.

"Did you use that look on your high school students?" I asked, trying my best to stop laughing. "It must have been very effective."

"It was," he said dryly. "You must not be worried about failing my English class."

"I can hold my own in an English class. Math, too," I grinned. "How much do you still owe on your credit cards, and why haven't I seen a statement lying around?"

He had the nerve to look embarrassed. "I have most of my mail delivered to Ellen and Ryan's." Reading the question on my face, he continued. "At first, I was too lazy to change my address, and I figured there was no point in changing it just to have to redo the paperwork in a year. Then after you paid off my student loan, I didn't want you to see them and get the wrong idea."

I refused to be sorry for paying off his student loan. "How much do you owe?"

The figure he named was significantly more than I made in a year. I swallowed a crack about him wishing Helene shared my excellence in math. Still, it wasn't out of reach for me.

"Jonas, I can—"

He cut me off. "Do not offer to pay off my ex-wife's debt. It was my mistake, and now it's my penance."

"Well, I can see now why you get so upset when I go shopping." Shyly I reached across the small space to rest my hand on his. "I promise I won't leave you with credit card debt. I don't even own a credit card." I used a check card. Grandpa taught me to always pay with cash. Paying later never did any good for anyone who wasn't charging interest on the loan. "And maybe you should consider letting me loan you the money. I'd charge you significantly less interest and you could pay it off faster." And I wouldn't care if he paid me back at all.

"I'll think about it," he said, turning his palm up to hold my hand. "Tell me about this Stephen who broke your heart."

"I broke his heart," I confessed. He wasn't surprised. "Stephen and I were fourteen when we first met. We flirted and passed notes for two years because neither of us was allowed to date. Junior year, he asked me to the Homecoming Dance, and we spent the next six years together. We attended the same university so we wouldn't have to be separated. The fall after we both graduated from college, he proposed, and I broke up with him."

Jonas stared at me after I finished my short story, waiting for a shoe to drop. After a long silence, he asked, "What was wrong with him?"

"Nothing."

"Did you live together?"

"No. My grandfather would have had a heart attack. My mom probably would have been okay with it, but I didn't want to chance it."

"He was controlling? Lazy? Drank excessively?"

I shook my head. "No. He was a great guy, but the sex sucked, and I realized I wasn't in love with him enough for that not to matter."

That gave him pause. "I thought you were exaggerating when you said I gave you your first orgasm."

"I wish." The words were out before I realized how they sounded. My cheeks heated, and I turned to Jonas. "I don't regret not marrying Stephen. He was kind and considerate. He treated me very well, and he would have been a good husband and father. He was willing to take me as I was, lackluster sex and all, but I wanted more. And frankly, he deserved more as well."

I sighed. Breaking up with Stephen had marked my entry into the world of serial dating and sex on the second date, sometimes the first if he kissed well. I often thought of him and various "what if" scenarios, but I never once considered looking him up or trying to rekindle anything.

"He just let you go? After six years of bliss?"

I looked for the sarcasm in his question, but I couldn't find it. "No. He stepped back to give me time to come to my senses. He enlisted my grandfather's help in trying to change my mind. Our families had us married for some time before Stephen actually proposed. It was difficult to stick to my decision, but I knew it was the right one for both of us."

"What happened to him?"

Though I knew the vague details of his life now, I shrugged. "One day he stopped coming around. We had been the best of friends, and so I missed him at first, but I was mostly happy to not have someone constantly checking up on me. I ran into his brother a few years ago. He told me Stephen moved to Chicago to open a new branch of their family business. Last I heard, he was engaged."

"Family business," Jonas repeated. "Why do I get the feeling this isn't a chain store?"

I laughed at that one and named the company Stephen and his siblings were set to inherit. "Galen Enterprises have their hands in many pots. If I were less scrupulous, I might use my connections to pursue an account with them."

"You know," he said conspiratorially, "a wise woman once advised me to use my resources and connections."

I thought about that for a long time. What would it take to contact Mr. Galen and land a chance to pitch to them? They were larger than the cat food company. My entire team would earn promotions and bonuses.

Later, when we were in bed and the room was dark, he asked me something else. "Why me? You were with him for six years. I assume you were both virgins, but six years is plenty of time to work out the kinks. We made good progress the first week, and things have improved since then."

It was a question I'd never asked myself. "I don't know. I suppose neither of us figured out what else to try. He didn't force the issue, and I was too busy being mortified about my inadequacies to bring it up. He certainly never did the things to me that you do." I waited a beat before adding, "I didn't know some of those things were possible."

He laughed, probably at the irony of an ignorant, inexperienced, sexually-active thirty-year-old woman. I didn't ask because I didn't want to know. Pulling me to him, he spooned me and repeated his question. "But why me?"

I understood the analytical Jonas. He wasn't asking for compliments. He was asking for data. "You make me forget myself. I'm someone else when I'm with you. I'm a voyeur, an exhibitionist. I'm a sexually-adventurous middle-level executive. I'm a bored housewife amusing herself with the gardener, the pool boy, the delivery man, or a random stranger I found in the grocery store. I don't know why, but it makes a difference."

"Well, then we need to get to work on the gardener, the pool boy, the delivery man, and anything else you've dreamed up." His hand traveled over my hip. "But right now, I'm starving. You haven't let me touch you in almost a week. That's not living up to our twice-a-day agreement."

I pushed his hand away playfully. "That's twice a week, and I think you used up your allotment for the year."

He wrapped an arm around me, palming my bare breast and pinning my back to his front. "Are you turning down an orgasm? You need me, you know."

I did know, but I giggled to keep the mood light. "Maybe, maybe not. In your absence, I have learned to use the vibrator."

With a low growl, he flipped me onto my back and used his body to pin me to the mattress. "You can't replace me with a vibrator. That's for supplemental purposes only."

I traced a fingertip up each of his arms, and then I walked them across his shoulders. "It's doing one hell of a job, and we get along quite well. I might marry it next."

He reached over and flipped the switch on the lamp next to his side of the bed. Dim light flooded over us. I winced and blinked, but he was already out of bed. He disappeared into the closet and came out with several pairs of panty hose. Since I'd been wearing the sexy stockings Ginny had bought for me, my full-length pairs had languished, forgotten in the bottom of the drawer.

Curious, I sat up. The sheet fell, revealing my nakedness. When we'd first met, I'd been scandalized that he slept wearing only underwear, and now he regularly wore more clothes to bed than I did. I smiled at the irony and the fact he looked so damn sexy in his dark blue jockey shorts.

"You won't be smiling in a few minutes." He threw most of the hose on the bed. Stretching the pair he kept in hand, his gaze swept the headboard. White and pretty, it had decorative, carved spindles—definitely more my taste than his.

"If you try to put those on, I will be."

Kneeling next to me, he took my wrist and wrapped the end of the leg around it and tied a knot. "I'll teach you the difference between a vibrator and a real man." He looped the hose around the bed post with one hand and jerked my covers away with the other.

"A vibrator doesn't complain when I cook or have to bring work home."

He pulled the hose taut, lifted my leg, and wound the other end around my thigh just above my knee. His lips were pressed together in a grim line that sent juices surging to my pussy.

"It isn't stubborn or moody. It never pouts. It always agrees with me, and it never complains."

"You said that already." He tied my other side the same way. I tugged on the hose to find that it only served to lift and spread my legs more.

"About anything," I added. "And it can last for hours without getting tired. Even then, a fresh pair of batteries, and we're good to go."

Plumping my breast, he took the last pair and wound it snugly around the base. My eyes widened. He'd never done anything like this before. Bondage for restraint—yes. Bondage for whatever reason he'd tie panty hose around my boob—no. Trapped blood pooled, darkening my areola. The tightness made me tingle.

"That shut you up better than a gag."

I looked from my bound breasts to him. "You find that attractive?"

"Hell, yes. I also find it attractive when you beg, and you will be doing a lot of that tonight."

"We have to work in the morning," I reminded him as he got comfortable on his stomach with his face near my pussy. "And you get cranky when you don't get enough sleep."

He dragged a finger through my wetness. "I might be a full-out bastard tomorrow, honey. Until you pass out from exhaustion, I'm not going to let you sleep. Even then, I'll probably just wake you up."

With that, he closed his lips around my clit and sucked it into his mouth. Sharp pain shot through my core. Reflexively I cried out and pulled against the restraints, but it only opened my legs further. He released the nub and chuckled.

Then he rocketed up my body and seared me with a kiss. Our tongues danced until he took over and forced me to submit to his mastery. When he finally released me, I panted with wanting him. He grinned. "A vibrator can't do that, Sabrina."

"No," I agreed. Nobody could kiss like him, but I wasn't going to tell him that. Inflating his ego right now wasn't in my game plan. "But when it's between my legs, it goes the distance."

Arching his brows, he reached between us. The next thing I knew, he was inside me, fucking with short, quick strokes. I wanted to lift my hips to meet his thrusts, but I couldn't move my core. Fire burned low in my abdomen. With a grunt and a cry, he came—and then he withdrew.

I snorted a protest. "That's not going the distance."

Pressing a finger to my lips, he silenced any further taunts I might hurl. "Do you remember the safeword?"

Imagining he might spank me, or perhaps whip out a flogger, excitement gripped me. My breath caught in my throat. I closed my eyes. Ellen had explained risk aware consensual kink, and I reminded myself that he wouldn't do any of those things without first asking— and he hadn't asked. No matter. He'd promised to make me beg, and he hadn't done it yet.

Opening my eyes, I met his gaze and nodded. "Vibrators talk less and do more, you know. With a vibrator, I'd be having an orgasm by now."

He smiled at my taunt and locked his mouth onto my nipple, sucking hard. It hurt. I arched and tried to buck, but this position robbed me of leverage. He tortured my breasts, alternating between using his teeth, tongue, and lips. Every now and again he'd throw in a vicious pinch. Just when I thought I could stand no more, he loosened the hose and blood flowed into starved capillaries. I screamed at the hot, pins-and-needles sensations suffusing my breasts. Tears leaked from my eyes as I tried to figure out if I liked the pain. It left an unsettled feeling in the rest of my body. Coupled with the fact he hadn't given me an orgasm, I nearly lost it.

"Inhale." The order penetrated the cloud surrounding my brain. "There you go. Breathe through it, honey."

If I hadn't been bound, I might have smacked him. And then I would have jumped on top of him and ridden him hard. I'd ride his face if his dick wasn't ready for the next round. Instead I had to settle for glaring. "That hurt."

He *tsked*. "It's not like you to complain. Sounds like somebody wishes her vibrator would grow legs and walk over here."

Considering his tone matched mine, I deduced that his climax hadn't sated him enough. I took heart from that. "You have legs. It's in the nightstand. Be a good *friend* and help me out."

Tilting his head, he pretended to think about it. "I don't see why not." He not only got the vibrator, but he returned with a bottle of lube, which I didn't need.

I studied him anxiously, knowing he had some insidious trick up his sleeve. "Thank you." He'd really liked when I'd said it the last time he'd helped me out like this while I was bound. I hoped he liked that I didn't require prompting.

"You're quite welcome." He twisted the base, and the thing purred to life. "I'm going to make you come, honey—hard and multiple times."

That sounded good to me. "Thank you."

214

He chuckled. "You might not mean that in about an hour." Grazing the tip against my clit cut off any reply I might have made. He toyed with me, playing around my labia, clit, and the opening of my vagina with light touches that turned to harder presses. I moaned when he slid it into me. My body was a mass of tension, and it didn't take long to set it free. I'd learned to concentrate, to help the climax bloom. I did that now, crying out after a few minutes.

Jonas, true to form, didn't stop there. He kept it going, teasing me through an orgasm that robbed me of my strength. Then he played longer, and the pleasure became the torment. I whimpered and considered using the safeword. I was tired from the stress of the day. Making up with my husband was balm for my soul, but it didn't chase away the exhaustion.

"Oh, you've got to be kidding me. Aren't you horny yet?"

"Hard as a rock. Thanks for asking."

I gave in and begged. "Jonas, please."

"Please what?"

"Please fuck me. Please use me. I want to feel you inside me, not this plastic thing."

"Silicone," he corrected. I didn't have the strength to glare at him for that. "Damn, you are tired. Carrying the weight of the world on your shoulders will do that. Surrender to me, Sabrina. Let go, and I will make your body sing."

I wasn't sure what I was hanging onto, but I let it go anyway.

"Good." Removing the vibrator, he praised me with murmurs and soft touches. His fingers moved through my wetness, spreading it around. And then I felt his finger at my anus. Before I could warn him away, he penetrated the tight muscle there. "Relax, honey. This shouldn't hurt. Maybe a pinch, but no real pain. Remember to breathe, and when I tell you to exhale, I mean it."

My mind was too tired to fight. I surrendered—letting him have any part of me he wanted. I was completely in love with him, and I couldn't hold pieces of myself back. He stroked me there for a little while longer, and I grew used to the foreign touch, and the feeling of being invaded diminished. I felt him stretching me and massaging more lubricant into my sphincter.

"Exhale," he ordered.

I did, my breath whooshing out with a soft exclamation as he covered the vibrator with a condom and inserted it *into my ass*. I prayed for him not to turn it on. He crouched over me, resting his weight on his hands on either side of my head. He kissed me, unleashing passion and pure dominance. Then he slid into me, slowly filling me with his cock.

He fucked me to a languorous rhythm, his eyes tawny with dreams as he gazed at me. I knew, without a doubt, that he saw only me, thought of only me, wanted only me. My heart swelled, and I came hard, my pussy squeezing him with violent convulsions. Moments later, he cried out and collapsed on top of me.

I don't know how much time passed, but he produced scissors and cut away the hose binding my wrists to my thighs via the headboard. I lay still as he pressed a cool cloth between my legs and cleaned away the juices.

He held me as we slept on his half of the bed, which was a good thing because the wet spot was mostly on my side. And I really needed to be in his arms.

Chapter 18—Sabrina

The next few weeks passed quickly, and fall came in with a blast of cooler weather that made me wonder if Jonas would like to spend some time up north, watching the leaves change. We could drive up over the weekend—if he'd take a day off from his other job. We could wear the new jackets I'd purchased a few days ago. I pictured us holding hands and snuggling as we walked under a colorful fall canopy.

That particular day, we had driven in separately because he'd taken the morning off for a dentist appointment. The November afternoon was cloudy, and the oppressive, unrelenting steel grey infected everyone's attitudes. I wished for sun, and Jonas visited my office. Close enough.

Minnie buzzed me, and I gladly put aside my tedious tasks to see Jonas. He strode into my office, bringing his own internal sunshine. The green silk tie he wore that turned his eyes a brilliant shade of emerald had been an impromptu gift from me. He'd let his hair grow several inches on the top, but he kept the sides cut close. My fingers twitched, remembering the way his curls felt in my hands when I had straddled his face that morning. I brightened immediately.

Coming around my desk, I greeted him with a chaste kiss and led him to the sofa so we could sit closer together. "What brings you to this side of the world today?"

He placed a large, plain, rectangular box on the coffee table. "I bought you something."

"A present?" I eyed the box with a smile.

He caught my hands before I could open it and gave me a wily grin. "Not exactly." He set a sealed envelope on my knee. "When you come home today, I want you dressed in this outfit. Park in the driveway, and ring the doorbell." Leaning over, he kissed me on the cheek. "I'll be expecting you at five-thirty. Don't be late."

I didn't quite know how to respond. When we role-played, he usually sent me a text. This was unusual.

"Have a great afternoon." He flashed a smug smile before leaving.

As soon as the door closed, I tore the envelope open. Inside was a typed document.

Characters:

1. A male virgin named Matt, mid-twenties, never leaves the house unless it's to attend a comic book event. Enjoys online RPG. He has tons of friends, but he hasn't met most of them in person.

2. A beautiful, high-priced escort named Sabrina. She was recently arrested for solicitation. The District Attorney, young Matt's father, will give Sabrina a break if she agrees to initiate his son into the world of non-digital women.

Setting:

The house is an expensive Victorian in an exclusive suburb. Matt is home alone. He is expecting Sabrina at five-thirty sharp. His parents are out for the night and plan to stay overnight in the city. He's okay with the fact his father hired a woman to have sex with him. Due to his awkward social skills, he gave up on women at a time most boys were still discovering them. He's never been on a date. He skips all social events that might involve women, who leave him tongue-tied and insecure with an innocent look. Even his online characters avoid interacting with women.

Objective:

Sabrina must teach Matt how to please a woman.

The description made me laugh, but the contents of the box sobered me. Sleek and sexy, with just a hint of slutty, the little black dress looked like something Ginny would buy for me. I wondered if Jonas had been out shopping with her. I didn't keep close tabs on where he went and with whom, so it was entirely possible. I could see the two of them pawing through racks of dresses until one of them came across this. Since we had the same build and coloring, Ginny would try it on to make sure it fit and looked good.

Also in the box were black silk thigh-highs and a pair of sleek, high-heeled leather boots. A matching dress coat, long and belted, completed the ensemble. Jonas was very thorough—even including a lacy, strapless bra and a thong.

My office, thankfully, had a mirror in the closet. At the end of the day, I sent Minnie home on time and changed. When I returned to my office to study my outfit in the full-length mirror, I heard a low whistle. Looking up, I saw Ty standing in the middle of my office.

"You look hot, Sabrina. Is Jonas taking you out tonight?"

Not having heard the door open, I shifted uncomfortably. "We have plans."

"Damn. If my girlfriend wore that, we wouldn't be going out, I can tell you that much. I don't envy your guy tonight."

I blushed and smoothed the skirt part that was poofy and also short. "It's too slutty?"

Ty shook his head. "It's just slutty enough. Every guy is going to be looking at you and wondering how Jonas landed a catch like that. Hell, we all wonder that anyway. You have to take Vanessa shopping with you the next time you go, Sabrina. If you have any mercy inside of you, please take my woman shopping. At the very least, she needs those shoes."

I looked down at the boots. They were very sexy. "Jonas bought them."

Ty helped me into my jacket, his bottom lip clasped between his teeth. Something was on his mind. I hoped he was more at ease with Jonas by now. They seemed to get along fine, even going out for lunch every now and again.

"What brings you in here when you should be halfway home?"

"I wanted a woman's perspective on something."

I had packed my clothes into the box Jonas brought. I picked that up and grabbed my purse. "Is it something we can discuss on the way to the parking garage?"

Ty nodded and took the box from me. "I'm going to ask Vanessa to marry me tonight."

"Congratulations," I said. I hadn't known he was that serious about anyone.

"I knew you would understand," he said. "You and Jonas didn't date that long, but you knew it was right."

I wasn't remotely tempted to tell him the true circumstances. "How long have you and Vanessa been together?"

"A month. I knew the first moment I saw her that she was the one. However, she's more like you, all level-headed and analytical. How did Jonas convince you?"

I blushed at the memory of how bold I had been. "I asked him."

Ty was speechless as we stepped into the elevator, but he recovered before we had descended two floors. "What made you ask him?"

Shrugging, I said, "It was an impulsive, irrational situation. I didn't even know his name. We hadn't met, or had one conversation. It was actually the first thing I said to him. Does that blow your theory about me out of the water?"

Ty laughed. "No. That happened when you finished my sentence by telling me that Jonas holding your hands behind your back means he knows how to please a woman."

The elevator dinged to let us know we had reached the ground level parking. Ty put my box in the trunk of my car. I laid my hand on his arm. "Be yourself. If Vanessa is a decent person, she's dating you because she likes you. If you think the woman and the moment are right, go for it."

As I stepped into my car, he said, "Have fun tonight."

I grinned at him. "Oh, don't worry about me. I will definitely be having fun tonight." *I think.* It had been a long, long time since I'd had a virgin.

The drive home gave me a great chance to think. I had always wondered at men's fascination with female virgins, but I chalked it up to possessiveness. Jonas could be possessive of me, but I wasn't the virgin in this scenario. I would be the one to initiate him into the art of pleasuring a woman. A thrill ran through me. Did he know he was giving me a do-over? I was so glad he hadn't asked me to call him Stephen.

I rang the doorbell and my nipples hardened as the frigid wind bit through my jacket and the thin fabric of my dress. I had to ring three times before the door jerked open.

Jonas stood before me, transformed. His hair, which he had been growing out, was straight, falling over his eyes like straw. I didn't want to think about what he did to those sexy curls to get them to lie down like that. He wore his glasses, but he had added tape to the bridge.

His shirt, a plaid, button-down dress shirt, was too tight. It was tucked sloppily, with half of it not making it into the waistband at all. I think he intended to look nerdy, but he was too well-built to pull it off.

On him, even the pocket protector was sexy. His pants were awkwardly tight as well, but again, it simply emphasized his iron thighs. His belt missed at least one loop, and his tube socks were mismatched. I bit my lip to keep from laughing.

He stared at me while I checked him out. The wind whipped my hair across my face and chafed against my cheeks.

"Matt?" It was his middle name, so the transition wasn't too difficult.

He nodded, a slow blush spreading up his neck to stain his cheeks.

I was impressed he could blush on cue. I wished I could control my blushing that well. "I'm Sabrina. You are expecting me, right?"

He nodded again, staring at my feet.

"Are you going to invite me in?"

"Oh," he slapped his hand to his forehead. "Come in." He moved aside to let me pass.

There was plenty of room, but I managed to let my shoulder brush against his chest. I shrugged out of my jacket and held it out. He stared blankly at the coat.

"When one entertains a guest, he hangs up her coat."

He clapped his hands together and rubbed them nervously. "Right. My mom told me that." Gingerly, he took my jacket and slid it onto a hanger. Then he turned back to face me, his eyes traveling from my feet to my face and back down. He blushed again when he realized I watched him. "My dad said I should feed you because you'll be here for dinner."

I went to him and took his hand in mine. He shook and his palms were sweaty. "I think you're too anxious to eat right now," I said. "How about we work up an appetite first?"

His eyes were firmly locked on the floor. "Where do you want to do it?"

"Why don't you take me to your bedroom?"

Without looking at me, he led the way up the grand curving staircase, turning right at the top instead of left. I was glad he was avoiding our bedroom for this. I stopped cold at the door of the guest room.

It was transformed. Instead of the tastefully decorated, gender-neutral décor, it was the den of a man who dreamed of women slightly less than the newest Battle Fever game, but never got to taste them.

Posters covered the walls. Some were for video games, others for movies. Several were highly-airbrushed shots of centerfold models.

The bedspread was vintage *Star Wars*. Action figures lined the shelves. Science fiction books and cheat manuals for video games were stacked around the room. Clothes were thrown all over the floor. The television was on, paused in the middle of a violent and bloody video game battle.

"We should probably close the door," he said, shoving his hands deeper into his pockets. "In case my mom and dad come home early. They said they would stay out late because you were coming, but they don't always do that if my mom gets a headache."

He reached behind me to close the door. Turning, I saw a swimsuit calendar from this year.

"My dad gets *Sports Illustrated*," he said. "I don't read it, though."

Scanning his room, I found my portable satellite radio system and tuned it to a soft jazz station. A lone, mellow horn filled the air.

"I like metal," he said. "With lots of heavy guitar. I have Guitar Hero. I'm pretty good at it."

"It's background noise," I said. "We're not listening to it." I went to him, stopping less than two feet away.

He peeked at the low neckline of my dress, and then he dropped his eyes to the floor when he saw me watching him. "Sorry."

Gently I lifted his chin until his eyes met mine. "Don't apologize for finding me attractive. A woman who is about to sleep with you likes to know you find her attractive."

"You're pretty," he said. "But a lot shorter than I thought a hooker would be."

I winced at his crudity. "I'm an escort, darling, not a hooker, and there isn't a height requirement. Does my lack of stature bother you?"

He shook his head. "What's the difference between an escort and a hooker?"

Caught off guard, I laughed. "The price."

"How much do you cost?"

Taking a step closer put me inches from him. "I think you're stalling."

He ran a hand through his hair. Some of it settled down, but most of it stayed in the air. It was an improvement in his style. "I don't know what to do first."

Resting my hands against his chest, I tilted my head up. "I like to start with a kiss."

Nervous green eyes flickered to my lips and away. "What if I'm not any good?"

"I'll teach you." I waited for a long time, but he only stared. "I know you've never been with a woman, Matt. Have you never kissed one?"

He blushed again. "I've never been out with a woman before. Well, not one that I wasn't related to."

I slid my hands up his chest, not stopping until I captured his face in my hands. "You're very tall, Matt. I can't kiss you if you don't meet me halfway."

He leaned down slowly and rested his lips against mine. I felt his tension, and his playacting sucked me further into my role. With slow, feathery strokes, I brushed my lips against his until he relaxed, and then I slipped my tongue into his mouth, exploring him that way. Little by little, I coaxed him into the kiss, and when I drew back, he was breathing hard.

I would be lying if I said he didn't affect me just as much. Even when he wasn't trying, he kissed too well. I was heady with power and moist for him already.

"Did that suck?" he asked hoarsely.

Smiling up at him, I said, "No, that didn't suck."

"Now what?"

"Now we get serious."

"More kissing?"

I nodded. "More kissing."

This time, his lips were firm when they landed on mine. He used the same tricks on me I had used on him. I tugged his hands from his pockets and put them on my waist. He gripped me tightly, and I pressed my body into his.

Instantly he grew hard and pushed himself away from me. "Sorry."

Cupping his cheek, I smiled reassuringly. "It's okay for you to be turned on by me. It's a little necessary if we're going to get anywhere today." His quick rise gave me pause. Jonas was playing this as if he were a sex-starved man in his early twenties. I steered him to a ratty old armchair set up in front of the television, no doubt so he could play his games. The chair was a new addition to the house. I had never seen it before. I would have thrown it out or had it reupholstered if I had.

"You want to play? I have another controller."

"Honey, I'm here to play with you." I draped myself across his lap, letting the neckline of my dress dip to preview coming attractions. "Now tell me truthfully. When is the last time you masturbated?"

He blushed. "I don't know."

"Was it more than an hour ago?"

His blush deepened. "I don't see why it matters."

"Because, darling, I like a man with stamina. If it's been a while for you, then you won't be able to please me. I'm here to teach you how to please a woman. Trust that I know what I'm doing."

"You want me to go masturbate?" He stammered the words, forcing them out as if he'd never before voiced the thought.

I shook my head and slid to kneel in front of him. With sure hands, I whipped off his belt and lowered his pants. It was hard to not laugh at the tight, white underwear he wore beneath, but I managed. His long, wide cock sprang forth, fully erect. He tried to cover it from my view, but I patiently moved his hands. "What are you doing?" he asked frantically as I licked his length.

I didn't answer with words. Taking him into my mouth, I sucked him hard, the way I knew he liked, and fondled his sac with a light touch. Anything he might have said was lost as he moaned, rocking his hips to the rhythm I set. He didn't hold back. Before long, he came, shouting incoherently as he tangled his hands in my hair. He pulled me up to him, kissing me long and hard. It was slightly out of character, but I didn't care. I loved the way he kissed.

Still breathing hard, he rested his forehead against mine. "Are we finished?"

I laughed. "We're just getting started. You're going to make me feel the way I just made you feel."

He blushed when I caught him staring at my chest again. "Sorry. My mom said it's rude to stare at a woman..." His blush deepened as he indicated the general area of my breasts, refusing to say the word. "...there."

I let out my breath in a controlled stream. "Matt, never bring up your mother when you want a woman to fuck you. That's one person who needs to stay firmly out of your bedroom and your sex life. Now say the word you don't want to say." I fondled my breasts while he watched. "What are these?"

His jaw dropped. It took him a few tries, but he finally managed the word. "Breasts."

"Louder. Come on. You can do this."

"Can I touch your breasts?" His tone bordered on innocent, but his eyes were riveted to my chest.

"Yes."

His fingers trembled as he reached for me, cradling one round globe in his hand through the thin fabric of my dress.

"Would you like me to take it off?" I asked. "Or would you like to undress me?"

He swallowed, his eyes still firmly on my low neckline. Against my thigh, I felt the stirring of his arousal. "Should we go on the bed?"

"We'll make it there eventually. There's no hurry." With one finger, I moved his hair out of his expressive eyes. As an afterthought, I removed his glasses and set them on the windowsill.

He reached for them. "I can't see without those."

Shifting, I straddled him. "Then you'll have to get closer and feel your way around." Leaning up on my knees, I placed his hands on my thighs and directed them upward until he understood that I wanted him to remove my dress.

Jonas would have run with that permission, but Matt didn't. He stared at me, taking in the strapless, black lacy bra, matching thong, and thigh-highs. He gripped the arms of the chair so hard his knuckles turned white.

I took advantage of his speechlessness to remove his shirt. He had a magnificent chest, lean and well-muscled. I couldn't resist running my hands over his taut skin. My lips soon joined in. He felt good, he smelled good, and he tasted heavenly.

When my mouth again met his, gone were the innocent kisses. Passion took over, and he met my challenge, responding with only his mouth. I don't know what it cost him to maintain his role, but his restraint brought me back to my role.

Breaking the kiss, I pulled back. "Where would you like to touch me now?"

His hand came up, hovering uncertainly in the air. "Where should I touch you?"

"Wherever you want. Start here." I put his warm hands on my hips and caressed his arms and chest. "Do you like the way I'm touching you?" My hands slid into his open pants.

Suddenly breathless, he nodded.

"Touch me the same way."

Hesitantly, he slid his hands up my body, stopping just below my bra.

"If it's in your way, take it off."

Light, tentative touches trailed to my back, unhooking the bra with practiced expertise. I shrugged out of it and tossed it onto the floor with my dress and his shirt. He stared at my breasts, mesmerized. Then slowly, he cupped them both. He explored them with unhurried, light caresses.

Growing impatient, I guided his fingertip over my nipple, teaching him to tease it to a peak. "Now," I said, breathing hard, "take it in your mouth. Use your tongue on it the same way."

He didn't need additional urging. Lightning quick, his mouth locked around my nipple, sucking and nibbling at the sensitive tip.

"Yes, Matt, like that." I moaned. "Oh, yes. Like that."

He caught on to the game, kneading one breast with his hand and the other with his mouth, then switching to take me higher. Heat swirled from his tongue, unfurling in my core. He buried his face between my breasts before his lips traced a trail up my neck and claimed me for a long, deep kiss. Pushing him away, I stood before him on trembling legs and removed my boots. Then I tugged him to his feet, and I finished undressing him. I planted a kiss on his full erection before leading him to the bed, where I ripped back the covers and guided him to lay on the mattress. I shed my thong and joined him, straddling him in a display of my utter control of the situation—control I had because he allowed me to have it.

He grasped his erection, intending to enter me, but I stopped him.

"No?" He whined his question.

"Soon, darling. You must prepare me better than this."

"How?" he whispered, straining toward me. "Tell me how."

"Touch me."

Immediately, his hands were on me, roaming from my breasts to my waist, grasping my hips and caressing my legs. I caught his right hand and guided him to my wetness.

"Touch me here."

Panic lit his topaz eyes. "I don't know how. I don't know what you like."

"Then find out," I said. "If you make me gasp, then you've found something I like. If you make me moan, you've found something I really like. And if you make me scream, you're onto something wonderful."

He slid two fingers between my lips. "You're so hot, Sabrina. It's like you're on fire."

"I'm on fire for you, Matt. You did this to me."

His touch was light, tentative. He fumbled, touching me clumsily. I gasped anyway, and Jonas took over. He knew full well how I liked to be touched. "Can I taste you?"

"Not this time, honey." I moaned, unable to resist him any longer. Positioning myself over him, I guided his cock into me, sliding slowly until I was sealed to him.

He looked up at me expectantly, his eyes a smoky topaz. Defiantly, he moved his hips, bucking them beneath me.

Placing my hands on his stomach to hold him down, I smiled and squeezed him inside me until he gasped. "Do you like the way this feels, Matt?" I lifted myself, slamming down on him.

He gasped.

"Answer me, Matt. Do you like the way this feels?"

"Yes," he breathed. "God, yes. You feel like heaven."

"Would you like it to get better?"

Wordlessly, he nodded, his smoky topaz eyes impaling me as he struggled to maintain his role. There was no doubt in my mind that Jonas wanted nothing more than to flip me over, hook my knees over his shoulders, and make me scream incoherently.

"Listen to me, Matt. This is important. When I come, the feel of my orgasm milking your cock is like nothing you've ever experienced. If you come before I do, you'll miss out on that feeling, and I will be very, very upset with you."

He stared at me, brows knit together.

"Hold back, Matt. Hold back until I tell you it's okay to let go. That's all you have to do, darling. Just hold on until I tell you it's okay to let go. Do you understand?"

At his nod, I rocked my hips back and forth. He touched me, roaming my body with strokes that were tentative at first, and then firm with purpose when I moaned with pleasure. I rode him hard and fast until I came, milking him the way I promised I would. His orgasm followed mine.

I collapsed on top of him.

"That was incredible," he said. "You must make a lot of money."

I wanted to smack him for that comment, but I couldn't break character. We were just beginning. Completely ignoring his crass comment, I asked, "What did you have planned for dinner?"

"Um, the cook left something. I could heat it up for us."

Gathering the bare minimum of clothing, I snagged his shirt. He watched me button most of it and roll up the sleeves. Glancing up, the fiercely possessive look I caught in his eyes was not in character. "You don't mind, right?"

Blushing, he shook his head and wiggled back into character, donning a pair of tattered dark blue sweat pants. Dinner was leftover Thai food from last night. Straddling him as he tried to slump over his cardboard container, I took his food away.

"I'm still hungry," he said, but his hands were already on my thighs, pushing the hem of his shirt upward to expose my nakedness.

Licking my lips, I stabbed at the spicy shrimp inside and held it between us. "Hungry for what?"

His voice rose an octave. "The shrimp?"

The prawn disappeared into my mouth. I chewed slowly and as sensually as I could. "Good boys get to eat, Matt. For everything you do well, you will be rewarded."

Regarding me with wary eyes, he asked, "What if I do something wrong?"

"Then you'll have to do it over and over until you get it right." I leaned back, letting the edge of the table press into my back. "And if you please me enough, you can have dessert. You do want to please me, don't you Matt?"

Wordlessly, he nodded.

"Touch me."

Confusion crossed his features. He pushed his hair out of eyes that were firmly attached to my chest. Slowly, he unbuttoned the shirt and slid his hands to cover my breasts. I fed us each one forkful. Unable to remain still, his hands caressed my soft flesh, teasing the nipple into arousal. I fed him again.

"Pinch them," I said.

His touch was tentative.

"Harder." I gasped as he followed my command, not only pinching them, but rolling them between his fingers. Sweet sensations spread through me. I fed him more. "What comes next?"

"You didn't say there would be a quiz." His mouth pursed and his tone became petulant.

"This is all a test, darling. If you know you can please a woman, then nothing will stand between you and the woman you want."

He snorted derisively. "I've looked in the mirror."

I stared at him. Years of hurt permeated his voice in a way that had nothing to do with the role he'd assumed. "It's nothing some new clothes won't fix. You have an incredible body. Never let anyone tell you otherwise. When I finish with you, you'll know how to bring a woman to orgasm with your hands and your mouth."

"Why would I want to do that?" His eyes glittered hard. "I just wanted to know how to fuck, and we already did that."

"I fucked you, Matt. You didn't actually do anything but lay there and take it. By the time I leave, you'll know how to take matters into your own hands." I took his face between my hands and kissed him until we both gasped for air. "Giving a woman an orgasm—that's power, that's control." I rained kisses over his face. "You want that, Matt, don't you? You want to know that you can make your woman wet with a look or a word. You want to know she lies awake at night, alone in her bed while you're at work, wishing you were inside her."

His words were so quiet, so strained, that I barely heard him. "No woman will ever want me like that."

"You don't know how wrong you are," I said, thinking reverently of the way Jonas affected me. "Touch me. Make me want you."

Placing his hot hands on my thighs, he caressed and massaged the tender skin there, circling closer and closer to the inferno he'd coaxed to life. My breathing came harder, encouraging him to circle closer.

When I felt he had mastered how he should be touching me, I lifted my lips to his, capturing them in a long, slow, deep kiss, and pressing my breasts against his bare chest. "Yes," I urged him. "Touch me, Matt. Don't be afraid."

His thumbs parted me as he massaged deeper and deeper, teasing gasps from me.

"Do you want me now?" he asked.

"Yes," I said, struggling to catch my breath. "But make me wait. Show me what you promise. Tease me with those strong hands."

"What if I'm too rough? What if I get carried away, and I hurt you?"

My eyes clouded over at the memory of the wonderful ways he hurt me. "You can be rough, Matt. I'll tell you if you go too far. Don't hold back your passion. I get off on how much you want me."

He was an apt pupil. Shoving two long fingers deep inside me, he rocked them slowly in and out, teasing me to the point of frenzy. I rocked on him, the heat spiraling from him into me, fanning the flames.

He bent his head to suck my breasts, biting and rolling my nipples with his teeth and tongue.

Remembering my role, I eased away from him, laying myself open on the table. "Finish with your tongue," I commanded. "Make me come with your mouth."

Pushing my legs farther apart, he continued to touch me, tracing his fingertips through my wetness as though memorizing every surface, every fold. Then his tongue was on me, burning me with its heat. My hips rose from the table, and I moaned.

Sliding his hands beneath my ass, he lifted my hips, tilting me for better access. He licked my pussy, his hot tongue tracing flames until he locked onto my clitoris, his teeth scraping as passion took him. He sucked me hard, slurping and making insistent moans in the back of his throat as if he had been starved, and I was the only sustenance that could save him.

I gasped his name—his real name. I wanted to thread my fingers through his hair, to feel his soft, silken locks wrapping around them, but I had to grasp the table for leverage and balance. He slid two fingers into my pussy, rocking me fast and furious until I came, screaming at the riot of waves washing over me.

Then his heat was gone for a moment as he stood, shifting his position. He grabbed me by the back of my neck and drew me to him, kissing me hard, and I tasted myself on his lips and tongue.

He lifted me, impaling me on his cock, and carried me upstairs to lay me down on his *Star Wars* comforter. Wild hands roamed my body, desperate and wondering at the same time.

I wrapped my legs around him tightly and returned the favor, luxuriating in the texture of his smooth skin as he moved against me, thrusting deep and slow.

With all the gentleness of a virgin, he made love to me. If I hadn't known him the way I did, I would have thought he was actually in love with me, so reverent were his caresses. It was bittersweet, almost heartbreaking, except I had hope and time on my side. He gazed down at me, his eyes heavy-lidded with passion, his movements deliberate and unhurried.

The fire he stoked in me grew, and he carefully fed it with each measured thrust. He locked me to him with his topaz eyes and welded me to him with each slow lunge, refusing to give into an easy frenzy.

My hips rocked beneath his, rising slowly to meet him each time. The fire smoldering in my core was unlike anything I had ever experienced before, and it frightened me with what it forced me to give to him. I had felt close to Jonas before, but never like this, as if we were two halves of a whole, our souls meeting and joining for the first and last time.

He felt it too. I saw it in his eyes, innocent and undisguised, just as I saw his determination. He could have climaxed at any time, but he tenaciously waited for me. Then the slow burn culminated, pushing me over that pinnacle. I lost all sense of myself as I climaxed, calling his name over and over until he joined me in the abyss.

Much, much later, after I had lured him firmly away from virgin territory, I lay in Jonas' arms, my head on his shoulder, hoping nothing had changed between us. "Jonas?"

"Hmmm?" He hovered on the edge of sleep.

"Where did you get all this stuff?"

"What stuff?" He was waking up. I heard the humor in his voice.

"Don't be obtuse. The posters, the books, the chair, the clothes." I lost it on the last word. Laughter rocked me, making me gasp for air.

"Are you laughing at me?" His voice held mock reproof. "Sabrina, that's not nice. Even nerds like hot women."

"I'm not disputing that," I said once I brought my amusement under control. "But how long have you been planning this? It must have taken you a long time to find all that stuff."

"Not as long as you think," he mumbled. "Most of this *stuff* is mine. It's been in my parents' basement forever. The Wii is Ryan's. Ellen bribed me to take it out of the house. We've got it for the weekend. I was going to challenge you to a game of bowling tomorrow, but now I'm not sure I want to play with you. Maybe I'll kick your ass at boxing or golf or Dance Dance Revolution. As you may recall, I'm not a bad dancer. I have good rhythm, a fact I dare you to dispute, and stamina."

Understanding dawned on me. It wasn't the first time he had brought up the topic of a geek liking hot women. "You were a geek in high school, weren't you?"

"You wouldn't have looked at me twice unless you needed help with your calculus or AP English."

"Maybe you underestimate yourself." I hated to think I would have missed out on this because he didn't fit into my social circle. I conveniently forgot I had been with Stephen in high school, and that Jonas would have been in college at the time.

He shifted me to his chest. "Honey, I've seen pictures of you in high school. You were hot then, and you're hot now. There are, no doubt, legions of girls from your graduating class that are extremely bitter about the fact that you're still so damn sexy twelve years later. Don't pretend you weren't popular. You wouldn't have noticed me at all. I was quiet and geeky. I didn't date until college. I'm different now, but you still didn't look at me at all until you needed a husband."

"That's not true," I said. "I noticed you before then. I thought you were cute."

"But not cute enough to talk to."

"You shouldn't take it personally, Jonas. I don't date people from work. It creates too many complications." I traced circles on his chest.

He stopped me. "I think it's a mistake to allow you around virgins."

Lazily, I slapped at his chest. "You enjoyed it. Don't pretend like you didn't."

"Hell, yes, I enjoyed it. But honey, you'll ruin a guy for life."

I was tired. Deflowering a virgin and stepping around an ego was hard work. Yet Jonas wasn't being as appreciative as I thought he should be. "Watch it, Spencer. You're treading on thin ice."

He laughed, the deep, rich sound rumbling under my ear. "Simmer down, hot stuff. If this was a guy's first sexual experience, no other woman could hope to ever measure up."

I let him fall asleep under me while I pondered his last statement. In so many ways, he was my first sexual experience. I didn't want to look elsewhere. Even if all things were equal, no one could hope to measure up to Jonas. I had it bad. I closed my eyes and tried not to think about Ellen's firm conviction that I would need to trick him into staying with me once the year was over. With enough time, wouldn't he just fall in love with me?

Chapter 19—Jonas

I'd spent my twenties being introspective about my experiences. Not only did the training Ellen and other mentors had put me through require it, but I had wanted to learn more about myself and my relationships with others. I watched people—not just in public D/s scenes or training scenarios—but everywhere, analyzing their actions and reactions. I tried to see inside their hearts, to read their souls. I was looking for more than love; I'd wanted the perfect relationship. After settling on the traits of the ideal woman, I searched for her relentlessly. She'd be pretty, of course, but she'd also be that perfect balance of strong and needy. She'd be intelligent and driven to seek perfection, just like me.

I'd been innocent and naively hopeful, and I'd gotten my ass handed to me by a cold-hearted bitch.

For the past five years, I'd cruised through life on autopilot, delving into my vast well of experience to deal with whatever crap life threw my way. I didn't think about the *person* doing the deed; I riffled through my memories to come up with an appropriate response, did what needed doing, and moved on. My last few years of teaching, I'd stopped being able to differentiate one year's slew of students from the others. I forgot names, backgrounds, and I'd stopped forging the connections that had made me a good teacher. Ellen liked to tell me I needed to get out there and take chances, but I had no desire to go through any of that again. Having a wonderful family and great friends meant there was no reason to put myself in a vulnerable position again. I liked having my life structured this way.

Sabrina didn't seek to change any of that. She didn't force me to give anything I didn't want to give. Yet I found myself slipping, and that was dangerous. The protocols and experiences I'd used to keep everyone at arm's length were in place to protect them as much as they protected me, and I wasn't adhering to them with her. I was doing it wrong—all wrong.

If I were to take a minute to think about it, to analyze why I was throwing protocol out the window, I knew I wouldn't like what I found. And so I didn't delve beneath my fucked-up surface. It wasn't worth the hassle.

Instead I sat back and enjoyed life with a woman who gazed at me with trust and affection every time I touched her; who laughed, joked, and conversed with me at all hours of the day and night; and who submitted to me completely when I demanded it. Life was good. Perfect, even.

Thanksgiving was a bit of a messy holiday. Sabrina's mother was back from one of her many vacations, but she hadn't originally planned to be here, and so Sabrina and I had committed to spending the day at my sister's house. Thankfully Amanda had given permission for us to invite Melinda. Sabrina had reluctantly extended the invitation, and her mother had accepted. Though Ginny and Lara had plans with Lara's family, they'd promised to show up in time for dessert.

Whenever her mother was around, Sabrina turned into an uptight mess. I didn't like to see her so stressed, and I didn't understand why she couldn't relax. Though her relationship with her mother was tense at times, I could see that Melinda loved Sabrina unconditionally, and I didn't know why Sabrina couldn't seem to come to terms with her mother's domineering personality. After all, she seemed to have no problem with mine.

Sex would calm her down a bit, but the effects would wear off by the time we made it to Amanda's, so I went with Plan B.

"Are you getting dressed?" I called up the stairs from the foyer. She hated when I yelled from other rooms, but old habits die hard. I'd grown up in a house where yelling from the kitchen to the basement was an everyday occurrence.

She came to the railing that kept people from plunging to the foyer floor from the upstairs hallway. Peering over it, she frowned in annoyance. "Is there a reason you can't come up here and talk to me?"

"That's not an answer." Judging from the towel wrapped around her and the dry state of her hair, I deduced she'd finally finished showering. Water calmed her a lot, and though I thought it was too cold to swim, she'd merely shrugged and did laps anyway. The pool was heated, but the air outside would make my balls crawl into my ass for the warmth. But I accepted this part of her—she had to possess a certain amount of crazy to put up with me.

Instead of answering, she disappeared back into the bedroom. With a grin, I mounted the stairs and went after her. She hadn't thrown me a sexy smile or dropped her towel to indicate she wanted me to follow her, but I knew she wouldn't refuse me if I captured her wrists and caged her against anything. In the five months we'd been together, she'd never once refused me, not even when I knew she had a headache. Since she was no longer sex-starved, that was the submissive in her, responding on a level she didn't question. If I was a good man, I'd make her question it. I'd make her think about it, analyze what she truly wanted out of our relationship. But I wasn't a good man, and I didn't want to be. After me, she could find someone who could love her the way she deserved to be loved—someone who could treasure the beauty and preciousness of her gifts.

I found her putting on mascara.

"Are you nervous?"

"Why would I be nervous?" She looked at me in the mirror, meeting my eyes with a challenge. And then her focus moved lower, her appreciative gaze roaming over the message printed on my long-sleeved shirt. Just when I thought she'd blush or smile, she frowned. "You're not wearing that. I bought you a suit for a reason."

I spent my time wearing entirely too many suits. This holiday had always been about family, good food, and football. "Thanksgiving with your mom might be a formal occasion, but I assure you that everybody at Amanda's will be wearing jeans."

She pressed her lips together. "Slacks, then. You can wear slacks and a nice shirt."

I thought her adherence to a nonexistent dress code was cute. "I'll wear slacks if you will. Same color. And matching shirts." She liked to buy clothes for me. After our talk about what she could afford, I'd stopped protesting, but I'd noticed she liked to dress me in a style similar to hers. She had good taste, so I didn't really have room to argue.

She tried to wait me out, but that was a game she never won. After a few moments, she sighed. "You're serious, aren't you?"

"Yes."

"I bought a dress."

"Wear the dress." I grinned. "And I'll wear this."

She wasn't amused. "You'll wear slacks and a nice shirt. No tie. I'll wear the dress. It's a very nice dress. You'll like it."

I'm sure I would, but that was beside the point. "That wasn't an option. How about we both wear jeans, and then when we get home, I'll tie you to my table and make you so exhausted, you'll forget to obsess all night about not dressing formally for an informal occasion?"

Her gaze clouded over and wandered to the closet door where she'd hung the garment. The knee-length deep emerald dress had long sleeves and a modest neckline, but it would hug her curves and have me looking at her instead of the game.

"I'll take you out to dinner this weekend. You can wear it then."

Her attention snapped to me, and she studied me intently. She did this sometimes, and I could never figure out quite what she was looking for. When her gaze sidled away and shades of disappointment flashed through her eyes, I pulled her into my arms. She didn't fight me, but she also didn't melt into my body. "What do you have against dressing nicely?"

"Nothing. This weekend, I'll wear a suit on our date. Today I want you to relax, and that starts with dressing in something conducive to kicking back."

"My mother will comment on my attire. And yours."

I sincerely wished she would stop taking to heart every offhand comment her mother made. Sometimes I think Melinda said things to Sabrina because she didn't know how to talk to her daughter. The two of them definitely had issues. "Why do you care? I told her it was casual. Maybe she'll show up in jeans too."

Her laugh came out so suddenly it turned to a snort. "I don't think she owns any."

I turned her to face me, and then I hooked my finger under her chin and made her look at me. "The only person who sets the rules for your life is you, Sabrina. Your mom may comment out of surprise, but she probably won't mean anything by it. Even if she does, so what? Wear jeans. Relax. Be a rebel. It's okay."

Jerking her chin away, she whirled out of my grasp. I kept her towel, but she didn't seem to notice her nudity. "I don't want to be a rebel. I want to have a nice dinner with our families."

"Nothing bad will happen. The Spencers aren't the kind of people who fight at holidays, and your mother would die before she'd say anything unpleasant while she was a guest in someone's home."

236

She put on a dark green bra that matched the dress. "Fine. I'll wear jeans. You owe me a date—that includes dinner and dancing—and exhaustion on your table tonight."

From the triumphant gleam in her dark eyes, I couldn't tell who'd won this negotiation. We were both getting what we wanted, so I guess we'd both won, but those odds didn't sit well with me. I always wanted a little more. "It's a deal, but don't put underwear on yet."

She lifted a scrap of delicate fabric that matched her bra and shook her head emphatically. "Jonas, we sincerely don't have time. You'll make me sweaty, and then I will have to shower again. Wearing jeans is one thing; late is another problem entirely."

I chuckled at her chagrin. "Don't worry—I have to conserve energy, so your chastity is safe until we get back. This is a one-minute delay."

The bottom drawer of her vanity had become mine. I didn't mind not having as much space because I didn't have as much stuff. As long as I had a toothbrush and some hair gel, I was good to go. Even the hair gel was largely optional. Since she respected my privacy, I had stowed something I knew she'd like, and this was the perfect time to bring it out.

I opened the package in the bathroom and washed the object in the sink. She hovered in the doorway. "Jonas, is that what I think it is?"

"What do you think it is?"

"A butt plug."

She'd come so far so quickly. The woman I'd met five months ago would not have uttered that term. Now she didn't hesitate. I flashed a devious grin. "I'm impressed—you didn't stammer or blush."

"Ginny had to put those on a cake before. I was there when she made it. This one is a bit smaller than the ones she was given."

"At least you're not shocked at the size."

"You're not putting that thing in me."

I had to get her to agree. Threatening to hold her down and forcing my will upon her would have her sopping wet. Following through on my threat would have her near orgasm. I dried my hands. "You can bend over the counter here, or we can do this in the bedroom."

"Jonas, you're not listening. I said it's not happening."

Crossing my arms, I leaned my hip casually against the edge of the sink. "Why not?"

Now she blushed. "The outline of the base will show through the jeans. People will know."

"I think you're overestimating the number of people who will be looking at your ass. However, if you're worried, you can wear a long shirt."

"Ginny will not only look, but she'll comment repeatedly and for the next several years." She pursed her lips. "I have a tunic with an empire waist that's long enough, but it won't go with jeans. Are leggings okay?"

If I wasn't careful, I was going to fall for this woman. I nodded. She went into the bedroom. I found her bent over the side of the bed, waiting patiently. First I took a moment to admire her luscious, heart-shaped ass and her shapely legs.

As I applied lube, I forced myself to refrain from taking liberties. The plug had two bulbs, the second one larger than the first. I lined it up with her anus. "This shouldn't hurt. Exhale." She followed instructions beautifully. "Good girl. One more time." When it was in, I was tempted to swat her ass, but I helped her stand instead. "Get dressed, honey. I'm going to finish up the potatoes."

Au gratin potatoes were our contribution to dinner. I stuck them into a travel container that would keep them warm, and by the time I was ready to go, Sabrina appeared. She moved slowly, and I could tell she was concentrating on walking normally. The butt plug did not diminish her grace, but I kept that thought to myself. She had a hard time accepting compliments, and saying anything would only make her more self-conscious.

Dinner went off without a hitch. Nobody noticed anything—I knew they wouldn't—and she garnered a lot of compliments on her outfit. Though it was comfortable, her shirt and leggings were dressy, so she got her way on that too. I found myself watching her a lot—admiring her sexy legs, the way the rounded tops of her breasts peeked out of her shirt, or simply marveling at her smile.

During a commercial break in the game, I cornered her in the front hall. Amanda's front door opened to a hall with a closet and stairs to the left. It was fairly private as long as nobody came to the door. I pulled her to me, grabbing a handful of her ass to see if I could feel the base of the plug. I could. Power surged through me, not just desire, but the pride a Dominant gets when his submissive behaves, when she does something simply because he wants her to—and she likes it. I inhaled to maintain control of my body, but her warm scent filled my lungs and made me want to take her home.

Smiling, she leaned in close and grazed her teeth against my earlobe. She knew my sensitive spots well. "You're bad."

"You like it," I teased.

"Very much," she agreed, and I captured her lips with a kiss that robbed me of my iron control. I pressed her to the closet door and ground my erection against her stomach. I wanted to lift her against me, but some voice of reason in my head counseled against it. That voice must not have been in her head because she tried to climb me. Since my hand was already on her ass and I'm such a helpful guy, I picked her up. She felt good in my arms. I gripped her hair and forced her head back to expose her throat. As I kissed a path toward the soft tops of her breasts, the doorbell rang.

She froze, her fists tightening in my hair. And then she laughed. "My mom caught us making out. I feel like a teenager again."

I set her down slowly, glad she found humor in the situation. She smoothed her shirt, and I kept her in front of me as we answered the door.

"Hi Mom." She leaned forward to hug her mother. "How was the drive?"

Melinda kissed Sabrina's cheek. "Uneventful, thankfully."

"Did you have dinner? Because there are plenty of leftovers. If you're hungry, I can make you a plate."

"I'm fine. I had dinner with old friends. You remember Dmitri Morozov?" At Sabrina's nod, she continued. "His kids were out of town, so he had a bunch of the old group over. The Overbergs, the Bancrofts, the MacIvers, and the Galens were all there. I had a nice time."

Sabrina seemed to simultaneously brighten and bristle nervously. "That's wonderful. I'm glad you went."

Melinda lifted her gaze and gave me a brief, polite smile, the kind your girlfriend's parent gives when she's issuing a warning. I wasn't sure whether she disapproved of what she'd seen or of me. "Good evening, Jonas. I trust you've been fine?"

Amanda and our mother came into the front hall, preempting my response. My mom held her arms out and hugged Melinda. "I'm so glad you could make it, Melinda. We're almost ready to dive into the sweets."

Melinda hugged my mom back, genuine affection in her smile. "It's great to see you, Alyssa. Amanda, thanks for having me."

Ginny and Lara rang the bell next, and I scooted out of the way as more hugging and greeting ensued. Sabrina was much better at handling her mother when Ginny was around, and that plug had left her very relaxed, far more than I'd thought it would.

An hour later, I cornered Melinda in the empty dining room. Most of the family was either in the kitchen helping clean up or in the living room socializing. Melinda had come into the dining room to gather dirty dishes, and I followed.

I piled miscellaneous flatware onto a plate. Skipping the preamble, I plunged right in. "She's happy."

Melinda didn't pretend ignorance. I liked that about her. She stacked plates, sorting them according to size. "For now."

For some reason, I felt judged. I defended myself, and Sabrina too. "We're having fun. We set ground rules, and we both know the score. There's no harm in that."

"If you ever become a father, you'll eventually understand my position. Children are stubborn creatures. They often can't be told things. They need to learn from experience. My daughters have always been stubborn. I love that about them, and I wouldn't change either of them for the world. But experience leaves behind wisdom. I've been married and divorced twice. I know what lies ahead for Sabrina, and for you too." She looked at the table, watching the cloth as she wiped crumbs across Amanda's tablecloth. "I can't do anything now but stand by and hold my tongue. When I look at you, when I see the joy you bring her, I also see the misery that will follow. When the time comes, I'll be here to help my daughter put her life back together. If I'm not entirely friendly, it's not personal. Under other circumstances, I'm sure you'd make a fine son-in-law."

In that moment, I finally understood Melinda. But I didn't think she really knew her daughter. "She's stronger than you think."

Her lips set in a tight, sad smile. "Strong, proud, and so very fragile. Just be gentle, okay? If you have to leave before the year is up, wait to file for divorce. I'll make my father's will work for her."

I frowned. I'd given Sabrina my word. I would fulfill my end of the bargain, and then I'd fade from her life. In a year, I'd be a distant memory that brought a vague smile to her lips every now and again, and she'd be the same for me. The thought made me a little melancholy. I shook the feeling away and sent a curt nod in Melinda's direction.

On the way home, Sabrina reached across the console and twined her fingers with mind. "I had a nice time today."

"Even though your mom caught us kissing?"

It was dark, but I knew she was blushing. "At least it wasn't your dad. He'd have been nudging and winking at you all night. He seems very proud of your sexual conquests."

He wanted more grandkids, but I wasn't going to tell her that. I tried for levity. "He's just relieved. There was a time he thought he'd have to hire an expensive hooker to get me laid."

As expected, she laughed. "Are we playing roles tonight?"

Roles protected us from getting emotionally involved. "How about I'm a sex demon and you're my captive?"

She giggled. "Will you wear devil horns?"

I picked up on her playfulness. "They're hidden in my hair. I'll have to keep you tied up so you can't find them. If you touch them, it'll rob me of all my power."

"And then you might end up tied to that table." She rubbed her hands together gleefully.

Her reaction surprised me. I hadn't seen even the glimmer of a switch in her yet. "You want to tie me up?"

"Do you want to be tied up?"

Not really, but if she wanted to explore a possible Domme side to her personality, I'd indulge her. "If that would turn you on, then I'd do it. If it wouldn't, then there's no point."

She pursed her lips. "I don't know. Not tonight, at any rate. I'll think about it and let you know."

I pulled into the garage and turned to her. "Do you want me to remove the plug, or do you want to do it yourself?"

Nailing me with a steady look, she said, "I don't want to tie you up. Are you okay with that?"

It took me a second to answer because I had expected her to spend a few weeks considering the idea, and it wasn't a response to my question. "It's fine." Staring expectantly, I waited for her answer. When she merely cocked her head and stared back, I shook my head. "I'll take it out. Go upstairs and take off all your clothes."

She frowned. "I'm trying to figure out if that will be gross or not."

I laughed. "Don't worry about it."

Her look spoke volumes. I liked the fact that I had grown so adept at reading them. She wanted me to take it out, but she didn't anything to happen that might ruin the night. Therefore she looked at me like I was an idiot.

"You have two minutes, honey. I will undress you if need be, and that will infuriate the sex demon who might take it out on that pretty mouth of yours."

Seconds ticked by. At last she smiled. "Sex demon," she muttered as she got out of the car. "Slave to his captive."

Two minutes wasn't a lot of time, especially not since I wanted to change before I joined her. When I came upstairs, I found her standing in the center of the bedroom, her dark brown hair cascading over one shoulder to cover a breast. The rest of her was delightfully nude. Her arms rested casually at her sides, and her feet were shoulder-width apart. I hadn't taught her any special stances or poses, and the fact she naturally assumed this one made my slacks tight.

She lifted her gaze when I came in, openly checking me out. A soft smile curved her lips as she saw that I'd put on slacks and a nice shirt. "Sex demons are snappy dressers."

"Disguise," I returned. "We adapt to whatever works for our captives. Bend over and grab your ankles."

A laugh bubbled up, but she realized I wasn't kidding before it made it past her lips, so she swallowed it down. She bent slowly, a move she managed to make both graceful and elegant. I traced my hand down her back so she could keep track of where I was. Startling her wasn't in my plan tonight. With quick efficiency, I extracted the plug.

"I'd like a few moments to freshen up," she said. It wasn't really a request.

If she were my submissive, if I were to be above-board about the realities of our dynamic, I wouldn't have let her speak at will. But since I wasn't willing to go there with her, I agreed. "Sure. I'll meet you in my office. Bring your vibrator—and don't keep me waiting."

On a whim, I went to the kitchen and grabbed a few things for later. When I returned, she still hadn't emerged from the bathroom. I lounged on the futon in my office, the only other contribution I'd made to the furniture in the house. Before too long, she joined me. She'd put her hair up to jump in the shower, and she'd left it that way. I rose, closed the distance, and removed the pins, watching each lock of satiny hair tumble down her back. Then I secured Velcro cuffs around her wrists and thighs.

Gripping her waist, I lifted her onto the table. "Lie back." Once she did that, I moved her around, situating her limbs so that her back and neck would be comfortable on the hard surface. She cooperated as I forced her legs wide open and bound her thighs to the sides of the table. The vibrator was still in her hand. "Ready yourself, captive. Use the vibrator while I watch."

I knew she'd been using it on the nights I worked. Often I came home to find it on the bathroom sink, taunting me for not being there to satisfy her needs. This was the first time I'd asked her to use it in front of me. I drizzled some warming lubricant over her clit and down her slit. She started at a low setting, pressing it softly to her tissues as she moved it along the inside of her labia. After a few minutes, she turned it up and used it on her clit. Quiet sounds of enjoyment issued from her throat. I looked up to find her gaze fastened firmly on me.

"Put it in that ripe little cunt, captive. I want to see you fuck yourself. I will hear your cries of pleasure."

Her pink tongue made a circuit around her lips, moistening them and whetting my appetite. "Yes, Demon."

My cock hardened instantly, just from the acquiescence in her tone. I watched as she fucked herself to the edge, and then I snatched the vibrator away.

"Hey!" The mutinous slant to her mouth and the fury in her eyes confirmed that I'd chosen the right moment. I planned to keep her on the edge for a long, long time. She may only have one or two orgasms tonight, but she'd work hard for them. "Hellspawn."

After turning it off, I licked it like a sucker. She eyed my tongue hungrily, probably hoping I gave her pussy the same treatment. I set the toy on my desk and prepared my next device. Ellen would kill me if she knew what I had planned, but I knew Sabrina would love/hate what I was about to do. If it was the wrong kind of hate, she could always safeword. Speaking of which, I'd better remind her it was an option. She'd never used it before. "Do you remember the safeword?"

"Yeah." Excitement laced her voice, and I knew she was looking forward to whatever mayhem I had in store. She cooperated as I bound her wrists to the table.

I didn't show her the finger of ginger root that I'd carved into a plug. I simply inserted it into her ass. Before it took effect, I placed a thin sliver on her clit. She lifted her head to try to see what I'd done, but it was useless. In this instance, her ineptitude in the kitchen worked to my advantage. She relaxed her neck and stared at me. "Now what?"

243

"Now you lick my balls." The table didn't lower down, so I put a low step I'd built at the head. She smacked her lips together as I unzipped and lowered my slacks. I pumped my hand up and down my cock a few times, teasing her until she made a short mewling noise. Then I leaned over and held my balls over her mouth. She opened up, tonguing and mouthing them gently. I could tell when the ginger kicked in because she got rough. Wisely, I pulled back and tucked my junk back into my shorts.

"Demon, what did you do to me?" She did her best to squirm, but I hadn't left much slack.

Bending down, I smoothed her hair away from her temple and murmured in her ear. "Magic, my captive. You will soon be desperate for my cock."

"It burns," she complained.

I laughed evilly. "It'll get worse before it gets better." And then I made myself comfortable on the futon sofa. Her performance was mesmerizing. Over the next fifteen minutes, which I'm sure felt like an hour to her, she begged, screamed, threatened, and cried. Several times she forgot her role and swore at me. The loss of her composure was beautiful and precious to witness. When the ginger should have started to lose effectiveness, I kissed her face and stroked her hair, speaking words of honest and heartfelt praise.

"So beautiful," I said as I extracted the root. "I'm going to fuck your ass, captive, and you're going to love it." I tugged on the Velcro to free her wrists and trembling thighs. Then I slid her down the table, bent her over it, and bound her wrists behind her back. She cooperated when I lifted each leg to pass it through the straps of a butterfly. This device was new to her, but staring at me with desire blazing from her eyes, she questioned nothing.

I covered my cock with a condom and added some lube. Having her wear the plug all afternoon had prepared her well. She sighed as I breached her opening. "Hard," she begged. "And fast. Please, Demon."

I flipped the switch to turn on the butterfly, and then I fucked her mercilessly—exactly the way she liked. Her ass was tight and hot around my cock. Her cunt began quivering almost immediately, and the hard pulses rocked me as well. She screamed, a long, loud cry that went on and on. When she went silent, I peeked to make sure she was okay, and I found her mouth still open in a soundless cry.

Fucking her harder made her body come to life. She fought me, pushing and bucking with all her strength, and she was a very strong woman. I pinned her bound wrists to her back, but that didn't stop her upper body from thrashing dangerously. Instinctively I grabbed a fistful of hair and jerked her head back, arching her so that she wouldn't hit her face on the table. I swear she came even harder. The convulsions became too much for me, and I'd held out for too long anyway. My balls drew up. Fire shot up my spine and down my legs. With a couple of jerky thrusts, I climaxed and collapsed on top of her.

I don't know how long it took to get my shit together, but when I finally did, her pliant body trembled as I carried her to the bathroom for aftercare. She opened her eyes when I propped her up in the shower, and she peered at me.

"The hair pulling," she said, her raw throat making her voice scratchy. "I really liked that."

My body stiffened, but she was too tired to notice. I chuckled to cover up my real reaction. Helene had said the same thing to me once upon a time. It was one more similarity in sexual preferences that I'd rather Sabrina not share with my ex. The only real difference was that Helene hadn't liked to role-play. Our scenes had been for real, and that was the single reason I refused to share that side of my life with Sabrina.

I finished rinsing her, dried her off, and tucked her into bed. When her soft body rolled toward mine, seeking warmth and comfort, I didn't move. She snuggled against my shoulder and fell right asleep.

Chapter 20—Jonas

On a freezing day in mid-December, Sabrina took me out to lunch. She pulled her coat tightly around her as she scurried from the restaurant to her car in the parking lot. Since I had the keys, she ended up standing next to it, shivering and stomping her feet. I clicked the remote from ten feet away. It couldn't have been warmer inside the car, but if she thought that would help, then I'd oblige.

She slid into the driver's seat. I frowned. Usually I drove. I preferred to be the one in control, and she hated driving anyway. Still, I climbed into the passenger seat and handed her the keys. "Is everything okay?"

"Yep." She started the car and set the heat on full blast. "Why do I wear dresses and heels in the winter?"

I put my seatbelt on. "Because you like when I check out your sexy legs."

That didn't get much of a laugh. She held her hands in front of the vent and shivered. The engine hadn't warmed yet, so the air was cold. "I've been thinking a lot about what I want to get you for Christmas."

"You don't have to get me anything." The response was automatic. Sabrina liked to give gifts, though she didn't like when she had to give them for a particular reason. She had no problem choosing gifts for the hell of it, but throw in a birthday or holiday, and she fell apart.

Her look said *shut up*, but her mouth didn't. "I was going to buy you a car, but I decided against it."

My beater now lacked heat, and the battery needed a jump to get started most days. I needed another car, but that wasn't something I wanted Sabrina to buy for me. "Good."

"I got you something else, something you may not immediately appreciate, but you will in retrospect."

246

That uneasy feeling that flittered by when she mentioned buying a car came back, but this time it settled like lead in my stomach. "What did you do?"

She put the car in gear. "Jonas, it's non-refundable, so please humor me."

My mind raced, trying to figure out what it could be, and I came up empty. I defaulted to my Dom voice, which had a hit-or-miss effectiveness with her. "Sabrina, what did you do?"

"I'm not going to tell you until we get there, so there's no point in asking."

Scanning the street, I realized she wasn't heading back to the office. "Does my boss know I'm not coming back after lunch?"

She smiled smugly. "Yep. He tried to argue, but now that he's afraid of my husband beating the crap out of him, he gave in gracefully."

Since she'd played that card, I had no choice but to humor her. Sabrina wasn't manipulative. This was the first time she'd mentioned when I'd stepped in to tell Jared not to speak to my wife disrespectfully, so whatever she'd decided to give me meant a lot. "Is this a present I can open?"

She shot a disapproving frown in my direction. "No clues."

I'd seen her looking up travel plans, but sometimes she did that for research. "Do I have to pack a bag? Will I be taking a long weekend this week?"

"You're nervous. I think I like it."

"Payback's a bitch, Sabrina."

"Ooh," she crooned. "Are you going to tie me up to a table again?"

"I can get some more ginger at the grocery store tonight."

She glanced at me. "If you try that again, you're going to have to earn it. I'll not go gentle into that goodnight."

Since she had come out in favor of figging, I knew her aim was to add a layer of struggle to the bondage. Enjoying the banter, I grinned. "Rage all you want. I'll just gag you with my tie."

"Hmm. You haven't tried that before. I'm not sure I'd like it."

I squeezed her thigh. "I might like that you don't like it."

She sucked her top lip between her teeth, but otherwise she didn't respond, and I was glad for that. I'd crept too close to the line.

Wherever she was taking me was located in a tall building that housed a shitload of businesses. No clues here. She popped the trunk and hefted out an opaque plastic bin.

"Can I carry that for you?"

"I got it. You can close the trunk and hold doors for me."

The weight of the bin didn't concern me, but it was a little on the unwieldy side, and she was wearing heels. And though the parking lot was clear, the sidewalk could be icy. I hovered close so I could catch her if she slipped. Inside the building, we got on an elevator that came out in the posh lobby of a law firm.

Biting back a barrage of questions, I glanced at Sabrina. She set the bin on the floor next to the receptionist. "Hi. I'm Sabrina Breszewski. I have an appointment with Becca Overberg."

The sleek, modern design of the waiting room gave no clue as to the kinds of law practiced here. What was in the box? Was Sabrina already preparing for the divorce? It had taken more than six months to sever my marriage to Helene, but the bitch had fought everything. Sabrina and I had planned for a nice, amicable, easy divorce. It should only take a few weeks. Afterward I could invite her for a drink, and perhaps we'd end up in bed.

The receptionist wore an efficient suit and an equally efficient smile. She came out from behind her desk. "Of course, Ms. Breszewski. If you and Mr. Spencer could follow me?"

Sabrina picked up the bin. I was tempted to get there first, but I refrained. If she'd changed her mind about needing my help, she'd let me know. As I followed behind the ladies, I bent to whisper to Sabrina. "What's going on, Sabrina?"

She threw a devilish smile over her shoulder. "It's killing you, isn't it?"

"A little."

"Ms. Overberg will be right with you." The receptionist waited in front of an open door. "There's water and coffee on the table. Can I get you anything else?"

"Thank you," Sabrina said as she breezed into the room and set the bin on a table. "We're fine."

The décor of the office matched the lobby, but personal touches differentiated it. Looking around, I noticed photographs of a woman with various people, and I deduced she must be Rebecca Overberg. My guess was confirmed a few seconds later when the very same woman came in. She had short blonde hair cut in a sleek, angled style. It drew attention to her blue eyes. Her suit was professional and classy, much like something Sabrina would wear. She was pretty, but in a completely different way than Sabrina.

Her eyes sparkled as they landed on my wife, and she let out a squeal as she flew across the room to engulf Sabrina in a tight hug. "Oh my God, Sabrina! I haven't seen you in forever, and then you call out of the blue. We have to get together for lunch so we can catch up."

Sabrina smiled uncertainly, and so I intervened. "Hi, Rebecca. I'm Jonas Spencer, Sabrina's husband."

Rebecca released Sabrina and offered her hand to me. "Yes, I've heard about you. Not nearly enough, though. Melinda has always been so tight-lipped." We shook, and she turned back to Sabrina. "I didn't see your mom, of course, but she had Thanksgiving dinner with my parents, and they told me all the latest on the old gang."

From this, I surmised that Sabrina's family was friends with Rebecca's family. The two had probably grown up together. Sabrina rubbed her hands together. "Lunch sounds fun, but I'm busy until after the holidays. Why don't you text me in January and let me know when you have some free time? I'd love to catch up."

"Great," Rebecca said. "Let's get to work. Are you going to stay for this, or maybe you want to wait outside?"

Sabrina backed toward the door. "I'll wait in the reception room. Take as long as you need."

I grabbed her arm. "Sabrina—"

She turned to me and smoothed her thumb along the line of my jaw. "Trust me, okay?"

Damn woman trapped me again. I released my grip on her arm. "Okay."

When we were alone, Rebecca gestured to a chair near the bin Sabrina had left. I sat, and she followed suit. "I know Sabrina didn't tell you why you were here."

"No, she didn't."

"She said you needed help structuring your debt."

Sitting back, I rested an elbow on the table to affect a casual pose, and I stared with my most potent Dom expression. "It's fine."

Rebecca wasn't impressed. "I understand that you and your ex-wife split the debt in the divorce?"

I nodded.

"You paid your half, and then when you were finished, they came after you for your ex-wife's portion?"

Though I'd shared generalities with Sabrina, I hadn't discussed anything this specific. I wondered where Sabrina had learned these details, and then I placed the blame firmly on Ellen. "Rebecca, I fail to see what you think you can do about this. Credit card companies and banks don't care what the court said. They want their money."

"Call me Becca." She flashed a sunshine-y smile. "From a legal standpoint, there's actually a lot I can do. First I need to see your divorce papers and financial statements, any correspondence you've had as well."

I'd brought nothing with me. As I opened my mouth to say that, I looked at the bin Sabrina had carried here. I opened it to find all my stuff neatly filed and labeled. Truly I didn't know whether I wanted to be angry with Sabrina for butting into my business or touched that she cared so much. "How do you know Sabrina?"

Becca's smile dimmed. "She dated my big brother, but that was a long time ago."

"Your brother? Stephen?" She'd told me Stephen's last name, and it wasn't Overberg. A look at her left hand confirmed that she was married, and so perhaps Overberg wasn't her original name.

"Yes. She's five years older than me, but she was always so nice. She never made me feel unwelcome or like I didn't belong with the big kids. I idolized her growing up, and now she's trusting me to help you out. So that's what I'm going to do."

Becca was one of the few people who recognized the supportive and nurturing tendencies that hid behind Sabrina's shyness. Even though she was Sabrina's ex-boyfriend's sister, I liked her.

"Anything you share with me is confidential, Jonas. You're my client."

"But Sabrina paid you."

"Doesn't matter who signs the check. You're still my client. Now, let's get down to business. I suspect that you've paid more than your fair share, and I'm going to do something about it."

"Don't involve my ex-wife. That's not a can of worms I'm willing to open."

"I don't think that will be necessary."

Opening the bin, I slid it toward her. "Have at it."

Three hours later, I found Sabrina sitting on a sofa in the reception room. She'd gone back to the car at some point because she had her laptop set up in a mini workstation. When she saw me come out with the bin tucked under one arm, she closed the cover and stood, regarding me with a hesitant smile.

Payback for keeping me in the dark was going to be fun. "Let's go. You can buy me a drink."

She packed up and followed me to the elevator. "Jonas, are you angry?"

"Oh, *you* don't have to tell me anything, but *I'm* supposed to spill my guts? No way. Not without persuasion."

The bell dinged, and we joined others in the tiny metal box. "Alcohol persuasion or sexual persuasion?"

I got a twinge of whiplash from turning to look at her so quickly. I couldn't believe what had come out of her mouth in front of strangers who had no choice but to hear her. Though a light blush made its way up her neck, her proud grin trumped it.

"You're planning to get me drunk and take advantage of me?"

Her expression didn't waver. "If you like. Or I could just take advantage of you. Alcohol tends to interfere with stamina and blood flow to the genitals. And you're getting older, so you probably don't want to chance it."

We left the elevator amid amused snickers and pure shock. I did some mental math, calculating the time it would take for us to get home. "Forty minutes, Sabrina. I'll show you 'older' in exactly forty minutes." To prove I was serious, I set the countdown timer on my phone.

As she started the car, she said, "That might prove problematic. We have one more stop to make."

"I don't need a drink, honey. I need you."

"Not that. I bought a car, and we need to go pick it up."

I stared at her with silent reproof. She didn't notice until the next stoplight.

"Not for you. I already told you I didn't buy you a car. I bought me a car. It's red. I've always wanted a red car, but it never seemed sensible to buy one."

"And it does now?"

"Sure. Why not? Are you going to tell me about your meeting with Becca or not? I know you're not mad at me, but I can't tell if you're flirting because you're happy or because you're planning revenge."

Perhaps a little of both. "I'm not a hundred percent sure. She managed to settle all the debt for what I've already paid. She even threatened to sue three of the companies for coming after me for debt

I hadn't incurred. I'm getting about three thousand dollars back. Not having all those bills hanging over me is a little surreal. Why did you do it?"

She pushed a strand of hair away from her face. It had fallen from the upswept style she'd wrangled it into that morning. I removed the clip so that it all fell out. I liked when she wore her hair down, and I suspected she wore it up because she liked when I messed it up.

"To set you free."

I had the sense she didn't mean debt-free. "How so?"

"It's the last claw Helene has in you. Now you're free—free to start over, to move forward, to live your life how you want. You gave me a new lease on life, and I wanted to give you the same thing."

Touched by the depth of her friendship, I had no response. I simply stared, basking in the beauty of her gesture and her profile. At last, I took her hand in mine. "Thank you."

Her expression turned smug. "You're quite welcome."

"I'm still going to fuck you in thirty minutes, even if we're at the dealership."

"I know."

Chapter 21—Sabrina

Relief flowed through me. He'd accepted my gift at face value. Part of me was a little disappointed that he hadn't dug deeper, that he hadn't pushed to find out the real reason I wanted him free of his ex-wife's legacy. I knew there was no way he could fall in love with me when he was still under her shadow.

At the dealership, Jonas was greeted immediately by a salesperson whose nametag identified him as Joe. I hated how car salespeople always ignored me because I was a woman. Buying online alleviated only part of this problem. Jonas grinned while I glared and said, "I'm here to pick up my car."

"It's red," Jonas added helpfully. Then he looked at his phone. "Twenty-eight minutes."

Joe the Salesperson looked confused.

I explained. "We're going to have sex in twenty-eight minutes. If you don't want that happening in this showroom, you might tell Jay Crandall that Sabrina Breszewski is here, and to get my car and the paperwork sooner rather than later."

Joe scrambled off, and I linked my arm through Jonas's. "I think I like that threat."

"It's a promise." He kissed the top of my head.

I had no doubt what we'd be doing in twenty-seven minutes, no matter where we were. Jay, the person who was supposed to be taking care of my purchase, appeared and ushered us to his office. The walls were thin, and the front one had a window that overlooked the showroom. "Your paperwork is almost ready."

I was a little late for my appointment, so I found it irritating that he wasn't ready. Jonas sat in a chair, and I sat on his lap. Jay chattered about nothing, and Jonas's hands roamed my hips and thighs. "Twenty."

"Excuse me?" Jay asked.

Jonas brushed my hair off my shoulder and kissed my neck. "In twenty minutes, we're going to have sex. If we're still in your office, then we're going to have sex in your office."

I think Jay thought Jonas was kidding. After a polite but uncomfortable laugh, he continued doing whatever time-sucking crap they do at dealerships. In keeping with the general schmooziness of car salespersons, Jay tried to converse, but Jonas kept kissing and biting me, which I found distracting—and hot. An audience did it for Jonas, but Jonas did it for me with his knowing touches and the desire kindling in his eyes. Every once in a while, Jay would leave the room to get something from a printer, which was apparently on the other side of the city. The countdown alarm on Jonas's phone went off during one of Jay's trips.

Jonas lifted me as he stood, backed me against the desk, and kissed me breathless. We made out, groping each other shamelessly. I didn't look at the window to see who was watching, but Jonas did several times, so I knew we'd been spotted. The desk was angled away from the door, probably to prevent potential customers from escaping, but in this instance it served to protect my modesty. People watching could tell what we were doing, but they couldn't see any flesh. His hard cock pressed against my leg. He pushed my dress up, opened his pants, and entered me swiftly.

Gripping his shoulders, I threw my head back and let him take me. Hard and fast, he pumped into me, pushing me to the edge quickly, and we fell over together, tangled in each other's arms. I clung to him, my heart thumping madly against his chest as we came down. "Damn. You are good at this."

He chuckled, zipping his pants before fixing my dress. "That was so fucking hot."

I settled back on his lap. As Jay returned, red-faced and avoiding eye contact, I said, "Set your timer for thirty minutes."

Jonas obliged. "Okay, but it'll take me longer to get there since I'm getting older and everything. We might need to clear the desk instead of just push things to the side."

Jay miraculously managed to turn over the keys and papers to my brand new red car within five minutes. I kept my old car. It was in great shape, and Jonas really needed something else to drive around. His car needed a funeral in the worst way.

Ellen had put me in touch with reputable sex clubs in Amsterdam and Sydney. Since I'd packed days of sightseeing and other excursions into our itinerary, our vacation would last ten days. Jared wasn't happy with me for insisting he give Jonas the time off, and I wasn't sure Jonas would be happy to learn I'd used up his five vacation days, but I went forward with my plan—without informing Jonas.

The more I came to know Jonas, the less of an enigma he became. I knew he had secrets, some darker than others, that he kept from me because he wasn't in a place where he felt he could be emotionally vulnerable with me. Yet he couldn't hide the essential pieces of himself. He loved to be in charge, and it was more than his natural leadership abilities. It was a need, an innate authority that couldn't be denied. In small ways, he came to control my life. Most days, he picked out what I wore. This wasn't an overt power grab. He'd come in while I was dressing and ask me to wear a certain piece of clothing, and the next thing I knew, he'd chosen my entire outfit.

He controlled what I ate and when I ate it. This began out of frustration when he found out I was too lazy most days to make a proper meal, but it evolved into something more. I didn't mind one bit. In fact, I preferred to turn over these kinds of decisions to him. It lifted a weight from my shoulders I hadn't known was there. Yes, I was capable of doing all these things myself, but I didn't want to. I wanted to be told what to do.

His approach was nonthreatening. He always asked. He always made it seem like I had a choice. I suppose I did, but his preferences became mine as soon as he uttered them. Nobody knew about this part of our dynamic, and I very much wished I could discuss it with a sympathetic party. I didn't want to change anything, but I wanted to understand why I wanted to embrace these old-fashioned gender roles. Ellen was available to some extent, and though our friendship had blossomed, she was first and foremost Jonas's best friend. I liked Ryan, but I didn't feel close enough with him to confide what was going on.

And though I was welcome to initiate sex anytime I wanted, he chose when, where, and how it would happen. Sometimes he had me dress or fix my hair a certain way, especially if it was for a role. Other times he just held me down and made me his.

Yet he didn't mind one bit if I rejected or amended his choice. If I turned down a skirt, he'd simply shrug and put it away. In some ways, that reaction affected me worse than if he'd argued or insisted. He also didn't mind when I took the lead. In those instances, he was supportive and encouraging. When I redecorated the dining room without consulting him, he told me it looked great. If I wanted to go out with friends, he would wish me a nice time. If I had people over—even his friends or family—he welcomed them.

Of course, none of those things crossed the invisible line he'd drawn, the line that screamed the demise of our arrangement if I breached it. I had been afraid that even having a third party assess his monetary obligations would infringe upon that boundary. Thankfully he'd accepted the gift of help. This trip, a second Christmas gift, was really for both of us. We needed some time away with just the two of us. I had high hopes that good things would happen now that he was free of the past.

We boarded a plane the day after Christmas. I'd given him the itinerary as his gift on Christmas Eve. Jonas was nonplussed by the short notice.

"You knew," I accused.

"I didn't know."

"You haven't asked about time off work or how I knew your passport was up to date or anything."

"I trust that you've taken care of the details, and I already know you've gone through my personal papers."

"Just to find your passport." And to organize his bills. And find his divorce papers, which I hadn't read.

He regarded me with barely disguised amusement. "It's okay, Sabrina." His tone didn't communicate trust. In fact, I deduced that anything he didn't want me to see or know about wasn't in our house. He set a possessive hand on my thigh. "I've forgiven you for being nosy. You had good intentions, and good things came of it. Next time just ask, okay? I'd rather you respect my privacy."

That stung, mostly because I still felt guilty for invading his privacy in the first place. I decided to change the subject. "Ellen said you've never been to Amsterdam or Sydney."

"Nope. This'll be fun. I've always wanted to visit Anne Frank's house and lounge on a nude beach in Australia."

I gripped the arms of my seat, and not only because the plane was taking off. "They have nude beaches in Australia?"

"Yep. You're going to come home with tanned boobs."

I'd been to Australia once before, but I'd obviously missed something. Okay, I also missed the fact there were sex clubs, but I attributed that to the fact that I'd been with my family the last time I'd visited. Go to a sex club with my mother? Hell, no.

"We'll see." Though I knew I would if he wanted, I wasn't going to give in easily. Where was the fun in that?

Chapter 22—Jonas

Amsterdam was gorgeous. The weather we'd escaped in Michigan was cold and grey. Amsterdam was warm by comparison, though still cold, but the day was bright and sunny. I'd always wanted to see Europe for the sheer historical significance. I'd taught Anne Frank's memoir to freshmen before, and I'd always been fascinated by the tragic tale of the vivacious teen.

A driver from the InterContinental Amstel Hotel met us at the airport. On the way to the hotel, he chattered about the accommodations and, when he found out neither of us had been there before, he informed us of several places we should visit. Sabrina had arranged for us to spend five days here and five in Australia.

The hotel blew my mind. I thought we'd stayed in luxury that one night in Louisville, but this took it to a whole new level. The lobby had high ceilings, painted a beautiful shade of light blue. Italian marble and ornate moldings surrounded us, yet it felt warm and inviting. Sabrina had booked the Royal Suite, an elegant set of rooms decorated in a classic French style. Everything was in shades of cream, peach, and gold. The concierge talked us through the features of the room, and then he put our bags in the bedroom.

Sabrina stood in the center of the living room and looked back at me. Framed by fancy drapes and windows that stretched the height of the room, she looked utterly gorgeous and a little ethereal. She'd been made to stand in rooms like this.

When the concierge came out, he looked from me to her, and then excused himself from the room. I don't know what expression was on my face, but I was hungry for this woman. I wanted more than sex. I wanted to possess her, to own her. I knew it would never happen—I wouldn't allow myself to fall prey to a woman's charms again—but I could pretend. We were very good at making believe.

"Do you like it?"

"Love it."

At last she smiled, and her eyes lit to an inviting golden brown. "I thought we could relax tonight. I've made reservations at La Rive. And then tomorrow I thought we could visit the Anne Frank museum. There are lots of things to see and do here, but if you want, we could also spend a day in Rotterdam or Antwerp. I have tickets to see the ballet in The Hague, but we don't have to go if you don't want to. I got them from a friend who wasn't using them."

As she talked, I came closer, and when I stopped in front of her, she fell silent. "We can do whatever you want. I know you researched the area, and I know you chose things to do that you thought I would like."

"I wasn't sure about the ballet, but it's supposed to be one of the best in the world."

I took her hand in mine. "I'm looking forward to it. I'm looking forward to everything."

She lowered her gaze, a submissive gesture that sent blood rushing to my cock. "There's a sex museum in the Red Light District. It's near the club."

I pulled her to me and held her pliant body against mine. "I'm going to make you climax in every room in this place." And then I kissed her.

Though we managed to visit a number of places—in addition to the Anne Frank house, we went to Van Gogh Museum, saw old churches and cathedrals, walked all over the place, shopped at local stores, and ate at a variety of restaurants—we spent a lot of time in our suite. It was a vacation in and of itself, and having Sabrina there made it perfect. She was more than willing to do anything I wanted whenever I wanted to do it. If I wasn't careful, I was going to become spoiled.

The fourth night, we visited The Temple of Venus, Amsterdam's sex museum. At the entrance, a plaster statue of Venus greeted us. It had some campy exhibits—Mata Hari with a bunch of lovers and Marilyn Monroe with a fan blowing her skirt up—but it also had a number of historical items. I could have done without the acoustics. We'd hear actual people having sex very soon, so I didn't need to hear recordings of people gasping and moaning.

Due to the cool weather, I had her wear a long skirt and a sweater under a long coat. She looked great, and once we got to Amsterdam's City Club, she could reveal the sexy lingerie hiding underneath. Inspired by our room, I'd picked out a peach and black half corset to go with matching thigh-highs and a garter. No panties. Tonight she'd be exposed. I'd show off what was mine while I still had a right to it.

Sabrina seemed more amused than aroused by the sex museum, so I cut our visit short. Slinging an arm around her waist, I leaned down to nuzzle her neck. "Let's go, honey. There are things I want to do to you tonight."

She rested her fingertips on my cheek, a gentle caress I was coming to recognize as a passive statement of affection. She smiled shyly. "Yes, Jonas."

Damn, but she could drive me from mildly horny to insane with such simple gestures and statements.

I held her hand as we navigated the crowded streets on the way to the club. "What made you decide to go into marketing?"

She glanced up, a frown marring the space between her eyebrows. "It's inconsequential now. I stay with it because it's challenging and I'm good at it."

Those were things I already knew. "But why did you originally choose it?" I'd been motivated by the challenge, but mostly I'd been attracted to the income potential.

"That's an odd question to ask right now. I would have thought you'd be asking if had I any special requests for tonight."

"I hadn't planned to give you a choice in what happened tonight." A shiver of anticipation traveled up her spine and made her shoulders twitch. I loved when she reacted so viscerally to me. "And now I'm wondering why you're avoiding an answer."

She let out a short huff of breath. "Stephen got his degree in international business. His father owns a diverse interest in businesses around the world, as did my grandfather. I didn't want to be so involved with the business side of things, but I knew I had to do something. If we were going to run an empire, I felt marketing paired well with international business."

From the start, she'd planned to uphold her duty to her family, even going so far as to choose her career—and her husband—based on what would benefit them the most. I measured my response carefully. "But you don't run your grandfather's business interests now. What happened?"

"Grandpa knew where my heart lay. He sold most of it to Morozov Industries, putting everything into trusts for me, Ginny, and my mom. Then he told me to forge my own path. At first I was upset—I'd just broken things off with Stephen, and I felt he was punishing me for it— and then I saw it for the gift it was."

"He set you free so that you could realize your dreams."

"Yes." She held my hand tighter and huddled closer. A cold breeze whipped through the street, but I think she did it because she needed to know I wasn't jealous. "Free—just like you."

I put my arm around her and held her to my side, but I didn't respond. We had arrived. The exterior marked an historic building, but the interior was completely modern. In the reception area, I gave my name. Working for Ellen netted us a discount, and we benefitted from professional courtesy that meant we didn't have to wait in line. Though Ellen didn't run a sex club anymore, she had until it had stopped being profitable. I'd always been a service top, and at some clubs, that meant I was in high demand.

Once inside, I scanned the place to get a lay of the land. It had a bar, seating at tables or couches, and as we walked through, I saw different open rooms that were filled with huge red pleather beds. No floor space was available at all. It was wall-to-wall bed. Each room was open on at least one side. In addition to the bed, they had pleather pillows of various shapes, including long rectangular ones that ran the length of the bed.

It wasn't organized with any kind of logic in mind. The whole place had a casual, laid-back atmosphere, which I liked. I took Sabrina to the locker room to store our clothes. She undressed slowly, neatly folding everything before putting it away.

"Nervous?"

She shook her head. "I'm with you."

I studied her and came up with a different guess. "You look reticent. Uncertain."

Looking down, she took in her outfit. The corset pushed her breasts up so they swelled over the top, and the garter held up her silk stockings. I'd asked her to get a wax at the hotel spa the day before, and she sported an inviting landing strip. "I'm wearing next to nothing, and you kept your jeans. It doesn't seem fair."

Grinning, I shrugged. I wanted to tell her to suck it up, that I'd display her because it's what I wanted, but I couldn't go there with her. Ever. "If it bothers you that much, I'll let you keep your skirt."

She held the skirt up to her waist, and then she put it on. I didn't want her to wear it, but I kept my mouth shut. There was a difference between asking and telling, and I wanted her to feel comfortable here.

Holding hands loosely, we wandered the club to see the sights. Though it was early, the place was filled with patrons, many of whom wore a lot less than either Sabrina or me. She stopped in front of a woman in a hanging cage. The way she was placed in there forced her to sit bent over, exposing her pussy and ass at a level perfect for fucking. It was a tight fit otherwise. The woman couldn't move around. Not only were her wrists bound to the bars, but the odd shape of the cage meant her ass was stuck in one place, and her head and legs had to cram into the rest of the space. She was a little too tall, and the cage forced her to keep her neck bent to the side. I wouldn't have done that to my submissive because it was too easy to pull a muscle in her neck or shoulder. She'd be sore for days.

Nonetheless she seemed to be quite content with her situation. Two people stood guard, and I assumed they were her Dominants or owners. The one nearest her ass, a woman, poked the blunt end of a bamboo rod at the caged slave's pussy. Whenever the slave yelped or wiggled to get away, the Dominant woman brought the small cane down across the slave's buttocks. At the front of the cage, the male Dominant stuck his fingers into the slave's mouth and reached through the bars to pinch her nipples.

I leaned down to Sabrina. "Does that bother you?"

She shook her head. "She looks like she's in heaven."

I didn't hear wistfulness or envy in her tone, so I left it alone. We watched as the female Dominant greeted a friend. They talked for several minutes, and then the friend dropped his pants and fucked the slave in the cage. I couldn't tell whether he was in her pussy or her ass. Hazarding another glance at Sabrina, I saw her lips parted in shock. "Are you still okay?"

"Does she even know him?" She whispered so only I could hear. She'd learned early on not to appear judgmental, but that didn't mean she didn't have questions.

"She might. People who play like that set up ground rules beforehand."

Sabrina relaxed. "So she has a safeword."

I had no way of knowing. Though this club belonged to a network of clubs, it was a sex club, not exclusively a BDSM club, and I wasn't familiar with their rules. "Whether she does or not, you do. Remember that."

The caged slave made sounds of pleasure, and the male Dominant near her face whispered things as he viciously twisted and pulled her nipples. Pleasure and pain transformed her face, and she cried out. Next to me, Sabrina's sharp intake of breath caught my attention. Her grip on my hand tightened. "She had an orgasm."

"Looks that way."

We turned away, and Sabrina's iron hold loosened. "That was damn hot, but I don't think I would like to be in a cage. It would be too lonely."

"She wasn't alone. She had two people with her."

"Still, it separated her. When you tie me up, you're right there with me. Most of the time." She tugged me in another direction. This time she stopped next to a man in a stockade. Ankle restraints kept his feet spread, and the neck restraint was positioned at waist height. A man in leather pants inserted a huge dildo into the bottom's ass, and then he went around to the front and fucked the man's mouth. He was rough, sliding his cock all the way in so that his submissive had to control his gag reflex.

Sabrina watched in fascination, and I watched her, wondering exactly which part she liked best—gay sex, the massive dildo, the brutal blowjob, or the way the submissive was bound. Taking a chance, I moved to stand behind her. Slowly I lifted her skirt, not stopping until her pussy was exposed. She drew a shaky breath as I traced my fingertip along the edge of her slit. It was damp already, and so I parted her lips and explored her folds.

A woman came closer, stopping to our right so she didn't block our view of the men going at it. She was a curvy blonde, a little taller than Sabrina, and she wore a low cut shirt that barely contained her ample breasts. She said something, but I didn't speak Dutch.

Sabrina answered in French. At the hotel, I'd been surprised to hear her speak French to the staff. She'd assured me she only spoke conversational French, enough to get by on vacation. The woman set her lips firmly and spoke again. Sabrina tilted her head to look back at me. "She wants to know if you want her to lick my pussy."

Once upon a time, I hadn't minded sharing a submissive or playing around with occasional thirds. Then my ex-wife had started playing around with those thirds while I wasn't around. Sharing Sabrina was off the table. She'd assured me she wanted the same thing. "What did you tell her?"

"I told her that we weren't into that, but she's insisting I ask you. Apparently you're the boss of me."

What Sabrina attributed to natural leadership, others labeled as Dominant. I couldn't help my bearing or the proprietary air with which I regarded my wife. I smiled at the woman as I inserted a finger into Sabrina's hole. "No, thank you."

Sabrina gasped and let her head fall against my chest. I added another finger, pushing them as deep as I could. The woman looked Sabrina up and down regretfully, said something in rapid French, and walked away.

"How did you know she speaks French?"

"She spoke Dutch with a French accent."

"What did she just say?" I kept my still fingers inside her.

"She said maybe next time."

I pressed my thumb against her clit. "She said more than that."

She trembled, and I wrapped my other arm around her waist. "She said I was too pretty for one lover and if I got tired of you, she would show me pleasures of my dreams. Or something like that. I don't know the exact translation."

The primal pieces of me asserted themselves. I had known that people would proposition us here—that was a normal thing. I even knew a woman would do it. Single men weren't allowed in sex clubs, otherwise they would overwhelm the female population and change the atmosphere of the place. Still I couldn't help the surge of possessiveness that made me want to tie her up and make her look at me while I did things to her.

I withdrew my fingers and shoved them in her mouth, making her suck them clean. Pressed against my body, she had nowhere to go. She gave me what I wanted, but I couldn't see her face, so I whirled her around. "I'll show you pleasures of your dreams."

With my fingers in her mouth, she couldn't respond. She stared at me, watching my actions more than listening to my words. I bent down, leveled a shoulder at her midsection, and lifted her. She was light and easy to carry—and she didn't struggle. I lifted her skirt, throwing it over her torso to expose her ass. I wanted to smack it a few times, but I refrained, and it cost me some of my patience. Looking for an empty bed sapped even more of it. I ended up on the second level, which turned out to be a long room littered with pleather-covered beds of various shapes and sizes. Couches were scattered throughout. Curtains hanging from the ceiling provided a semblance of privacy for some people. I wasn't looking for that. I found an unoccupied bed near the center of the room, and I threw her down. Sabrina blinked up at me, but there were no questions in her deep brown eyes, only abject desire.

"Take off the skirt. Now."

She scrambled to obey, tossing it to the edge of the bed. I pushed her back down, lifted her legs, and buried my face in her pussy. I sucked and bit. She grasped my hair hard and cried out, pleasure and pain mixing in the wondrous sound.

The bed had large eyelets sewn into a fringe on the seams. When I came up for air, I peeled away her stockings. One I used to bind her wrists together, and the other I threaded through a couple eyelets. Now she was tied with her hands over her head, and that attracted more attention than me simply ravaging her. Being watched did things to me. It ramped up my excitement in a way nothing else could. I had to close my eyes and count until I regained some of my composure.

When I opened them, I found Sabrina waiting patiently. Understanding had joined the desire shining in her eyes. I laid on top of her, crushing her with my weight because I liked to, and kissed her with a mixture of tenderness and urgency. When I broke it off to trail sucking kisses and stinging bites down her neck and shoulders, she arched her back, begging for more. I touched her all over, removing her corset to expose her ribs and stomach. My caresses were rough, and I squeezed her delicate flesh anywhere I could get a handhold— her arms, her breasts, her waist, and her thighs. I wasn't careful, and she would likely have bruises, but I was too far gone to temper myself. And she neither resisted nor safeworded.

I set my mouth on her pussy again, but this time I plunged my fingers into her dripping vagina as I bit her clit. She yelped and cried out, coming hard on my hand and in my mouth. I kept going, drawing out her climax until her thighs trembled too hard to support her efforts to thrash.

Then I kissed her again, and I found her mouth slack because she was still in the throes of orgasm. "You were made for this, Sabrina. You were made to be fucked hard, used relentlessly, and watched. You're so fucking beautiful, especially when you come, and you taste so fucking good." I stopped before I said too much, before I called her mine and told her that I would never share her, that I'd never let her go. Because it didn't matter how much I wanted to keep her, she was a rental. We'd agreed on a year, and that's all the time I would allow myself to get lost in her bliss.

She murmured my name, and I turned her over. I opened my jeans, careful not to touch my erection too much. I was primed, and I didn't want to come on her ass. With the way she was bound and the fact her entire body shook, there was no way she was going to be able to hold herself up. I pushed her knees apart and up, and then I threaded her skirt under her hips. This would allow me to hold her up, and it would further inhibit her movements. It would also keep me from squeezing fingerprint bruises into her hips. She was a vessel, waiting for me to fill her with my cock. I plunged into her pussy, wound the ends of her skirt around my fists, and fucked her with hard, punishing strokes.

Her body softened even more, and she submitted to me completely, yielding and welcoming my demands. I held off as long as I could, but when she came, her hot pussy pulsating around my cock and desperate sounds heaving from her chest, I only lasted two more thrusts. I fell to the side so I didn't crush her, and I held her in my arms. She'd given me everything, and she needed to know I would take care of her.

Later, back at the hotel, we soaked in the huge tub, and I made her come again.

We left Amsterdam the next day and headed to Australia, where it was summer. The moment I stepped out of the airport, warm air surrounded me. There was a sense of relief and freedom that comes with summer, and it was extra special when it happened while it was winter at home.

A driver met us at the airport and took us to the InterContinental Sydney Hotel. Though it wasn't as historical and awe-inspiring as the one in Amsterdam, it was still very nice. When we got to our luxury suite, the view out the window stole my breath. It had two walls—in two different rooms—of solid windows that overlooked the harbor. I could see the Sydney Opera House and the lights from the bridge.

Sabrina stood by my side, silently taking in the view.

"You sure don't half-ass anything."

She laughed. "I booked it based on reviews and the pictures I saw online. They were gorgeous, but nothing compares to seeing it in person."

No, it didn't. "What do you have planned for our five days here?"

"We're only here four days. We lose a day because of the time difference. I thought we'd see the Royal Botanic Gardens. We have tickets to see a performance at the Opera House tomorrow night and reservations for dinner. Our last day here I booked a tour in a little plane that will take us to a romantic spot for dinner. I thought you would want take it easy and spend a lot of time relaxing."

That left two nights open to visit the Sydney City Club. She'd left that decision up to me. "I've always wanted to see the zoo here, and we have to go to a nude beach so we can get some sun on your boobs."

"Do tanned breasts turn you on?"

I shrugged. "I've never thought about it. We'll see, won't we?"

She rolled her eyes and shook her head in a what-am-I-going-to-do-with-you way. I tried to kiss her, but she yawned. "Sorry. I'm exhausted from the plane ride."

"Let's order room service, and then we can go to bed. It's almost morning anyway."

We slept late. I woke Sabrina by pinning her hands to the mattress and having my way with her, which she very much liked. I was programmed for a morning quickie, and I liked having a lover who got off on the fact that I wanted to use her for sex.

The day was magical. We strolled through the gardens, holding hands and talking about anything and everything. I loved talking to Sabrina. She was intelligent and interesting, and she was a really good listener. She was easy to be with, and sometimes I felt so close to her. It scared me, yet I couldn't seem to pull back. Over the next two days, we did everything together. Though there was an entire floor with a huge swimming pool, she didn't leave me once to do laps.

The third night, we went to the sex club. This one wasn't attached to a dance club. The entryway was manned by a huge guard. He checked our identification against a list before letting us inside. Once there, we paid the fee and signed waivers, and then we were admitted to the main room. This one wasn't as relaxed as the one in Amsterdam, and I immediately realized why. Ellen had sent Sabrina to a BDSM club. The people here had clear roles, as delineated by their dress. I probably should have read the waiver. I parked a possessive hand on the back of Sabrina's neck.

A host greeted us before we'd taken more than three steps. He wore tiny black leather shorts and kept his gaze lowered as he addressed me. "Good evening, Sir. Welcome to City Club. I'm Adam."

Half of my mouth lifted in an uncomfortable smile. "This is our first time. What's the protocol here?"

Adam flashed a genuine smile. "I'm happy to help, Sir. You're fine, of course. But submissives aren't permitted shoes or shirts. Corsets, lingerie, or any kind of bondage or fetish wear are acceptable. Our changing rooms are separated into Dominant and submissive instead of by gender. If your submissive requires help getting into her outfit, we have smaller, single-person changing rooms available, or you may instruct her to use the submissive attendant stationed in the submissive changing room."

I looked at Sabrina. "Give us a moment?" Adam stepped back, hovering a respectful distance. "This isn't strictly a sex club. We don't have to stay here. They're into stuff we're not."

She tilted her head and regarded me with a mischievous smile. "I've never been to a club like this before. I've heard about them, of course. We should stay. It'll be interesting. You're pretty bossy, so you can act all dominant, and I can say 'Yes, Sir' a lot."

I shouldn't have given her a choice in the first place. "You're going to see things that will disturb you."

She lifted a brow. "I think you underestimate how thoroughly you've debauched me. Besides, they're bound to have interesting bondage stuff, like the table in your office that we like so much. And you won't have to use my stockings."

I wanted to tie her up. I wanted to bind her to a cross or a spanking bench or put her in a training stockade. I wanted her to feel the sting of my flogger, the snap of my crop, and the thud of my cane. I wanted to see tears track down her cheeks as I took her through the pain to subspace. I wanted to see her body with my marks on her thighs, ass, and breasts. I wanted to see her kneel at my feet, look up at me, thank me, and beg for more.

Violently I flung those thoughts and desires away. I didn't want that with Sabrina. I never wanted her to look at me and ask for those things, because one day she would look at me and only see those things, and I would hate her for it. Yet it was an integral part of who I was—and that's why I was doomed to never fall in love again.

"Bondage." I said it through gritted teeth. "Okay. We can do that. But we're not looking around. You'll stay by my side with your gaze on the floor at all times. Do not look up unless I instruct you to do so. Do not speak unless I ask you something or tell you to respond to someone. Do you understand?"

With a tolerant smile, she nodded. "Yes, Sir."

"Jonas. Say 'Yes, Jonas,' okay?" Her smile slipped a bit, but she nodded. "Take off your shirt and skirt. Wear only your bra and panties. After you change, wait right here for me."

Slowly she lowered her gaze until it was fastened on the floor. She folded her hands meekly in front of her, and when she spoke, her tone was soft and submissive. "Yes, Jonas."

My pants tightened, and that pissed me off a little. "Clasp your hands behind your back." No matter what, people would know she was untrained. They would expect me to correct her, and I didn't want to do that. *Fuck them*, I decided. I'd do what I wanted. As long as she stuck close to me and didn't talk to anybody but me, we'd be fine. People at sex clubs were usually a friendly lot. They liked to converse on a variety of topics, and they liked to have sex. People at BDSM clubs were very similar, only there was a protocol in place that had to be followed.

Sabrina waited for me in the exact spot I'd told her to wait. She was even on the same floor tile. Her gaze was lowered, and she waited with her hands dangling loosely at her sides. It was a submissive pose, and she lent it an elegant grace that was more beautiful than Sydney Harbor. I closed my arms around her, pulled her to me, and kissed her until we were both panting for oxygen.

She kept her arms by her sides the entire time.

I led her through the place, looking for something semi-private. Normally I liked a crowd, but tonight I wanted something a little less public. I heard the swish of a flogger and the slap of leather on flesh. Screams, cries, and the sounds of submissives and slaves begging for release filtered through the music, which wasn't nearly loud enough. I glanced back at Sabrina several times to find her following my instructions to the letter. She didn't flinch at the sound of things she'd never seen or heard, and that made me question her inexperience.

Finding an empty table near the bar didn't take long. I sat down and pulled her onto my lap. "Are you okay?"

"Yes, Jonas."

"It's just the two of us. You can speak freely. Nobody's listening."

She lifted her gaze and met mine. I don't know what she saw, but her smile vanished. She stroked my cheek. "I'm fine. Really. But you're not. Do you want to leave? Oh, Jonas, we don't have to stay if this kind of thing turns you off. We can go back to the hotel, and I'll let you do whatever you want to me."

As she generally let me do whatever I wanted—or whatever I was willing to ask for—that wasn't surprising. "People are flogging other people. They're inflicting pain. Are you sure you're okay with that?"

Spreading her fingers, she cupped the side of my head. "When I'm with you, like this, I only see you. It doesn't matter what other people are doing. It only matters to me what you do. If this makes you uncomfortable and you want to leave, I'm okay with that. Just like you'd never force me to do anything I didn't want to do, I would never force you either. But if you're this tense because you're worried about me, don't be. I'm a big girl. I can live and let live."

My heart thumped painfully.

"I won't ask you any questions, though, because I know you can't answer them. If it's really puzzling to me, I can research it when we get home." Before I could respond, she kissed me. It was a slow foray, meant to be comforting and affectionate. When she pulled away, her lips hovered inches from mine. "I just want to have sex with you really, really badly, and I want to do it in public. We came all this way so I could bring you to a sex club because you like performing in front of an audience. I don't care what kind of a club it is—I just want to give you this because you give me so much. Let me give back to you, Jonas. Please?"

How could I refuse a plea like that?

I flagged down a passing server. She wore a corset top, a chastity belt, and a thick collar around her neck. "Does this club have a swing?"

"Yes, Sir. On the second floor, we have a number of private rooms, and some of them have swings. Would you like me to see if one is open?"

"I'd like a public swing."

She tapped her lips. "Master Christian has it right now, but he's due to give an oral sex demonstration in about a half hour, so it'll be free soon. Would you like me to see if I can book it for you?"

"That would be wonderful."

"Can I get you anything else, Sir?"

I took her pad and wrote an order on it. I'd angled it so Sabrina couldn't see. I gave the paper back to the server and smirked at Sabrina. "I'll take a beer, whatever is on tap, and my lovely sub would like a glass of water so she doesn't get dehydrated."

She went off to get our drinks, and Sabrina said, "Don't you want to watch the oral sex demonstration?"

I shook my head. I'd seen many of those before. I'd even given demonstrations on that topic—and many others. Mostly I was afraid that if I took her around the club, something would capture her imagination, or worse—mine. I frowned at her in mock reproof. "You've already forgotten my oral sex prowess?" I hefted her onto the table and wrenched her knees apart.

She giggled and tried to close her legs, and I found myself doing something I'd never done before. During the course of our association, I'd discovered her reaction to different kinds of touches in different places. Sabrina was ticklish along her hips, upper thighs, and if she was in the right mood, her ribs and knees. Jumping to my feet, I attacked her, mercilessly tackling all her tickle spots. Shrieking, she tried to curl up in a ball and twist away from me, but I held her so that she wouldn't fall off the table.

I loved hearing her laugh, and so I tortured her this way for longer than I should have. When I stopped, I helped her sit up. She regarded me with wide, tear-bright eyes. "Nobody's ever done that to me before."

That struck me as sad, a tragic comment on her upbringing. "Did you like it?"

She thought for a moment. "I don't know. You utterly stripped me of control, but you do that all the time. This was somehow different."

I knew exactly where I'd erred. I should have stopped after about thirty seconds. "Too intense?"

"Maybe. It's not something I expected to be intense at all." She smoothed a strand of hair away from her cheek. "But you have a way of intensifying everyday things."

I wasn't sure if that was good or bad.

"I thought you were going to remind me of your oral sex prowess. I didn't expect to be tickled at all, so perhaps I am not a good judge of whether or not it was too intense."

"Since it involved you, your judgment is the only one that matters."

She pursed her lips. "Then no, it wasn't too intense. It was very *you*, and I like you."

I planted a firm kiss on her lips. Around us, the audience we'd attracted started to drift away. Perhaps they'd thought I had more torture planned. I didn't, not until I got her in the swing. The server brought our drinks, and I had Sabrina sit back on my lap. Many clubs had rules about where submissives could sit, but I had her on my lap because I wanted her there.

The place was growing crowded, and two other couples joined us. Mistress Kate had her sub kneel on the floor, and Master Blair had his sub sit in a chair. We chatted, sharing basic information the way kinky people do when the first meet. I pretended to be new to the scene, and so I received an earful of advice, some of which I agreed with. Sabrina followed the conversation, though she remained quiet. I let my hands wander carelessly over her skin as we talked. From the occasional shivers that would travel through her, I knew she found it arousing to be caressed like this. Since this normally didn't get her going all that much, I knew the situation contributed greatly to her arousal.

Casually I fished an ice cube from her water. Then I wound her hair around my fist and leaned down to speak to her. "I'm going to put this inside you. I want you to clench around it until it melts. Don't let it slip out."

I'm not sure what kind of reaction I expected, but her meek nod wasn't it. She parted her legs and didn't offer an objection when I moved aside the crotch of her panties and pushed the cube into her vagina. It wasn't large, but it was cold. I waited for it to hit. From the intent way she stared at the floor, I figured she was waiting too.

"You doing okay?" I spoke low so only she could hear.

"It's cold."

"Uncomfortable?"

"No, but I can see how it could be. I think it melted."

"Let's try another." This time I fished out two larger pieces. When I inserted them, I got the reaction I'd expected. She pressed her lips together to muffle her squeak.

"I have a mold that I think was to make ice cubes that would fit into a water bottle, but I found they were perfect for making dildo-shaped icicles," Kate said. "I like to tie him up, stick them up his ass, and listen to him howl."

A small tremor of anticipation went through her sub's shoulders.

Master Blair grinned. "My subbie likes to play with hot wax. I use the ice with it, of course, but she prefers hot to cold. She loves knife play as well, so I use a knife to remove the wax."

There was no way in hell I was bringing up the subjects of hot wax or knife play with Sabrina. Releasing her hair, I smoothed a hand down her back. "Since we're just starting out, we're taking things slowly."

I noticed the server waiting patiently next to me. When I gave her my attention, she said, "The swing will be open in five minutes. If you're not there when it becomes available, the dungeon monitor will give it to someone else."

Tapping Sabrina's ass, I said, "Time to tell everybody it was nice to meet them, gorgeous."

She stood, and I rose behind her. Facing the group, she kept her gaze lowered. "Thank you. It was lovely to meet everybody."

I took her to the swing, which was empty by the time we arrived. It was located in a corner of a larger room that had several stockades and sex benches in various configurations. I wiped it down, and she eyed the contraption suspiciously. "It's not what I pictured when you mentioned a swing."

"What did you picture?"

"A swing—the kind you find on a playground. I thought you'd sit on it, and then I'd get on you, and we'd swing. And you know, have sex."

"That position is possible. I can sit in the sling, you can climb on, and I can bind your wrists. It's versatile, but that's not how we're going to use it." I patted the rectangular piece of reinforced pleather. "Hop on."

I helped her, of course. Fucking height for me meant she would have to jump into it, and I didn't want to chance her missing the seat. I wouldn't mind her ass reddened, but not accidentally. Once I had her situated, I wrapped the restraints around her wrists and ankles. She tested her ability to move and found she could, though her range of motion was diminished.

"This isn't bad."

I adjusted the ankle straps, tightening the slack until her legs were high in the air. She was splayed wide open, and I realized I'd forgotten to remove her panties. I flagged the monitor. "Can I borrow your scissors for a minute?"

She chuckled as she took an industrial pair from her satchel. "Those look like expensive panties."

I had no doubt they were. "They served their purpose." Two snips, and Sabrina's panties weren't in the way anymore. I glanced up to see if she was pissed, but she wasn't. In fact, a blush of desire had bloomed on her chest and neck. I handed the scissors back to the monitor. "Thanks."

I snagged a padded chair that sat against a wall and sat so that I had easy access to her pussy. After her earlier crack, I had to remind her of my oral sex prowess. Our server came over with the item I'd ordered on a tray. She set it up on a stand. Sabrina peeked over, but her leg was in the way, so she didn't see much.

The vibrator had been cleaned and sanitized, and they'd included condoms. I'd get to it soon enough. Placing my hands on the backs of her thighs, I gave her a level look. "You can get as loud as you want, but unless you safeword, I won't stop."

She nodded, but her eyes were wide. She'd guessed that I was going to jog her memory. I started with my tongue, licking her pussy with long, slow strokes. She was wet, dripping with desire just from being restrained. I loved the way she tasted. I kept an eye on her face as I worked her to the point of frenzy. She cycled from enjoyment to pleasure, and when her face scrunched up like it did when she was close, I got rough. In seconds, she cried out.

Adding my fingers to the mix, I plunged two into her pussy and felt around for her sweet spot. Chains rattled as she tugged on her restraints. "Son of a bitch," she gasped.

We'd attracted a small crowd. Ten years ago, I would have choreographed a performance that included nipple clamps, a violet wand, vibrators, dildos, and anything else I felt would torture my sub. Now I performed simply for my pleasure and hers. I liked the crowd, but with Sabrina, I was finding they were no longer the point—they were just a bonus, like having a soft lining inside a set of restraints.

I heard murmurs of smart-assed masochist and predictions of punishment, but I ignored them. Driving Sabrina to the point of swearing meant she'd submitted to me and she'd forgotten herself. Her mouth was my reward, and hearing her curse made me hard. I played with her for a while longer, prolonging her orgasm until she realized she could grasp the chain to which her restraints were attached and hoist herself up. I followed her, and I forced her to another climax.

As I licked my fingers clean, I watched her arms slowly relax and release the chain. I bent over her and kissed her sloppily. Her juices were still on my lips and tongue, and I smeared them on her face. When I finished, I closed my hands around her upper arms. "Don't pull yourself up like that, honey. I know you're strong enough, but you could injure yourself if you're not careful, and you're not in the right frame of mind to be careful."

She twitched and flinched, and I knew she wanted to wipe the wetness from around her mouth. "You did this on purpose."

"Of course I did. Leave it alone, or I will ejaculate on your breasts, and I'll leave it there for as long as I want." I squeezed one plump globe for emphasis.

She glanced at her boobs, thinking about my ultimatum. Her tan showed through the white lace, evidence that she'd come a long way from the uptight woman I'd first met. "If that's what you want, then I'm okay with it."

My cock swelled, not at her permission, but at how thoroughly she'd submitted to me. I kissed her again, accidentally wiping away some of the mess. "Vixen. You were supposed to be shocked by that."

She laughed. "Very little that you do shocks me."

If she knew all I did, she'd be so shocked she might never speak to me again. Ice clawed at my heart, warning me that I was letting her get too close. Steeling myself, I called up the impassive façade I used as a service top. Her eyes widened, and her lips parted as her breathing sped up. I may have dented her trust by withdrawing emotionally, but it was necessary to protect us both.

Pushing my jeans down, I entered her with one hard thrust. She gasped and let her head drop back. I focused on her breasts as I fucked her, tucking the cup underneath so I could play with her nipples. I didn't count her climaxes, but I did notice that a vicious twist to her nipple when she was coming made her pussy contract harder around me.

I varied my rhythm, exchanging long thrusts for short jabs whenever I got too close. At one point, I grabbed the vibrator, threw a condom over it, and pressed it to her clit. She screamed and tried to thrash to get away, but there was nowhere to go. I kept an eye on her hands, but she was too weak to form a fist, much less pull herself up. I fucked her until her cries turned to soft utterances and whimpers, and then I pulled out. Hot jets of semen shot across her stomach and splashed onto her bra.

She watched me with a soft, affectionate, and sleepy expression.

The nice thing about BDSM clubs were that they provided areas for aftercare. Sabrina could barely walk after what I'd done to her. I cleaned her up, massaged her shoulders and hips, and held her until her muscles worked again.

On the way out, she stopped in front of a man being flogged. She stared at the scene for the longest time, enough to make me worry that she wanted to try it. Then she shook her head, the glaze vanished from her eyes, and she snuggled against my arm. "Goodness, I'm tired."

Thankful she hadn't been hypnotized by the skilled top's technique, I kissed the top of her head. "Let's get out of here. I can't have you falling asleep on the tour you planned tomorrow."

She had no trouble dropping off, but I lay awake for most of the night. Images of Sabrina in various positions danced through the darkened room, and when I closed my eyes, they only intensified. I wanted to see her skin turn pink and red from the kiss of my lash. She was strong—enough of a masochist to take everything I dished out and thank me for it afterward.

I wanted her to ask for it—beg, even. I wanted to see her features twist with pain, and I wanted to watch it turn to ecstasy.

And yet, I knew it would ruin her. She would become dependent on it, and on me to give it to her. She would learn to manipulate me so I'd give her what she wanted. It would turn her hard and cold. This past six months had been incredible. In some ways, this was the best time in my life. I would lose her soon enough; I didn't have to wreck her in the process.

And so I fought the sadist in me, beating him back down with promises that he'd be fed when I returned to work. Eventually he settled down, but his intermittent growls let me know that he wanted Sabrina, and anything else wouldn't satisfy him.

Chapter 23—Sabrina

The New Year dawned bright and fresh and full of promise. I couldn't help but feel a little deflated. Vacation was over, and it marked the beginning of the end of my time with Jonas.

I sat in my office, staring into the middle distance instead of preparing for the preliminary interview I was about to conduct with a large firm that had contacted us about putting together a proposal. I tried to quiet the ticking of my biological clock, which had never bothered me before but refused to cooperate now. Images of children with Jonas' eyes and my hair kept appearing, mocking and distracting me from the task at hand.

Minnie called to announce my appointment had arrived. I took a deep breath and squared my shoulders, preparing to meet with the people who had requested me, specifically. I wish I had been more prepared. I hadn't even looked at the name of the company. Since I'd been on vacation, Veronica had done the research and put together a report for me—a report I should have been reading instead of daydreaming about having kids.

I opened the door and froze in shock, recognizing Stephen immediately. In eight years, he had changed so little. His dark brown hair was shorter, but he hadn't been able to tame the unruly waves. It didn't take much for me to see it moving with a breeze or to remember the silky feel of it against my skin. His face was distinguished, marked by a jaw that was square and strong. He had a wide smile and friendly brown eyes.

He was only 5'8, but he commanded attention as if he were much taller.

"Stephen!" His name had not been on the account. I would notice a detail like that. Though the name "Galen Enterprises" should have

277

tipped me off. Perhaps my mind had dismissed it as correspondence from Rebecca regarding the settlement of Jonas' debt.

His smile widened, and delight danced in his warm eyes. "I wanted to surprise you. I see I was successful."

He took me in his arms and kissed my cheek, lingering a little too long. It was a comfortable feeling, though slightly alien. My entire team and my assistant watched me greet the man I'd nearly spent my life with. I ushered him into my office and tried not to see the questioning and disapproving looks five people sent my way. At least Ophelia's internship was over, otherwise she would have been sending me one too.

I'd expected a team, a contingent of several people, but Stephen had come alone. Minnie took his coat, while I directed Stephen to the sofa. He reached for my hand and pulled me down next to him. The visit had a dreamlike quality. I kept expecting to wake up to the sight of Jonas sound asleep next to me.

Minnie offered coffee. He accepted and turned to me, never once relinquishing my hand. "You look absolutely incredible, Sabrina. It's been far too long. Tell me how you've been."

I needed time to compose my thoughts because the first thing that came to mind was the number of men I'd slept with since I'd last seen him. I smiled, a genuine one that reached my eyes in a way a business smile never could. "Why don't you go first? Brett told me you moved to Chicago and got married." Other than vague statements, Becca and I hadn't talked about our families.

"I did," he said. Minnie handed him a mug of fresh coffee. "Thanks." He waited until she closed the door behind her to continue. "The divorce will be final in April."

I nodded in understanding. "I'm sorry to hear that." I wasn't sure this was actually a business meeting. I'd sent out tentative queries to Galen Enterprises for a couple months, but I hadn't heard back. "Why are you moving back, though? I thought you had established an arm of your company there?"

"I missed you," he said candidly. "We were good together."

I had a slightly different recollection, but I wasn't about to bring that up now. "Stephen, I'm married."

He nodded, running his thumb and his gaze over my wedding rings. "I heard. Jonas Spencer, former teacher. Mid-life career change and a crappy car. I hear he shows promise."

"Who is your spy?" I hadn't talked to Rebecca about those things, and she wouldn't go around discussing her clients if she wanted to have any kind of success as a lawyer. She wasn't stupid.

He laughed. "If I tell you that, I'll have to tell you how I know all about your grandfather's will and the real reason you married Mr. Spencer." He looked up, meeting my eyes, and I realized that my mother was the loose-lipped one. She'd rekindled her friendship with Dmitri Morozov, and that meant she was hanging around the old gang again, which included Stephen's parents. "When will your divorce be final?"

"Stephen." It was a warning. Not only was it a rude question, I didn't want to think about what life would be like without Jonas.

"Sorry. I wanted to lay all the cards on the table right away. We never played games before, and I don't want to start now. I sent flowers to the funeral, Sabrina. I would have divorced Kelly in a heartbeat for you."

I remembered seeing the flowers. I'd sent a thank-you note. "If you're being completely honest, then why did you want to meet me here? Does this have anything to do with business, or is this entirely personal?"

He sighed. "I thought I'd try personal first, but this is primarily a business meeting. Dad wants to explore options for expanding his market base for several of our products, and he cut our internal marketing division when we downsized. Your name made the list of finalists, though that's not shocking. You've always been creative and intelligent."

"Thank you." I was concentrating on turning our discussion to business matters, so I didn't see him lean in to kiss me until it was too late.

It was a short foray. His lips brushed against mine. They were cool and soft, just like I remembered. He was testing the waters. I drew back and rose to my feet.

"Stephen, I told you I was married." I kept my tone gentle, even a little regretful, but it had an underlying firmness that couldn't be missed.

His eyes lit wistfully. "Normally, I'd love that you're so loyal. I haven't heard you say you were in love with him."

I thought Jonas should hear something like that from me first. "It's really none of your business."

His smile grew. He thought he knew me so well. "I'll wait."

"Can we discuss what it is you want Rife and Company to do for you?"

Two hours later, I had a sizable list in my hand. Stephen's father wanted one firm to handle all of the marketing. Since Rife was a midsize company ripe for growth, they thought it was a good fit. However, they were giving eight pitch spots to different companies. Rife would receive two. My team had to take one. The other team would be chosen by my supervisor, Joy White. That meant Jared's team would get it. Another representative had met with Joy while Stephen had met with me.

Now Jonas and I would be in direct competition for an account that could make either of our careers. It wasn't the first time I'd competed with Jared, but it was the first time since I'd married Jonas. I wondered if Stephen knew about the dynamic he'd engineered?

The competition didn't worry me; the fact that Stephen seemed determined to win me back did. I didn't put it past Stephen to try to sow discord, or Jared to help. My stomach twisted, refusing to consider lunch.

I asked Minnie to set up a meeting with Joy, but Joy had already beat me to the punch. She was ecstatic, but my stomach wouldn't stop heaving. How would Jonas handle it if I won the account? I didn't fool myself by thinking I didn't have an edge. Mr. Galen had always liked me. He'd been friends with my mother, and he'd bought pieces of my grandfather's companies as he'd sold them off.

Joy had Jared there already. She knew Galen Enterprises was a large firm with diverse holdings. We usually had to nibble away at a company, account by account, until they trusted us with their prize possessions. This could double shareholder values in a very short time.

Jared smelled a rat. Accounts this lucrative didn't fall from the sky. Life wasn't that serendipitous. "Why us?"

"I've known the Galens for years, and so I've been querying them. But it won't be an easy sell. My acquaintance with them won us two spots of eight. If either of us lands this account, it will be because we earned it. My connections won't get us special treatment with the people hearing our pitches."

He wouldn't let up. "Why now?"

Because Stephen wanted to reestablish a connection with me, and this was his excuse. I used Stephen's reasoning for my verbal answer. "We're a midsize company ripe for expansion. You'll find our competitors will all be similarly sized and positioned."

I was quiet at dinner, trying to figure out how to broach the subject with Jonas. I was sure Jared had already told him and Timothy about the project. After the mistake he'd made with the cat food account, Jared had cut back on his tee time and was actually seen in the office during business hours.

Also, he had been given permission to temporarily hire another team member. I had asked him to interview Ophelia, because she was good, but I wasn't sure that was a nice thing for me to do for her. I'd called to warn her either way.

"Worried?" Jonas reached across the table and took my hand. It was the middle of winter, and I was wearing a sweater, thick socks, and slippers—even though the floor was heated. He wore his customary T-shirt and jeans, and his feet were bare. It was Tuesday, so he would leave for work right after dinner. "I promise not to peek at your notes if you promise not to peek at mine."

My tiny smile matched my laugh. Confession time. "It's Stephen's father's company. Stephen met with me today as the representative from Galen Enterprises."

"Ahhh," he said, as if it explained everything. "I wondered who would have the nerve to kiss you."

Nobody had been in the room. My jaw dropped. "How did you hear about that?"

"I guess when somebody rich and handsome lays one on somebody else's wife in front of a roomful of witnesses, news inevitably travels directly to the husband. They meant well, of course." He was amused. "Don't worry. I won't kill him for such a small token of affection."

It dawned on me that he was talking about the kiss on the cheek. I waved away his words. "That was nothing. He kissed me again when we were alone." I thought I'd sounded nonchalant, but the way Jonas' features hardened had me rethinking my delivery.

"On the mouth?"

I'd fumbled this badly and now I paused, searching for the best way to recover. I took too long.

Jonas was far from pleased. "I thought he was married and living in Chicago. From the way you've described him, he didn't seem the type to cheat on his wife."

"His divorce will be final in April."

Jonas stood, grabbing his plate. His dinner was only half-eaten. I jumped to my feet and used my body to block his exit. "I told him I was married."

Some of the tension left him. "Before or after he kissed you?"

I had to think about that one. "Both."

He evaded me, and I was forced to follow him into the kitchen. "He's still in love with you."

Maybe he was, maybe he wasn't. I wasn't about to debate Stephen's feelings with Jonas. "He's probably upset that his marriage is ending, and he's trying to recreate simpler times."

He cleared his plate into the disposal and started in on the dishes.

"Damn it, Jonas, don't do this. I didn't kiss him—he kissed me. I reminded him I was married, and then I steered the conversation toward business matters. I did everything right. You have no reason to be mad at me." I hated feeling like I had to be defensive. I hadn't done anything wrong.

He stopped, staring out the window above the sink. "I'm not mad at you."

"Then why are you acting like this?" I stomped my foot, a useless gesture. "This is why I didn't want to tell you. But it didn't feel right to keep it from you, either."

"Because we're friends." He said it quietly, as if he was reminding himself.

"Because we're lovers." *Because I love you.* "Because we promised to be honest with each other. And yes, because we're friends."

He whirled, grabbed me around the waist, and pinned me against the counter, kissing me roughly as if he sought to erase the memory of Stephen's brief brush. I gripped his shoulders to hold him close until his hands moved up my back. Then I threaded my fingers through his short curls and deepened the kiss.

It was different from the way he usually kissed me. Though it was erotic and I was wet for him, he didn't do it to arouse me. He did it to mark me, to brand me, to bind me to him. Didn't he know it was unnecessary? He broke the kiss, resting his forehead against mine as our chests heaved, starved for air.

"I have to go to work." His voice was heavy with the weight of his demons. He left the room without looking back.

Trembling, I watched him go, wishing I could call out—tell him that he wasn't alone, not if he didn't want to be.

But I didn't. I couldn't.

The next month passed in a rush. Work was insane. In addition to our regular accounts, my team was putting in extra time on the Galen pitch. They knew it meant promotions and significant bonuses for us all.

I had pulled back drastically from the way I used to control my team's every move. It turned out to be a good thing because now I could spend more time managing the Galen proposal and filling in the holes when we ran short on staff.

Jonas worked no less than I did. Where we had reached an unspoken agreement to leave work at work, mostly due to the fact that he monopolized my time when he was home, we now set aside time each night for work. It left less time for the role playing I loved to do with him, but we found time elsewhere.

We woke up earlier in the morning. We ordered out for dinner. We showered together. Most significantly, he began waking me up when he got home from work. Those encounters were invariably frantic and rough. I didn't complain. I loved it hard and fast, and I understood why he needed it to be like that. He ceased prompting me to use dirty language. He didn't ask me to speak at all. Instead, he murmured my name desperately, as if each night was our last time together. After a month of this, I began to worry. Which of his demons had him now? Was it a new one, or an old one tired of being dormant?

On a frosty Tuesday in February, restlessness invaded me, and I couldn't make it go away. I wanted him. I wanted him home, and I wanted him inside me—pounding me until he made me come. I had the vibrator he had so thoughtfully bought me, but it wasn't the same.

It was never brutal, never cruel and demanding. It did the job, but it didn't push me to the heights Jonas could make me reach. To be fair, Jonas was never brutal or cruel. He was rough when I wanted it and gentle at any other time. I secretly craved the ruthlessness I sensed in him, that he saved for his clients. The BDSM club we'd visited on our vacation was the closest he'd come to unleashing that part of him, and that wasn't even close.

I heard him come in downstairs sometime around midnight. He crept through the darkened room, disappearing into the bathroom. I knew he would shower before climbing into bed. I didn't know if I would feel his hand on my hip in invitation or if he was too exhausted to do more than fall asleep.

Boldly, or perhaps a little cowardly, I donned my silk dressing gown and followed him into the bathroom. Though it was cold outside, I still slept naked most nights. It was easier to do with Jonas in bed beside me because he generated more body heat than should be humanly possible.

In the eight months we'd been married, I had never disturbed him in the bathroom after he worked. I wanted him to have time to lay his demons to rest. However, that hadn't been happening since Stephen had reappeared. Though Jonas refused to acknowledge it, I knew having my ex back in my life affected him.

He wasn't in the shower as I expected. Instead he was bent over the sink, gripping the edge so hard his knuckles had turned white. Lost in thought, he stared at the floor and didn't hear me come in. He was fully dressed, but the hard, lean muscles of his shoulders and arms were visible through the thin cotton of his shirt.

Tentatively, I caressed his shoulder. He tensed under my light touch. "Jonas? What's wrong?"

"Nothing," he said tightly. "Go back to bed."

I didn't buy his lie. I leaned against the counter and watched stress lines deepen around his mouth. His head turned slightly, and I knew he was looking at my legs. The dressing gown only fell to mid-thigh.

"At least tell me what you're thinking about."

Without moving, he answered, the strain in his body reflected in his voice. "I'm trying to convince myself I should masturbate and leave you alone."

"I'm awake. You don't have to leave me alone."

"Go to bed, Sabrina." Finally his gaze met mine, and I saw the misery there, the internal battle ravaging his psyche. I had no idea why he was fighting it—I was more than willing. "You have no idea what you're asking."

"No?" I challenged him because I couldn't help myself. I wanted more from him, and he withheld vital pieces of himself from me for no good reason. "Then tell me."

Slowly, his eyes darkened. When he was aroused, they were liquid gold. Now they reflected bronze. He caged me with his arms and that look. I was instantly wet. My nipples hardened and my breasts swelled, yearning for the feel of his palm and the pinch of his fingers. Anticipation flowed through me, and I could barely breathe. I struggled to refrain from leaning close and kissing him. Something in me knew he wouldn't be able to handle it right now. It wasn't what he wanted. He hadn't meant to turn me on.

"You won't like it."

My lips curled with a wicked smile. I wasn't about to run away from this challenge. Something dangerous and reckless in his demeanor beckoned to something primal in me. "Why don't you let me decide?"

The bronze light intensified. I'd never seen him like this. He leaned closer, and I felt his lips tracing the curve of my neck, though their pressure never materialized, leaving me longing for the physical contact.

"I want to hurt you, Sabrina. I want to turn your skin pink with my flogger, heating it until you cry out for mercy that I won't give. I want to see tears streaming down your cheeks because you ache with pain and wanting, and you know you have no control over any of it. I want to hear you beg until I can't stand it anymore."

He finally looked into my eyes. "I want to hear you say you belong to me and no one else. I want to hear you say that no one can make you feel the way I make you feel, that nobody can give you what I can. I want you to scream my name because it's the only word you know, because it's *everything* to you."

I think he was hoping to scare me, and he did a little. I held his gaze, searching for hate, anger, or malice, but I saw only his need. I'd never been able to deny him, and I wanted this as much as he did, maybe more because I was in love with him and I desperately wanted him to be in love with me.

Slowly I loosened the satin belt of my short robe and let it fall open. Rolling my shoulders ever so delicately, I released the fabric. It slid down my body with the whisper of a caress, taking Jonas' attention with it.

His eyes feasted on the sight of my naked body for a long time. As potent as if he was actually touching me, he caressed the curve of my hip, the lines of my inner thighs, and my calves before changing direction. He lingered on the sight of my breasts with their pebbled nipples tipped toward him, begging for his mouth.

When he met my eyes again, their color had returned to olive green. He shook his head, a tiny, desperate movement. "You have no idea what you're asking."

"I trust you." The words came out on a breath colored with need, but they were completely true.

"It will hurt, Sabrina." Desperation was back.

Now I understood the look he gave me when I misbehaved during our bondage activities. He wanted to discipline me, but he was afraid of hurting me in a way that would irrevocably damage our relationship.

"I know the safeword," I said, throwing him a cheeky grin that quickly morphed it into something infinitely more seductive. I assumed the role of the bored housewife because I knew he needed to pretend it wasn't just him and me. I traced his lips with a seductive finger. "I've been a naughty wife, Jonas. I've amused myself with the delivery man, the pool boy, the gardener, and random men from the street. I've been to sex clubs—without you. You're away so much, you see, but now you're back, and you know everything."

He stopped breathing. I let my finger wander, and I knew I was trailing fire in my wake.

"Better than anyone else, you know what kind of a woman I am. Did you send those morsels as gifts? Have you come home now to remind me that nobody measures up to you? That nobody can come close to making me feel the way you can?" I had him, but he hadn't realized it yet. "Tie me up. Flog me. Make me come, Jonas. Make me scream your name because it's everything to me."

"If you go to bed now, I will forget all of this." He trembled with the effort to refrain from touching me.

I shook my head. "No, you won't, and neither will I. You told me not to be ashamed of what turns me on. You told me it was okay to want this, to want you like this." As I spoke, I let my fingers stroke his face and trail south. "I've been waiting for you, Jonas. I ache to feel your touch."

He stilled my fingers with his iron grip before I could release the snap on his jeans.

Without a word, the desperation vanished, as did the pain and anguish. His dark olive eyes regarded me without compassion or mercy as his hands encircled my wrists. He pinned them behind my back and kissed me savagely.

I was so wet, and my legs trembled. I tried to press my body to his, but he threaded his fingers through my hair and pulled me back, breaking the kiss. Still gripping my hair, he forced me to my knees. My heart sped up in anticipation. If he were merely going to bind me, I knew what came next. Because this was all new, I had no idea what he was going to do, and that was the best part.

Faced with evidence of his erection at eye level, an impish impulse kicked in. Licking my lips hungrily, I ran my hands up his inner thighs, encircling the area of his arousal wantonly. Usually that would be enough for him to open his pants and press me toward him. This time was different. He lifted me, tossing me over his shoulder and knocking the air from my lungs in a long whoosh.

I protested, pushing myself up after we cleared the doorway. "You know you want me to suck your cock." Words like that from me never failed to excite him, but they fell on deaf ears this time. For the first time in a long time, I felt helpless, and my clit swelled at my predicament.

He threw me on the bed so hard I bounced, but he didn't follow me down. "Don't move." He turned to leave.

"Or what? You'll punish me?" All of my bravado was false. I may have agreed to let him flog me, but the thought petrified me. I'd seen it done twice now, and though it fascinated me, I was still afraid of the unknown.

The look he threw over his shoulder promised much. "I'm going to punish you anyway. If you move, I'll punish you even worse."

When he returned, I had moved, and not just in an effort to adjust my position. He caught me in the bathroom door, having just come from hanging up my robe. I may have dropped it in an effort to be sultry, but I hated leaving clothing on the floor. Having been the victim of my exasperation on the topic often enough, he knew exactly what I was doing.

Ripping the robe from its hanger, he tossed it to the middle of the bedroom floor where it would taunt me. Then he set me gently on the edge of the bed with my feet on the floor. All business, he ignored everything except his task, which was to secure leather bindings to my wrists. He cuffed me to the foot of the bed.

"Really? Because I hung up a robe? Don't be petty." I don't know why I goaded him, perhaps it was the role or maybe it was anxiety. Before I could utter another word, he forced a ball gag in my mouth. I glared at him furiously, promising retribution.

He smirked, mirroring my earlier impudence. "One day, you'll learn, but I hope that day doesn't come anytime soon." And then he left the room again.

When he tied me up, he invariably left me to stew, though usually in a far less comfortable position. Waiting was part of the game, and I had developed patience. Tonight, trepidation made the wait unbearable. I heard the echo of the back door closing, and I nearly wept. He couldn't leave me here like this. The robe on the floor I couldn't reach became unimportant. I was wet and curious and waiting.

Relief flooded through me when I heard the door again. Moments trickled past until at last, he was back with me, tossing an unfamiliar duffle bag on the bed. He unzipped it and rummaged around. The odor of canvas and leather wafted to me. Because of the angle, I couldn't see what was in the bag, but I didn't have to. This was the bag he took to work.

He lifted out a flogger. The handle was bound tightly in black leather. The end that would soon be licking my flesh was also black leather, a bundle of leather falls that spilled from the handle in a riot of promise. Turning it in his hand, he adjusted his grip easily. He held it in front of me, rotating it so that the individual strips of leather tumbled over one other. "I've been around the world with this thing, my dear wife. I've tested it on hundreds, making sure it was properly broken in for you."

I stared at the thing, caught between the fear common sense told me I should feel and the anticipation I couldn't help but feel.

He opened his hand, balancing the handle on his palm. "It's perfectly weighted, and the grip is comfortable and familiar. You need to be taught a lesson, my dear." Abruptly, he closed his hand around the handle and released my handcuffs with his other hand. I hadn't even noticed he was holding the key, something that had always caught my attention in the past. He removed my gag.

"I want to hear you scream. Now stand up, darling. You're going to take this without the benefit of restraint."

Now I was afraid. I'd assumed he would tie me down. After all, I was wearing his cuffs. In my fantasies, I was always tied down for this part, if not the whole thing. I panicked. "You would do this to me? Your wife? I married you when no one else would have you. I let you have me whenever you wanted and however you chose, and this is how you repay me?"

Okay, maybe that was going a little too far, but I was completely unnerved by the fact he had released the handcuffs. It was one thing to be tied down, to passively accept what he dished out because I had no choice but to trust him. It was something else entirely to stand there and take it, to become an active participant. No matter how much I wanted it, no matter how much I had fantasized about it, I didn't have the courage to follow through like this.

Then I saw a glimmer of satisfaction in his eyes. The bastard was doing this on purpose. He was counting on me to safeword. Well, I could play this game at least as well as he could.

Ignoring my nakedness, I stood proudly and glared at him with a disdain I did not feel. "You can't do this to me. I made you. I can break you." My words forced him to use his skills to dominate me other ways. If he refused to tie me up, then I was going to make him use force.

A slow smile curved his lips, but it didn't reach his eyes. My stomach muscles clenched, and I was aware that I had become uncomfortably moist. My breath was shallow, but I didn't look away from the promise he made and kept from me.

He threw the flogger on the bed and took one step, closing the distance between us and forcing my head back in order to keep challenging him. His fingertips traced a path down my arms that made me tremble. I thought he would imprison my wrists, but his hands jumped to my waist and he spun me around to face the post at the foot of the bed.

It was shorter than the posts on the headboard, reaching only to the height of my shoulders. His hands closed over mine, a gentle caress when I wanted rough treatment. With infinite tenderness, he placed my hands so I gripped the post. He lifted my hair and secured it out of the way. I felt his breath on my neck below my ear where he knew it would drive me insane with the need for his touch.

"Hold on, darling. This is all you're going to get." He brushed a feathery kiss across the sensitized skin and stepped back, snagging his flogger. "Now, this is a precision operation, as I'm sure you know." He had dropped all pretense of intimacy. His tone was brusque. "If you move too much, you'll mess up my aim. If you tense too much, it will hurt even more. I don't wish to harm you, my sweet, fickle wife, so relax and be still."

I think the waiting was the worst part. Until that point, I thought I was so good at waiting. It was a mind game, one I had learned to play, or so I'd thought. The time it took for him to find his grip and tell me to hold still stretched my coiled nerves. If he kept this up, I would come at his first touch.

The first blow landed on the back and side of my right leg. The second landed in the same place, but on the left side. They came so quickly I didn't have time to process the first, much less recover from it, before he struck a third, fourth, and fifth time.

It stung.

It was nothing like I thought it would be.

Air escaped my lungs in a low, brief moan which I didn't think could be heard over the swish of the falls through the air or the sound it made smacking against my virgin skin. My hands tightened on the smooth, polished antique wood.

The stinging moved up my body, claiming my ass, my hips, continuing on to torture the sensitive skin of my upper back. The blows came too fast for me to anticipate them. I tensed all over and the singing of the leather stopped.

I still felt every sting of the lash. Every nerve was awake and protesting, every muscle supporting the picket line. Tears welled in my eyes, and I couldn't make a sound.

He moved closer, and I could feel the brush of his clothes against my skin even though he wasn't touching me. The fingertip he ran from my shoulder to my thigh and back up the other side nearly sent me over the edge. I couldn't squelch one miserable moan. If I touched my clitoris now, I had no doubt I would come.

"Relax," he directed. "You're no good to me if you don't relax."

I tried. I willed my muscles to respond, but they were granite. Ironically, I knew he had barely begun. According to Ellen, clients typically lasted for fifteen to forty-five minutes. This was pathetic. I strengthened my resolve, but it didn't relax me.

He kicked at my feet, forcing me to widen my stance. Reaching under me, he found my wetness. I trembled, my entire body shaking at his touch. He pressed my swollen nub hard, and I came. It was a small release, but it allowed me to relax.

The throbbing hadn't subsided when he started again. The stinging, which had begun as hundreds of separate lines, merged into one mass. I was on fire. Dropping my head against the bedpost, my entire body relaxed into the rhythm he set. My hips moved back and forth, wanting more but afraid of asking for fear he would stop.

He moved around me and the tips of the falls stung the front of my thighs and my stomach. They were light licks, I knew, but my skin was more sensitive there. My moans and gasps came louder, and I knew he could hear them over the sound of the falls whistling through the air.

Then he stopped, and I cried out in protest. I turned my head to see him reach into the bag for another flogger, a shorter implement that looked like it packed a wicked punch, and a length of rope. He crossed to the rounded area of the room where a window seat ringed the bank of windows. Gossamer curtains covered them, but anyone standing outside the house could see our silhouettes. Most of the lights in our room were on.

I had removed the chandelier an earlier occupant had placed in that spot because the idea of that much glass hanging from the ceiling in my bedroom didn't sit well with me. I'd left the anchor behind. Jonas pushed an end table over and looped the rope through the anchor.

He beckoned to me. "Come here."

Willing to do almost anything to make him continue, I obeyed.

He handed me both ends of the rope. "Hold this." They fell to a point that was still above my head. Reaching up, I grasped one end in each hand.

He put the table back, and then he picked up the longer flogger. The falls of this one were longer and thinner. There were fewer of them, but I knew it would sting more. Lifting his eyes to the rope in my hands, he smirked. "Don't let go."

The rope was to anchor me and keep my arms out of the way. He had no intention of restraining me, of giving me that release. Like he had in that club in Lexington, he was going to make me work for it. "Bastard." I muttered the word under my breath, but he heard it anyway.

He laughed. "Oh, honey, you truly have no idea. When you shower, when you dress, and every time your clothing shifts against your skin, you will remember exactly how much of a bastard I am."

He began, working me with a feverish intensity. I thought the first flogger hurt, but it was nothing compared to this. He spared no part of me. My skin burned. A glance down showed my flesh was streaked pink and red. An inferno smoldered inside me, a chemical bomb set to explode if only he would light the fuse. Every once in a while, he would stop the flogger and smack the sticklike thing against my ass or upper thighs. It thudded against my muscles, and the pain penetrated deeper. Then he would resume using the flogger, never giving me time to acclimate to the rhythm.

I begged. I sobbed. I pleaded with him, apologizing profusely, but forgetting why. The reasons no longer mattered. Just when I thought I could stand no more, peace came to me in a foggy cloud, and I submitted completely. I had submitted to him before. Each time, the release had been soul-deep, incomparable to anything else. This time was even more so.

I heard the dull thump as he tossed the flogger onto the window seat. Cold hands shocked the hot skin of my waist. "Let go," he said.

"I have," I sighed.

He chuckled gently, and the rumble sent waves through my skin, though his chest touched me only slightly. Tears blurred my vision. I felt his hands pry my fingers loose and lower my arms. He leaned me against him, putting his arms around me. Without hesitating, he slid his hand between my legs.

He slid several fingers inside me, and I rode his hand hard, scraping my clitoris on his palm until I came. I cried out his name, and tears coursed down my cheeks, mingling with the ones that had already dried.

He released the tie holding my hair out of the way and kissed me, the gentle affection in direct contrast to what he had just done and how he usually kissed me after he spent the evening punishing clients.

It was my undoing.

He picked me up, hooking his arm under my legs and cradling me against his chest, and he carried me to the bed. Laying me down, he caressed me with his eyes and his words, praising me as he undressed. "That was beautiful, honey. You took your punishment with grace and dignity."

He lay down on top of me, settling his weight so that he slowly pressed me into the mattress. His touch was soft, reverent, but my skin was so sensitized that every caress was amplified. Because he hadn't restrained me, I didn't feel trained to keep my hands away from him. I let them explore, reveling in my power to exact gasps and moans he hadn't wanted to give.

I made love to him. I wasn't sure he was aware that he was making love to me too, and I wasn't about to bring it to his attention.

Chapter 24—Sabrina

In the morning, he examined every inch of me. The redness had mostly subsided. A few places on my thighs and ass were still pink, and I had three long bruises from the instrument he called a cane. Though the evidence was fairly absent, my skin was still tender and extra sensitive. I felt it when I showered. My muscles, which I'd tensed after he'd warned me not to, were sore. When my clothes shifted over my body, which happens far more often in the course of a day than I ever thought it could, it was a reminder of his touch.

And I was tired. We were both going on three hours of sleep, which I knew made him irritable. I also suspected he had realized that not only had he made love to me, but I had made love right back to him. Both were enough to render him a bear.

I ordered takeout to be delivered right after we arrived home, and I sent him to bed when he finished eating. He tried to argue with me, but he didn't have the energy. Of course, that meant he woke up at four in the morning ready to start the day, which meant he woke me up for a couple of hours of slow love. I didn't mind at all.

Ellen invited me out that Friday night. We made a point to have a girls' night out at least once a month. However this time we were alone. Ginny and Lara were out of town, Amanda was taking her turn with the family flu, and Samantha was traveling for work.

"Let's go to my club," Ellen suggested as she picked me up. We were both dressed to kill and freezing in the icy February wind. "We won't have to pay for drinks."

"Okay, but you can't work while we're there." Every time we went to her club, she invariably ended up having to deal with some kind of problem. "What do they do when you're not there to put out fires?"

She laughed. "I hired a new manager. She's pretty good, so we shouldn't have our night interrupted."

She took me to the VIP lounge, and we both ordered our usual drinks. She was partial to tequila shots, and I tended toward anything with coconut rum. I liked hanging out with Ellen. She wasn't demanding or high-maintenance. I didn't have to watch what I said around her or worry how she would take something. Ginny was the same way, but both Lara and Amanda could be easily offended.

After we gossiped for an hour about the usual stuff, she turned to me with that expression she got when she wanted to broach a subject and she wasn't sure how I would react.

"So," she began, "what's going on with our boy?"

Though I really hadn't seen him much, Jonas seemed fine to me—at least, as fine as he'd been. "What do you mean?"

"He has some serious angst issues."

I knew what she was talking about. Every night when he came home from work and woke me up, his angst was palpable, yet we didn't talk. It bothered me that he wouldn't come to me with his problems. "What did he say?"

"He hasn't said anything," she shrugged. "I've barely seen either of you in a month."

"Things have been hectic at work. We've both been keeping insane hours." I explained about the competition for the Galen Enterprises account, amazed he hadn't told her already.

"He told me about that." She frowned thoughtfully. "I get the feeling it's something else."

I shrugged and shook my head. "I have no idea. He seems fine at home."

Just then, her floor manager ran up and whispered urgently. I sighed. I knew we should have gone somewhere else. Now she would look at me apologetically and promise to be right back. Very few emergencies took under twenty minutes. The woman left after a rapid back-and-forth.

Ellen turned to me. "Can you come with me?"

That was unexpected. "Why?"

She pursed her lips. "There's been an accident. Things like this happen once in a while. It's why we make clients sign consent forms and pay huge membership fees. But we still send home everyone involved for the night. It's protocol."

I thought she wanted me to spy on Jonas. I was against it for two reasons. First, it wasn't nice to spy. If he wanted me there, he would invite me. Second, I would probably be jealous of anyone I saw him flog. I opted for obfuscation. "What kind of accident?"

She looked me in the eyes, her expression grave. "Jonas drew blood from a client. No one has been hurt, and our house doctor has cleared the client for release, but I'm still sending him home."

My jaw dropped, and not just because he'd made someone bleed. "He's going to be pissed."

"Yes," she confirmed. "He's been pissed since you guys got back from vacation. I figure that if you're with me, he might go quietly. Maybe you can take him home."

"Ellen, he doesn't know I know what he does."

"Don't you think this has gone on long enough?" Ellen rolled her eyes when I pressed my lips together, and then she tugged at my arm. "He's in the break room. I can take you there through the bar, so if the two of you want to keep up this little pretense, you can."

We found him seated in a chair across the room, watching the door. No doubt he planned to ambush Ellen as soon as she arrived. He was wearing a different shirt than what he'd put on to leave the house. Momentary shock registered when he saw me, and then he snarled at Ellen. "There is no reason for me to leave."

"Policy," she said placidly.

He shot a glance at me. "Nothing happened."

"Great," she said, her voice dripping with sarcasm. "Then we cut our girls' night out short for no reason. Thanks."

"Ellen," I said. The warning and sympathy in my tone were real. The angst issues she'd mentioned were in full force. "I'm sure Jonas didn't mean..." I let the sentence trail off, waving my hand in the air vaguely. "...whatever it is that happened."

"Still," she continued, narrowing her eyes at him, "policy dictates you go home. No exceptions. I'll remind you that getting snarky with me has never worked in your favor."

He glared at her, but she merely regarded him impassively. I reached out my hand to him. "Jonas, let's go home. Where is your coat?"

"Elle, be a dear and get my things." My presence didn't seem to mitigate his anger.

She left, and we were alone in the room together. He studied me in a way that set my heart pounding and not in a good way. I didn't entertain the idea that he might want me later because I knew, given his mood, I'd be fortunate if he spoke to me at all.

The ride home was long, icy, and desolately silent.

In the kitchen, he threw the keys to his car on the counter and perched his hands near the waist of his jeans. "How long have you known?"

I wasn't about to play games with him, but it did take me a minute to do the math. "Six months. Since before we went to Kentucky."

"Ellen told you." He was looking for someone to blame.

"If it helps, I found out you were lying to me by accident. I thought you were cheating on me with Sophia. Ellen set me straight."

"You met Sophia?" Steel was softer than his question.

I closed my eyes, realizing my error. I'd identified a second friend who'd betrayed his trust. "Briefly. She was nice." I moved closer, laying a hand on his arm. "Does it really matter? It's out in the open now. You don't have to hide what you do, and I won't have to wonder how in the world a bartender pulls in so much money."

"You... You don't care?" That question was much softer, but he was looking at his shoes as he asked it.

"I do care. I care about anything you do, especially something that takes you away from me three nights each week." My voice was surprisingly steady given the way my emotions strangled me.

He looked me in the eye. "Why have you never said anything?"

I drowned in the olive green and took a chance. "You once told me you have some pretty dark secrets. I figured out there were mainly three. But they're your secrets. I wasn't going to pry or force you to tell me things you didn't feel comfortable sharing with me. I hoped one day you would trust me, know me well enough to understand that I can handle your secrets."

He tensed. "Did Ellen show you or tell you what I do? Is this why you let me flog you? Because you thought it was what I wanted?"

"You did want it." I choked down a laugh. He had been very descriptive about exactly what he'd wanted. "But I wanted it too. I've fantasized about it for some time, but I didn't want to tell you because then you would know I knew one of your secrets. Oh, Jonas, I wanted you to confide in me when you were ready. That's why I haven't said anything."

He swallowed, and bitterness twisted his lips. "You said three secrets. What were the other two?"

"Helene, obviously. But we've already dealt with that issue." Mostly. His third secret was a direct result of the second.

He jolted me out of my thoughts with a prompt. "And the third?"

I bit my lip, stalling in the hope he would relent. "Wouldn't you rather deal with that when you're ready? I really don't want to force you on the last one." Especially since he was nearly there.

"Sabrina."

I responded to his note of desperation, knowing it was a mistake and unable to stop myself. "You're terrified of falling in love with me."

His eyes glittered hard, but his voice was soft. "I'm not in love with you."

I dropped my hand from his arm and turned away. I couldn't let him see how his words cut. "I'm aware." Painfully so. I didn't mind thinking it in the confines of my head, where optimism could creep in to tell me there was time. Patience, as he had taught me, always paid off.

"You're not in love with me." It was an order, a directive, not an observation.

I couldn't lie to him. "Yes, I am." Tiny cracks formed in my heart. They hurt.

"No, you're not." Someone who didn't know him would have been deceived by the softness of his voice. I wasn't.

"Just because you're afraid I'll crush you like Helene did doesn't mean you get to dictate my feelings." He caught my arm, but I refused to face him. I knew I would lose it if I saw the coldness, the remoteness that he wore for armor. "I liked you from the beginning. I've loved you for longer than I care to admit." It had most likely started with the rosebush.

"You love the way I make you feel." He talked to me as if I were a child to whom he was explaining a common misconception. *Thunder is a noise; it can't hurt you.* But watch out for that lightning. "You love that I set you free, that I taught you how to let go and enjoy sex, to have fun with it. You can have that with anyone, Sabrina. Stephen seems interested."

I looked at him then, incredulity rendering me momentarily speechless. "I'm not a confused teenager with a crush on her English teacher," I shot back hotly. "I don't have stars in my eyes. I'm painfully aware of your faults."

"Sabrina," he began.

"I know the difference between love and sex." It came out much louder than I intended. He could try the patience of a saint, and I was at least six incarnations away from anything approaching sainthood.

The hard remoteness took over. I didn't have a chance of reaching him, not that I thought this was the right time to have this discussion in the first place. "I never meant for this to happen. I never wanted to hurt you." He was quiet, but I could see he had already arrived at a decision. The cracks in my heart multiplied. The pain was crippling. "Time away from me will give you perspective. I will wait until June to file for divorce."

The hand around my arm loosened and dropped away. With the posture of a defeated man, he left the kitchen, heading toward the stairs. His intention didn't register. It sounded like he said he was leaving, but it looked like he was going up to bed. Wordlessly I followed and found him in the closet. He tore through the racks and drawers, tossing his clothes into suitcases and stuffing them into bags. "I'll come back for the rest when you're not home."

Tears coursed down my cheeks, and I choked back a sob. "You don't have to do this. I'm not asking you to leave." I desperately didn't want him to leave. I couldn't breathe. I could barely think.

He froze at the pain in my voice, but he didn't look at me. Maybe it would have been his undoing. "I can't do this, Sabrina. Maybe you are in love with me. Maybe what you feel is real and not the product of our role playing, but it doesn't matter either way. I can't stay here and lie to you. I can't hurt you more than I already have."

"Then don't go." I begged, sagging against a row of drawers, powerless to stop him. Each article of clothing he punched into a bag pummeled my heart, chipping away at something slowly shattering. I thought breaking a heart was a faster thing, a momentary process. I didn't know it kept breaking. "Don't run away from me, from us."

"There is no us!" He yelled his denial, as if the volume would give it validity. His skin reddened, ruddy in fury.

I wasn't afraid of him. I'd never been afraid of him. I'd been afraid of falling for him, of what he might make me feel, but never of him. My legs gave way, and I slid to the floor. In a trance, I watched him pack his arms with his things and try to step over me.

He stopped in mid-stride to stare down at me. I can't imagine how desperate and pathetic I must have looked. "I can't love you the way you want, the way you deserve. There are things broken inside me that have nothing to do with you, and you can't fix them. Nothing can fix me. Go back to Stephen. He never stopped loving you."

Then he was gone.

Time took on vague and ethereal qualities. I don't remember moving, but I woke in my bed to find my mother lying next to me. Instantly, I was transported back to when I was five and Ginny's dad had left. I had been bereft at having lost the only dad I'd ever known. It would have been better for me if he'd died.

When Ginny was with her dad, Mom always let me sleep with her. I was a poor sleeper in those times. Ginny and I shared a room by choice. We had always been close. I knew when she wasn't there, and I knew why. I'd cried a lot.

I don't know how many times I slept, or sobbed, or just laid there in a stupor, but every time awareness returned, Mom was there to smooth my hair back and hold me.

I have indistinct impressions of being forced to eat soup and use the bathroom. I sat on the edge of the bed, wondering when I'd changed out of my dress, and wrinkled a brow at my mother. "Don't you have a flight to catch this morning?"

Tears sprang to her eyes, but didn't fall. She shook her head. "My trip was cancelled. Don't you worry about that. There's nowhere else in the world I'd rather be."

Later I lay on the sofa with my head in her lap and no tears left in my body. Forgotten memories flooded back. I had several moments of clarity in that time. The first came then. Memories of Mom, holding me when I cried, and more significantly, when I couldn't cry. Taking mother-daughter art classes with me, even though she had no attitude for it. She still had a collection of badly-painted pottery which she displayed with pride. My name was printed on the bottom of every piece in blocky, childish handwriting.

She used to hug me all the time. When had she stopped? When had I begun to see her as cold and bitter? She was neither. The bitterness was the same shyness I had that people so often mistook for something haughty and aloof. I'd pushed her away when I was a teen. It began with asking her to drop me off a block away from school, and it never ended. She'd only respected my wishes, just as I had respected

Jonas'. I saw it clearly. My mistakes stretched before me like the Yellow Brick Road.

"Mom?"

"Yeah, baby?"

I used to get so mad when she used terms of endearment. Even a month ago, it made a place deep inside me shrivel up to escape the implied bond. "I'm sorry."

"For what? You haven't done anything."

Her voice soothed me far more than I deserved. "For being such a horrible daughter."

"No, sweetie, don't you think that for a minute." The sob she swallowed made it worse. "You're a fabulous daughter. You're intelligent, sensitive, and kind. Not a day goes by that I don't think of you and almost cry from the pride I have in you."

"I've thought unkind things about you," I confessed.

She laughed, a sad kind of laugh, and tucked my hair behind my ear. "Every daughter thinks unkind things about their mothers. It's part of growing up, of forging your own identity away from her. As wonderful as Grandma was, honey, I thought some really nasty things about her. Some of them I said to her face. I was always thankful you refrained."

The second moment of clarity came when I was alone. He thought I was like Helene. He'd passed unfair judgment on me after he swore he'd never judge me. Our physical similarities had made him see her when he looked at me. Logic fled. The clouds cleared briefly. I went into the bathroom and found shears in a vanity drawer. I gathered my hair into a ponytail, secured it with a band, and cut it off.

The third moment of clarity was Ginny's doing.

I woke from a nap to find her sitting on the edge of the bed next to me. I sat up, astonished to see her. She had a competition in Madrid this weekend. What was she doing here?

She laughed. "I missed the stench of Paris. So I came to see you. It was very thoughtful of you to recreate it for me in your bedroom." She turned on the light next to the bed.

I shielded my eyes from the brightness. I hadn't remembered the reading lamp being that brilliant. "What the hell are you talking about? Why aren't you in Spain?"

"I won second place." She stared at me without smiling. "The competition ended Sunday. Today is Wednesday. You don't remember having this conversation before, do you?"

Dumbfounded, I stared at her. "It's Saturday."

"Four days ago, it was Saturday. Today is Wednesday. You haven't showered in five days, big sister. Time for a soak. When by soak, I mean shower. The filth on you isn't something in which you should bask."

She helped me out of bed. My legs were weak, and I leaned on her for support. In the name of sisterly love, she grabbed one of my bathing suits and joined me in the shower, washing my hair at least four times and directing me in how to wash the rest of my body until I snarled at her to get out.

I did feel better once I was clean and dressed. Ginny was drying my hair when Mom came in and said, "Oh, thank God. I tried getting you in here, but you're far too heavy for me to carry."

Mom looked tired. She had dark circles under her eyes, and she was uncharacteristically pale.

"Mom, are you sick?"

Tears made her eyes glisten. "Yes, Sabrina. When my baby girl is in so much pain she can't get out of bed, it makes me sick."

"Maybe you should go home and get some rest," I suggested. "I'll be fine."

I wasn't fine, but I was alert, and that was an improvement. Mom left for a couple of hours because Ginny promised to babysit me. I didn't bristle in the slightest over the way they talked about me like I wasn't there. My full capacity for logic and rational thought took a little longer to return. I was depressed.

It was during one of Ginny's turns that Ellen came to see me. I was on the sofa in my room, which I hadn't left in a week, trying to work a crossword puzzle.

She looked me over critically before sitting in the chair next to the sofa. "You look like shit."

"Thanks," I said, unsure how to respond. Why was she here? What had Jonas told her? I defaulted to my manners. "You're looking well."

Rolling her eyes, she slapped the arm of the chair forcefully. "Are you going to let him win this? I never thought you were the kind to roll over and play dead."

I closed my pen in the puzzle book and set it on the end table Jonas had stood on when he'd rigged that rope to the hook in the ceiling. "I'm sorry, Ellen. I don't quite know what you mean."

"I'm on your side," she said. "Don't use your manners on me." I was going to tell her that I didn't know what she was talking about whether or not I phrased it politely, but she jumped to her feet and

301

continued. I hadn't seen that much movement near me in a long time. "Jonas, Sabrina. I'm talking about Jonas. Your idiot husband."

I flinched. Ginny and Mom had assiduously avoided mentioning his name. "He isn't here."

"I'm well aware of that," she said. "He's at my house, but not for long. Ryan is on the verge of kicking his irritating ass out."

I didn't see what it had to do with me. "I didn't make him leave."

"I know," she said. "He told me. I had to drag it out of him, and it took a few days, but I think I got all the details. I won't make you relive them."

"Thank you."

"Ginny tells me you haven't been to work in a week. You've got a huge bouquet of flowers down there from Stephen, who I understand is an old boyfriend of yours."

I had trouble following simple conversations. Ellen was impossible. I waited, hoping she would eventually arrive at a point.

She plopped down next to me. "Can I have the flowers?"

I shrugged. I really didn't care.

"Great. I know the perfect place for them." Suddenly, she threw her arms around me and hugged me so tightly I wondered how my bones didn't break. "You can't let him do this, Sabrina. You can't let him go."

Stiffening, I pushed her away. "I can't force him to stay," I said when I felt my dignity had been restored. "I don't want him on those terms."

"He's going to take forever to come around if you don't do something," she warned.

"He's filing for divorce in June, on my birthday." I recited the fact without thinking about what it meant.

She clapped happily. "Then we have time. Let's start with your hair. What in the world possessed you to cut it?"

I regarded her solemnly. "I'm not Helene." It made perfect sense to me.

Ellen cried.

Shocked, I unbent enough to rub her shoulders soothingly.

"That bastard."

Funny—I had called him the same thing, but I hadn't meant it at the time.

In the end, Ginny brought over a friend who she swore could work miracles with hair. I had chopped it so unevenly that I ended up with a pixie cut. My head felt naked, but they assured me it was an attractive look.

The reflection in the mirror wasn't that bad. If my face hadn't been gaunt or my eyes so sunken, it would have been an attractive look. Ginny brought food, and Ellen kept up a steady stream of chatter. Between the two of them, they managed to distract me for a long time.

Ellen had a plan, which she didn't reveal to me until Sunday night. She was right that I couldn't afford to take all this time away from work with my big proposal only a week away. Since I almost never ran into Jonas at work, I wasn't overly worried about going back to work for that reason.

Due to my unexpected leave, my team had been on their own for a week. I didn't know what unpleasant surprises awaited.

Ellen and Ginny agreed that I needed to focus on work. Ellen would work on Jonas. I objected, and she promised to leave him alone. I think she said it more to placate me than because she meant it. The bouquet of flowers she took from me appeared on her dining room table, complete with the card from Stephen.

Chapter 25

Jonas

I'd called Melinda as I left the house. She'd seen this coming, and I'd discounted her warning. "She needs you."

"She needs me? What's wrong?"

"She's in this too deep. I had to leave. I'm sorry. Can you go over there? She shouldn't be alone right now."

"I'm on my way."

I slept all weekend, waking only to go into work Saturday night. Neither Ellen nor Ryan bothered me. I gathered that Ellen thought Sabrina and I had a fight, and I was just staying here for a few days to cool off. I'd been pissed that Sabrina knew, and that Ellen had told her, but my anger was gone, leaving exhaustion in its wake. That wasn't surprising. I'd been burning the candle at both ends for months. It was bound to catch up with me eventually.

Monday, I bumped into Randall on my way into the copy room. He was on his way out, but he smiled when he saw me. "Hey, buddy. How's Sabrina doing?"

Though I didn't know Sabrina's meeting schedule, I knew she always touched base with her team members. I frowned. "She's fine."

He nodded. "So it's just a cold. That's good to hear. Give her my best."

He left, and I peered after him. The last image of her, crumpled on the floor of the closet, her face frozen in shock and misery, flashed through my mind, pummeling me with guilt and other emotions I'd rather not identify.

The next day I managed to avoid the members of her team, but I overheard Jared complaining that she was out again. On Wednesday, Veronica caught me in the break room.

"Hey there, Jonas. How is Sabrina? What did the doctor say?"

I scowled into my empty coffee mug. "She's fine."

Veronica snorted a short laugh. "She can't return a phone call or an email. She's not fine. Is it a nasty virus with lots of puking and diarrhea, or is it worse?"

This wasn't like Sabrina. She was made of stronger stuff. We'd been together less than nine months. It wouldn't take her long to get over the end of our relationship, and there was no way she would allow personal problems to sideline her professionally. And I wanted her to be fine. It would prove that I was right.

"Something like that." I got up and left the room. My manner was abrupt, but I couldn't sit there and be grilled about Sabrina. I'd wronged her. I'd fucked up, and she was paying the price.

Ellen ambushed me when I got to her house. I set my laptop bag on the bed in the guest room where I had been sleeping, and she came in behind me. I loosened my tie as she closed the door. "You're not my type."

"Please. You couldn't even get me with roofies." She perched on the edge of the bed and faced me, worrying her lower lip with her teeth.

I jerked my head in the general direction of rest of the house. "Where are Jake and Ryan?"

"Infant swim class. Ryan wants Jake to know self-preservation swim techniques if we're going to be spending so much time over at your house. You know, the one with the pool?"

Rolling my tie carefully, I set it in a drawer. "It's not my house."

"Jonas, why are you here? I've left you alone to pout long enough, and Sabrina's not answering her phone or returning calls. You can't honestly be this upset about her finding out you're a Dom."

"Honestly I'm relieved she found out. Now I can stop pretending, and so can she. It's been a tedious year."

"You're an ass. If you were really okay with it, you'd be at home teaching her how to be a good submissive."

"I don't want that kind of a relationship." I'd been over this with Ellen a hundred times, especially when she'd tried to set me up with submissives over the years. "What I had with her was good until you interfered."

Standing, Ellen snorted. "Six months ago, I showed her what you do. She's known about your kinky side for a long time, and what you have with her has only been getting better."

My temper flared. "I'm not talking about that—though I am pissed at you for betraying our friendship. You had no right to share that with her." A thought occurred, and I closed my eyes. Sabrina hadn't said she'd seen me in action. "You *showed* her? She saw me at work?"

Ellen shrugged. "We were at the club, and Sophia joined us for a drink. Sabrina nearly freaked out when she started connecting the wrong dots. She thought you were having an affair with Sophia, and then she thought you were having sex with your clients, so I took her up on the catwalk to show her what you were doing. She told me she'd fantasized about you spanking her. I told her to talk to you about it, but she said she wouldn't say a word. She wanted you to tell her yourself. She wanted to wait for you to trust her enough to confide in her. God, I think she was in love with you even then."

"She's not in love with me." I growled through clenched teeth. "She's in love with the way I make her feel. Before me, she'd never had an orgasm. She thinks I'm magic because I can make her come. She'll find someone else who doesn't suck in bed, and she'll realize I'm nothing special."

"You're being a stubborn asshole. Go back to her. Talk about this. You know that what you've been doing isn't enough. You want more—you *need* more—and so does she. It's a perfect match."

"I don't want more." I shouted. Ellen was the most exasperating person I knew, and at times like this, I wondered why the hell I kept her around as a friend. "I wanted *less*. We agreed that we'd screw around for one year, and then we'd go our separate ways. But you went and put ideas in her head, and now she thinks she's in love with me and if she waits long enough I'll love her back. She's hurting because you couldn't leave well enough alone."

"Don't you blame this on me, clueless motherfucker. *You* left *her*. She was never going to throw you out. At the end of the year, she would have asked you to stay, and you know it. You're afraid. You're terrified that she's going to hurt you, so you're hurting her first. That's a chickenshit move, dickhead! She's perfect for you, and if you let her go, you deserve to be alone."

It's what I wanted. Being alone had been my plan from the moment I'd caught Helene in our bed with another man. He'd tied her up using my restraints. But Ellen didn't seem to care what I wanted.

Ellen set her hands gently on my shoulders. "Jonas, give her a chance. She's a good person and a born submissive."

Sabrina was definitely both, and she deserved better than a yearlong fling. I closed my eyes and leaned my forehead against hers. "Elle, I fucked up."

"I know you did, but it isn't too late. Apologize—on your knees if you have to. Plant another rosebush. She gets dreamy-eyed whenever she looks at the one you put in last summer."

"It's too late. It's been too late since you gave her the address of a fetish club in Sydney instead of a sex club."

Ellen leaned back to see me better. A frown line brought her eyebrows closer together. "What happened in Sydney?"

"You admit sending us there on purpose?"

She shrugged. "It has a great reputation. I've met the owners many times."

"You knew I didn't want to take her to a BDSM club."

"Maybe I was hoping you'd extract your balls from your ass and admit you did want to take her to a BDSM club. You had fun. She told me you put her in a swing."

"Yeah, and you put her in a BDSM club so that I would have that image in my head. You wanted it to haunt me, and it did. I wanted to tie her to a St. Andrew's Cross and flog her. I wanted to hurt her, to see her cry. I wanted to break her down because I knew it would be precious and beautiful."

"Well, you are a sadist. From what you've told me, she's a masochist. Those are some pretty huge compatibility points."

"I did all those things. I flogged her. I even used a cane." She'd unraveled, revealing herself to me in a way she'd probably never dreamed possible. She'd given me a gift I didn't want, a gift that should only be given to someone who could treasure it.

Ellen's face lit with hope.

I turned my back on her and took off my belt. "I ruined her. I fell into Domspace, and I sent her to subspace. I left before she could become addicted to it, before she could figure out how to use her position to manipulate me."

That hope turned to incredulity. "I'm struggling really hard to control the impulse to punch you in the gut. You can't possibly be this much of an idiot."

"I don't love her. She deserves to be with someone who does."

Ellen headed for the door. She paused with her hand on the knob. "She definitely deserves better than what you've given her. Maybe I'll help her with that."

She slammed the door behind her. I glared at the place she'd been, seething with anger and jealousy at the thought of Sabrina with another man—because I knew Ellen would find her a Dom who would give her what I couldn't.

Sabrina

Work was a pleasant surprise. Randall enveloped me in his very large arms as soon as he saw me. "You *were* sick, weren't you?"

"We weren't sure," Veronica chimed in. "Jonas didn't seem to know anything about it, and he became very rude whenever anyone asked."

"I like your hair," Clare said quietly. "It looks really good on you. Different, but good. It makes your eyes look bigger, not that you needed help in that department."

Minnie and Ty stared at me. I smiled weakly. "Thank you for the flowers," I said, "and the card. I'm sorry this happened now, with so much at stake."

"Don't worry about it," Minnie said in the tone that meant she knew more to the story than everyone else and she wasn't about to dish. "We took care of everything. I have some papers for you to sign, and some personal emails to answer, but we've handled everything else."

I searched her face, wondering whether or not to be happy about that. The control freak in me was chomping at the bit. This was the only aspect of my life where I still felt some measure of control.

Looking at the rest of them gathered around me like I was a long-lost friend, I felt guilty for more than abandoning them.

Ty spoke up at last. "I stopped by to see how you were doing a couple of times."

I hadn't known. Mom either didn't tell me, or I had been too out of it when she had.

"Your mother is a lovely woman," he continued.

I closed my eyes and looked away. It would have to come out sooner or later. "Jonas and I separated. He moved out."

Ty put a heavy hand on my shoulder. He had asked Vanessa to marry him based on my apparent success. They'd tied the knot on New Year's Eve, when Jonas and I were exploring foreign sex clubs. "I thought so."

Before they could start drowning me with their condolences, I turned to Minnie. "Give me about ten minutes, and then meet me in my office." I turned back to my team. "Then I'll be around to catch up on things."

They had made tremendous progress during my absence. Minnie shared with me how hard each of them had worked to make sure we weren't behind when I returned. The week passed with incredible speed. I was very pleased with our presentation. Knowing the Galens like I did proved to be quite useful in making decisions about what to include and which direction to take.

We traveled to the Galen building, which was just twelve blocks away, to make our case bright and early Friday morning. This was the second day of proposals. We were the second group to present that day. Jared's had been the first.

Jared had hired Ophelia as his temporary team member. She bounded over to me as we passed in the lobby, thanking me again for recommending her and gushing over my hair. I was able to smile and accept the compliment without self-consciously feeling for what I had donated to Locks of Love.

When she released me, I glanced around, my eyes automatically searching out Jonas. I hadn't seen him since he'd walked out on me.

The color finished draining from his face as I watched. The sight of my absent tresses hit him like a physical blow. He had loved my hair from the beginning.

Our eyes met briefly, and then I turned away to give my team last minute instructions. They surrounded me on purpose, creating a protective barrier. Veronica squeezed my hand hard. I caught myself before I shot her a dirty look. It made me stop thinking about Jonas, and it helped me to stop shaking.

The group around me didn't stop someone from politely shoving through. Stephen took both my hands in his and kissed my cheek. "I'm not part of the board, so I have no say in this decision," he warned. "I just wanted to wish you luck."

I had no trouble giving him a genuine smile. "You were just looking for an excuse to kiss me again."

"Guilty," he said, reaching out to touch my hair. "I like this. It reminds me of when you cut it short to make the Varsity swim team sophomore year."

I smiled nostalgically. "It did improve my time." By a whole four seconds, which did get me on the team. I knew from the outset that I had neither the talent nor the drive to swim for college or try for the Olympics. It was fun and it kept me in shape. I had immediately begun growing my hair back out.

Stephen escorted us to the conference room we would be using. When he left, Ty gave me such a curious look that I snapped at him. "What are you looking at?"

"You flirted with the son of the CEO." He sounded impressed.

"I told you I've known the Galens since high school."

He grinned. "You didn't say Junior had a thing for you. We could have dressed you up in sexier clothes. He may pretend he doesn't have a say, but I'll bet he does."

I blushed. "Knowing Mr. Galen, Stephen will have a significant say in the decision, but not a vote. And Stephen doesn't have a thing for me. We dated in high school."

Clare raised a brow.

"And college," I added.

Veronica laughed so hard she snorted. Randall muttered something under his breath. I think he was thanking God.

The presentation went extremely well. If we landed this account, it would be because my team earned it, not because Stephen was entertaining some belated fantasies about getting into my panties, which I was definitely wearing these days.

The next week crept by. We still had plenty of work to do, but not nearly the amount we had become used to handling for the past six weeks. Then Stephen called to let me know his father was notifying Joy White that we had been awarded the account. They wanted to take me to lunch to discuss timelines.

It wasn't an intimate lunch by any stretch of the imagination. In addition to Stephen and Mr. Galen, Joy and Mr. Rife rounded out the crew. Stephen and Mr. Galen met me as soon as I exited the elevator in the restaurant's lobby.

Mr. Galen took each of my hands in his and kissed me on the cheek, just as Stephen had done. He treated me with warmth and respect. He asked after my mother and Ginny. He expressed his condolences about my grandfather, with whom he had golfed regularly until Grandpa had declined too much to enjoy the game.

He directed me to call him by his first name, which I found weird because I'd called him by another name my whole life.

The only unexpected thing to happen was that Mr. Galen— Steve—insisted on naming one of my team leaders. Apparently, Jonas had singularly impressed him in the presentation. When Stephen told Mr. Galen that Jonas was my husband, Mr. Galen's dilemma was solved. Surely I wouldn't mind putting my own husband on the team?

With Mr. Rife smiling indulgently as if he were personally responsible for the way things turned out, I swallowed my pride and nodded. Jonas was brilliant and talented. I would cope.

Ellen jumped up and down and actually turned a cartwheel in the middle of my living room. A well-executed cartwheel. "What?" she said when she caught my expression. "I took twelve years of gymnastics."

I did not share her excitement. "I don't know why you're so excited. It's going to be torture."

"For him," she smiled. In that moment, I hoped with all my heart I never did anything to piss her off. Every insidious piece of her soul showed in that smile. "He has to watch you every day, knowing he could have had you, but he blew his chance. Even better, he has to do what you say because you'll be his boss. Oh, that's going to chap his ass."

I probably shouldn't have told Ellen the news before Jonas knew or had a chance to decide, but I foolishly thought she'd help me through my panic attack. I knew Jared wouldn't have said anything to Jonas today, even though he was supposed to inform him of the promotion. I knew that job would fall to me, and I did not relish it.

"You don't think that's going to torture me more than him?"

She waved away my concern. "The jerk is in love with you, but he's too busy trying to keep his head from slipping out of his ass to admit it. Now he's gotta watch you take meetings with Stephen, go out to lunch with him, laughing, flirting. You have to flirt with him."

"That's not fair to Stephen." And I didn't like games.

Her shoulders dropped and so did the starry look in her eyes. "You have to play dirty in this game if you want to win. I've already started. He saw the card Stephen sent with the get-well flowers."

I hadn't seen the card, but I knew Stephen too well to think he'd written anything unusual or suggestive. "I don't want to win that way. That isn't how you ended up with Ryan."

"No," she admitted. "Ryan didn't have this problem. He knew his number was up the moment he met me. Jonas lacks self-awareness."

I slumped back on the sofa, defeated. "I wish you could whip him into shape like you did when he nearly flunked out of college."

She narrowed her eyes at me. The look that inspired fear in the hearts of millions—or at least mine—appeared on her face. "Come on. I'm taking you to the Service part of the club. Sophia should be able to help with some of that stress."

I winced. "Sophia?" Sophia had said she wouldn't hold it against me that I asked her if she was a prostitute, but I didn't know her well enough to evaluate her sincerity.

"She's really very good. I go to her when I need a good flogging." She had her coat on before I moved. "Ryan is too much of a submissive to deliver for me. Get moving. Sophie leaves early tonight."

"I don't know," I said. The idea appealed to me more than I let on. The release of total submission for non-sexual purposes was something I desperately needed. It was still too cold to swim. I really needed to enclose the pool. "What if Jonas is there? I don't think I could—"

She stopped me with a wave of her hand. "He won't be there. I fired him."

I gaped at her. "Why?"

"It was time he moved on."

"But he needs that job. It helps him emotionally."

Ellen exhaled hard. "I guess he's going to have to do some soul searching and come up with another way of coping because this one is no longer working for him or me. Now drop the subject."

I wondered how Ryan got anywhere arguing with her because I knew he prevailed in as many disagreements as he lost. She seemed to have a knack for barreling right over me.

Sophia squeezed me in as her last client of the evening. Dressed in a simple black lace baby tee and jeans, she was incredibly lovely. Her long black hair was pulled back in a ponytail and her large eyes were accented with dark eyeliner, giving her a harder, more severe appearance that did not hide her softness.

However, I wasn't there to admire her exotic beauty. Ellen handed me over and disappeared. I hadn't changed after work, so I still looked like an executive. Sophia wasn't impressed.

"Take off your clothes," she said. "Strip down to your underwear."

I didn't have a problem stripping to my panties in front of strangers. Having sex in front of people all over the world changes one's perspective on things like that. My problem was that I wasn't wearing underwear. Of all the days to take up the habit again, I'd picked this one.

Sophia regarded me stonily. I recognized the expression as one Jonas and Ellen both used. I stripped to my bra and thigh-highs. Before I could fully stand back up from removing my shoes, she had me cuffed to a padded bar. It was thick enough so that my torso curved around it and my feet could still reach the floor.

Curiously, I was not aroused. If Jonas had done this, I would be drenched. If he were watching, I would be drenched. Because it was just the two of us, it changed the whole dynamic.

She didn't hesitate before she began flogging me. She also wasn't gentle after she'd warmed me up. It hurt worse than what Jonas had done because it was so impersonal. At first, I held it in. The sting of the lash came predictably after I heard it whistle through the air. I tried to concentrate on relaxing, but my body wouldn't cooperate.

She concentrated on my upper thighs, butt, and shoulders. Her purpose was not to turn me pink; it was to make me submit. When the burning pain became unbearable, I cried out. The sting concentrated, forcing tears. Gradually, I relaxed, submitting to the leather stinging my skin. The person wielding the flogger didn't matter, only the kernel of peace inside me that steadily grew as hot tears bathed my cheeks, dripping onto the padded bar where I rested my head.

Then it was done. My wrists were free. I dressed.

Sophia squirted water from a bottle into her mouth and leaned against another piece of equipment. "You'll want to rub something into those welts," she suggested. "Otherwise they could become bothersome. You have sensitive skin."

I found it ironic that she could say that after having spent twenty minutes flogging me. Ellen returned with a timing that made me think she had watched. She led me to a locker room and handed me a small bottle of cream.

"Come out when you're done," she said. "We'll get a drink."

Sophia joined us for the drink. Neither woman mentioned Jonas, and I was very grateful for that. He was on my mind enough.

It was difficult to sit. I constantly shifted in my seat, finally settling on the very edge of the chair so that my body made minimal contact.

Sophia laughed at my discomfort. "You're a natural sub, you know that, right? You can come back and see me anytime."

"We'll have to get you a membership card," Ellen said, sipping her herbal tea. "There's an application. I assume you'll want to run a tab."

"You think I'll be back?" I asked, laughing. "I can barely sit. I can't imagine working like this all the time."

Sophia leaned closer. "Most of it will be gone by tomorrow. I gave you a really nice line on your upper thigh that should stay for a few days. Let me know if it works for you."

I opened my mouth to ask, but realized what she meant in time. If most of the evidence was gone, I would have freedom of movement. By leaving me one welt where she had, I could lean it against the edge of a desk. The pain would relax me. I wondered if I could capitalize on this to masturbate, something I still couldn't seem to do successfully unless I was sore. Jonas had left me crippled in so many ways.

The next morning, I had Minnie summon Jonas for a meeting. Jared was supposed to have notified Jonas of the opportunity for promotion, but nobody had seen Jared around since it had been announced my team won the account. His streak of responsibility had come to an end.

Minnie escorted Jonas into my office. I was on the sofa, studying the timelines and to-do lists scattered over my coffee table. Winning the account was proving to be a phenomenal amount of work. It was so large that it would involve the restructuring of the entire advertising department. I would have five teams to manage. Each team would have a leader who reported to me. I had to figure out which teams would handle the different pieces of the campaign.

Additionally, we would move to a new floor, which was being remodeled according to my specifications. I wanted a lot of open space, a few comfortably appointed conference centers, a digital media lab, and several offices. The technology would be state-of-the-art and easily upgradable.

I crossed the room to greet him, offering him my hand to shake. This was a business meeting. Nothing personal was involved. "Thanks for coming. Can I offer you something to drink? Coffee?"

He shook his head, staring at me as if I had lost my mind. He didn't shake my hand. "No, thanks."

Minnie gave me the look that let me know she would be available if I needed anything and left the room, closing the door behind her.

Jonas eyed me suspiciously. "What's going on?"

"Why don't you have a seat?" I indicated the sofa and chair grouping at the other end of my office, trying not to recall the number of times we'd had sex there.

"Sabrina," he began.

"This is business, Jonas. You're aware we won the Galen account."

His jaw ticked and his lips pressed together. "I meant to congratulate you on that, but then, you knew all along you would get the account."

"Don't be nasty," I chastised. "You know that's not true."

"I saw him kiss you before your presentation. Nobody else received the same treatment." He sounded jealous. I wished he would sit down and have conversation like a normal person.

Leaning against my desk caused me to wince. I had forgotten about Sophia's gift. I used it now to help me focus on the reason he was here instead of his apparent bitterness. "Both Stephen and Steve are like that. Over time, you'll see them greet dozens of women the same way, especially ones they've known since childhood."

"Are you sleeping with him?" The fury in his olive green eyes was palpable.

I massaged the space between my eyes where a headache was forming. I leaned harder against the desk and breathed into the pain. "For the love of God, Jonas, that's none of your business, but since you're so intent on being a jerk, I'll clear the air."

Dropping my hand and fisting it on my hip, I glared at him. "I am not sleeping with Stephen. Just because you told me to fuck someone isn't enough of a reason for me to actually do it. He is an old friend and now our client. And you have no right to question me either way. You walked out on me, not the other way around. This is how *you* wanted things to be. Let it go."

He turned on his heel to leave, but I wasn't finished.

"Don't even think about it," I growled at him. "I didn't ask you here because I want to discuss the mess that passes for our relationship. I asked you here to offer you a job. Steve Galen, the CEO, was impressed with you. He wants you to head one of the teams, specifically the one in charge of the feel-good campaigns."

He froze. Without turning, he said, "You called me here to offer me a job?"

"And a promotion. You'll have your own team. You would have to report to me, of course, but you'd be free to develop projects as you see fit." I couldn't resist a jab at him. It was a low blow, but he pushed me to it. "And seeing as how you're down to just the one job now, you might appreciate the raise that comes with it."

When he turned back to me, he had a wry smile on his face. "You've been hanging out with Ellen way too much."

I ignored his comment. "There's a staffing meeting at two. I'll need an outline of how many people you think you'll need to hire and their expected duties."

Bitterness crept into that tight expression. "You're assuming I'll take the job. Don't I get some time to think about it? This is a big decision."

He had a point, but we didn't have the time. "Jared was supposed to have this conversation with you yesterday. You were supposed to have an answer for me by this morning."

He stuck his hands in his pockets. It was a casual gesture that reminded me of better times. He wore one of the many green silk ties I'd bought him. This one had a subtle diamond pattern that caught the light when he moved. I liked how it brought out the green of his eyes. The tawny color was something I liked to save for just the two of us. I wondered if he'd thought of me when he picked it out that morning.

He nodded knowingly. "Jared went out for lunch yesterday and was picked up for a DUI. He won't be back for a while. I don't know if Joy can save him this time. Apparently it wasn't his first offense."

I hadn't known any of that, but it explained why I hadn't been able to get in contact with Jared. I took a deep breath and continued with the informal job interview. "If you're going to work for me, I expect that we maintain a professional working relationship. There will not be a repeat of the way this started out today."

While I was laying down the law, I leaned back against my desk, inadvertently bumping my welt. Jonas noticed the way I stiffened briefly from the contact. He narrowed his eyes with that look he got when he studied me thoughtfully. "Sleep wrong?"

"I'm fine," I said, brushing away his concern, which brought a fresh pain all its own. "Do you think you can check the baggage at the door?"

"What did you do?" He wasn't going to let it go.

I crossed my arms over my chest. "After all, we'll be divorced in a few months, both moving on with our lives. This job is a great opportunity. You shouldn't let your fear of me keep you from it."

"You went to the club."

"I go all the time with Ellen," I said dismissively. Sometimes I hated how single-minded he could be. "Can you focus on this conversation? This is your job interview. You and I don't have a personal life in common anymore."

"We'll always have Amsterdam," he said. He'd meant it as a joke, to lighten the mood. It had the opposite effect. The bliss of Amsterdam hit me hard, not just the club we had visited, but of all the touristy things we had done and the nights spent in his arms. I had been in love with him then. It had meant more to me than it had to him.

"I'd like to forget Amsterdam. And Sydney," I said quietly, masking my pain inexpertly. "We work together, nothing more. Feel free to pretend we just met this morning." I turned away to avoid seeing his reaction, but I wasn't fast enough, catching the flash of regret that made me think he still cared.

It kept me up at night.

Chapter 26

Jonas

"You took her to the club. Who serviced her?"

Ellen sat on the floor across from Jake. She stacked blocks, and he knocked them down, laughing hysterically the whole time. "Say hi to Uncle Jonas."

He looked up at me with a huge smile lighting his face. Two teeth showed. Though he could say hi, he chose to open and close his hand in a wave.

I smiled back, though it wasn't enough to quell the jealous tidal wave that kept slamming my stomach. "Ellen, don't do this to her."

Ryan came in from the kitchen. He had a towel thrown over a shoulder. They'd eaten dinner already, and he was cleaning up the mess. "Jonas, I put a plate of food in the fridge for you."

"Thanks."

"Maybe you two want to go into the kitchen and talk about this. I'll take Jake. It's time for his bath."

Ellen frowned. "You did the dishes. It's my turn to bathe Jake." Jake clapped and scrambled to his feet, chanting something that might have been "bath, bath."

"Mistress, I live to serve you."

"Don't be a martyr. You worked all day. You need some down time."

I waited for them to finish their negotiation. Though Ryan did, in fact, live to serve Ellen, they had an even division of household and family duties.

Ryan spread his hands wide. "If you head upstairs, Jonas will follow you, and when you two yell, Jake cries. I'd rather him have a good bath experience. He'll have plenty of time as he grows up to listen to you yell at Jonas."

I wasn't sure I liked Ryan's assessment. "I'm not planning to get in an argument, and we aren't that bad."

"Normally, no. But your head's messed up, and Ellen finds it frustrating. Given the way you led off your greeting, I'm predicting a fight." He scooped up Jake and turned away. "If you feel like rewarding me later, Mistress, I will be ever so grateful."

I peered after him as he disappeared up the stairs. "You let him get away with too much."

Ellen got up from the floor and headed to the kitchen. "Yep. He's manipulating me, all right. That what he does—manipulation. He spends all his time thinking about ways to make me do what he wants and absolutely none thinking about my needs, our son's needs, or even your needs. He's one selfish motherfucker."

Her tone was so dry it almost started a brush fire. She got her point across, so I held my hands up in defeat. "Okay, sorry. He's one of the few who has good intentions. I know that."

"You know Sabrina's a good one as well. She's hurting, Jonas. Go to her. Talk it out. She needs you."

From what I'd seen today, she didn't need anybody. I extracted the plate Ryan had put away for me and slid it into the microwave. The light inside went on, and my mood blackened. "She seemed fine when I saw her today, and she doesn't want to talk about our relationship. She made that very clear."

"This wouldn't have been when she was offering you a promotion, was it?" Ellen poured herself a glass of wine and sat at the kitchen table. "Because even I know she doesn't mix her personal and professional lives. She gives me nasty looks when I take her to my bar and the employees need me to deal with crap."

I whirled to face her. "She told you about the promotion before she talked to me?"

Ellen shrugged. "We're friends. You wanted us to like and accept her. We did that. Unlike you, we can admit we love her and want her to continue being part of our lives. You don't get to control when my friendships end."

"Wonderful. You're choosing her over me." I saw red when I thought about Ellen's threat to help Sabrina find someone she deserved. I set my heated plate on the table. "Who topped her, Ellen?"

"That's none of your business. She needs it, Jonas. I watched her submit, and it was stunningly beautiful."

Fury wrapped around my cold heart, but I forced it away. I had no right to be upset. Sabrina needed to move on with her life. "I'm going to kill whoever it was. I will find out, you know."

She arched a superior brow. "No you won't. I meant to tell you—you're fired."

I'd been shoveling mashed potatoes into my mouth, and I froze. "You can't fire me."

"I can do whatever I want. You're done at City Club. You're finished as a service top. You're going to have to find another outlet for your sadistic impulses."

Rage took over. In an uncharacteristic display of temper, I threw my plate at the wall. It smacked hard and food went everywhere. "You think taking that away from me will force me to go back to Sabrina? Well, you're wrong. Hell will start hosting ice skating competitions before I make that mistake. I may have started ruining her, but you're finishing the job. In six months, she's going to turn into Helene, and this time it'll be your fault."

Ellen eyed the mess with detachment, though I knew she was moments from kicking me in the balls. She settled for screaming at me as loudly as I'd screamed at her. "First, you didn't make Helene into a heartless bitch. She was always that way, but you didn't want to see it. None of us liked her. We put up with her because we love you, not because she had a single redeeming quality. Sabrina is nothing like Helene. I thought she was at first—we all made that mistake—but once we got to know her, we realized she's just introverted."

"She wasn't meant to be in the lifestyle." Though I stood less than two feet away, I roared at Ellen.

"You're so far down the wrong road, you can't even see where you left the path. God, you're an idiot. Maybe I'll mentor Stephen in how to be a Dominant. She deserves someone who will treasure her loyalty and submission, because you sure as hell don't."

I'd pushed her at Stephen. I wanted her to fall for someone else so she'd forget me, so why did the idea of him as her Dom feel like a kick to the gut? I lashed out at Ellen. "You fucking bitch."

She drew up to her full height and set her fists on her hips. Leaning closer, she spoke quietly. "Coward."

I left, not because I was a coward, but because I was tired of arguing with Ellen. She was frustratingly stubborn, and I didn't have the patience to deal with it. I snagged my suitcases and started pouring my clothes into them. Thanks to Sabrina's love of shopping, I had a shitload of stuff to pack.

"Are you going back to Sabrina?"

"No, but I can't stay here anymore. I don't love her, and I never will, but you can't seem to get that through your thick skull. You don't want me to work at the club? Fine. I'm finished there. It doesn't do it for me anyway. I have to work with Sabrina, and I'm going to make the best of it. We were friends once, and we can at least be collegial now." I smashed one suitcase to zip it and started on the other. "You want to be friends with her, then be friends with her. You want to find someone to train her and ruin her, then find someone to ruin her."

She laughed nervously. "You've lost it."

The image of Sabrina on her knees in front of a faceless man slammed into my brain. I punched clothes into a gym bag. Turning to the closet, I saw her standing there in a swim suit, water dripping down her body as she smiled a greeting. I stepped around the image, grabbed an armload of hanging clothes, rolled them into a ball, and shoved them into the bag.

"We had an agreement. We had rules and boundaries. I never wanted to hurt her." Pale and drawn, Sabrina hovered in front of me, shorn of all that glorious hair. I knew exactly why she'd cut it.

"I know you didn't." Ellen took the bag from me and set it on the floor. "It's not too late, Jonas. You can make this right."

I looked at Ellen, a world of misery buzzing through my head. "That's why I left—to make it right. I don't have anything to give her."

The next few months passed quickly. I tried to make things as easy as possible on Sabrina. I kept things courteous and professional, even when I caught her looking at me with soul-crushing sadness in those bottomless brown eyes. I argued with her a lot, mostly because it had the effect of focusing her mind on work.

Our new office space was completed and we moved up four floors. I had an office of my own, though I mostly spent time in the open area where my group had their desks. It was easier to collaborate that way.

Every couple weeks, I would notice Sabrina walking stiffly or fidgeting to find a comfortable way to sit, and I knew she'd visited Ellen's club. Sophia had let it slip that Sabrina was seeing her, and I decided I was okay with that. Sophia was an excellent service top, and she didn't let her submissives—she kept several—come to the club. I also knew that my family still saw Sabrina. After leaving Ellen's, I'd moved into my parents' basement and I'd caught my mom making plans that included Sabrina several times. She'd look at me, daring me to challenge her, but I never did.

Ellen and Ryan saw Sabrina all the time, and they didn't bother to hide it from me.

And I swallowed my pride whenever Stephen Galen showed up to meet with Sabrina. Invariably he took her out to lunch and kept her out of the office for the rest of the day. I reminded myself that she was happy. When she smiled, it reached her eyes, and that was all I wanted—her happiness.

Sabrina

Now that I was separated, I almost never had an evening to myself. If Ellen didn't ask me to do something, then my mother, Ginny, or Amanda and Sam did. I even spent time with Jonas' parents. Stephen and I had lunch or dinner at least twice each week. We mostly talked about business, but personal things crept into the conversation. I'd known him since I was fourteen, and it was easy to fall back into the simple friendship we'd once shared.

On the day Stephen's divorce was final, I took him out to celebrate. We had drinks. After the toast, he leaned over and kissed me. I let him. His lips moved softly over mine, seeking a spark that never came. He pulled back before it came to the point where he might try to deepen it.

He gave me a lopsided smile. "That answers that question."

We'd spent a lot of time together, and I'd wondered whether I would let him take our relationship in this direction. "It certainly does."

Our eyes met, and we laughed. I lifted my glass. "To friendship."

He clinked his glass against mine and echoed my sentiment.

Ellen continued her campaign to convince Jonas he was making the biggest mistake of his life. She worked on him by dropping hints about what I might be doing and with whom. I had more faith in his stubbornness and inability to cope with the lack of control being with me brought than in the possibility of his eventual enlightenment, especially as time passed. He became too comfortable around me at work, striking up conversations about topics that didn't relate to the job. He interrupted an important phone call to ask me the name of the restaurant in Lexington where we had dined before we'd visited the sex club.

Stephen began sending flowers to the office and dropping by to take me to lunch. He always made certain to visit with Ty, Randall, Clare, Veronica and Jonas. After all, each was in charge of developing ad campaigns for Galen Enterprises. Then he would kiss me on each cheek and whisk me away to lunch.

I regretted my inability to keep anything from Ellen. She was wickedly good at making me tell her things I didn't mean to divulge. The subtle tightening of Jonas' jaw whenever he saw Stephen made me feel guilty for my part in the game. It brought me a fleeting joy to know he still cared for me on some level.

Ellen spent time educating me on the customs of a D/s relationship. The more she told me, the more I realized Jonas and I had engaged in that dynamic, to some degree, from the beginning. We hadn't used any of the protocol, but Ellen explained that she and Ryan changed their protocol depending on their moods or the environment. Over the years, they'd developed signals so they'd always have clear communication.

"Communication," Ellen had said, shaking her head. "That's not Jonas's strength."

He did fine communicating—as long as it was something he wanted to discuss.

One warm June day exactly two weeks before my birthday, I arrived home from work to find Jonas waiting on the patio in back. Well, near the patio. He had opened the garage to access the gardening tools we'd amassed as he'd put in flower beds last summer.

He was digging around near my rosebush.

A shot of pain went through me, arcing like an electrical burn through my torso, and a dozen Sunday mornings watching him fool around in the dirt replayed in my mind. I had an irrational fear that he was taking the bush back as part of the divorce settlement. By the time

I had parked my car next to his in the garage and made it to the patio, I was angry. When I spoke, my words came out harsher than they should have.

"What are you doing?"

Without looking up, he said, "Weeding." He was wearing the same suit he'd worn to the office. The striped red tie made his eyes turn gold. His mother had picked it up last weekend when we'd gone shopping. He poked at the ground a few more times, expertly dislodging several clumps of weeds with his trowel. "And feeding. Your service isn't keeping this up."

I looked at the rosebush clinging to the trellis for support and envied it. "I haven't had a chance to talk to them about it. I don't know if they'll do flowers."

He wiped the trowel on the grass and disappeared into the garage. I followed him. "What are you doing here?"

"I tried to see you this afternoon, but you were at a meeting with Stephen. You weren't back by the time I had to leave, so here I am." His delivery made it seem like it was normal for one of my employees to wait for me at my house.

Logical, maybe. It just didn't make sense. He replaced the trowel and washed his hands.

"I have something to give you. I didn't want to leave it on your desk because I didn't know if you would return to the office before coming home, and I know you'll want some kind of explanation with it."

He dried his hands and pulled an envelope from his pocket, which he handed to me. I stared at it blankly.

"You'll have to open it to read it."

I wasn't under the impression that it was personal, and I was right—sort of. It was his letter of resignation. My heart stopped. Strands of ice formed in my veins, and their sharp points jabbed me painfully. I stared up at him, shock and amazement communicating a question my lips couldn't form.

He shifted, regret flashing on his face before it strengthened with resolve. "I've done a lot of soul searching in the past few months. Something about being thirty-five and living in your parents' basement will do that to a guy. Advertising is a job. I'm good at it. I've proven that I can be successful doing pretty much anything I want. I needed to do that."

He'd done it, all right. He was easily one of the best employees I'd ever had and one of the best advertising minds with which I'd worked.

"I'm going back to teaching. I had my final interview this morning, and they offered me the position. It's at the same school where I worked before. I'll be making less. A lot less, but it's what I want to do. Teaching fulfills me in a way nothing else can."

That explained why he had been late to work today. Numbly, I nodded. I understood what he was doing and why. The pain that prevented me from speaking was because I knew I had no chance with him anymore. He was breaking all ties to me.

"I failed at something too." He reached out to finger a strand of my short hair, his expression regretful. It had grown over the last few months, and now it was chin-length. "You are nothing like her, Sabrina. I never meant to hurt you. I hate what I did to you. I wish I could take it all back."

I shook my head, denying his line of reasoning. I did not regret our time together. As painful as it was now, he had changed my life in profound ways. I wanted to tell him that, but I couldn't speak without choking on the heart I thought had already been safely broken.

He seemed oblivious to my struggle. "You knew me better than I liked. You saw inside me, and the mess didn't make you run in the other direction. You were right about everything. I am desperately and irrevocably in love with you, only I was too terrified to admit it. And now it's too late."

He kissed me on the cheek and turned toward his car.

Hope surged through me, suspending all pain. "Where are you going?"

The muscle along his jaw tightened. "Home." The single word hung in the air, an unasked question.

My jaw dropped at his stupidity. "I've waited how many months for you to finally realize you love me, and this is all I get? A kiss on the cheek?"

The look of confusion that crossed his face morphed into one of incredulity. "What about Stephen? It's no secret that the two of you have been spending time together."

"He's a friend. You'll have to get used to that."

He pointed, a vague gesture. "Ellen said you were more than friends."

I shrugged. Nobody could control Ellen but Ellen. "She thought it would help you come to your senses before you divorced me, but I hoped for after. I thought it would be nice to have another wedding. We could invite our families this time. They weren't too happy about missing the first one."

The expression on his face didn't change, so I kept talking. "And I always wanted to wear a beautiful white dress with a long train and matching veil. Your mother and I found a really nice one last weekend, but I'm not sure about it. I was going to wait until my mom got back from Mexico City tomorrow to get her opinion on it. Your dad said he would walk me down the aisle, if that was okay with you."

He grabbed me roughly, his hands encircling my arms. He shut me up with a gentle shake. "You want to be married to me? For real?"

"Somebody called my mom to take care of me when you left. Since you were the only one who knew you left..." My heart softened with love, and I melted toward him. "I never doubted that you cared, Jonas, only that you would realize it."

His expression matched mine. "I'll never give you reason to doubt me again."

An impish smile played on my lips. "How about you do the getting-down-on-one-knee thing? That would be far more romantic than shaking me. Then you can carry me into the house and we can get started on the makeup sex. It's going to take a long, long time for you to make this up to me."

He tried to kiss me, but I slapped a palm over his mouth. I looked at him expectantly. "Do it right, Jonas. This time is for real."

Kneeling on the concrete garage floor, he took my hand in his. "Sabrina Breszewski, will you do me the honor of becoming my wife?"

I cupped his face between my hands. "Yes, Jonas. I want nothing more than to be your wife."

He rose, took me in his arms, and kissed me tenderly, finally letting out all the love he'd kept bottled up inside. I missed the feel of his body against mine. Any residual anger or hurt fled, and I kissed him back, unleashing everything I'd kept at bay for the last eight months. Affection turned to ardor, and I arched, offering myself to him.

Breaking the kiss, he scooped me up and strode toward the house. "I feel it's necessary to warn you that I'm a sadist."

"And a Dominant. Did you want me to call you Sir?"

He fumbled with the door. "It's locked."

"Well, I did just get home from work."

He set me down and rooted around in my purse for the keys. "I want my keys back."

"I want my rings back. Sir."

"I'd rather you called me by my name, and unless you have a hankering to be called 'sub,' I'll just call you by your name." He pushed the door open and picked me up again.

"My wedding rings," I reminded him.

"I'll give you the engagement ring, but you don't get the band until the actual wedding."

That sounded good to me. "I've missed having you here. Nobody cooks for me like you do."

He grunted as he carried me up the stairs. "You haven't lost weight, so I think you did okay."

I smacked his chest, but it was the limp-wristed kind, so I know he took it in the spirit with which it was intended. "Things are going to change around here."

"No shit." He put me down. "First, you're going to get naked."

I shrugged out of my jacket. "I stopped taking birth control." I'd forgotten when I'd been in a depressed stupor, and I'd never started again.

"That's okay. I want at least two kids before I turn forty, so we can get started on that."

I'd been unbuttoning my shirt. Freezing, I stared at him. We'd never discussed having children. "I don't want to be fat in my wedding dress."

"Pregnant isn't fat. If you don't want to show, then you'd better get moving on planning the ceremony. You've got three, four months tops."

Nodding, I resumed unbuttoning. "It turns out I'm a masochist. I've been seeing Sophia as a service top."

"She told me."

Naked, I faced him. "You've kept a lot of your life hidden from me, Jonas. That can't continue."

He shook his head gently. "No more secrets. My life is an open book."

I ran my fingertip down his tie. "If you peel back your cover, we can get right to the sex part."

He combed his fingers through my hair. "Business first, honey. You cut your hair."

My gaze dropped. "I didn't want—"

"I know why you did it, and I'm sorry. Since it was my fault, I won't punish you for it. But I will spank you."

Looking into his liquid gold eyes, I saw the parts of him that he'd kept from me. "How is that not a punishment? Ellen said those things are negotiated. To my recollection, we've negotiated rings, keys, and getting pregnant."

With a cocky grin, he turned away. Ten seconds later, he settled on the sofa and patted his lap. "It's not a punishment, honey; it's my atonement. Lay down with your ass right here. I'll help you learn the correct position."

I didn't know how me being spanked could be his apology, but I'd wanted this from him for far too long. I draped my body across his lap. He lifted my hips and repositioned my shoulders.

"I'm expecting you to have at least one orgasm from this."

In the past two months, Sophia had used different floggers, canes, and even a single tail whip on me. None of it had made me orgasm. Knowing I would probably like it anyway, I relaxed. He warmed me up with smacks that got blood flowing to my skin, and then he laid into me. I yelped and squirmed.

He pushed down firmly on the back of my neck. "Don't move."

That firmness was balm to my soul. Wetness flooded between my legs, and when he resumed spanking me, it felt different. I hadn't wanted atonement—I wanted the man who took control of my body and made me have orgasms. He must have sensed that because he stepped up his game, alternating a series of spanks with pinches to my clit. I cried out and buried my face in the cushion, but I didn't squirm. Before long, an orgasm washed over me.

He lifted me, turning me so he could kiss me. His hands roamed my body, and he settled his weight over me, crushing me to the sofa. I tugged at his tie, loosening it so I could get to his skin, but he was too frantic. His hands were everywhere, caressing and shoving my limbs around. The next thing I knew, he was inside me. At last he paused, and his gaze locked to mine.

"I love you, Sabrina."

My heart warmed and swelled. I'd never get tired of hearing him say that. "I love you too, Jonas."

"I'm never going to let you go."

I traced my knuckles down his face and touched his lower lip. "You'd better not."

He hiked one of my legs up so he could slide in even deeper. "Hang on tight, honey. I'm not going to be gentle."

I grasped his shoulders and wrapped my free leg around his waist. "Just the way I like it."

Michele Zurlo

Michele Zurlo is the author of the Awakenings, Doms of the FBI, and the SAFE Security series and many other stories. She write contemporary and paranormal, BDSM and mainstream—whatever it takes to give her characters the happy endings they deserve.

Her childhood dream was to be a librarian so she could read all day. Some words of wisdom from an inspiring lady had her tapping out stories on her first laptop, and writing blossomed from a hobby to a career. Find out more at www.michelezurloauthor.com or @MZurloAuthor.

Lost Goddess Publishing

The Doms of the FBI Series
Re/Bound (Doms of the FBI 1)
Re/Paired (Doms of the FBI 2)
Re/Claimed (Doms of the FBI 3)
Re/Defined (Doms of the FBI 4)
Re/Leased (Doms of the FBI 5)
Re/Viewed (Doms of the FBI 6)
Re/Captured (Doms of the FBI 7)

The SAFE Security Series
Treasure Me (SAFE Security 1)
Switching It Up (SAFE Security 2)
Unlocking Temptation (A SAFE Security Short)

The SAFE Security Trilogy: Jesse and Jessica
Forging Love (A SAFE Security Novella: Jesse and Jessica prequel)
Coming Fall 2019:
Drawing On Love (Jesse and Jessica 1)
Broken Love (Jesse and Jessica 2)
Shards of Love (Jesse and Jessica 3)

Awakenings
Letting Go
Hanging On
Owning Up (Summer 2019)

Safeword: Oasis Series by Michele Zurlo
Wanting Wilder
Mina's Heart

Paranormal by Michele Zurlo
Dragon Kisses 1-3
Blade's Ghost

MM Romance by Nicoline Tiernan
Nexus #1: Tristan's Lover by Nicoline Tiernan
Nexus #2: The Man of His Dreams by Nicoline Tiernan

Anthologies
BDSM Anthology/Club Alegria #1-3 by Michele Zurlo and Nicoline Tiernan
New Adult Anthology/Lovin' U #1-4 by Nicoline Tiernan
Menage Anthology/Club Alegria #4-7 by Michele Zurlo and Nicoline Tiernan
Discovering Desires Anthology by Michele Zurlo

Bear's Cove Series (MM/MPreg) by A. J. Stone
Dak's Omega
Tanzil's Second Chance
Perfect Blend: Kofi's Omega

Draco International (MM/MPreg) by A. J. Stone
Amaricio's Omega
Koren's Omega Neighbor
Zeke's Reluctant Omega

Letting Go: Bonus Material—The Pool Boy

Sabrina peeked out the window of her breakfast nook. In the distance, past the deck, the trellis bursting with tangerine and white roses, and a large expanse of lawn, the sun glinted from the water, beckoning her closer.

With the kids at her in-laws for the afternoon, she had some free time, and it had been a few days since she'd been able to get in a good, punishing workout in the water. She opted for a bikini—the hot-as-hell pool boy was due sometime today—grabbed a towel, and rushed to the pool.

As she got closer, she noticed the man with a long pole stuck into the water, and she slowed her pace. Too late. Now she would have to wait for the pool boy to finish cleaning it before she could swim.

With a sigh, she heaved herself onto a lounger and sent a baleful look in his direction. He wasn't supposed to show up until later, after she'd worked out. She had planned to pull herself, dripping wet, out of the water, throw her hair back so that the sun caught some of the highlights. She'd squeeze away the excess, letting it drip over her breasts to draw his gaze to the gentle swells there.

He'd ruined everything by showing up early. There was so little variety in her life—she spent most of the day looking after her one-and-three-year-olds—that the chance to put herself on display to torment the pool boy was one she hated missing. While her afternoon wouldn't be completely ruined, she did prefer to do things her way.

After all, a girl had to have fun, right? Her husband worked long hours and traveled all the time, so she had to get her kicks however she could.

"Good afternoon, Mrs. Spencer." He grinned at her from across the pool.

He wasn't wearing a shirt. She spent some time admiring the way his lithe, lean muscles bunched and strained as he methodically worked his way toward the far end of the pool. The tan darkening his skin testified to many hours spent under the punishing rays of the sun.

Her gaze traveled lower, taking in the way his shorts hung low on his hips. Too low. One tug and she'd catch an eyeful. The hipbones jutting forward were tanned as well. It made her wonder if his gorgeous ass enjoyed the same freedom as his chiseled chest.

"Armand, I thought I told you to not wear those shorts anymore. They're positively scandalous." She spoke to him in a tone that managed to be both haughty and lazy. "And put a shirt on. My husband will not look kindly upon you if he sees you walking around here almost naked."

He didn't respond. Nothing in the set of his shoulders or the tilt of his mouth gave her a hint as to his reaction, but she knew he had one. She knew he'd heard her. He hadn't stopped looking at her for a single second.

After forever, he extracted the vacuum from the pool and set it on the concrete patio. Ever so slowly, he rounded the pool, not stopping until his shadow loomed over her. This close, she could see the danger glittering from his olive green eyes.

"Mrs. Spencer, your husband is half a world away. And you know as well as I do that you like when I wear these shorts. You think they're sexy. After all, you bought them for me." Like a cobra, his hand shot out. He caught the end of the string tied behind her neck to hold up her bikini top, and he tugged.

She felt the small pop that indicated it was no longer tied. She knew she should put her hands over the fabric to shield herself before he peeled the scrap of material away, but she was paralyzed by the hard expression on his face. The planes and angles that made up his visage were what some might call handsome. She might think it, but she knew better than to say it to his face. And his lips were positively sensual. She imagined what they'd feel like traveling down her neck, sucking her nipple inside, and then slipping lower.

"Armand, this is highly inappropriate. My husband wouldn't like this." Her voice came out breathy, colored by desire.

The mask slipped away for a second, revealing Jonas's humor at her remark. They hadn't planned to role play today. She knew he was pleased with her improvisation, and she loved how quickly he'd understood both what she was doing and what she wanted from him.

"He's a busy man, your husband. I'm doing him a favor by putting you in your place." With that, he tugged again, and the last string holding up her top came loose. "I'm going to make you beg, Mrs. Spencer."

And just like that, she was wet. It only took one look from him to make her knees weak, and he was using it on her now.

She'd wrangled her hair into a braid to make it easier to get under her swim cap. Reaching back, he grasped her by the long rope and pulled, urging her to stand up. He turned her around, so that her back was to his front, and he guided her back against him. Only then did it become apparent exactly how hard his muscles were. Before she could think to struggle, he banded one iron arm around her midsection.

Because she was half a foot shorter, her head fit neatly under his chin. He rested it on her now, another tool to keep her close. "Last chance, Mrs. Spencer."

"Really?" She didn't honestly think he'd let her off the hook so easily. Men as dominant and virile as this didn't take kindly to her haughtiness.

He chuckled, a low, sinister tone that sent a shiver down her spine. "No, not really. Your fate is sealed."

With that, he peeled away the fabric clinging to her breasts and squeezed one hard, his calloused palm scraping her sensitive skin. She whimpered with the effort it cost to not beg for more.

He ground his pelvis into her ass, and she realized he was hard and ready. That could only mean one thing.

Without baring her further, he pushed her into the pool house. While he loved being an exhibitionist, she'd drawn the line when it came to overly graphic displays where their neighbors could see. Of course, he liked to counter that by saying their neighbors shouldn't be using binoculars to see into the backyard if they didn't want to see the kind of shows they put on.

In the cool darkness, she could barely make out his shape. The temperature difference made her nipples stand on end. She had to stop leaving the air conditioning turned up so high.

He ran his fingers through her hair, roughly combing out her careful braid, and then he pushed her to her knees.

"Hands behind you, Mrs. Spencer."

She complied, assuming one of the submissive positions he'd taught her, and she licked her lips in anticipation.

One shove, and those shorts fell to his ankles, proving her assessment correct. They were entirely too loose. He kicked them away, but she didn't pay much attention to them. Instead, she focused her gaze on his engorged cock. The thick purple head demanded the caress of her tongue.

She leaned forward and licked a path around the tip, widening her circles until she had him in her mouth. She sucked lightly, knowing it would drive him crazy until he was compelled to take over.

Until then, she took her time, exploring him with her lips and tongue. She loved his texture and the salty, musky flavor that leaked from the tip. After a few minutes, she heard him groan, and then his hands gripped the sides of her head. He set the pace now, fucking her mouth with long, slow strokes.

She relaxed her jaw and swallowed every time he came to the back of her throat, urging him deeper. His moans came faster and shorter. Crude language sprinkled from his lips.

"Fuck, baby. Take my cock deeper. Suck harder. That's right. Your little cunt is dripping, isn't it?"

She made a noise of agreement in the back of her throat. The vibrations shut him up for a second. He knew how much that kind of language embarrassed and excited her. Five years of marriage, and certain words still made her blush. Of course, that was why he used them. He loved to see her cheeks turn red.

And then he groaned loudly and his hot semen shot down her throat. When he withdrew, she used the back of her hand to wipe away the extra saliva that coated her lips and chin. Giving head could be so very messy.

Always amused by her need for neatness and order, he laughed at her as he pulled his shorts back into place.

She lifted a brow. "Is that all you have, hot stuff? I expected more."

It was a dangerous move, mouthing off when he was in Dom mode, but she always loved the outcome. Jonas had a magic touch when it came to making her body sing in all the right ways. He didn't disappoint now.

The room upended and she found herself over his shoulder. The pool house wasn't large. It had a shower room that could accommodate four, and that was the main feature. Otherwise, it comprised two large rooms. One was a combination kitchen, living, and gaming area. The other was a bedroom. Shortly after she had it built, Jonas had turned it into a man cave. It housed so many electronics that she'd installed an alarm. She didn't mind, especially after the children were born and it became an escape for her too. She'd even bought him a pool table.

He threw her down on the sofa. She landed on her ass, sinking deep into the cushion. It was too soft to provide any bounce. Knowing what was coming next, she scrambled out of the way, but he was too quick.

Before she knew what had happened, he had her face down over his lap. He threw one leg over her knees to hold her in place, and he placed one firm hand on her lower back.

Knowing she would be eagerly anticipating what was about to happen, he lowered her bikini bottoms slowly. She squirmed a little bit more now, trying to get him to slap her ass to make her stop, but he was too smart to fall for her ploy. He halted his actions completely.

Seconds ticked by. Her half-naked ass waited. He'd positioned her so that she was up a little on her knees, her ass presented prettily, her legs spread wide enough so that he could spank her pussy if he wanted. It didn't take long for her to give in. "Please, Armand. I'm sorry. I'll be good. I promise."

"Ask for it, Mrs. Spencer."

The moment she'd taken his name, he'd begun calling her 'Mrs. Spencer' during most of their games. He used it often as a way to stake his claim. She didn't mind. She liked belonging to him.

"I've been bad, Armand. I need to be spanked."

"That's not asking." He rubbed his palm over her flesh, a little fresh incentive.

"Please spank me. Please? I need a good spanking. My husband is away and I'm going to be very bad."

His hand stilled. "You're going to be?"

"Yes," she said. "With you. I'll do anything you want if you'll just spank me. Hard."

The first time she'd gathered the courage to ask him for what she wanted, it had turned into the most blissful and bittersweet night of their marriage. Since then, Jonas had steadily initiated into the world of bondage and submission. And she'd discovered her inner masochist.

She could feel it already, the burn that would morph into a steady tingle, but he didn't deliver.

"Anything?"

"Anything."

A loud crack rent the air. He spanked her so hard her body scooted forward. The leg he'd thrown over the backs of her knees pulled her back into place, and she braced her hands against the arm of the sofa. "I'll keep that for later."

Before she could process his comment, he delivered another blow. Knowing he wouldn't stop until she climaxed, she didn't bother to count how many times he spanked her. As he warmed her up, he rested between each smack, taking time to caress her heated flesh. Soon he switched up the rhythm, and she could no longer distinguish one blow from the next. It blurred together as an inferno coiled low in her abdomen.

And he stopped.

She wailed a protest.

He lifted her and set her on her feel. "I never promised you an orgasm. You begged for a spanking, sweetheart, and that's what you got."

She was about to beg when he stood and moved into her personal space, thrusting his chest forward to bully her into walking backward.

Puzzled, she took one step after another until she bumped into an old, scarred table he'd owned for longer than he'd been with her. With a devious grin, he gripped her hips and lifted her on top. "A spanking only increases your attitude. You still think you're in control."

She didn't, not really. Sure, they had a safeword, which she could use if she needed him to stop, but almost nothing could induce her to call "onion." He could do pretty much anything he wanted to her and she would most likely love it.

Automatically, she lowered her gaze. Though they didn't use titles and Jonas typically didn't make her ask for permission before coming, he was as demanding—sometimes more so—than the Doms in those erotic romances she'd begun reading during her first maternity leave. And he always made her beg for an orgasm, so she really didn't see a distinction. She still only climaxed when he let her.

The coolness of the lacquer faded due to the warmth radiating from her ass. Somewhere between the lounge chair and now, he'd completely disrobed her. It hadn't taken much to get rid of the scraps of material that passed for a swimsuit, which wasn't something she'd wear for a serious workout anyway.

He shoved at her shoulders, and she found herself flat on her back. The tone of their encounter was set. Moisture pooled between her legs because she knew he wasn't going to be gentle.

With efficient movements, he buckled cuffs around her wrists and ankles. In short order, he used snaps to bind her arms above her head. The table might be ugly, but it served a purpose. It had hooks strategically placed along the legs and underneath the top. Jonas had modified it over the past five years to fit her body and all the positions he choreographed for their scenes.

Normally he would immobilize her legs next, but he threw her for a loop when he snapped the cuffs around her ankles together. Then he pulled a chair over, climbed on top, and pulled a chain from behind a panel in the ceiling. It looked like he had modified a few things other than his orgasm table.

When he finished, her legs were stuck straight up in the air. She could lift her ass if she used her abdomen muscles, but those weren't as strong as they once had been, so she couldn't hold the position.

He stood at the foot of the table with his hands on his hips. Her legs hid half his body from view. "That's a damn fine cunt you have there. It's red and swollen from your spanking and dripping with juices."

She felt the swipe of his finger over those inflamed tissues, and she shuddered from the lightning it sent careening up her torso.

"I think you want me, Mrs. Spencer. Is that true?"

"Yes." No hesitation on her part. He'd denied her an orgasm and she was ready to beg. This was his favorite part. "Armand, please don't be cruel."

She knew he wouldn't be too cruel. Each of his personas had a distinct personality that had developed over the course of their relationship. Master J was a demon who was cruel in all the right ways; Matt, the former virgin, was obsessed with a call girl; and Armand fucked like a marathoner. There were more, but these were her favorites. She'd signaled the terms of the scene with only the use of that name.

God, she loved this man. He made her dreams come true, and then when she thought up new dreams, he made those come true too.

He rechecked her bindings before disappearing across the room. She heard evidence of him shuffling items around in a drawer or cabinet, but he had left her field of vision and her position didn't allow her to shift.

She tended toward impatience, and Jonas loved to exploit this weakness. Tugging with her arms, she tested the give of her wrist bindings. Then she tried to move her torso. In this she was more successful. However it yielded no relief. The motion only made her more aware of her acute need.

"Armand." She breathed his name, a plea and a sigh. "Please fuck me. Please don't leave me here all alone."

He appeared on her other side, chuckling at her pathetic begging. Holding his hand over her body with his palm up, he paused. "You're going to stay still while I fuck you. This will ensure your cooperation."

She could see the glint of light from something silver. He tilted his palm, and a delicate chain slithered to land on her stomach. She recognized nipple clamps on a long chain.

From his other hand, he produced a ball gag. Sabrina wasn't a fan of the way it felt in her mouth or of the drooling mess it necessitated. She shook her head. "No, Armand, please. I promise I'll be good. I'll be silent."

He cupped her jaw and forced her mouth open. Wearing a gag made her feel more helpless than being bound. She struggled against it, but she lost the fight. She always lost these fights. He popped the ball between her teeth, brought the strap around her head, and buckled it on the side of her head.

Sabrina sank back against the table, feeling every inch of her body cede control to Armand. She didn't have the ability to just submit, and Jonas always knew exactly what he needed to do to force the issue.

"One more thing, and then you'll realize exactly how little control you have over anything, Mrs. Spencer. And then I'm going to fuck this tight, hot little cunt all afternoon. When your husband returns later today, you'll still be walking funny."

She tried to say something, breathe a shade of protest, but the gag turned her words into a whimper.

He pinched one nipple hard and twisted it viciously. Her back arched off the table, trying to ease the sudden pressure. No longer worried about making too much noise, she screamed against the sharpness, even as it ebbed into a pleasing sting.

He toyed with that tender bud, an arrogant slant to his lips as he ignored her desperate noises. When he tired of that kind of play, he clipped the clover onto her sore nipple and gave the other the same treatment.

Then he secured the chains—two, not one—to hooks on the underside of the table on each side of her body. Now her wrist and ankles were bound, and he'd used her nipples as the third point of security. If she shifted to the left, it eased the tug on that side, but it intensified the pain on the right side. A similar thing happened when she tried to wiggle to the right.

He watched while she tested the limits of her movement and the consequences of trying for something other than what he allowed. When he was satisfied with everything, he untied the string holding his shorts around his slim hips and let them slide to the ground.

She watched as his body was revealed. The chiseled perfection never ceased to amaze her. He'd installed a workout room in the basement, and he used it regularly now that he didn't have a separate job as a service top to keep his muscles as hard as iron.

His erection sprang from a nest of curls. If the gag hadn't been in her mouth, she would have licked her lips, inviting him to let her taste him again. As it was, he fisted his cock and pumped his hand up and down the length in slow motions that drove her insane with unsated need.

The thick scent of her arousal filled the room, her body's way of sending out insistent signal flares. She whimpered and wiggled. The pain brought a sheen of wetness to her eyes, forcing her to call up on the shallow well of patience that frequently ran dry. He would fuck her when he wanted, and she couldn't say or do anything to entice him closer, harder, or faster.

The topaz of his eyes betrayed the level of his desire and gave her hope. After an eternity, he rounded to the end of the table. She felt the nudge of his cockhead against her entrance. With her legs tied together, it was going to be a tight fit. She wouldn't be able to lift her hips or spread her legs wider to ease the way for him. He shoved inside roughly and abruptly, her plentiful cream providing all the help necessary.

She moaned and gave herself over to the conflicting sensations running rampant inside and outside of her body. Soon the climax he'd denied her loomed close. She fought the urge to writhe and was only half-successful. Each tug of the clover clamp on a nipple drove her further from reason. Behind the gag, she screamed out an orgasm.

Jonas—Armand—ignored her climax. He didn't slow down or take into account how sensitive her tissues became after an orgasm. A shiver wracked her body. Accepting her helplessness, she sank into a deeper level of submission. He hadn't asked for it, but he'd taken it just the same. Goodness, how she loved this man.

Another climax rocked her body. Tears streamed from her eyes. He just might kill her with pleasure. She felt bathed in her own juices, full and thoroughly used. When she came again, he came with her.

She floated in a vast sea of blissful semi-consciousness for the longest time before fire ripped her from heaven. He'd removed one of the clamps. The other followed rapidly. If the gag hadn't still been in her mouth, the neighbors definitely would have heard her scream.

The fire lingered, growing and receding, pulsing in time with her heart. Jonas made no move to soothe it away.

He leaned down and nipped her earlobe. "That was stunning, Mrs. Spencer. Thank you for the gift of your submission." Now he closed one hand on her breast and plumped that tender globe.

She arched into his hold. That, coupled with the insistent moan she forced out from behind her gag, begged for more of his touch. Moving around the table to stand at her head, he gave her what she wanted. He remained on the gentle side, as though he knew he couldn't handle more right then.

His caress moved up her body, over her arms and to her wrists. She felt the slight tug and heard the scrape of metal-on-metal as he released her arms. He brought them down one at a time, massaging the protest from her aching muscles.

Then he removed her gag and wiped away the moisture from her face before massaging a reverent kiss across her lips. Now that her hands were free, she cupped his face and kissed him back. His submissive wasn't gone, but she had definitely grown bolder now that he had partly freed her from the restraints.

When the kiss ended, he drew a finger over her swollen bottom lip. He moved down her body and stood at the end of the table that would give him a prime view of her exposed pussy. She knew what was coming next. The man was a stallion, and she knew he wouldn't be able to resist one more bit of torture.

He drew a finger along her dripping tissues. Her entire body flinched in protest, even though she knew this was the best part. When she was bruised and tender like this, it was the only time she could masturbate successfully.

The soft pressure of his digit on her flesh increased. He pressed her clit flat. In the absence of bindings on her arms, she gripped the edges of the table. "Armand, you're a beast."

With that, he plunged at least two fingers deep inside. He worked her into a fine frenzy, and when he reached up and twisted her nipple, she came hard one last time. It was a shorter-lived climax, intense and pulsing, but not lingering.

Then he used a cold, damp cloth to clean her pussy before releasing her legs from the hook on the ceiling. As he helped her stand, she resigned herself to the fact that she'd be walking funny for the rest of the afternoon. Her legs were rubbery at best, and her ass, thighs, breasts, and pussy throbbed with remembered pleasure and pain.

He helped her back into her bikini and carried her to the sofa. She slumped against him, resting her head on his shoulder, and closed her eyes.

"I love you, Jonas."

He kissed her forehead. "I love you too, honey."

Made in the USA
Middletown, DE
09 November 2019

78330057R00203